BURY YOUR HORSES

BURY

YOUR

HORSES

DAN DOWHAL

DUNDURN
TORONTO

Publisher: Scott Fraser | Editor: Allison Hirst
Cover designer: Sophie Paas-Lang
Cover image: istock.com/ilbusca
Printer: Webcom, a division of Marquis Book Printing Inc.

Library and Archives Canada Cataloguing in Publication

Title: Bury your horses / Dan Dowhal.
Names: Dowhal, Dan, 1954- author.
Identifiers: Canadiana (print) 20190194898 | Canadiana (ebook) 20190194928 | ISBN 9781459745391 (softcover) | ISBN 9781459745407 (PDF) | ISBN 9781459745414 (EPUB)
Classification: LCC PS8607.O98744 B87 2020 | DDC C813/.6—dc23

We acknowledge the support of the Canada Council for the Arts and the Ontario Arts Council for our publishing program. We also acknowledge the financial support of the Government of Ontario, through the Ontario Book Publishing Tax Credit and Ontario Creates, and the Government of Canada.

Care has been taken to trace the ownership of copyright material used in this book. The author and the publisher welcome any information enabling them to rectify any references or credits in subsequent editions.

The publisher is not responsible for websites or their content unless they are owned by the publisher.

Printed and bound in Canada.

VISIT US AT

dundurn.com | @dundurnpress | dundurnpress | dundurnpress

Dundurn
3 Church Street, Suite 500
Toronto, Ontario, Canada
M5E 1M2

To Harry,
who was always ahead of me on the path.

ONE

To a northerner's eye, this corner of the Chihuahuan Desert looks desolate, like some vast empty lot forsaken and left to sprout weeds and scrub brush. If you look more closely, though, you'll see it's not barren. Here, too, the ageless struggle to survive continues. Gaze up into the faded blue sky and you'll see a turkey vulture circling lazily with the patience of death itself. Down on the ground, lizards and rodents, scorpions and snakes scurry and slither in the unrelenting dance of hunter and prey. If you sit and wait patiently, which is not easy to do in the brain-baking heat of a spring afternoon, you might even see one of the larger denizens — a puma, or a mule deer — moving through this deceptively bleak environment, exploiting the niche Nature has afforded it.

There is a perfectly straight black line down the middle of the thorn scrub landscape, showing that the ultimate predator has also staked a claim. But although humans have been industrious enough to place a highway here, it seems at first they are not so foolish as to inhabit the place.

But then, as the asphalt shimmers in the sun, a lone figure crests the horizon. Riding a motorcycle that costs several times more than most inhabitants of this New Mexico county earn in a year, the man is racing at full throttle, achieving speeds approaching two hundred miles per hour. It's unclear whether he is momentarily taking advantage of the straight and deserted stretch of highway to test the vehicle's capabilities, or is really in such a hurry to get to the small border town at the end of the road. In either case, he is pushing both his own limits and the machine's.

A desert box turtle begins crossing the highway. Having waited out the winter in hibernation, the creature has been coaxed it out of its burrow by the late-April warmth, and evidently it has business on the other side of the road. The creature is, by nature, in no hurry, and steadfastly crawls toward its goal. The rider of the motorcycle spots the reptile traversing the road, and for a few seconds it appears he is planning to run over the turtle, but at the last moment, he veers abruptly out of the way.

This is a mistake. At such high speed the rapid jerking movement interrupts the motorcycle's gyroscopic stability and causes its rear to fishtail violently. The man fights desperately to steer his machine, and as he rides the thin edge between control and calamity, the adrenalin-soaked battle for balance feels very familiar. The motorcycle leaves the road. While this reduces the speed, it also makes any chance of control impossible as the machine bounces over the rough terrain. Separated from his bike, the rider becomes a projectile, passing through and obliterating two large yucca plants before landing in a patch of creosote bushes. He is fortunate to be alive, though he feels far from it as he lies on the ground, awash in pain.

"Fuck!" he screams. "You stupid asshole, Shane!"

Self-recrimination is nothing new for Shane, but since it is currently counterproductive, not to mention historically ineffective, he abandons the exercise and instead inventories his injuries. On top of sundry contusions and sprains, his left arm, he realizes, is broken.

With his operable hand, Shane removes his motorcycle helmet, then pulls the glove off his right hand using his teeth. Slowly, he struggles to his feet, but when he places weight on his right leg, the knee buckles and almost sends him back to the ground. He does a frantic little dance on his uninjured leg, his fractured arm dangling at his side, and manages to retain his balance.

It feels to him, from experience, that the kneecap has popped out. He looks around for his motorcycle, which is fifty yards away, lying on its side and still idling.

"This ought to be fun," he mutters, and hops toward the machine. He is halfway there when his foot catches on something in the soft soil, and he trips. He twists in mid-air to ensure he doesn't land on his broken arm, and with practised expertise keeps his head forward, allowing his back and shoulders to absorb the impact.

As he lies there, summoning up the energy to rise again, he notices there are now three buzzards circling overhead, gliding in and out of the sun's glare. The scavengers' presence actually causes him to laugh.

"How about that. Just like in the movies." Not much of one for reading, Shane loves cinema — especially old Westerns — having devoured film after film during the extensive travel involved in his past profession.

He watches the lazy aerial display until its significance hits home, then he rolls over and struggles to stand up again. By now glistening with perspiration, he manages to hop over to the motorcycle without losing his balance this time.

Despite his injuries, his first priority is to turn off the idling engine and examine his bike. He's obviously not in any condition to try to right the motorcycle and ride it, but he loves the Ducati nevertheless and regrets any damage it has sustained. He ascertains that, in fact, the motorcycle has fared far better in the accident than he has. Relieved, he turns his attention to the saddlebags.

"Shit. It figures." Shane realizes that the motorcycle has landed on the side where his cellular phone was stowed. The easiest thing to do now is sit and wait for help, but based on the paucity of vehicles he has encountered on this particular highway, it could be a while before someone happens along.

He decides to try moving the motorcycle, reasoning that he need only raise the bike far enough to access the saddlebag underneath. He looks around for something to use as a lever, but the scrub brush of the Chihuahuan Desert offers no usable timber. Shane opts to use his head like a bull — an animal which, coincidentally, he has been compared to in the past. The best spot for leverage seems to be the seat, so he tries to get his head under it. Unable to achieve good purchase, he decides to make a hollow in the ground to allow for a better angle of leverage, and begins scooping out the soil with his good hand.

His digging dislodges a striped bark scorpion from its burrow. Unaware that this particular arachnid's sting is almost never fatal, Shane lurches backward in a panicked reflex, jolting his fractured wrist. The pain — which had previously subsided to a tolerable throbbing — spikes beyond endurance, and he passes out.

When he regains consciousness, the scorpion has disappeared. He climbs to his feet and pats himself down with his one operable hand to make sure the creature has not crawled inside his clothes or some bodily crevice. Satisfied he is in no immediate danger of being stung, he is nevertheless reluctant to resume excavating. He looks around for something to use as a digging tool, cursing when the search proves futile.

The heat is oppressive, and Shane feels his face beginning to burn, so he picks up his motorcycle helmet, puts it on, and lowers the tinted visor against the glare. This reminds him of his resistance to using a visor in his former profession, and that remembrance makes him smile, despite his dire situation.

He looks down at his hole and pokes around with his boot to unearth any critters that might lie in wait. Even so, he has no desire to stick his hand or his head into the depression. Finally, he uses his teeth to pull on his glove, trusting the thick leather will protect him against scorpions, and cautiously resumes digging.

Nothing crawls out to disturb Shane's excavation, and soon there is adequate space for him to get his bare head beneath the motorcycle seat. Removing his helmet, he pulls his broken arm against his belly, distributes his weight as evenly as possible, and — emitting a grunt — lifts with his head and shoulders.

He is elated to feel the motorcycle lifting, but it is evident that he will only be able to raise the bike a foot or so. Still, he can see that the flap of the trapped saddlebag is now clear of the ground. Straining to support the weight, he uses the elbow of his injured arm to shove his discarded helmet underneath the vehicle's frame before relinquishing the weight and exhaling with a loud whoosh.

"Woo-hoo! You the man, Shane," he hollers, permitting himself a little horizontal victory dance. Pivoting onto his good shoulder, he reaches underneath to unfasten the flap of the saddlebag and fishes through his belongings, retrieving the cellphone by touch alone.

When he looks down at the phone's screen, he realizes there is no signal in this remote place. All his effort has been for nothing. He erupts in a scream of rage, but manages to refrain from hurling the offending phone into the scrub brush — no small feat, for Shane's rage-filled attacks on inanimate objects are well documented. Instead, he covers his face with his good hand and begins to sob.

The pent-up tears flow easily, not only for his current predicament, but for the sea of angst that has been swelling over his torturous past week. Crying does not prove therapeutic, however, for in Shane's mind, it is unmanly. Still, he cannot seem to stop — not, that is, until he realizes that millions of people would relish seeing his despair. Pride and stubbornness kick in, and he wipes away his tears.

"Stop it, you big pussy," he chides himself. He really has no choice now but to wait for help. Reasoning that it would be unlikely a passing vehicle would have the ability to carry his motorcycle, he transfers his possessions to his alligator leather toiletry kit — it is a tight fit and the zipper won't close. He considers donning the dental plate that holds the five artificial upper teeth replacing the ones he has lost over the years. But looking presentable is the least of his problems, and removing the dentures would only buy a little space, so he discards his can of shaving cream instead. He hasn't shaved in three weeks anyway.

He stuffs in his wallet, passport, and traitorous cellphone, sticks the pouch under his arm, and hops back to the highway. Squinting at the blazing sun to gauge its bearing, he chooses the far side of a creosote bush, then removes his black leather jacket and drapes it over the branches to form a crude canopy before dropping to the ground.

Keeping a wary eye on the bare earth around him, he sits and watches the highway, which shimmers hypnotically in the afternoon heat. Finally, in the distance a rumbling engine announces a vehicle approaching. Shane climbs to his feet, fighting dizziness. Struggling for balance, he shouts and waves his good arm at an odd-looking vehicle. He makes out a vintage Indian brand motorcycle with sidecar, apparently piloted by unskilled hands, weaving across the lanes. As the bike draws near, the young male driver stares bug-eyed, unsure what to make of the scene.

"Stop! For the love of God, I need help! I'm hurt!" Shane screams. For a horrific few seconds he is convinced the motorbike is not going to stop. But relief washes over him as its brake lights go on and it veers onto the shoulder.

There is something peculiar about the gangly, bumpkin-like teenager who climbs off the motorcycle. His sandy-blond hair is cropped in a crude bowl cut, and his attire is like something from another century. The collarless shirt is filthy, and some of its myriad stains appear to be blood. The coarse black pants are torn and worn away at the knees and heavily soiled, as if the teen has been rolling in the dirt. Only the ankle-high leather clodhopper boots are in sound shape.

"You been in an accident, Mister?"

"My bike went off the road," Shane says, indicating his overturned motorcycle. "My arm's broken, and my knee's screwed up pretty bad, too."

"You bust your head?" the teenager asks.

Shane realizes the teen is referring to the missing teeth, cuts, and black eye Shane is sporting.

"Nah, I had these already. Listen, dude, can you call me an ambulance?"

The teen shakes his head, avoiding eye contact as he does so. "I'm not from around here, Mister," he mutters in a low voice. "Don't know about no ambulance. I think maybe there's a hospital in Deming."

"Okay, how about a lift, then? How far's Deming?"

The teen looks down the road before answering. "Sorry. I got to get going. I'm in a hurry. There's bound to be a car along soon."

"Aw, for fuck's sake, you can't just leave me here!" Shane protests. "Look, I'll pay you a hundred dollars for a lift."

Shane hops over to his shelter and reaches into his toiletry kit to extract a roll of hundred-dollar bills. He peels one off and waves it at the teen, whose eyes widen. He walks over to silently grab the proffered money.

"Okay, now we're getting somewhere," Shane says. "Help me over to your bike, will you?" He zips up the toiletry bag and is about to tuck it under his uninjured arm, but realizes the best approach will be to wrap that good limb around the teen's shoulder for support.

"Here, hang on to this, will you?" he asks, handing over his kit. The teenager freezes, holding the bag far out in front of him like it's some sort of dangerous animal. Then, abruptly, he turns and dashes back to the motorcycle. Shane stands transfixed, refusing to believe what he is seeing ... until the engine starts up and the Indian zigzags away. Now Shane has plenty of words, all of them expletives, but it's too late, as the bike vanishes down the highway. His anger sustains him for a little while, but when it subsides, he is left feeling weaker than before. He hops back to the shade of his makeshift canopy and resumes his vigil.

TWO

The desert stirs as the wind picks up. At first the moving air has a welcome cooling effect, then grit starts blowing into Shane's face. He covers his head with his leather jacket, peeking out periodically to scan the road and eat a little dust. With time on his hands it is inevitable he should start reflecting on his predicament.

"How the hell did you get yourself into this mess?" he asks himself aloud. The question is rhetorical, for he has mentally replayed the events of the past week over and over. Admittedly, today's motorcycle crash and robbery add troubling new footage to his highlight reel of regrets.

Feeling drowsy, he closes his eyes and drifts off. Awoken by a loud rumbling in his ears, he throws off the jacket covering his head and sees a large four-by-four pickup idling on the highway. The truck is completely decked out in off-road accessories, and the chassis has been lifted to accommodate five-foot monster tires.

The young, black-haired, olive-skinned driver is leaning out the window, peering at Shane through mirrored sunglasses, while two older, hard-looking, moustachioed Hispanic men in straw cowboy hats stand in the back of the truck, clinging to a roll bar and glaring at him.

"Help me!" Shane calls out, but his throat is so dry the words come out as an unintelligible croak.

"*Que? No hablo Inglés*," the driver replies, giving the men in back cause to chortle.

Shane swallows hard and tries again.

"I need help. I had an accident and my arm's broken. Then some kid on an old Indian motorcycle robbed me. I need an ambulance."

At the word *Indian*, the driver's bemused expression disappears. He climbs out of the cab and approaches Shane.

"The Indian. Was it black with a sidecar?" he demands in perfect English.

"Yeah, that's it. This punk-ass blond kid was driving it. He stole my wallet, my cellphone … everything I had."

"When?"

"I don't fucking know. Maybe twenty minutes ago. Look, dude, I need a hospital."

The driver ignores this last part, barking orders to the men in the back of the truck, then jumping back inside and putting the pickup into gear.

"You're not going to just leave me here, are you? Holy fuck! I just had a nasty accident. I came off my Ducati and my arm's busted bad."

When he hears *Ducati*, the driver perks up and scans the terrain. Spotting Shane's overturned cycle, he catapults out of the truck with the eagerness of a child on Christmas morning.

"*Hijole! Es uno Panigale!*" the driver exclaims, running over to the motorcycle.

"Yeah, that's right, a Ducati 1199 Panigale R Superleggera," Shane confirms, pride transcending pain for the moment. "So ... are you going to help me or what?"

At the driver's command, the two outriders leap out of the back of the pickup and hustle over to right the bike. The driver climbs on and, seeing the key in the ignition, fires up the machine.

"*Escuche ese motor!*" he shouts, revving the engine, and the two moustachioed men, clearly the driver's minions, gush sycophantic enthusiasm. The boss pops a wheelie and races off on the Ducati, creating a cloud of dust while his underlings wave their hats and holler like hands at a rodeo. Shane is unhappy with this turn of events, but hopes allowing the joyride will work to his advantage.

The motorcycle weaves through the scrub brush and onto the highway. Now the boss opens up the throttle and zooms off down the blacktop for a few hundred yards before making a skidding turn and racing back to brake behind the four-by-four.

"*Padre, qué máquina,*" he says admiringly, and his two companions bob their heads frenetically in agreement. The boss man gestures at the motorcycle. "*Ayúdeme lo levanto en el camión.*"

They start lifting the Ducati into the truck — no easy task given the bike's weight and how high the truck bed is jacked up — and Shane is relieved they will take the motorcycle along with him. After much heaving and grunting, the bike is secured and the tailgate slammed shut. The boss calls out, "*Vayamos,*" and everyone begins climbing back into the pickup.

Shane is miffed that no one is helping him, but thinks he now has a good measure of these men and their machismo. He hops to the passenger side on his own. The door is locked, so he raps on the window. The boss lets out a big laugh and starts up the engine. Realizing they mean to leave him and abscond with the Ducati, Shane bellows in rage and starts pounding on the truck.

That elicits from the boss a string of expletives that need no translation. He leaps from the vehicle and races around to come at Shane, who, injured or not, is prepared to take the guy on. But he suddenly finds himself staring down the barrel of a large silver-plated handgun. He feels a wobble in his abdomen and knows that if he weren't so dehydrated, he'd probably be pissing his pants.

The boss is shouting as he forces Shane to his knees, presses the pistol against his forehead, and cocks the hammer. Shane is certain he is about to be die. His insides lurch in terror. But one of the minions starts yelling entreaties at his pistol-toting boss from the back. At first Shane figures the tirade is against the firing of the gun, but when he hears the words *la migra* — which he knows from watching movies is Mexican slang for "border patrol" — he realizes the henchman's only concern is trouble with the authorities.

The boss relents, uncocking the pistol with a pronounced flick of his thumb to underscore his displeasure. He mutters unhappily as he sticks his weapon into the back of his waistband, and Shane realizes the young punk is actually angry at being deprived of the opportunity to commit murder. Unloosing a final curse, the boss shoves Shane down hard onto the ground with the sole of his boot. Shane's broken wrist bangs against the asphalt, and although the pain is excruciating, he fights hard not to black out, fearing the men now mean to run him over with the pickup and make his death look like an accident.

He is wrong on that account at least, for the truck peels off, leaving him curled up on the highway clutching his injured hand. His heart wants to hammer its way out of his chest, so he stays put, willing himself to calm down. The surface of the highway is scorching hot, while the wind blows a steady veil of dust over his face and lips. He rises, picks up his leather jacket, and labours back toward the creosote bushes by the roadside to once again shelter from the sun and wind.

As he is hopping over, the sunlight glints off of something. Shane sees that it is the helmet he used earlier to prop up the motorcycle. The helmet is of questionable use to Shane now, but he has so few possessions left, and he holds out some hope of getting his Ducati back, so he summons the energy to hop over and fetch the helmet.

When he picks it up, hiding underneath is what looks like the same scorpion he encountered previously. Whereas earlier, the sight of the arachnid made Shane recoil in fear, now he is filled with rage — although it has little to do with the creature itself. He starts pounding at the scorpion with the helmet. The ground is relatively soft, but finally he catches the creature against a rock and mashes it into a messy pulp.

A little wiser now to the ways of the desert, Shane gives the helmet a shake to ensure nothing else lurks inside before pushing it onto his head. The instant shade and especially the protection from the blowing dirt make the effort to retrieve the helmet worthwhile. He returns to the roadside and plops himself down to wait for help.

✻ ✻ ✖ ✻ ✻

Lapsing in and out of consciousness, and without a watch, Shane loses all track of time. His pain and nausea become as constant as the blowing desert wind that covers him with a layer of grey grit. At first, he periodically wipes away the film from his visor, but eventually, too tired and discouraged to bother, he lets the world outside grow dimmer and more distorted, as if some giant cancer is eating away at reality.

When a vehicle does finally appear down the highway, Shane tries to rise, but instead keels over onto his side. As he struggles to his knees, fearful the vehicle will pass him by, a wave of nausea overwhelms him. Failing to remove his helmet in time, he throws up inside it. The smell of his own vomit generates a second spewing, and violent spasms make him feel as if his insides are tearing themselves apart. Clawing with his good hand, he finally manages to remove the helmet and crawl toward the road. The wind blows dirt into his face, blinding him in one eye, but he crawls on.

To his relief, the vehicle stops. He hears doors slamming, followed by the sound of approaching feet. Two pairs of legs, one pair adult-sized and the other child-sized, enter his field of vision, but Shane has no strength to look up at the associated faces. He is fighting just to keep the inky vortex of unconsciousness at bay.

The child's legs move away to the side, and when they crouch downward, Shane can see they belong to a girl of about eight or nine. She has a stick in her hand, and with it she flips over rocks and pokes around in the dirt. Something she unearths makes a sound, and Shane feels a pang of horror grab his groin, for although he is new to this environment, movies have taught him what a rattlesnake sounds like. Sure enough, he sees the serpent hoisted up on the girl's stick. Its triangular head is raised in his direction, and the two holes in its face that distinguish it as a pit viper are clearly visible.

Shane abhors snakes, and the sight of this venomous reptile with its cold, catlike eyes causes him to tremble uncontrollably. At the same time, he is mesmerized and unable to look away.

"It's a big one, Mommy," the girl squeals gleefully, as if talking about a puppy. Shane wants to shout at her to be careful, but his dry lips seem to be glued together. He can only watch in dismay as the girl lowers the rattlesnake to the ground, pins it with the stick, calmly seizes the serpent just behind its head, and proceeds to hold up her prize triumphantly.

He fully expects to hear the mother scream in alarm, but instead she quietly chides the girl. "Stop playing with it, Gracie. Get it in a sack and let's see what's wrong with this fella."

It's all too much for Shane, and he begins to pass out. His last thought before blackness spills in to mercifully eclipse the unrelenting sun is that everyone in this part of New Mexico is either a criminal or, to quote the movies, just plumb loco.

THREE

When Shane comes to, there is a woman hovering over him, backlit by the sun. There is something angelic about her, although, judging from the worry lines etched on her face, she doesn't exactly reside in paradise.

"Is he a bum, Mommy?" Gracie's voice asks from behind the woman. Although she was fearless earlier with the rattlesnake, the girl now keeps her distance, as if frightened of Shane.

"Hush, child. It ain't polite to talk about folks like that. I'm sure he can't help it if he's fallen on hard times."

"My arm's broken," Shane manages to croak.

"I can see that," the woman replies. "Someone beat you up, Mister? They sure did a number on you."

Shane wants to explain about the crash and the robberies, but doesn't have the words in him.

"Water," is all he manages.

"Sorry, ain't carrying none, Mister. Our spread's not far from here, though. We can call the doc and get you tended to. Can you make it to the truck?"

Shane nods and, with the woman's help, struggles to his feet. Swallowing hard, he explains, "Knee's screwed, too."

The woman looks at the leg he is favouring and slides under his good arm to take up the weight. When Shane's hand is resting across her bicep, he can feel the firm definition of muscles beneath her denim shirt.

"Grab his stuff, Gracie," the mother instructs, and the daughter scampers to obey.

"Ew!" she complains as she picks up the vomit-splattered helmet and holds it as far from her body as her little arms will allow. Shane and the woman move in unison toward the pickup truck, an old Dodge that looks like it's from the '70s. It is rusted and dented, with various body parts having been replaced over the years, resulting in a mishmash of colours. The truck looks as worn as Shane feels.

The woman helps Shane hop to the passenger side, and he crawls in, noting without comment the abundant cracks in the seat's upholstery, some of which are spilling stuffing. Gracie enters from the driver side and seems reluctant to get close to Shane, causing her mother to growl, "Git over, child, you're crowding me." Gracie grudgingly complies, but stuffs Shane's leather jacket and helmet in between them, and then, for added separation, reaches down onto the floor and retrieves a canvas sack.

"Don't squish 'im," she tells Shane, placing the bag on the seat. He realizes it holds the rattlesnake they encountered earlier and presses up against the door, giving Gracie her desired space.

The truck has a manual transmission. The mother puts it into gear, and there is an audible grinding as the clutch engages. The girl keeps stealing glances at Shane, while he warily keeps his eye on the bag with the snake. Eventually, once he's reasonably sure it won't come crawling out, his gaze wanders to the woman who's helping him.

He estimates she is in her midthirties. Her dirty-blond hair is pulled back into a utilitarian ponytail and shows a few wisps of early frost. In addition to the lines he noted earlier, there is a puffiness under her grey eyes, plus a scar on her chin that to Shane, a possessor and creator of scars in his own right, looks fresh. Still, he likes what he sees.

"Thank you," he offers.

"Uh-huh," she says without glancing his way. He gets the impression that she feels inconvenienced helping him. The pickup pulls onto a dirt side road, then, after a few dusty miles, turns into a gate overhung by a large sign that says *Rancho Crótalo*, the letters burnt crudely into a rough slab of barn board.

The property is composed of the same desert scrub brush as the rest of the godforsaken terrain, and Shane wonders what kind of a ranch it is that manages to prosper here. As they drive farther, he makes out a one-storey dwelling flanked by a cluster of tin-roofed outbuildings. There's no livestock in sight.

They pull up in front of the ranch house, and the driver gets out and hollers, "I need some help here!" Gracie grabs the sack with the snake, much to Shane's relief, and dashes straight toward a big barnlike building. She passes a shirtless boy in coveralls who has emerged in response to the call, but stands watching with a slack-jawed look.

Two women come out of the ranch house. One of them, a buxom, solidly built Hispanic woman, is carrying a shotgun, cradling it with confidence. Worried the Chicana has misinterpreted the call for help, Shane stays in the cab. The other one, however, a slender thirtysomething redhead wearing a sundress, comes bounding straight out to the vehicle.

"What's the matter, Tammy, Tammy, tell me true?" she asks the driver in a singsong voice.

"Found this fella lying out near the highway. He's busted up pretty bad. Call Doc Sanchez, will ya, Maybelline."

The redhead tears back into the house, her waist-length hair forming a flowing mane behind her, and Shane is relieved that someone is finally taking his condition seriously.

"For cryin' out loud, Yolanda, put down that goshdurned gun and give me a hand," Tammy calls out as she comes around to Shane's side of the truck. "You, too, Vern," she adds, spotting the boy standing there. "Git over here."

The command stirs Vern from his trance, and he hastens over to assist. In his eagerness he seizes Shane by the broken hand, eliciting a howl of pain. Tammy slaps the boy across the back of his head.

"Mercy, child, can't you see it's broke?"

Vern blushes all the way to his hairline. This time he is careful to grab Shane by the armpit. Collectively, they help him out of the truck. As Shane stands up, there is a loud ringing in his ears, and he blacks out again.

When he comes to, he is lying inside on a sofa in what appears to be a parlour or living room. He looks around the sparsely furnished space and guesses from the construction that this is one of the homestead's original rooms. In addition to the cloth-upholstered sofa on which he lies, there are three mismatched wooden chairs clustered around a large, scuffed-up steamer trunk that serves as a coffee table. The only attempt at decor is an old sepia-toned photograph that dominates one wall. It shows a serious-looking couple in frontier attire posed in front of a crooked canvas tent. Everything about the picture's subjects screams hard luck and desperation, and if they were the founders of this ranch, he surmises that their descendants have not fared much better.

In the adjoining room an argument has ensued, and as its volume escalates to audible levels, Shane realizes he is the subject of the debate.

"What was I supposed to do, just leave him lying there to die?" Tammy shouts.

"He's *un vagabundo*," another voice shoots back, and from its Hispanic flavouring, Shane deduces it belongs to the gun-toting Chicana. "He'll rob us blind … or worse. And who's going to pay Sanchez? Does that bum even have any money?"

"I brought him here, I'll take care of it!"

Presently Tammy steps back into the living room and stands looking critically at Shane.

"Doctor's on his way, Mister. Listen, I don't mean to sound cold, but you carrying any money?"

"This kid out on the highway stole my wallet. I've got nothing on me right now, but I swear I'm good for it. I'll get some sent."

"Where you from, Mister?"

"Shane. My name's Shane." She grins at this, as if he's just told a joke. The smile softens her face, letting its prettiness surface.

"Okay, Shane, so where do you hail from?"

"The Yukon, Canada — way up north. But I've been living in Columbus, Ohio, the past couple of years."

"Well, you're in Columbus, New Mexico, now, Shane. How'd you end up all the way down here?"

Shane sees no advantage in relating the specifics of his recent tortuous odyssey. "It's a long story," he says.

"Yeah … always is. Bet it's a real tear-jerker, too. The thing is, Doc Sanchez usually likes to be paid in cash."

"Look … it's Tammy, right? Tammy, I meant what I said about being good for the money. If you can bring me a phone, I'll make a call right now."

"Phone's on the kitchen wall. I can help you over if you're up to it."

"Thanks." He smiles, forgetting that he's not wearing his dentures. He reads the distaste in Tammy's face. Her aversion is apparent in the uncertain way she approaches him to offer support. Embarrassed, Shane waves her off and hops into the kitchen on his own, sending tremors through the ancient floorboards with each jump.

Unlike the stark parlour, the kitchen is cozy and well used. A jumble of blackened, well-tempered cast-iron pans and skillets hang in an array from the ceiling above an open grill. A crudely mortared brick wall holds an oven big enough to roast an entire side of beef. Garlic braids and herb garlands are hung wherever there is space above rows of simple wooden cupboards all painted a uniform glossy white. Instead of a tap, an iron hand pump overhangs the sink. It is clear that this room is where most of the house's activity takes place.

Yolanda and Maybelline sit at a long plank-top table with bench seats, watching Shane hop into the room. Tammy gestures toward the phone — an old rotary model the likes of which Shane hasn't seen in years — hanging on the wall.

When he picks up the handset, it occurs to him that calling someone to ask for money will not be a simple matter. His live-in girlfriend, Brandi, recently kicked him out, cleaning out their joint bank account in the process. For tax purposes, and as a sign of his commitment and trust (now proven to be misguided), the million-dollar condominium they shared was deeded in her name. The bottom line is, he has no home to telephone, and no ready funds to access. As he ponders who might lend him some money, he realizes, too, that all his telephone numbers were stored in his cellphone, which was among the possessions stolen by the youth on the highway.

There is one person he can definitely reach, and who will wire him some money, but there is a tightening in the pit of Shane's stomach at the thought. He and his father have not spoken in over two years, and their last exchange was not a pleasant one.

"It's a long-distance call to Canada," he explains, and he sees Yolanda flash Tammy a triumphant look. As much as he'd like to avoid the added humiliation of calling his father collect, he needs to reward Tammy's faith in him. "It's okay, I'll reverse the charges ... it won't cost you anything."

He doesn't need directory assistance. Although he hasn't lived in Peel Crossing for over twenty years, his boyhood phone number is tattooed on his memory. He connects with the operator, delivers the instructions, and waits while the line rings. His father is an invalid. Shane can picture the old man sitting in front of the television in the same La-Z-Boy he has occupied since his stroke five years ago.

The call connects on the third ring.

"This is a person-to-person call from Shane Bronkovsky. Will you accept the charges?" the operator asks.

"What? No, Shane doesn't live here anymore," his father answers. His voice sounds slurred, disoriented. Perhaps he was napping.

"Dad, Dad, it's me," Shane cuts in. "Tell them you'll accept the charges."

There is a pause as the old man absorbs the situation. "Okay," he finally responds, and Shane hears the operator click off.

His father starts in on him right away. "Why the hell are you reversing the charges, Mr. Big Shot? All that money you make and you won't even pay for a damned phone call."

"Nice to talk to you, too, Dad." Shane keeps the sarcasm out of his voice, sensitive to the fact the three women are listening to every word, not even making a pretence at affording him privacy.

"Listen, Dad," he continues, "I'm in a bind. I crashed my bike. My arm's broken, and my knee's hurt, too. The thing is, I've been robbed. Some kid took my wallet with all my cash and credit cards. And if that wasn't enough, these other guys came along and stole my motorcycle. I really need you to wire me some money to pay for the doctor and tide me over until I get things sorted out."

He's glad the women can't hear the ensuing silence at the other end of the line. After his father still hasn't said anything for several seconds, he adds, "I'm in New Mexico."

That finally garners a response. "New Mexico? What the hell you doing there? If I was you, I'd keep going all the way to *Old* Mexico. There's talk on the TV they're going to charge you."

"It was an accident." Shane is no longer talking about the motorcycle crash, but hopes his audience won't pick up on it.

"Maybe so ... I must have watched it a hundred times, and it looked that way to me, too. But the kid's dead, and a lot of people got a serious hate on for you. And now some camera-loving DA is making noises about charging you."

Shane feels the bottom fall out of his stomach. "I can't do anything about that right now. Listen, Dad, about the cash ..."

"Did you say some guy stole your wallet?"

"Yeah."

"Well, Mr. Smarty Pants, how the hell do you expect to pick up a wire transfer when you got no ID, huh? Tell me that."

Shane feels anger ignite in him. He would like nothing better than to curse the man and slam the phone down hard, but he chokes back the impulse.

He turns to Tammy. "What's your last name?"

She exchanges glances with the other women before answering. "DeWitt."

"Where's the closest place to wire some money?"

"Western Union office in Columbus, I reckon."

"Listen, Tammy, since I've got no ID, I'm going to have my dad wire you the money. Is that okay?"

Tammy shrugs her consent.

Shane returns to the phone. "Okay, Dad. I've got some people here helping me out. You can wire the money to one of them, care of the Western Union office in Columbus, New Mexico. Got that?"

"*Can* I now? Lucky me. So just how much you need?"

"I don't know. Fifteen hundred ought to do it ... at least until I can get my credit cards replaced. You know I wouldn't be asking, but it's an emergency. I'll pay you back double, I promise."

What is meant to be a concession only inflames his father. "Screw you, Big Shot. I don't need your money. You think I can't afford a couple thousand dollars? I can damn well fend for myself, but from the sound of things you still need me to take care of you. Yes, sir, all that big money you made and you still got to come crying to me for help."

The words are meant to sting, and Shane again feels his rage rising, causing his face to redden all the way up to his scalp. So many times in the past, he has let his anger erupt freely, usually with the result of something being broken, but this time he does not succumb to his father's taunts.

"You're right. I still need your help," he says, eyeing the watching women.

"You're damned right, you do. You'd be nowhere without me — not that you ever gave me one ounce of appreciation for it." Shane's father pauses, as if leaving room for Shane's usual angry retort. When no outburst comes, the old man heaves a sigh, like an ancient boiler letting out steam. When he speaks again, his voice is calmer, almost friendly. "All right, then, who am I sending it to?"

"Tammy DeWitt, care of Columbus, New Mexico."

"Too late to get anyone to drive me into town today, but Oksana's here tomorrow morning."

"Who's Oksana?" Shane asks. As far as he can recall, his father lives alone.

"My caregiver. You know her from when you were kids. Oksana Kravchuk, remember? Anyway, I'll get a lift from her in the morning and send the money out right away, don't you worry." All the gruffness and resentment has disappeared from the old man's voice. Shane can't remember the last time their conversation didn't end in a shouting match.

"Thanks, Dad. For everything. I do appreciate it. Honest."

His father grunts. "Always knew one of those motorcycles of yours would get you, if some goon didn't. You sure you're all right?"

"I'll live."

"Hope it's not inside a jail cell."

"Yeah, me too, but I guess I'll worry about that later. I got other problems right now." Their business has concluded, but Shane finds himself reluctant to end the conversation, revelling in its rare amiability. "So, how's the weather back there, anyway?" he asks. "Snow gone yet?"

"Pretty much, except for what's hiding in the woods. We don't get the weather we used to anymore. Remember how frigging cold it used to get? You kids had your shinny game going on the pond pretty much into May."

"Sure I remember. I gotta say, it's pretty darn hot down here. We could use some of that cool air."

"Don't complain. I'd trade you for hot any day of the week. Listen, Shane, someone else is trying to phone me. Probably Oksana making sure I took all my pills. Great girl, but she sure does nag. I'll let you go now. Take care, son."

"Okay, thanks again, Dad. I'll phone again soon to confirm I got the money, and, well, you know … to let you know how I'm making out."

"Do that, son."

"Bye, Dad."

Shane hangs up and turns to face his audience. "He'll wire it first thing tomorrow morning, okay?"

Tammy shakes her head. "Tomorrow? Gosh, no. Tomorrow's milking day. It'll have to be the day after."

"All right. Can I stay here until then?"

The reactions are immediate. Maybelline cackles, and Yolanda slams her fist onto the table.

"No, sir, you can't stay with us," Tammy tells him. "When Doc Sanchez gets here you'll have to get him to give you a lift into town — drop you off at a motel or something."

"For fuck's sake, I already told you! I have no money ... no credit cards, no ID, nothing. How the fuck am I supposed to pay for a motel?"

"I said no, and that's that. And I'll thank you not to use cuss words in this house."

Regretting his error, Shane tries another tack. "I'm sorry, Tammy, I really am. Here you are being a Good Samaritan, and I'm being a royal pain in the ... um, butt. But, listen, I'm not asking for a free ride. I'd pay you for it. How about a hundred dollars for the night? The money from my dad's going to be wired in your name, so you know you'll get it."

"I already told you I'm too busy to go into Columbus tomorrow, so it wouldn't be just one night now, would it?"

"All right, then, two hundred dollars for two nights."

"Four hundred dollars," Yolanda interjects from the table. "And you sleep in the stable."

Clearly caught by surprise, Tammy gives Yolanda a questioning look, and the Chicana nods in response. Shane senses money is in short supply on this hardscrabble ranch.

"Okay. Four hundred dollars, then," he offers, sticking out his still-operable right hand. Maybelline squeals and begins bouncing up and down on her bench with delight. "*Gimme gimme money, honey*," she sings. Although she helped negotiate the arrangement, Yolanda still looks hostile.

Tammy looks at Shane's proffered hand, then spits in her own palm and shakes his to seal the contract. Her grip is surprisingly strong.

"Deal," she says. "But don't go thinking this is some hotel. You'll eat what we eat, and once the doc patches you up, you bunk in the stable. There's a room at the back where we keep the tools 'n' such, and there's a mattress in there we can drop on the floor. Should be cozy enough."

✗ ✗ ✖ ✗ ✗

Doc Sanchez is a short, corpulent man in his forties sporting a large walrus moustache. He enters the house without knocking, drops a black leather satchel on the floor of the parlour, and bellows for someone to bring him a basin of water and a washcloth. When the doctor removes his mammoth stetson, Shane sees that his salt-and-pepper hair has been slicked back, revealing a pronounced widow's peak that hangs down his forehead like a buzzard's beak.

There is a buzzing in the kitchen. Shane gets the impression that none of the women wants to be the one to attend to the good doctor. Finally, Tammy comes out carrying the requested items. Doc Sanchez breaks into a big, toothy grin and rises to greet her.

"Hiya, Tammy darlin'. You're looking mighty fine, as always," he coos. He takes the basin of water, but instead of using it for his patient, mops down his own face and hands.

"That's better," he says, picking up his satchel and dragging a chair over so he can scrutinize Shane. Rather than survey any injuries, he examines Shane's features. "What have we got?"

Shane holds up the broken arm for inspection, supporting it with his good hand.

"Had a motorcycle accident back on the highway. The ulna's definitely fractured … maybe the radius, too." He gestures to where his leg is being supported by a pillow. "The patella's dislocated, but it's happened before. I think you'll be able to just pop in back into place."

The doctor seems more interested in the stitches and scars on Shane's face than the fresh injuries. "You know a lot about anatomy for a biker," Sanchez comments, and he unbuttons his suit jacket, which flaps open to reveal a revolver hanging from his belt in a decorative black-leather holster. The gun's handle is ornately carved, and the weapon has an antique appearance, although Shane wagers it's fully functional.

"Look, I'm just a traveller who's had some bad luck. And then some. I don't know if they told you on the phone, but I was robbed, too."

Sanchez has finally started to study Shane's injuries, starting with a probing of the kneecap through Shane's jeans. He raises his head and bellows at the kitchen door.

"Hey, Tammy! Git in here. I need a hand." When Tammy enters, he instructs, "Take his pants off, will ya, darlin'."

Tammy hesitates, and Shane can see she is trying to decide whether this is a necessary medical procedure or some sort of ribald prank.

"I need to examine his knee … he says it's dislocated," the doctor explains, although the smile on his face betrays his amusement at Tammy's discomfort.

"Why can't you do it yourself?" she asks, not budging.

"It's a nurse's job, not a doctor's," Sanchez replies. "Besides, I figure you're better equipped to deal with whatever might come crawling out. Of course, it's been a while, hasn't it, darlin'?"

Tammy's face reddens, and Shane can endure her discomfort no longer. He begins tugging at his belt buckle with his good hand. "I'll do it myself," he tells Tammy.

She watches him struggle for a few seconds, then sighs and begins helping. She pulls off his boots, then grabs his jeans at the ankles and tugs them off in one smooth motion.

Shane has always been proud of the musculature of his legs, and he thinks Tammy is impressed, too, although when her eyes make the inevitable trip upstream to Shane's ultra-brief designer underwear, she immediately averts her gaze and focuses her attention on folding his jeans.

"Anything else y'all want?" she asks.

"Plenty," Sanchez replies with a wink, "but I know you're not selling."

Tammy flings the jeans at him and storms out of the room.

The amusement disappears from the doctor's face, however, when he returns to examining Shane's leg. The scar of previous reconstructive surgery runs up one side of the knee and makes a large crescent below it, and the doctor traces it with a finger.

"You say you were robbed. I guess that means you've got no insurance card or money to pay for treatment."

"Don't worry," Shane says testily, "I've wired for cash. Tammy's picking it up the day after tomorrow. So you'll get your —"

The last statement remains unfinished as Shane lets out a howl of pain. Doc Sanchez has grasped the injured knee with both hands and given it a sudden twist.

"How about that? Just like you said," the doctor says, chortling. "The patella just popped right back into place."

The door to the kitchen opens and Yolanda sticks her head out. She seems pleased to see Shane grimacing in pain, but when Sanchez calls out, "Hola, bonita Yolanda," her face hardens, and she disappears.

"Geez, Doc. You might have given me some painkillers first," Shane complains.

"I figured a big macho biker like you could take it, but okay." Sanchez grunts as he bends to open his satchel. He fishes around inside and pulls out a pair of plastic pill containers. Holding one in each hand, he shakes them rhythmically like miniature maracas. "What's your pleasure — Vicodin or Percocet?"

"Percs, always. More punch, more buzz."

"Ah, a connoisseur." He dispenses a pair of pills into Shane's open palm and hands him a plastic water bottle.

The doctor now turns his attention to Shane's arm, squeezing the swollen areas and rotating the wrist's position. The pills have not yet taken effect, and Shane winces with pain.

"Looks broke, all right," Sanchez opines, "but I'll need to take an X-ray. Let's see if you can stand up."

Shane hoists himself to his feet, and when he shifts his weight onto his injured knee, it holds. He takes some steps to walk off the stiffness before stopping in front of Sanchez, who nods approvingly.

"Okay, then. We'll head out to my truck to take some pictures."

"Mind if I put my pants on first, Doc?"

"Whatever. Can you do it yourself, or do you need one of the ladies to help you?"

"I'll manage."

The doctor shrugs and occupies himself by jotting down some entries in a pad. Shane steps into his pants and pulls them up with one hand. He cannot do up the top button, but manages to fasten the belt. Finally he steps into his boots and stomps a couple of times to make sure they're secure before turning to Sanchez.

"Lead on, MacDoc."

FOUR

The doctor's vehicle is a converted cube van crammed with medical machinery and gear. A gurney with rumpled bedding sits against one wall. Sanchez first removes a bathrobe and a bag of potato chips to make room for his patient. Shane surmises that the van constitutes the doctor's home as well as his clinic.

The X-rays reveal that Shane's self-diagnosis was spot on. There is a perpendicular break across the entire width of the ulna — although luckily the bone has not separated — as well as two hairline fractures of the radius. Whatever his initial dislike of the doctor, Shane concedes that Sanchez is skilled at his craft, or at least at casting broken bones. Rather than use the pre-fab plastic variety, the doctor puts on a traditional cast, applying the plaster layers delicately, almost lovingly, as if moulding a sculpture.

Once he has completed the work, he wheels over to a small desk and begins writing.

"What name do I put on the bill?"

"Shane Bronkovsky — B-R-O-N-K-O-V-S-K-Y."

"What's that, some kind of Russian name?"

"Ukrainian, originally, but I'm pure Canadian — second generation."

"Do tell. Well, my people have been in this part of New Mexico for well over three hundred years, but a lot of folks still act like I came sneaking over the border yesterday." He hands Shane a handwritten bill. "You owe me four hundred and sixty bucks all told. Now, normally I get paid up front, but it seems I have no choice but to let it slide till Thursday."

Suddenly, Sanchez draws his revolver and shoves the barrel into Shane's groin. "And just so we're crystal clear, I don't care what kind of tough guy you think you are or who you're running with — nobody fucks with Frank Sanchez ... and I got badass friends of my own you do *not* want to mess with. *Comprende, hombre?*"

It is the second time today that someone has threatened Shane with a handgun, but this time he does not experience the same gut-wrenching fear, either because he knows the doctor is merely posturing, or because the drugs are working their way into his bloodstream.

"Okay, Doc ... how about tossing in a bunch more of those percs, and we'll call it an even five hundred."

Sanchez lets out a big belly laugh, withdraws his pistol from Shane's nether regions, and gives it an expert gunslinger-style twirl before re-holstering it.

"Why not?" He tosses Shane a pill bottle. "Here, knock yourself out."

"Thanks, Doc. Don't worry, you'll get your money. Come back Thursday and I'll have it."

"You're staying here at the *rancho*? No shit. Well, hopefully I won't have to charge you for reattaching your balls, too. Or for snakebite."

✕ ✕ ✖ ✕ ✕

Shane returns to the house and borrows the phone again to call the Sheriff's Department to report the robberies.

"Dispatcher says a deputy will be by in a while to take my report," he tells his audience after hanging up.

Tammy rises to usher Shane out of the room. "Wait in the parlour, then," she instructs him. "Once you're done with the law, we'll have supper, and then we'll get you set up in the stable. Meanwhile, we got chores to do, so stay put and out of our hair, okay?"

Shane exhales irritably, but complies. He stretches out on the couch and tries to nap, but the drugs have his brain buzzing, and memories of the day's events keep swarming relentlessly, like backwoods blackflies. He gets up and wanders the room, looking for something to occupy himself. There is no television set, no stereo, no magazines or books — except for an ancient and well-used Bible. Spirituality is not an affliction Shane has ever suffered, so he opens the Bible out of boredom, not interest.

The inside cover contains a record of births, deaths, and marriages in one branch of the DeWitt family, going back almost two centuries. Working through the genealogy, Shane deduces that the unhappy couple depicted in the photo on the wall are Jacob DeWitt and his wife Catherine DeWitt, née Stouffer, who moved to this place sometime before the birth of their first child in 1891.

Shane skims forward to the end of the handwritten entries. They show that Tammy's maiden name was Brand, and that the little girl Gracie, whose full name is Grace Roberta DeWitt, was born six months after Tammy's marriage to one Robert DeWitt. The final entry reads: "Pvt. R. DeWitt, killed in action, Bahrain,

Iraq, September 12, 2012." There is nothing to explain the identity of the other women or the boy also living on the ranch.

Feeling like he has violated Tammy's privacy, Shane softly closes the Bible and goes to the window. The wind outside has worsened, and he watches the swirling patterns of dust, grateful he is no longer sitting in the middle of it. It is hard to imagine anyone choosing to live here, let alone clinging to a patch of arid scrub brush for over a hundred years. Given his own nomadic history and the fact that as of a week ago, he has been technically homeless, there is something admirable about the household's tenacity.

He returns to the sofa and soon drifts off into an uneasy half sleep. He is awoken by the deputy sheriff rapping on the door. The short, big-boned woman introduces herself stiffly as Deputy Alvarez and never removes her stetson or mirrored sunglasses throughout the interview. While Shane relates his story, the deputy listens quietly and takes notes, her expression inscrutable. She then starts asking questions to fill in the details.

"Can you describe the kid who stole your wallet?"

"Tall and skinny. Sandy blond with a weird-ass bowl haircut. Dressed strange, too."

"How so?"

"Well, his clothes looked like something from an old movie. The pants were black and kind of crude, and held up by leather suspenders. He had these old-fashioned boots, too. Oh yeah, and his shirt didn't have a collar," Shane adds.

"What colour was the shirt?"

"White ... well, white originally. Had a lot of stains on it."

"And how much money was in your wallet?"

"Around four thousand. But that's not the half of it. He took my credit cards, my ID, my passport ... everything."

"Four thousand? You always carry that much cash?"

Shane shrugs. "I was travelling." He doesn't feel the need to explain that his assets were recently purloined, and that was all the money he could scrape together.

"And you say he was driving a black Indian motorcycle with a sidecar? What year would you guess?"

"It was vintage, maybe from the 1930s or so, but still in perfect shape."

"I don't suppose you got the licence plate number?"

"No. It happened too fast. By the time I realized what was going on, the bastard had driven off."

Deputy Alvarez flips through her notebook. "Six one. Around seventeen years old. A hundred and sixty pounds. Sound about right?"

"Yeah. You know him?"

"We know *of* him, although he's moving up in the world if he stole that motorbike. We figure he's one of the boys who got run off from Holy Waters."

"What's that?"

"Blessed Temple of the Holy Waters. It's a renegade offshoot of the Mormons ... started a farm up in the foothills about forty years ago. They're polygamists. The old guys run off the young men — don't want them competing for wives — and some end up hereabouts. They account for a fair bit of the petty crime. Don't really have what it takes to make it in the outside world."

"Isn't polygamy illegal?"

Alvarez smirks. "So's a lot of things, but people do 'em anyway. State's been trying to make a case against them for a few years now, but no luck. They've got those women brainwashed, and they circle their wagons whenever outsiders come around. Now, tell me about the men in the pickup who stole your motorcycle. Got a make and model on that one?"

"It was a 2017 Ducati 1199 Panigale R Superleggera. Mint condition … I just picked it up from a collector a month ago."

"I meant the truck."

"Oh. Sorry, no. I can tell you it was black with red detailing, but I haven't a clue what its make was originally. All tricked out now with big-ass monster tires, brush bars, running lights — the whole nine yards."

"Licence number?"

"Don't even recall seeing any plates. Wasn't exactly seeing straight by that point, though."

"And you say they were all Hispanic?"

"Yeah. The two riding in the back wore jeans, plaid shirts, and straw cowboy hats … looked to be in their forties. Both had big walrus moustaches. The guy driving was younger and clean-shaven. He was definitely the boss."

"And you say he's the one that pulled a gun on you?"

"That's right. I swear he wouldn't have thought twice about blowing me away, but one of the older guys called him off. They spoke in Spanish, but I made out 'la migra' — that's border patrol, right?"

Deputy Alvarez nods, but is clearly puzzled by the information. "That one's harder to figure. It's nobody local. Almost sounds like they were from one of the Mexican drug gangs down south, but we've never known them to operate on this side of the border. And then to pull a stunt like stealing a motor-cycle … just don't make sense."

"I got the feeling the boss man was into fine motorcycles. He damn near creamed his jeans when he saw mine."

"You don't say. What's the bike worth, you figure?"

"I paid almost ninety K for it with all the bells and whistles."

Deputy Alvarez's eyebrows arc above her mirrored sunglasses.

"Ninety thousand for a motorcycle! What do you do for a living, Mr. Bronkovsky? If you don't mind me saying so, you don't look like someone who can afford that kind of coin."

Shane feels the serpent of his anger stir within him. Somewhere, in the distance, like someone calling from far off in the woods, the voice of prudence tries to intercede, but he shoves it aside.

He rises to his feet and looms over Alvarez. "What the fuck are you grilling *me* for? I'm the victim here. Those motherfuckers robbed me. Shouldn't you be out trying to catch them instead of giving me a hard time?"

Only when he sees the deputy's hand slide down to the taser on her hip does he realize he has again let his rage possess him.

"Mr. Bronkovsky. I'm going to have to ask you to sit down and get a hold of yourself. I am investigating here, and I advise you to co-operate, if you know what's good for you."

Shane drops back onto the sofa and feels the familiar feeling of remorse wash over him. He has been like this as long as he can remember. There is a beast that lives coiled within him, a sly, powerful, and venomous thing that strikes without warning, then slithers away, leaving him swollen with guilt. He has received counselling for his anger in the past — learned tricks and techniques to mitigate his raw emotions — but these all proved to be clinical abstractions. Plus, the whole therapeutic exercise was rife with hypocrisy, since the people who'd sent him there were the same ones who expected him to let his fury erupt when it suited their purposes, then exploited it and banked on it, even while publicly condemning it.

"I'm ... or at least, I used to be a professional athlete," Shane says quietly, residual emotion causing his voice to tremble.

"Really? What sport?"

"Hockey."

"No fooling. What team?"

"Columbus Blue Jackets. Columbus, Ohio, that is."

Alvarez shrugs. "Never heard of them, but I don't really follow hockey. Now, my brother — he's a *huge* fan. Never missed a Scorpions game when they were still around." Shane has never heard of any hockey team called the Scorpions, but nods anyway. "Well, you being a hockey player, that explains a lot."

"What do you mean?"

"The missing teeth and those scars on your face, for one thing. But that shiner you're sporting looks kinda fresh."

"I was playing just last week — first round of the playoffs." He scratches the whiskers on his face. "I guess I never got around to shaving off my playoff beard, either. Anyway, we got eliminated, and my season's over." *My career, too*, he adds mentally.

Out of habit he runs his tongue through the gaps in his teeth. "Speaking of missing teeth, the little rat bastard stole my dentures, too."

Alvarez records that in her notebook. "Anything else?" she asks.

"My cellphone ... and the alligator leather bag I kept everything in. I guess that's it." He purposely omits the marijuana and cocaine he was also carrying. His supply of drugs was significantly depleted over the past few days, anyway.

"I'll be honest with you, Mr. Bronkovsky. Most of your stuff's probably been tossed in the desert somewhere." She tears off a slip of paper and hands it to Shane. "That's the police report details. You'll need it for your insurance company. My advice is, file a claim and start getting all your stuff replaced. Have you reported your credit cards missing?"

"No, not yet."

"Well, I'd start there, although I doubt that kid's got the savvy to use them. Now, we might have better luck with your bike. Given, from what you tell me, it's rare. Still, I wouldn't get my hopes up." She rises and flips her notebook shut with a practised flourish. "Where you staying, in case we need to get in touch with you?"

"I'll be here for the next couple of days until I can get some money wired to me. After that, I'm not sure, but I'll let you know."

"You're staying *here*? Hmm. Well, I guess a big macho hockey player like you should be able to take care of himself."

FIVE

Shane is dozing fitfully on the sofa when chattering voices and clattering dishes in the kitchen wake him. He opens his eyes and turns to gaze through the parlour's grimy window. Outside, the wind is blowing shifting pillars of dust across his field of view. In the far distance, a tumbleweed bounces down the driveway, dancing ever closer as if it, too, is coming to stay at the ranch house.

The sight makes Shane smile. Until a couple of days ago he had only ever seen tumbleweeds in cowboy movies, and he'd always assumed they had been a fixture of the Western landscape for eons. But last night, in a drunken conversation with a stranger at a roadhouse outside of Las Cruces, he learned that the plant was an invasive species called Russian thistle — although not really a thistle. According to the gabby stranger, it had been accidentally imported in shipments of flax seeds by Ukrainian immigrants to North Dakota in the 1870s. Clearly liking its new home, the Russian thistle had quickly spread throughout the Southwest, earning the name *tumbleweed* for its itinerant behaviour. The Hopi Indians, on the other hand, equating it with another invader, named it White Man's Plant.

Shane seldom goes out of his way to acquire new scientific or historical knowledge, but being of Ukrainian descent himself, manages to retain last night's facts. He even remembers that the plant is classified as a *diaspore* because it spreads hundreds of thousands of tiny seeds as it tumbles along. His father had often talked of the Great Diaspora that brought the family to Canada. Right now, watching the rootless invader spin in the wind, Shane can identify with the tumbleweed.

In the next room something smashes, and the sound is immediately followed by a woman's howl of indignation. From hunger as much as curiosity, Shane rises to investigate. When he enters the kitchen, the boy Vern is down on his knees picking up the pieces of a broken plate, while Tammy looms over him, scolding.

"I swear you're the stupidest, awkwardest child I ever met. Now you've gone and done it. There ain't enough plates to go around for supper. Well, you're just gonna have to eat from one of the tin bowls, that's all there is to it."

Vern says nothing, but when he looks up at Shane's entrance, there are visible tears forming at the edges of his eyes. Shane instantly feels sorry for the boy.

"That's okay," Shane says. "I don't mind eating from whatever's handy."

"No, sir, you're a guest in this house, and we ain't going to punish you on account of this one being so darn clumsy. It's only fair he pays for his mistake."

Over by the stove, Maybelline and Yolanda are fussing with pots and pans, uninterested in the spat.

"Well, something smells good, that's for sure," Shane comments, trying to steer the subject away from Vern.

41

"Nothing special. This ain't no restaurant, so you'll just have to eat what we eat."

"Silly, we're having chili willy-nilly," Maybelline calls over.

"*Con carne*," Yolanda adds. Something in her delivery makes Shane think he's missing a private joke. As the butt of countless locker room pranks in the past, he is a minor authority on the subject.

"There's rice, too, and biscuits in the oven," Tammy says.

"Oh, boy, biscuits!" Vern exclaims and jumps to his feet. He dumps the pieces of the broken plate into a trash can with a clatter and goes to hover near the oven. "Aunt Tammy makes the best biscuits."

"So, Vern's your nephew?" Shane asks.

"He's no blood kin of mine. He's my late husband's sister's son," Tammy says without enthusiasm. As if to reinforce the point, she swats the boy across the back of the head with a dish towel. "Git away from there, child. They're not ready yet. Make yourself useful and pump some water for cleaning up."

Vern's shoulders slump, but he obeys. As the boy approaches the sink, Shane again marvels at the ancient cast-iron pump in place of a faucet. Standing on the tips of his toes, with two hands, Vern begins to labour at the handle, which creaks with resistance.

"Here, let me help," Shane offers. He goes over and starts pumping, relishing the physicality of it. It takes a half-dozen strokes before a trickle of water emerges. By this time Vern has fetched a large kettle, and he gives Shane an appreciative smile.

"I took him in after both his folks were killed in a tornado over in Ector County," Tammy says. She jerks her thumb generally eastward. "That's in Texas."

Shane glances at the boy to see if there is any reaction to the mention of his parents' death, but Vern is watching him, bright-eyed, intrigued by the history of violence written on Shane's face. By now the water from the pump is flowing freely, and Shane pushes harder, feeling his biceps swell with the effort.

"Easy, *hombre*! That old thing isn't used to a big muscleman like you," Yolanda exclaims. "She won't be able to pump for a week after you've finished with her."

The other women erupt in laughter at the joke.

A veteran of locker room banter, Shane jumps reflexively into the play. "Maybe she's just out of practice. I bet with some proper lubrication she can pump all night."

"Maybe *she* can handle it, but I never met a man who could keep it up that long," Maybelline retorts, and does a curtsy.

The women all laugh again, and suddenly Shane feels like the joke is on him. He fumbles unsuccessfully for a witty retort and falls silent. The kettle is now full. Seeing Vern struggle to lift it from the sink, Shane hoists it out with ease and brings it to the stove.

His stomach growls, reminding him how long it's been since he last ate. "I'm so hungry I could eat a horse."

At this, the girl, Gracie, who has been sitting silently at the kitchen table grinding chili peppers with a stone mortar and pestle, begins to wail.

"We don't eat horses!" she screams, and pounds the table with the pestle.

"For heaven's sake, Gracie, he didn't mean nothing by it," Tammy sighs. "Tell her, Shane."

Shane squats down beside the girl. "That's right, Gracie. I didn't mean it. It's just a figure of speech."

"Oh," says Gracie. She stops blubbering, but looks unconvinced.

"I'd never really eat a horse," says Shane.

"Some folks do ... and dogs, too."

"Well, I've heard stories of them eating dogs in other countries, but they don't do that around here, do they?"

"No, silly, dogs eat horses … you know, they put 'em in dog food. I don't think it's right."

Shane's ex-girlfriend, Brandi, used to feed her Lhasa Apso the choicest food straight from the table, and frankly, Shane would have preferred for the spoiled little mutt to have been fed dog food made out of any kind of cheap animal by-product instead, but he does not say this to Gracie.

"No, I don't think it's right, either," he agrees, and that brightens her up. "My neighbour used to have a horse I was friendly with when I was growing up. His name was Opie."

"Did you ride him?"

"No, not really. He wasn't that kind of horse."

"Why? Was he too wild?"

"No, Opie was real tame. He'd eat out of my hand and let me pet his nose and stuff. But he wasn't a riding horse — he was a working horse. You know, like those ones you see in the Budweiser commercials on TV?"

"We don't got no TV," Vern interjects. He exchanges an antagonistic look with Tammy, and Shane understands that this is a point of contention within the household.

"Well, anyway, Opie was a big horse, so tall he wouldn't even fit into this room. My neighbour used him for hauling big logs from out of the woods."

"That sounds cruel," Gracie protests.

"Oh, no, Opie liked it. That's what he was born to do. He used to pull this big logging sled, and it was quite a sight to see, especially in winter. The snow could be up to a man's chest, but it didn't faze Opie at all. 'As good as a tractor, cheaper to fuel, and better company,' my neighbour used to say."

"You hear that, Mommy? A horse is cheap."

Tammy ignores her. "Dinner's ready. Here, hon. Give me them peppers, and you can dole out the cutlery. Sit down, everyone."

As Vern passes Shane, the boy runs a hand from the top of his own head and gauges where it lines up on Shane.

"Wow, if snow was up to your chest, it'd almost be over my head."

Tammy gives Vern a shove from behind. "I said sit down, child."

Shane hovers, unsure what's expected of him. Tammy's eyes circumnavigate the kitchen table, and she finally points to the head of it. "I suppose you'd best sit there," she says.

The serving bowls are brought to the table, where they send up a cloud of steam that hovers over the scene like morning mist. By now Shane's stomach is murmuring in anticipation, but no one has yet made a move toward the food.

"I guess it would be fitting if our guest said grace," Tammy announces. All eyes are on Shane. But if the invitation is meant to embarrass him, the gathering is in for a surprise. Shane spent two years of his junior hockey career billeted with a Baptist pastor and his family in Sault Ste. Marie and has learned this particular drill well.

He bows his head and begins the benediction. "Praise God, from whom all blessings flow. Bless us, O Lord, and bless this bounty we are about to receive, and grant that, healthily nourished by it, we may serve you better." Here, Shane adds a little improvisational sucking up. "And please, God, bless these good people, who as in the parable of the Good Samaritan related to us by Christ our Lord, stopped to show kindness to a stranger. We thank you in Jesus's name. Amen."

"Amen," the others echo, and before the last phoneme has faded, Vern has made a grab for the biscuits. While the others begin helping themselves to the food, Yolanda pulls out of her blouse an amulet that looks to Shane like a skull-faced Grim Reaper in a dress. She hastily murmurs a prayer in Spanish. Tammy's face tightens, but she says nothing, instead turning to Shane.

"That was a fine prayer, Shane. Care for something to drink?"

"I'd love a beer … doesn't matter what kind. I'm not fussy."

Down the table, Maybelline giggles. "*No beer here*," she sings, like it's an advertising jingle.

"I don't allow no alcohol in the house," Tammy explains. "We've got homemade lemonade, or there's ice water in the fridge."

"Lemonade'll be fine."

Tammy fills Shane's glass from a chipped china pitcher, then slides the chili his way. "Dig in before it's all gone."

Shane anchors the serving bowl with his cast and spoons out a helping. The rice and biscuits are passed his way, and he adds these to his plate. Even if he weren't practically starving, he would have found the well-spiced meal delectable. He is not used to eating without his denture plate and is grateful most of the food does not require a great amount of chewing. Even so, the pieces of meat he encounters, although tender, have to be moved around inside his mouth so his surviving teeth can chew them.

"The deputy thinks the kid who robbed me was probably run off from some place around here called Holy Waters," he says, in an attempt to start some discussion at the dinner table.

"They're not from around here. They're holed up in a big spread up north," Yolanda growls. "Pigs! *Capullos!*"

"They say the leaders keep a dozen wives apiece, some of them barely fifteen years old," Tammy adds. "Oh, they keep the women covered in them ankle-length dresses when they got them out working the fields all day, but you can be darn sure those dresses come off fast enough at night." The subject is clearly a sore point with Tammy; her face tints with anger as her words come louder and faster. "The church owns everything, so they don't even get paid for what they do. They're breeding like rabbits up there — must be a thousand of them now. The old goats want the women all to themselves, so they send the young bucks packing as soon as their juices start to flow. The elders say it's what God wants. Funny how the guys at the top always claim they got a direct private line to God's lips. Well, I hope they hear it loud and clear when the good Lord tells them to go burn in hell."

She practically shouts the last sentence, and a shocked silence descends on the gathering.

Gracie looks up from her food, wide-eyed. "Mommy, you swore."

"No, I didn't, sweetie. I was talking about H-E-double-hockey-sticks, the place bad people go when they die. I wasn't using it as a cuss word."

Vern is stuffing a third biscuit into his mouth, but his eyes widen. "Hockey sticks?" he asks.

"Oh, you and your confounded hockey," Tammy scolds. "How many times have I told you not to talk with your mouth full? And, dad gum it, boy, leave some of those biscuits for the rest of us."

The rebuke makes Vern slump in his seat, as though the words were blows that physically beat him down.

"You like hockey?" Shane asks the boy.

Vern instantly perks up. He starts to say something, but realizes his mouth is still full, so he nods vigorously instead.

"Who's your favourite team, then?"

Vern rushes to finish chewing so he can answer. "The Odessa Jackalopes! They're awesome. My dad used to take me to see them." He gives his aunt an uncertain glance, but keeps going. "The kids at school say I should cheer for the Mustangs 'cause they're from New Mexico, but I'm not gonna." He pauses for a second to catch his breath. "I guess I like the Killer Bees, too," he adds.

Shane has never heard of these teams and is uncertain how to react. He does know, however, that there is no such thing as a jackalope. Once, on a road trip to play the Dallas Stars, some teammates convinced him that the jackalope, a cross between a jackrabbit and an antelope, really did exist, and thereafter he was regularly teased about it in the dressing room — until he was traded to yet another team. He is also pretty certain that Odessa is a city in Ukraine, although he has often encountered instances of duplicitous geography. Still, something in the boy's earnest manner makes Shane believe he is sincere.

"Wow, I didn't realize hockey was so big this far south."

"I think hockey's the best! There's been a whole bunch of leagues around here … the Central Hockey League, Southern Professional Hockey League, Southern Hockey League, Western Professional Hockey League, International Hockey League. We still got the East Coast Hockey League and the North American Hockey League. That's the one the Jackalopes play in."

Gracie has been listening impatiently to her cousin, and now she interjects. "*I* like the Mustangs because mustangs are horses and because they're from New Mexico. That's why they're better." She punctuates her declaration by sticking her tongue out at Vern.

"Are not. The Jackalopes made the playoffs this year. The Mustangs were almost last."

"I don't care. Horses are way better than a bunch of crazy rabbits."

"You're the one that's crazy."

"That's enough, you two! Eat your supper," Tammy scolds, and the children fall silent but continue to glare at one another. She turns to Shane. "I expect hockey's real big up in Canada."

"I'll say. It's huge, from coast to coast to coast. Sort of Canada's religion."

"Sure, 'cause it's always covered in ice there," Yolanda chimes in. Her tone is derisive, but Shane just smiles. He is used to American misconceptions of his homeland.

"Brrr. I don't know how you stand it," Maybelline says. "We had snow this winter and I pretty near froze my *derrière* off."

"Snow? Here?" Shane is skeptical.

"Oh, it happens regular upstate in the mountains, especially 'round Christmastime and into January," Tammy confirms. "And from time to time, it blows down here, too. We usually get a dusting or two a year. But Maybelline's right — that storm last year was as bad as I've ever seen it since I moved here. Couldn't imagine dealing with that all the time, but I guess everyone's got to live somewhere."

"Personally, I'll take snow over that stuff blowing outside," Shane replies, "but I guess in the end, a man can pretty much get used to anything."

"More times than not it's the woman who's used, and expected to have to get used to it," Tammy shoots back. She looks around at the other women. "Just 'cause a body can get used to something don't mean they got to — assuming they can find someplace else to go. These ladies here will testify to that."

Tammy rises and clears her plate from the table. "Eat up, everyone, we don't want to see it go to waste." She turns to Shane. "We ain't got nothing sweet to nibble on tonight, but I'll put on a pot of coffee anyway, and then we'll see about getting you squared away for the night."

Shane takes another helping of rice and chili. Seeing only one biscuit left, he gestures for Vern to have it and is rewarded with a big smile of thanks. Together, they sit munching their food, looking up at each other periodically, and grinning.

Yolanda finishes her own meal, but stays at the table and watches Shane eat. The malevolent glimmer in her eye unnerves him. Since she offers no conversation, he avoids looking at her. Finally, when he has shovelled down the last of his food, she speaks up.

"That's quite an appetite you have. You liked it?"

"Yeah, everything was really delicious. Thanks."

"Know what kind of meat that was in the chili?"

"Not really." His intestines wobble in anticipation of a rude surprise.

"It was rattlesnake."

Anger and the contents of his stomach begin to rise, but he chokes them down. He refuses to give Yolanda the satisfaction of acknowledging she has landed a damaging shot. Besides, everyone at the table ate the same meal; it's not like he was singled out for a prank. Perhaps this is some kind of an initiation rite. If so, it's far from the worst he has ever endured.

"No kidding. Well, it went really good with the spices. My compliments to the chef."

Yolanda tries to call his bluff, pushing the chili bowl toward him. "Sure you don't want to finish it off?"

"Gosh, no. I wish I could, it was so delicious, but I'm stuffed. Thanks, anyway." He grins affably in a way that will not expose his missing teeth and locks onto Yolanda's brown eyes with an unwavering stare that says, *I can take anything you can dish out.*

Evidently having hoped for a bigger reaction, Yolanda looks away first and rises to start clearing the table.

"Coffee'll be ready in a minute," Tammy announces. "We'll put it in a travel mug so you can take it with you to the stable. It'll help warm you up until you get under the blankets. Gets cold mighty fast, now that the sun's gone down. Maybelline, round up a sleeping roll and a pillow. Vern, if you're done stuffing your stupid face with biscuits, go fetch a hurricane lantern and show Shane where he'll be sleeping."

SIX

Outside, the wind is still sandblasting the landscape, and no stars penetrate the darkness. Head down against the blowing grit, Shane follows Vern's bobbing lantern. When they reach the outbuilding and step inside, relief from the swirling dust is instantaneous. In the lantern's light, Shane discerns walls covered in rough-cut slabs of unpainted wooden siding. There is a faint scent of manure in the air, but the odour is far less pervasive than Shane had feared. A central gravel corridor runs the length of the building, and a half-dozen partitioned stalls branch off on each side.

"The toolroom's at the back," Vern says, heading down the pathway. "There's electric lights in here, but they ain't working." Their boots crunch audibly on the gravel underfoot. As Shane notes with curiosity that the stall doors are all fully open, a strange sound like a small orchestra of quaking tambourines sweeps through the stable.

"What's that noise?"

"Aw, they're just riled up. They always get antsy before feeding day, especially at night, but Aunt Tammy says we get more juice out of them if we hold off feeding till after they're milked."

As Vern's lantern light sweeps across the interior, Shane sees that the stalls do not contain any kind of farm animal, but rather stacks of cages, each one containing a very agitated rattlesnake. He realizes there are hundreds of the vipers housed in the stable.

"Holy fuck! You keep *snakes*?"

Vern turns his head and stares at Shane quizzically. "Sure, what else? *Rancho Crótalo* — Rattlesnake Ranch."

"Why the hell would anyone keep rattlesnakes?"

"Some for meat and hides, but mostly we milk 'em for the venom."

"The venom? What for?"

"They use it to make antivenom, you know, for folks who get snakebit. Well, more for animals ... dogs and horses and cattle 'n' such."

"There's money in that?"

Vern shrugs. "Some, but you'd have to ask Aunt Tammy about that. She keeps the accounts. It's not like we're rollin' in clover, I can tell you that much."

"Aren't you afraid of them?"

Vern grins bashfully. "I sure was when they first brought me here after my folks got killed. But Gracie, she grew up handling them, and she don't shy away from the rattlers at all. Well, I wasn't gonna let a girl show me up, was I? Once you get used to them, they ain't so bad. Got to be real careful-like, that's all, 'cause they're quick. It's all in how you handle them."

"I can't stay here," Shane protests.

"If you'd rather sleep outside, you're welcome to it," Vern says with a shrug. "But don't go thinking you can bunk in the ranch house. Heck, they don't even let *me* sleep inside. I got a cot in the potting shed back of the kitchen, and they send me out there and lock the doors … like I'm a dog being put out for the night. No, sir. Only womenfolk allowed."

"I … I hate snakes."

"Well, they ain't too fond of us, neither, I can tell you that, but hopefully you'll all calm down after a spell. C'mon, I'll show you where to sleep."

They resume walking, and with every crunching footstep, the snakes rattle their displeasure. At the end of the corridor is a room where tools and hardware lie in a clutter, including several rusty, worn implements that qualify as antiques. A large, chaotic workbench dominates one side of the space, and the smell of paint and gasoline hangs in the air.

A mattress stands against one wall, behind sheets of plywood and corrugated metal. Vern and Shane wrestle it out into the open, pound the dust off, and let it drop to the floor. The bed-roll, once loosened and spread out, at least looks warm and clean, and the pillow completes Shane's vague hope that this will be a suitable place to sleep. Without bothering to undress, he flops onto the bed with a sigh.

"Okay, then. I'll be getting to bed myself now," Vern says and turns to depart.

"Can you leave me the lantern?"

Vern hesitates, then sets the lamp down on the floor. "I expect I can find my way back in the dark. Careful you don't go knocking it over during the night."

The sound of his exit stirs up the caged rattlesnakes, and it takes a long time for the reptiles to settle down. Even afterward, there is never complete silence, but always the sound of one or another moving in its cage, scales rubbing against the wires, strumming them like some discordant string instrument. Shane finds his heart will not stop pounding.

"Snakes! Why did it have to be snakes?" he quotes aloud. He did once handle a garter snake as a boy during a visit to his mom's relations in Quebec, but he did it to frighten a girl cousin, and pride suppressed his squeamishness. But these needle-fanged, venom-dripping, demon-eyed, diamond-headed monstrosities squirm into the darkest recesses of his psyche and rattle him to his core.

His broken arm has begun to throb, so he fishes out some Percocet and washes down the drug with coffee. His mind briefly nags about the nighttime effects of oxycodone and caffeine, but he decides there is little chance of sleep, anyway. *Too bad I don't have a shot of something a little stronger to go with this,* he thinks, *or a nice fat joint to smoke … that would take the edge off.*

He closes his eyes and tries to relax. His body begins to numb as the narcotic goes to work, but his brain will not follow suit. His thoughts dash frantically from one end of his mind to the other, like some cornered animal. At one point he manages to doze, then he jerks upright, convinced he heard something slither into the room.

He cautiously hoists the kerosene lantern to illuminate the space around him. He hates the fact that the mattress is on the ground, right at snake level. Although logic tells him a rattler's bite wouldn't penetrate the protective wad of his bedroll, his gut remains unconvinced. The clutter in the room only makes matters worse, offering a hundred shadowy recesses where a viper could hide.

Although no slinking menace reveals itself, he rises to search for a defensive weapon. He rules out a hatchet, deciding its short length would bring him too close to a striking rattlesnake, and opts instead for a pitchfork with four nasty-looking tines. He places the weapon alongside his mattress.

Having thus garnered some peace of mind, he lies down again, shuts his eyes, and tries to calm himself, but the accident out on the highway keeps replaying itself in disturbing detail. The images are worsened by the guilt-soaked knowledge that he was at fault for his carelessness and excessive speed. But something far more menacing is gnawing its way into his consciousness, and despite his best efforts, he cannot suppress it. *Why was I going so fucking fast anyway? What if I was really trying to kill myself? Again?*

The other incidents wriggle their way back into his mind. There was the time he climbed over the balcony railing of his 41st-floor condo in Manhattan and balanced there, holding on with only five fingers ... then three ... then just one. *But you didn't let go. You climbed back over. And that was during the divorce, when you were really hurting.*

His traitorous memory moves on to the moment during his half season with Philadelphia when he learned that he had been traded again, the sixth time in nine years. Not even a heads-up swap for another player, but cast off for a fourth-round draft choice. On that occasion he had placed a hunting rifle under his chin and tested whether his arm was long enough to pull the trigger. (It was.) Even now he can distinctly feel the overwhelming bleakness of that moment, a heaviness pushing down on his chest that felt like it would never go away, as well as the tears he fought hard to contain because it was not manly to cry.

But you didn't pull the trigger, Shane. You felt it, hard and cold, against your finger ... all you had to do was squeeze, but you didn't. And that coach had it in for you from the beginning. Getting traded was the best thing that could have happened. You went to a playoff contender. They wanted you. Remember that game-winner you scored at home in Game Three of the first round? Wasn't that sweet?

It was sweet, but that was part of the problem. Those rare moments when he contributed to the team with more than his fists only made him feel worse when the glory faded into

56

memory, and he went back to his designated role. Enforcer. Fighter. Goon!

"You're what's wrong with the game!" fans would shout, and pundits would agree from the pulpit of the television screen.

"It's always been part of hockey ... it's what the fans want," others would say, and so, for eighteen years Shane has had steady work.

"Get him, Shane! Beat the crap out of him!" the hometown fans would scream when he and his opponent dropped their gloves, knotted up each other's jersey in one hand, and looked for an opening to deliver a lightning strike with the other. You'd circle around and around in that synchronized dance, the din from the cheering and jeering spectators overwhelming at times, the referees orbiting all the while, pretending they wanted to stop it, but purposely allowing it to continue.

Then there were the punches themselves. It was bad enough even when you won. The objective was to land one fully on the side of the head or in the face, but that was tricky; all too often you'd end up pounding your knuckles into a pulp on the side of someone's helmet. As for the punches you were on the receiving end of, better not to dwell on those bone-crunching blows that tilted the universe, sent a ringing through your ears, and caused a multitude of tiny flares to dance before your eyes. Blood, almost certainly, or you hadn't done your job, hadn't put on enough of a show. Stitches and lost teeth, other times. Sometimes, when you came up against someone meaner or better and got your lights punched out, the headaches afterward lasted for weeks. Lately, it seemed like they never fully went away.

He knows he is blessed just to have made it into the NHL, let alone to have played for so many years. A million kids out there would kill for his spot. He appreciates this, and thus feels guilty for the hopelessness and self-loathing he has felt, especially in the latter days of his career, which he has increasingly tried to wash away with alcohol and drugs. But he has never been able to talk to anyone about it, not even his ex-wife, Veronica, during their best years. And there were some good years — great ones, actually — especially out in California, where the fans were more interested in baseball and basketball. People didn't even recognize you, and nobody gave you a hard time, not even the media.

He and Veronica had even tried for a baby back then. Maybe things would have been different if they'd succeeded. But after the second miscarriage, she grew depressed, sometimes angry, blaming all the drugs in his system — the steroids, the painkillers — for the miscarriages. Hell, she didn't even know about all the booze and weed and coke and pills he went through, especially on the road, although that was mostly just to fit in. Especially when he had to earn his place in so many new locker rooms over the years. Perhaps he'd started out partying for kicks and camaraderie, but lately it felt like he did it to stay numb, to keep himself from losing it.

He doesn't blame Veronica for divorcing him. He made sure she was well taken care of, even when his lawyer and his agent complained he was bankrupting himself. Now he regrets not talking frankly to Veronica about the turmoil and confusion roiling within. Nor did he open up to any of the puck bunnies who came afterward, including Brandi, even after they'd shacked up together.

As these thoughts steamroll through Shane's mind, something brushes up against his foot. This time it is definitely not his imagination, and he flings himself upright in a giant spasm, jerking his knees up so high he hits himself in the chin. Earlier, he told himself that if a rattler should appear, the best thing to do would be to hold still and avoid sudden movement, but this stratagem dissipates in the face of blind, panic-driven reflex.

It is not a snake that has disturbed him, however. With a flood of relief that makes him want to laugh, he sees a mouse scurry toward the corner and meld into the shadows. Although he can practically taste the adrenalin still, Shane flops back into a prone position and feels himself relax. *You big pussy! It was only a mouse,* he chides himself. It dawns on him that if he really wanted to kill himself, he should have been hoping for an escaped rattlesnake to actually bite him. *Go stick your hand in one of those cages, if you're so hell-bent on doing yourself in, Shane. Not an appealing idea, is it?* He chooses to interpret his fear of the vipers as a will to survive.

From the corner the mouse disappeared into comes the loud snap of a mousetrap being sprung. When no follow-on squeaking or scraping ensues, he concludes that the spring-loaded bar has snapped the rodent's neck cleanly. He finds it ironic and somewhat sad that the rodent managed to elude hundreds of hissing, hellish vipers only to perish in a mousetrap. *But hey, that's life. At least it died quickly.*

Unfortunately, Shane cannot be quite so philosophical about his own recent misfortunes, especially not the incident that has ended his playing career and made him a pariah — and possibly a criminal. As has transpired every single night in the week since the tragedy took place in Chicago, Shane finds himself replaying and analyzing the fateful moment, freezing it in his mind, and viewing it from every conceivable angle.

It is not the final, fatal impact that troubles him most, although he knows he will never forget the sickening sight of Ken Linton's head smashing against the ice. No, it is the before and after of the incident that haunts Shane. He clings to the belief he did not deliberately injure Linton, although at the professional level, the game can be lightning fast, and even a veteran like Shane can find it all a disorienting blur at times.

He clearly remembers that Linton had just passed off the puck and wasn't looking where he was going — admiring his handiwork, cocky little bastard that he was. Whether or not Shane could have avoided the contact is moot. When it's the playoffs and you get a chance to catch the other team's top goal-scorer with his head down, you take it. What he did was completely within the rules of the game, and it was a clean hit, damn it — no dropped shoulder or raised elbow. Surely everyone could see that from the slow-motion replays that ran incessantly in the days afterward.

He believes Linton sensed the hit coming at the last second and started to try to dance around it, but it was too late. As a result, however, he was off balance when Shane's bulk struck his slight frame. Both players were spun around violently by the force of the collision, and Linton's helmet came flying off. It was a one-in-a-million occurrence. And then, in his mind, Shane sees it again, so vivid and real: himself fighting to stay on his feet, then rotating back just in time to see Linton's skull smash against the ice.

It was an accident, pure and simple, so what transpired afterward is equally hard for Shane to relive. An uncanny hush fell over United Center as the medical staff converged on Linton, but as he was wheeled away, with the paramedics performing CPR, a sound started — soft and low at first, but growing into an ear-numbing clamour. Twenty thousand livid Blackhawks fans were booing and screaming curses at Shane.

The game officials conferred amongst themselves, and then the referee pointed at Shane and signalled a game misconduct penalty. Shane wouldn't have thought it possible, but the crowd's decibel level shot up even higher. You could barely think in such a din, let alone conduct a conversation. He had been on the ice the entire time, hovering anxiously nearby in the hope that

Linton's eyes would flick open. When Shane saw the referee's gesture, he skated over immediately to protest the penalty. He knew the ref, Jack Olsen, fairly well, and had always considered him a fair dealer, so this was an outrage.

Olsen placed his hand on Shane's arm and shouted in his ear, "Look, I know it's not fair, but he's hurt real bad, and the crowd is screaming for blood. I'm doing this for your own protection ... to get you into the dressing room." In hindsight, Shane should have simply gone quietly. There wasn't a damn thing he could do about it. No referee ever changed his mind after a call.

But his damned temper kicked in. He shook off Olsen's hand and started berating him. All the other officials suddenly swarmed Shane — funny how they're not equally feisty when it comes to breaking up fights between players. It was drilled into Shane from a very early age that it's a grave sin to lay a hand on an on-ice official, so he actually gave up the argument the moment they converged on him. He was letting himself be towed toward the bench when one of the linesmen's skates got tangled up with Shane's, and they all went down in a heap. To the rest of the world it looked like he was resisting four officials and had to be wrestled to the ice. That clip also has been replayed constantly on television sets everywhere, second only in on-air popularity to the graphic image of Linton's lethal blow.

The Blue Jackets lost the game in overtime, and Shane could only watch the outcome helplessly from the visitors' dressing room. Afterward, not a single one of his teammates blamed him in any way. He had taken out their opponents' top sniper and given them a chance to win. Several made a point of coming over to assure him that it had been a clean hit. Of course, that was while there was still hope of a recovery for Linton. He never regained consciousness. Some announcers speculated that he'd died upon impact. They didn't release the news of his death until later.

Back in Columbus, his teammates closed ranks and helped him crash through the scrum of cameras and reporters at the airport. Ironically, his agent, Morrie Getz, was waiting to spirit him away in a cab. Ironic not because Brandi, his live-in lover and supposedly the one person in the world closest to him, hadn't shown up (she was, he'd learn shortly, too busy changing the locks on the condo, emptying out the bank account, and maxing out their joint credit cards), but because Morrie no longer had any financial incentive to help his client, given that Shane was out of a job and blackballed from the league. But Morrie has always had a soft heart, as far as agents go, and Shane supposes those eighteen years together counted for something, even if he was only paid the league minimum wage for many of those years.

Morrie dropped him off with platitudes that things could be worse. Those words soon turned out to be prophetic. Shane remembers his burning outrage upon discovering he was locked out of the home he shared with Brandi and that he'd paid for. The concierge and the building security guys were sympathetic, but firm. The condo was legally in her name — just a tax move for Shane's benefit, she had convinced him when arranging the purchase — and they had been specifically instructed that Shane no longer had access privileges. He recalls his volcanic eruption of rage in the condo's lobby, culminating with the smashing of a glass coffee table, and knows he's lucky that security didn't call the police.

In the end, Shane waited outside the building until someone was leaving the underground parking lot. Sneaking in before the automatic door closed, he punctured the tires of Brandi's BMW (also paid for by him) before riding off on the Ducati — the one remaining thing of worth that was truly his.

The rest is a hazy, vodka-soaked, cocaine-powdered half memory for Shane. He foraged as much cash as he could, climbed on his motorcycle, and rode west originally, toward Chicago, having some fuzzy notion of trying to explain himself to the media and fans there. But the idea made less sense the closer he got, and in central Illinois, he stumbled across signs for the legendary Route 66 and decided to follow it southwest. Not because the signs proclaimed Route 66 to be the "Mother Road" and the "Main Street of America," but rather because Mario Lemieux, Shane's biggest hockey hero, had worn number 66. They were comparable in physical size, though not scoring prowess. *I followed Number 66 into the NHL,* Shane reasoned. *Let's see where it takes me now.*

Where it took him was Missouri, Kansas, Oklahoma, the top of Texas, and finally New Mexico. During the day, he'd drive as far as his hockey-ravaged body and the Ducati's poor ergonomics allowed, before finding some cheap motel for the night and getting wasted. For company, he frequented roadhouses and dive saloons, conversing with anyone he met at the bar or behind it, but never divulging his true identity or occupation. His playoff beard helped disguise his now infamous face, and he wore sunglasses, even at night.

There was something appealing in the anonymity. It wasn't just avoiding the frenzy over Linton's death. People treated you differently when they found out you were a professional athlete — like a celebrity, or at least someone who should buy a round for the house. It was an eye-opener to see the world from the cheap seats, as just another Joe sitting on a barstool.

In New Mexico, Route 66 lost its appeal, or rather, the idea of ending up in California did. He decided to work his way down the back roads and eventually out of the country to Mexico, where his money would go further, and where no one had ever heard of Shane Bronkovsky. Or Kenny Linton. And so, that morning, after sleeping off his latest hangover, he checked out of a motel near Las Cruces and rode south. It was a beautiful day for it, sunny and warm, the highway practically deserted, with straightaways where he could really open up the Ducati ...

And look where you ended up, Shane. Busted up. Robbed blind, left with just the clothes on your back. Sleeping on a dirt floor surrounded by poisonous snakes.

He lies there in the dark, listening to the wind flinging grit against the stable, while inside, serpents sporadically strum the wires of their cages, and he ponders his misfortune. He doubts that the universe singled him out for special punishment, reasoning that this is more like one of those occasional one-sided hockey games where every bounce and rebound and call by the referee went the other team's way, and his side would get royally drubbed. "That's all right, boys," the coach would say then. "It was just one of those nights. We'll get 'em next time."

Yup, shit happens, Shane. What was it they used to say back home in Peel Crossing? Sometimes you eat the bear, and sometimes the bear eats you.

Shane doesn't know if there are any bears around this part of the States, but he supposes the locals have an equivalent aphorism. Given that Tammy seems to be fairly religious, he imagines her saying something like, "The Lord giveth, and the Lord taketh away."

Tammy. His restless mind, having run itself out stampeding across space and time, comes to roost at *Rancho Crótalo*. Despite the boy Vern's admonishment that men are not allowed inside the house — or perhaps because of it — his imagination takes him inside those tired, old walls. Although it would be impractical and highly improbable, he pictures himself and the ranch's three women sleeping together in one bed.

He dismisses the thought that even a fully functional man would have trouble satisfying three women. In his case, on top of the headaches and dizziness plaguing him for the past few years, there have been persistent bouts of impotence. But, hell, it's only a fantasy, so he pushes pragmatism aside, hoping to masturbate and ride the afterglow of orgasm into a deep sleep.

He struggles to remove his jeans one-handed. *Good thing I didn't break my right hand*, he jokes to himself. It is an old locker room barb. "Hey, buddy, there goes your sex life." The proper retort, he's learned, is: "Are you kidding? I've switched hands and now it feels like someone else."

But it is fruitless. No amount of fantasizing or rubbing can induce an erection. Sighing, he rolls over and resigns himself to a night of masturbatory celibacy.

SEVEN

Morning squeezes through the seams of the barn board and prods Shane awake. Despite a sleepless night, he is actually feeling pretty good, given it is the first time in a week he hasn't had a hangover. There's an unexpected chill on his nose, and he would prefer to stay bundled in the bedroll, but the need to urinate asserts itself.

The wind has died, and the low-slung sun is proclaiming its presence. Shane empties his bladder and takes a minute to study the landscape. As barren and alien as the Chihuahuan Desert first appeared, and despite the bad things that happened here, he's beginning to see that it possesses its own unique beauty. Different, certainly, than the in-your-face green upon green of the boreal forest where he grew up. No, this is more like the woods in winter, blanketed uniformly in white, but given infinite variety by the underlying topography. And there are mountains here, too, admittedly distant and hazy, but surrounding them on all four sides.

It's been a while since Shane has been up this early, but he doubts he's risen before the ranchers. He heads toward the ranch house in search of breakfast. The kitchen door is unlocked, a sign the women are up and about. He pushes through and finds himself in the middle of an argument, albeit a one-sided one.

"The teacher knows we need you here today," Tammy is telling an unhappy Vern. "We've talked with her about it a bunch of times."

"But I'm missing the lesson on fractions. It's hard enough already to keep up with the other kids. You're the one that told me how important it is for me to learn my 'rithmetic."

"Land's sake, child, missing one day of classes ain't gonna kill you. Most kids are just itching to skip school."

Shane takes this moment to interrupt. "Good morning, everyone."

"Ain't nothing good about it," Vern complains.

Tammy swipes him across the back with a dish towel. "Don't ever say that! Thank the good Lord you're alive and got a roof over your head ... got enough to eat."

"Er, speaking of enough to eat ..." Shane interjects, as much to defuse some of the flak Vern's taking as to get fed.

"Just putting on a fresh pot of coffee. There's oatmeal, if you want," Tammy replies.

"Well, maybe a small bowl. But a big mug of coffee for sure, when it's ready."

"Well, don't go expecting me to wait on you. Pot's on the stove. Bowls are in the cupboard. Sugar's in the pantry. Spoons are in the drawer."

"Listen, I couldn't help overhearing when I came in ... about Vern and school and whatnot. I don't mind helping out around here today. Maybe that way you can spell the kid."

"With a busted-up arm?" inquires Tammy.

"I still got one good right hand, and I'm pretty sure I can be as much help with one as Vern is with two."

The boy looks hopeful, but Tammy frowns. "I appreciate what you're trying to do, but it's going to be a crazy busy day, and we won't have time to be showing you the ropes. The boy already knows exactly what to do. Besides, it's gone on eight o'clock, and the school bus has passed by, anyway. But it's mighty kind of you to offer your services ... I'm pretty sure we can find something for that one good right hand of yours to do. You'd best eat up, now. We'll be starting work pretty soon."

Shane pours himself a cup of coffee, but hangs around the stove to watch Tammy at work. In profile, she's like a different woman. Her nose is petite, and although it's got a slight bump in the middle, there's an alluring appeal to that. Her bottom lip has a cute little permanent pout. The more he looks, the more he enjoys the view.

"Can I help with the dishes?" he offers.

"Not unless you're fixing to get that plaster wet."

"I could dry."

She considers that. "All right, give 'er a whirl. Dish towel's hanging there."

Shane passes behind Tammy, taking care not to touch or brush up against her, and leans in to secretly take in her scent, which has a sweet natural muskiness to it.

As he dries the dishes, he finds that his casted hand has limited grasp, so he switches to using it for towelling instead.

"That's supposed to be good for you," he comments, when Tammy notes the change.

"What is?"

"Switching up hands ... you know, doing things with your left hand you normally do with your right."

"Do tell."

"Yeah, something about carving new neural pathways in the brain. It's one of the reasons people get feebleminded as they get older. Their brains are stuck in a rut."

"Well, too bad you didn't break your other wrist, then. You'd get a heaping helping of new pathways that way."

Shane likes this wry sense of humour Tammy is revealing, and he smiles, careful to keep his lips pressed together so his missing teeth don't show. That action reminds him that he will eventually need to call his dentist to order a replacement plate, but the phone number is lost along with all the others in his stolen cellphone.

He's starting to realize just how troublesome piecing his life back together will be — further complicated by the fact he has no actual home address. He ponders all the places he has lived over the past two decades and realizes there isn't a single one he can call home.

"You're doing a great job," Tammy says. "We're almost done. You'll make someone a fine wife some day," she jokes.

"Been there, done that, bought the T-shirt," he replies. He wants her to know this about him — that he is not some shift-less drifter, that he is capable of commitment. Someone once saw enough in him to want to marry him and start building a life together, regardless of how it ended up.

"You don't say. Any kids?"

"No. We tried, but —"

"Oh," is all she has to say. Eventually, she pulls the plug out of the sink and declares, "I reckon we best be joining the others." The sudden end to their brief intimacy sours Shane's mood. Still, as a final demonstration of goodwill, he hastens to wash out his coffee mug in the ebbing dishwater.

Inside the front entrance of the stable, a crude plywood work platform has been set up on sawhorses. Tammy strolls up and instantly takes charge.

"All right, let's move 'em in," she commands, like some Hollywood trail boss.

Shane sits on the sidelines, clueless as to how to help. Only when he sees Vern struggling to reach over his head to bring down the top cage from the first stall does Shane sees an opportunity. He reaches for the cage, but freezes as the viper squirms and hisses. Its mouth opens impossibly wide, revealing an unsettlingly moist, pinkish maw and curved, needle-like fangs. He tells himself the reptile cannot possibly bite through the wires, even as some deeper instinct makes his body hair bristle. A tremor passes through him, like the cold kiss of a winter wind.

His trance is broken when the cage starts teetering. Vern's smaller fingers poke between the wires as the boy struggles to steady it. Shane grabs the top handle and, holding the crate well away from himself, easily hoists it down to the ground.

Vern mutters a quick, "Much obliged," and practically runs the cage over to the work platform that Tammy and Gracie are standing beside. The boy balances the crate on the edge and slides open the cage door. Gracie holds a rod with a semi-circular bend at its end, and she pokes it inside to lift the rattler around its middle. Perfectly balanced, the snake is suspended, tense but helpless.

Gracie hoists out the snake and dumps it onto the platform, where Tammy, wielding a short iron shaft with a T-shape at the end, presses down behind the rattlesnake's diamond-shaped head, immobilizing the business end.

Although he is at a safe distance, Shane's heart beats fiercely as he watches Tammy coolly grab the snake just behind its head. As she picks up the rattler, Gracie comes in to hold up the tail and support some of the weight. The girl sees Shane watching, and with an impish grin, gives the snake's rattle a shake, like it's a child's toy.

Together, mother and daughter bring the rattlesnake to a large glass jar whose opening is covered by a thin sheet of clear plastic film. Tammy presses the viper hard near the edges of its mouth, and the jaws swing fully open. Then she jams the exposed fangs through the top of the plastic and squeezes again. There is an explosion of yellowish fluid; the venom drips down to collect at the bottom of the jar.

The rattlesnake, thus milked, is dropped back onto the platform, then Gracie wrangles it back into its cage. Vern then takes away the coop and deposits it in a previously empty stall. As the boy approaches to fetch a new subject, Shane, having seen how the work flows, already has the next cage waiting. Vern offers up a big grin, nods, and carries off the snake to be milked.

Maybelline and Yolanda enter the stable carrying plastic pails. In the coolness of the morning air, steam wafts from the containers, and when Shane peeks inside, he discovers that they contain freezer bags stuffed full of frozen mice defrosting in a bath of hot water.

"You want to do the feeding?" Yolanda asks with a smirk.

Although her mocking attitude irritates him, Shane is reluctant to take up the challenge. "That's okay, I'll just watch for a bit … you know, to see how it's done."

Yolanda picks out a mouse, opens the cage belonging to the rattler just milked, tosses in the rodent corpse, and slams the hatch shut.

"There. Really complicated."

The snake slithers up to the dead mouse, its forked tongue flickering in the air. Then its mouth unhinges and spreads wide as it swallows the rodent whole, starting with the head. Shane feels a spasm of revulsion at the sight.

"*Buen apetito!*" Yolanda says, like a proud chef. She hands Shane the freezer bag. "Here, you feed them. Maybelline and I have a mess of meat and hides to make."

Shane peers inside without enthusiasm. There is little consistency in the size or even type of dead animal inside. There are mostly common brown field mice mixed with white lab mice, but also numerous other small rodents he cannot identify.

"Where do you get them all from?" he asks.

"Some we catch, some we trade for," Yolanda replies. "There's an old fellow up in the hills who collects them for us. The rest we buy when we have to. Got a lot of nasty big mouths to feed, don't we?" Yolanda and Maybelline head off toward one of the other stalls, chuckling between themselves as they go.

Shane has little time to reflect, as Vern is back with a freshly milked rattlesnake, and the process continues non-stop. He and the boy develop a rhythm, with Shane hoisting out the next cage in line and positioning it in the aisle, then hastening back to feed each devenomized snake. He uses his casted hand to slide open the cage doors and his good one to speedily toss in each meal. Then he stacks the cage and repeats the process.

After feeding a dozen rattlers, he feels himself relaxing around the reptiles. Not a single one has made so much as a casual lurch in his direction. They tend to be docile, either because they are dazed from the milking procedure, or because they are conditioned to await the arrival of their food. As Shane becomes used to them, he starts to appreciate other aspects of their appearance beyond the fearsome ones. The diamond pattern and the leathery texture of their skin are fascinating, as are their catlike eyes, which seem to miss nothing. By now, he is also starting to note the variation in their length and girth and adjust their meal selection accordingly. A few of the defrosted rodents are some kind of wild rat — at any rate, they are bigger and fatter than the mice — and he sets these aside to feed to the largest snakes.

At one point he goes to receive a returning cage and looks up to see Tammy holding it.

"Where are Yolanda and May?" she asks.

"Took off as soon as they brought the mousesicles. Said they had other work to do."

"You been helping here the whole time, then?"

"Sure have."

She smiles. "Yup, you'll make someone a good wife someday."

"Is this what wives normally do in New Mexico?"

"Mister, this ain't what wives normally do anywhere." She points down at the cage beside her. "Don't bother feeding that one. He's for butchering and tanning. Set him aside for the gals. We're making good time. Let's take a break, and I'll go rustle us up some coffee."

Shane picks up the snake earmarked for slaughter and finds the other women in a rear stall set up as a reptilian butcher shop. A large wood block dominates the middle, where Yolanda is carving up fillets of meat, a picnic cooler beside her. Meanwhile, Maybelline is seated against the wall, and on her knees is a wooden pegboard onto which she is stretching a snakeskin.

"Tammy said to bring you this one," Shane says.

"Put it on the table," Yolanda commands.

Shane complies, and watches as Yolanda pulls out a well-cared-for machete. Before proceeding, she reaches into her blouse, pulls out the death's-head necklace he noted earlier, and delivers it a quick kiss. Then she dexterously flicks open the cage door, reaches inside with the flat of the machete to hoist out the snake by its midsection, plops the victim onto the block, and before the rattler can react, chops off its head.

Both pieces of the serpent continue to thrash about. Yolanda holds down the head with the machete, grabs it from behind, and waves the halved snake, its face forward and mouth menacingly agape, at Shane.

"Did you know a rattlesnake can still bite you after its head is cut off?" she tells him. He doesn't know if this is true, but isn't about to find out the hard way.

73

"Stick it up your ass, then," he retorts, and leaves the laughing women to their bloody work.

Tammy returns with a Thermos, juice boxes for the kids, and a platter of snacks. She pours Shane a mug of coffee. He finds himself hoping she'll sit beside him for a while, but she leaves to deliver refreshments to Yolanda and Maybelline. Shane sits sipping and munching, studying the two children.

"I'm old enough to drink coffee if I want to, on account of I'm twelve years old now," Vern informs Shane, catching his gaze. "But I prefer juice."

"Juice is better for you, anyway," Shane replies.

"How old are *you*?" asks Gracie.

"I'm thirty-eight."

"You look a lot older."

"Thanks, that's sweet of you to say so."

Gracie misses the sarcasm and smiles at Shane. "My birthday is May thirteenth. I'm a Taurus."

"Bull!"

"No, it's true."

"I meant that Taurus is the sign of the bull."

"Oh." She thinks about that for a second and giggles. "You're funny."

"So your birthday is coming up soon."

She nods enthusiastically. "I'm going to be eight."

"What do you do on your birthday? Do you have, like, a party, with balloons and cake and ice cream and stuff?"

Gracie frowns. "I dunno." She looks down in the dirt and won't meet Shane's eyes.

Tammy comes crunching back down the corridor and instantly notices her daughter's expression.

"What's going on?" she asks.

"I was just asking about Gracie's birthday."

"Well, plenty of time to talk about that later. Right now we got work to do. C'mon, you two, let's get cracking. Vern, go fetch the next cage."

The children move to comply, but when Shane gets up to go with Vern, Tammy grabs his arm to hold him back.

"Listen," she says, lowering her voice, "I realize you didn't know better, not having kids of your own and all, but I don't want you filling their heads with any kind of crazy notions."

Shane has no idea exactly what he's done wrong, but is irritated by her insinuation that he has no sense in these matters, just because he hasn't fathered children. "We were talking, that's all."

"It's just we don't make a big deal of birthdays around here. It's tough enough makin' ends meet as it is. We really don't have money to spare on presents and parties and stuff."

"Sorry, I didn't know. Like I said, we were just shooting the breeze."

"Well, you'll be gone tomorrow, free as that breeze, but we're the ones that gotta stay behind and make do as best we can."

"Look, I said I was sorry. I'm going to go help Vern now, okay?"

"Okay." She looks like she wants to say something more, but bites back her words. Shane's not sure whether she feels she went too far, or not far enough.

With an extra helper, the rest of the morning goes smoothly. Except for yesterday's injuries, Shane is in end-of-season shape, and does not find the work taxing. However, he can see young Vern start to fatigue, even with Shane there to hoist the cages. Intermittently the boy does something to earn a verbal rebuke from Tammy, and in one case gets smacked on the ass with the metal wrangling rod.

"Lawd A'mighty, boy. If dumb was dirt, you'd cover about an acre," she chides him. Shane can see why the boy prefers school.

They break for a lunch of egg salad sandwiches and iced tea. Outside the stable, the sun shines brilliantly, and there is no wind to stir up dust, so he opts to take his meal in the fresh air. Despite Tammy's admonishment about talking to the children, he is glad when Vern follows and sits next to him.

"Hard work, eh?" Shane comments. Vern just shrugs.

"Say, Vern, last night you said something about the lights inside not working properly."

"Yeah, all the electricity inside the stable's screwed up. It's all old wiring from the 1920s, I think."

"Well, I know something about electricity. Me and my dad replaced all the old knob and tube wiring in our house when I was about your age. Actually, I've helped quite a few buddies wire cottages and houses over the years, too. Got a knack for it, if I do say so myself. How about you and me have a look after the milking?"

"Well, I'm supposed to do my homework …" Vern starts, but then he breaks into a toothy grin. "But, yeah, we can do it when Aunt Tammy goes to ship off the juice. It'd be kinda nice to have lights and a working fridge in there again, not to mention proper heaters for the critters in winter."

Shane gives him a playful punch on the arm. "Well, I'm sure it's something we men can figure out, eh?"

EIGHT

When, around midafternoon, Shane watches the final dead rodent being kneaded into a giant lump inside a rattlesnake's body, he feels a swell of pride, both for his work contribution and for overcoming his revulsion toward the vipers. He stacks the last of the cages and wanders out to check on the rest of the team.

Tammy is transferring the venom from the milking jar into a stainless-steel vessel that reminds Shane of a cocktail shaker. The day's extraction takes up just half of the container, and the liquid's yellowish colour gives it the appearance of a urine specimen.

"Liquid gold," he comments.

"I wish. Used to sell to a bunch of different places and get top dollar for it, but now a big lab up in New York has pretty much cornered the market, and that ain't been good for prices. Not to mention shipping costs ... got to send it expedited air freight. But at least they're still sticking to certified suppliers. If that ever changes, we'll be shoot out of luck."

"You're a certified facility?"

"Darn tootin'. Got the paperwork and everything."

"How do you get certified for something like this? Is there some kind of special rattlesnake milking test you have to take?" He means to be funny, but it comes out sounding like he's mocking her, and Tammy flashes him a displeased glance.

"Don't know, actually. It was my husband's doing. This whole dang place was my husband's doing." Resentment oozes from the statement.

"Have you thought about doing some other kind of ranching? Cattle or the like?"

"This ranch ran cattle for pretty near a hundred years. Fought off Mescaleros, rustlers, cattle barons, and even the government. Lived through disease and drought. Never amounted to much, but at least they kept it going all those years, and that's something, I reckon. Then Bobby — that's my husband — inherited the place and got it in his fool head he could get rich raising rattlesnakes. Gave away all the steers ... can you believe that? Didn't even sell them, just gave them away to anyone who showed up with a trailer. Said he never wanted to see another cow again as long as he lived. Well, that's one promise he managed to keep, all right."

"Where's he now, your husband?" he asks, knowing the answer but not the details.

"He's dead, okay? Died in Iraq, blown up so bad there weren't enough pieces to fill a shoebox. And I'm the one left standing, trying to keep everything together ... eating snake meat and can't even afford a decent beefsteak now."

Tammy is visibly upset by the subject. Shane senses that she takes pride in her strength and resents this loss of self-composure. She turns her back and begins fiddling with the venom containers. "Look, if you don't mind, some of us are trying to earn a living," she says.

Sorry to have stirred up lingering bitterness, Shane mumbles an apology and allows Tammy her privacy. He wanders off to see how the other women are progressing. Judging from the smell in the air, Maybelline has applied some kind of treatment to the stretched-out snakeskins, which she is now arranging to dry. Yolanda, meanwhile, is packing away a set of scales. Shane is surprised to see that most of the meat she's cut up has been weighed, packaged, and labelled, as if destined for a supermarket. There are several smaller Styrofoam containers on the ground with what appears to be dry ice inside them, generating a mini fog above each, and this strengthens his conviction that the meat is not meant for their consumption.

"You guys sell that meat?" he asks. He fully expects a sarcastic retort, or to be threatened with the machete, but Yolanda is surprisingly talkative.

"Grade A ranch-raised rattlesnake. That's us. Most of it goes to a distributor in Nevada for restaurants that want some exotic Southwestern dishes on the menu. They charge enough for it — what a joke. But we ship some of it to Chinese butchers in San Francisco and New York, too. They got clients who think the meat has special powers." She grabs her crotch suggestively, like men sometimes do. "Maybe we should have charged you extra for that meal you had last night. *Esta perron!*"

"I don't need performance enhancers," he lies. "So, rattlesnake for supper again tonight?"

"Nope. Tonight we're gonna celebrate. Tammy's taking the python piss and meat up to Deming for shipment. On the way home she'll buy a couple of chickens. We'll barbeque them up real good."

"I don't suppose there's any chance she'll pick up a bottle of *vino* while she's at it."

Maybelline laughs. "*It's dry in the desert*," she sings in a little girl's voice, then mimes like she's choking.

"*Puta loca*," Yolanda says, but she is laughing, too.

Tammy comes crunching up the aisle. "What's so funny?" she asks. Shane fears the women will snitch that he was asking after booze and is relieved when they keep his confidence.

"*Nada*. Shane here was just disappointed we wouldn't be grilling up any rattlesnake tonight, that's all."

"I think you'll find Yolanda's chicken is nearly as good. Speaking of rattlesnake, that meat good to go yet?"

"Almost. Just have to close and label the boxes."

"Well, hurry it up. I need to haul buns. Bring it out to the truck when you're done. *Rapido!*"

Once Tammy is out of earshot, Shane whistles. "She can be pretty bossy, huh?"

Expecting agreement, he is surprised to find himself between Yolanda's crosshairs again.

"What the fuck do you know, *hombre*? You try doing half of what that woman does in a day. If it wasn't for her, we'd all be screwed. Come to think of it, she saved your bacon yesterday, too, didn't she?" She reaches beneath the butcher's block, pulls out the machete, and embeds it in the wood with a demonstrative thud.

"Whoa. Peace. I was just making an observation. I didn't mean anything by it." But he feels no anger at Yolanda's hostility. He respects her loyalty and shares her high opinion of Tammy. "I'm going now. *Adios, señoritas*."

"*Señora. Soy una señora*," Yolanda calls after him.

Shane begins troubleshooting the stable's electrical issues. He starts with the overhead lights, whose exposed wires run the length of the building. He follows the line as it passes over several of the original porcelain insulating knobs, then finally snakes down a beam to an ancient wall switch near the entrance. He goes over and flicks the switch a couple of times, just to be sure, but unsurprisingly, nothing happens.

Maybelline and Yolanda hurry past him, each one toting a cooler. In the yard the pickup truck starts up, grinds its transmission, finds the gear, and drives off, lofting a tail of dust behind it. The truck is barely out of sight when Vern comes running out of the house, eager to help.

"Let's start by checking out the backroom and seeing what tools we got, okay?" Shane suggests. "Can't be handymen without tools, right?"

They pillage the cluttered toolroom for stuff that might be useful, collecting everything in an old carpenter's apron that Vern asks to wear. Then Shane has the boy fetch a ladder and, working from the fuse box forward, they start their diagnosis.

It turns out the light switch itself has failed — in a shower of sparks, Shane surmises from the carbon residue splattering the inside of the housing — but they do not have a replacement switch. The bulbs shine brightly overhead when they bypass the light switch altogether and connect the wires, but clearly it is not feasible to have lights burning non-stop.

"I'm not sure who'd hate it worse, the rattlers, or Aunt Tammy when she gets the electric bill," Vern comments.

It is Vern who comes up with the idea of cannibalizing the on-off switch from a discarded vacuum cleaner, and because of Shane's limited manual agility, the boy also performs the bulk of the wiring himself. When the impromptu replacement has been installed and successfully passes the flick test, the two handymen whoop and shake hands.

Phase Two is not quite as successful. They only manage to restore power to one lone receptacle, as it soon becomes obvious that the run of ancient wiring leading to the remaining outlets has degraded beyond usefulness. In the interest of safety, Shane has Vern disconnect those lines altogether.

"I'm surprised that fuse didn't pop," he comments, shaking his head. "Count yourself lucky you didn't have an electrical fire. One big accident waiting to happen, if you ask me."

"Wow," is the boy's only comment, but judging from how much his eyes widen, he's picturing the calamity that's been avoided.

"You should pick up a proper light switch next time you're in town," Shane counsels, "but the whole downstairs needs rewiring. Good industrial-gage wire. Junction boxes. Brand new receptacles. Cut over that antique of a fuse box to a new panel with some proper circuit breakers."

"That's … that's a lot of work. I wouldn't even know how."

"You can always do the basic stuff and hire an electrician for the tricky parts."

"Oh, geez. I don't think Aunt Tammy's gonna spend money on that. She keeps saying we got nothing to spare." Vern has grown visibly agitated by the financial implications of their surreptitious little repair job.

Shane puts his arm around the boy's shoulders. "Anyway, it's not something we have to worry about today. Besides, we did all right getting the lights and one outlet fixed, don't you think? Great job, Vern. High-five!"

The boy's humour returns, and he gives Shane's palm a celebratory smack.

"You should probably go and do that homework now, though, before your aunt comes back."

"Oh yeah, right. Okay. See ya later, Shane." Vern starts toward the house, then stops and turns. "You're leaving tomorrow, ain't you?"

Shane nods. The boy's face tightens, but he says nothing. As he walks away, he glances back over his shoulder.

The sun is tilting toward the western mountains, but there are a few hours of daylight left, and Shane ponders how to kill time. As often happens when he's idle, the desire for a drink or a snort of cocaine asserts itself. Although it's grown quite hot outside, he feels chilled. Everything around him seems a little blurry, and if he stares too long at the blue sky, the world begins to spin. His stomach has not been right all day, either, and he's been suffering occasional spasms in his lower abdomen.

Shane goes back to the toolroom, thinking he'll take a nap. When he lies down on his mattress, he starts to shiver, so he climbs beneath the bedroll and curls up into a tight ball. Eventually the tremors stop, and he slips into a dreamless, cavernous sleep.

✗ ✗ ✗ ✗ ✗

Someone is shaking his shoulder and trying to wake him. Shane sits up, disoriented, his mouth feeling like it's stuffed with cotton. Outside, everything is darkness, and Shane realizes he's slept past sunset. Maybelline is sitting beside him on the mattress, holding a hurricane lantern.

"Wow, I really conked out," Shane groans. "Is it time to eat?"

Maybelline gives her head a playful shake, causing her red hair to dance. "*Where were you at the barbeque?*" she sings. "*We ate and ate but Shane was late.*"

Shane is still groggy, but it sinks in that no one woke him for the meal. "I missed supper?"

"Yolanda tried to call you. Said if you'd rather sleep than eat, that was your problem." Maybelline produces a wicker basket and pulls out a cellophane-covered plate, waving it enticingly in front of him. "I saved you some, though. Chicken, potato salad, and corn niblets."

Shane's stomach growls on cue, and Maybelline giggles. "Someone's hungry," she says.

As Shane unwraps the plate, Maybelline suddenly gives a squeal of joy. "*Double, triple, we can tipple,*" she sings eagerly. "I brought something else." She reaches into the basket and holds up a quart mason jar half full of a clear liquid. Unscrewing the lid, she hands the jar to him. The inside of Shane's mouth feels like a skunk has crawled in there and emptied its sac before dying, so he takes a big swallow.

A wave of toxic fumes explodes up his nasal passage, and his eyeballs suddenly throb as if they're about to blow out of his skull. He gasps for air, realizing he has just taken a substantial undiluted chug of some potent alcoholic beverage.

"Whoa," he comments hoarsely, wagging his head to restore cranial function.

Maybelline giggles and takes a swig herself. "Good, huh? It's the best moonshine in Luna County."

Shane glances guiltily toward the doorway. Maybelline puts a finger to her lips. "Shhh. Tammy don't know nothing about it. She'd probably run me off the place if she did."

"It'll be our little secret," Shane promises her.

Making occasional noises of appreciation, he hastily eats the food, washing it down periodically with cautious sips from the liquor jar as it passes between them. Maybelline, meanwhile, has kicked off her shoes and cozied up beside him on the mattress. When he has finished with his plate, she leans over to take it and glances upward at him. In that instant it seems to Shane that Maybelline may want him to kiss her ... then again, it might just be side effect of the booze.

He has never been adept at divining female nuances, and one of his biggest fears is misinterpreting a signal and forcing himself upon an unwilling woman. As a consequence, he knows he has missed some sexual opportunities in the past by being too cautious — or too obtuse — to decipher an invitation. Still, he has seen teammates embroiled in nasty public scandals, and some have even faced criminal charges of rape or indecent assault, so he has always been content to take the better-safe-than-sorry approach.

He is doubly cautious because he knows his professional persona, cultivated by the showmen of his sport, is of some dangerous, violent beast. Certainly, his explosive, often spectacular acts of rage have fuelled this reputation, along with the bloody on-ice fights he engages in regularly in front of tens of thousands, sometimes millions of viewers. He resents that he is believed by extrapolation to be a brute by nature. With the exception of a couple of barroom brawls — which he did not initiate and where he acted in self-defence — he has never assaulted or battered someone off the ice. And he has certainly never hurt a woman, not even in moments of white-hot rage. To him this would be unthinkable.

"Thanks for thinking of me," he tells Maybelline.

"Nice to have someone to drink with. Not quite the same thing sneaking out back by yourself." She studies his face, making him self-conscious about his appearance. It's bad enough that he's missing his dentures, but it dawns on him that he's going on two days without a shower. "Tammy says you're married," Maybelline adds after a moment.

"I was. I'm divorced now."

"How long?"

"How long was I married, or how long since the divorce?"

She shrugs. "Both."

"I was married for six years. We got divorced five years ago."

She bites her lip as she digests the information. "I like you," she finally concludes, squeezing his bicep, although it somehow sounds like the pronouncement of a six-year-old. Shane can't glean whether it's meant to be a sexual come-on. His mind wrestles with the parameters of the problem — the degree of uncertainty, his bouts of sexual dysfunction, and something else, or rather *someone* else hovering at the periphery of his thoughts.

Abruptly, the overhead lights go on.

"See, Aunt Tammy, I told you we got 'em working," Vern's voice echoes down the stable.

Maybelline grabs the liquor jar from Shane's hands and leaps up to stuff it behind some paint cans in the corner. Handing the dinner plate back to him, she whispers, "Here, pretend like you're just finishing eating," as the crunching footsteps draw nearer. Shane complies, and Maybelline steps into her shoes, tugs down her dress, extracts some breath mints from a pocket, and pops them into her mouth. She flits to the far end of the room and leans against the workbench. When Tammy and Vern enter, Maybelline is pretending to fish through a box of bolts, not even looking in Shane's direction.

"Well, look who finally woke up," Tammy says.

"Can't believe I passed out like that," Shane says with a laugh. "Must have been the medicine the doc gave me. I really appreciate you saving dinner for me, though. It was delicious."

"Uh-huh," Tammy replies. She glances in Maybelline's direction, then scrutinizes Shane, but eventually her face softens. She gestures upward. "Vern says that's your doing."

Before he can answer, Maybelline comes over. "You finished?" she asks, acting indifferent. When Shane nods, she takes the plate, gives him a wink that Tammy can't see, and leaves the room. Shane makes a point of not watching the redhead's retreating backside, instead looking at Tammy and indicating the cast on his hand.

"I wasn't much help, really. Vern did most of the work."

The boy is as excited as a puppy being petted, but he refuses to hog the credit. "I couldn't have done it without Shane. He showed me what to do. We're a good team."

Tammy actually smiles at Vern's exuberance. "Well, we're much obliged."

"Shane says we could redo the whole stable if we had the materials." Vern cuts himself off, realizing what he's just said.

Tammy's grin evaporates. "Well, Shane's leaving tomorrow, ain't he, and we got no money for new wiring nohow." She prods Vern toward the door before turning to address Shane. "The Western Union office in Columbus opens at nine, so I figured we'd leave right after the kids are on the school bus. Okay with you?"

It's not really a question, and Shane nods assent.

"All right, then." Tammy gestures toward the kerosene lantern beside Shane's bed. "I reckon you'll be all right with just the lamp. We'll turn off the lights on the way out. Just because we got 'em don't mean we have to burn up electricity. See ya in the morning."

NINE

Shane wakes the next morning to discover he's over-slept and missed saying goodbye to the children. He is annoyed with himself, having intended to get up at the crack of dawn, although his throbbing head tells him he can partially blame it on the moonshine. Only Yolanda is in the kitchen when he finally shows up at the ranch house, scrubbing the tarnish off an old kettle. She looks up at Shane with antipathy when he enters.

"Where is everyone?" he asks.

"Died of old age waiting for you to get up. Going on ten o'clock."

"Why the hell didn't somebody wake me?"

She leaps to her feet and slams the kettle on the tabletop. "What the hell you think this is? A hotel? You want a wake-up call? Maybe you want the maids to come and make up your bed. Or fuck you in the bed while they're at it."

"Yolanda! Watch your language," Tammy shouts from the doorway behind them. Yolanda shrivels like a chastised child, but continues to mutter in Spanish under her breath. "You ready to go?" Tammy demands brusquely.

Shane had hoped for a cup of coffee and some breakfast and was even thinking of asking if he could impose on them for a bath or shower before heading to town, but now he abandons these notions.

"Sure. Um, where's Maybelline?"

"Why do you want to know?"

"Just wanted to say goodbye, that's all."

"She's busy. You got everything?"

"Didn't exactly come with much."

"Okey dokey, then. Meet me out front. I'll go bring around the truck."

Shane turns to address Yolanda. He can think of several sarcastic barbs, but really he bears no grudge toward her, despite her hostile attitude. "I truly appreciate everything you've done for me. *Adios, señora. Muchos gracias. Buena suerte.*" He knows his pronunciation is bad and half expects the kettle, or at least some choice words, to hit him in the back as he exits the kitchen, but Yolanda lets him go unmolested and in silence.

Shane and Tammy climb in, and the pickup truck starts to rattle toward the highway. Shane is surprised and delighted when Tammy rolls down her window and shakes out her hair. Though far shorter than Maybelline's, it still drapes below her shoulders and has a lovely sheen.

Shane observes that, although Tammy is again wearing jeans and a denim shirt, they are tighter-fitting, more feminine attire, not the loose-fitting men's clothes she wears around the ranch. The new garb reveals a pleasing, curvy figure. Presumably the change in her appearance is because they're going into town.

She turns and catches him staring. Instead of resenting it, though, she appears to be assessing his own appearance.

"I'm guessing the first thing you'll be wanting is a bath."

"And a change of clothes," he adds.

"Then what?"

"Good question. I guess I'll start by finding a Canadian consulate ... see what they can do for me. Listen, I really appreciate you helping me out the way you did. You were a lifesaver. And, well, sorry about this morning, you know, sleeping in and all. I hope I didn't screw up your day too bad."

"*No problemo.* It'll be worth it to have that money, I don't mind saying. We've been cutting it pretty close to the bone lately."

"Must be hard not having your husband around to help."

She snorts. "More calluses, fewer bruises."

"What do you mean?"

"Bobby was one mean son of a bitch, especially when he was all liquored up ... which was pretty much all the time once the rattlesnake business didn't pan out the way he'd hoped."

"He slapped you around?"

"Mister, slapping weren't the half of it. I've had more than my share of shiners, and he done busted my nose once, too." She reaches up to touch her face. "That's why I got this bump on my beak."

"I noticed that ... but I kind of like it."

She glances at him quickly to see if he's serious. "Anyway, he ain't around to hurt anyone no more," she says.

"How did he end up in Iraq?"

"Volunteered, if you can believe it. He was in the New Mexico National Guard, mostly to get away from me 'n' the pup on the weekends and play soldier, but then the dumb cuss goes and manages to hook up with a combat unit from Colorado. Said he wanted to see action. Well, he done saw it, all right. Wasn't over there more than a week when he got himself killed."

"I'm sorry."

"Truth is he done more for me and Gracie dead than alive. Left us mortgaged to the hilt, but at least his government death benefit helped us crawl outta our hole a bit."

"Why didn't you leave him?"

"I did, once. Took baby Gracie and ran off to a women's shelter in Santa Fe. That's where I met Yolanda and Maybelline. But I ain't one to live on welfare, plus Bobby sobered up — for a while, anyway — and came crying after me, saying he'd change, and couldn't we try again, that it would be like it was in the beginning, when we first started courting, before he knocked me up. And like the trusting fool I am, I came back."

"So, Yolanda and Maybelline, they were abused, too?"

"Yup. Different situations, but same kinda story. Well, worse in Yolanda's case — she spent time in prison because of it."

"What do you mean? If her husband was beating her, how come *she* went to prison?"

"Aggravated battery. Her husband tracked her down and tried to lay another beating on her, so she took a hunting knife to the sonabitch. Gashed him around the crotch something good. Said she was trying to cut off his balls ... that didn't do her any favours in court. She done spent two years at the women's pen in Grants — that's upstate, Albuquerque way. We kept in touch when she was inside, and when she got out, well, I took her in."

Shane can't help but smile. Tammy sees and raises an eyebrow.

"You're the first feller who ever found that funny. Most guys hear tell of a woman trying to cut off someone's testicles, they squirm in their seat."

"Sounds to me like the bastard had it coming, but it does explain her sunny disposition."

"Yeah, except that he's the one that got compensation and custody of their kid."

"I think she needed a better lawyer."

"Well, you get what you pay for, and she couldn't pay nothin'. Luckily the kid was pretty near full-grown, anyway. He lit out on his old man once he was of age. Up in Seattle now, working at some factory. He calls Yolanda every month, but she misses him something fierce."

"And Maybelline?"

Tammy hesitates. "Listen, I don't want you thinking I'm some kind of Chatty Cathy, gabbing about this kind of personal stuff, but at the shelter they counselled us to get it out into the open ... said that if we kept it quiet, 'cause we was ashamed or afraid or something, then we'd only make it easier for the abuse to continue. So I guess I just want you to know what we've been through, and where we're coming from, okay?"

"Sure."

"Besides, it's not like we're gonna see each other again anyway."

Shane feels a twinge of regret at the statement. It's not just that his future is dark and uncertain — he's starting to realize he has an attraction to Tammy. His recent relationships have trended toward self-serving party girls and star-struck hockey groupies. This is the first truly serious woman he's met since he and his wife parted ways.

"Maybelline's a different case," Tammy continues, "in that she was never married to the guy. The abuse really started at home, when she was a little girl, where her daddy used to beat her, and, well ... do things to her. She ran away when she was fifteen and ended up in Corpus Christi, living on the streets."

She glances over at Shane, looking for some kind of reaction.

"Poor kid," he says.

"I imagine you can guess the rest. She meets up with some guy who gives her a place to stay, and pretty soon they're sleeping in the same bed. They start partying together and, bingo, she ends up hooked on crack, or smack, or whack, or whatever ... I've never been into that scene. Before you know it, he's got her stripping in some sleazy bar, and then after a while, he starts pimping her out. Now, Maybelline don't want to be no whore, but when she tries to stop and get herself clean, the bastard takes to beating on her, and cutting her, to keep her in line. So, one night, after he's beaten the crap out of her and then passed out, she takes whatever money she can find in his pockets and starts heading west."

"And the shelter took her in?"

"Well, not right away. In case you ain't noticed, nothing's in a straight line with that gal. Oh, don't get me wrong, she's really sweet, but she ain't the sharpest tool in the shed. Didn't take her long before she was mixed up with some other no-good who was using and abusing her. But that guy got himself busted right quick, and Maybelline would have gone to jail, too, excepting she was lucky it was Alvarez who arrested her. You remember Deputy Alvarez ... she's the one you talked to at the house."

Shane nods, recalling the tough little officer who was ready to taser him.

"Well, Alvarez sees the marks and bruises on Maybelline, hears her story, and makes sure she goes into detox instead of jail. Afterward, on her own time, she drove her upstate and personally checked her into the shelter. I took a liking to Maybelline. She made me laugh. Weren't a lot to laugh about in those days. Still ain't."

"You said your husband went and brought you back. Did Maybelline come with you to the ranch?"

"No, she came a little later. It was just me, Bobby, and Gracie again, and he stuck to his word for all of a week, and then there he was back into the bottle and beating on me again. I was getting set to take Gracie and light out for a second time, when he got it into his head to go to Iraq. So, before I knew it, I had the spread to take care of by myself, and, well, I heard Maybelline was fixing to leave the shelter, and I knew if someone didn't look out for her, she'd only end up on the streets again."

"And Vern came later ... after your husband was already dead?"

Tammy nods. "Yeah, about two years ago. Even if he ain't my blood kin, the *rancho* does hail from his side of the family, and, well ... hell, somebody had to look out for him. Don't think he likes it much here, though. He was a big shot jock back in Texas, and he's been knocked down a peg or two since coming here. Well, boo hoo. Nobody said life's supposed to be fair. Waste of time, if you ask me. Sports, I mean. Bunch of men running around playing a stupid game and pounding on each other."

"Oh, I don't know. Women and children play, too. I think sports can be really good for you. Build character, teach you teamwork, that kind of thing."

"I reckon," she says, but sounds unconvinced. She stops talking for a while, but Shane wants the conversation to continue, if only so he can keep looking at her.

"You have a big heart, taking in the others like that."

"A soft spot for strays, you mean. Vern, that's family business, but Yolanda and Maybelline, I'm glad to help them. I wish I could do more for the rest of those poor women. Don't get me wrong. That shelter's a godsend, but we need more of them, and it's just a Band-Aid ... it ain't no cure. It's really hard taking that first step and leaving your man — giving up on a marriage and a home — but that ain't nothing compared to how hard it gets later. A lot of those women have never had to fend for themselves and got no clue how to get by, especially if they got kids to take care of. There's a reason a lot of women stay home and take the beatings."

Shane shakes his head. "It's not right, hitting a woman like that."

"Yeah, well, a lot of guys somehow figure it's their God-given right to pound on the missus and lord over her. And if you don't mind me saying, you look like you've been in a scrape or two in your time, Shane."

"Yeah, but never with a woman. Although Yolanda sure seemed to want to go a couple of rounds with me."

They both laugh at that one.

"So, you some kind of barroom brawler, then? Like to get a snootful and take on the world?"

Shane realizes just how low an impression of him Tammy has. "Don't let this face fool you. I'm a lover, not a fighter." He regrets the hackneyed line the second it leaves his lips.

Tammy snorts. "Is that what your ex would say if I asked her?"

"Who, my ex-wife? I don't think she'd say anything really bad about me. Sure, we quarrelled some at the end, but never what you'd call a real fight ... and I sure as hell never laid a hand on her. Like I told you, we didn't have kids. That's why the marriage fell apart in the end, I guess. She had a couple of miscarriages ... things were never the same after that. I travelled a fair bit, too, wasn't there for her to lean on."

"No kids ... that made it easier, I guess. Splittin' up and all, I mean."

He shrugs. "I always gave Veronica whatever she wanted, anyway. In the end I gave her the house, the bank account, and the divorce she was asking for. She's married again, now. Nice guy. He'll be good for her."

Tammy swivels her head to study him for a few seconds, then returns her gaze to the road. Despite Shane's best intentions, the conversation has dried up, so he resigns himself to watching the scrub brush roll by.

They arrive in Columbus and pull up to the Western Union agent. Shane gets out first, intending to open Tammy's door for her, but she is too quick for him. All business, she slides nimbly out of the truck and heads for the door with long, purposeful strides. She enters first, but waits for Shane to catch up, and they go up to the counter together.

"Howdy, Mr. Gassner," she greets the older man behind the glass. He is wearing gold-wire-rimmed glasses, has a blotchy bald pate, and carries the sour look of a lifelong clerk.

"Hiya, Mrs. DeWitt."

"Nice lookin' day today."

"They say the wind might pick up later."

"Is that a fact?"

"Yes, ma'am … that's what they say."

"Mr. Gassner, I'm expecting some money to be wired here. From Canada."

"From Canada? You don't say. Well, let's have a look-see." He starts painstakingly typing into a computer. The monitor is oriented so only the clerk can see it, and he repeatedly stops his typing to stare intently at the screen.

"Don't see it," Gassner finally decides. "When would it have been sent?"

"Yesterday."

"Hmmm. Should be here, then. No, sorry, there's nothing."

"Bastard," Tammy hisses at Shane under her breath. She stomps away, and Shane stands there for a moment, stunned that she's blaming him. He's torn between trying to sort things out with the clerk and going after her.

"There must be some mistake," he tells Gassner.

"No mistake, *sir*." There's enough of an emphasis on the last word for Shane to realize that the clerk is editorializing about his appearance. "I've dialed up all the incoming transactions for this location and there's nothing for Mrs. DeWitt."

"Look, I can straighten this out …" Shane starts to say, but stops when he hears the pickup truck's engine rev to life outside the building. He dashes through the doorway, but it is too late, and he helplessly watches Tammy pull away.

"Fuck!" Shane screams after her. It takes him a couple of minutes to regain his composure before returning to the counter inside.

"Hi again."

"Yes, sir?"

"Listen, you said there was no transaction for Tammy … er, Mrs. DeWitt at this location."

"That's correct, sir."

"Well, is there any way to check the name of the person sending the money? The sender's name is Peter Bronkovsky … Peel Crossing, Yukon, Canada."

"Well … I don't know," Gassner wavers, but after a few seconds of thought, he begins to painstakingly work the keys again. He glances at the screen and then types some more. "Well, I'll be," he finally says.

"What is it?"

"You won't believe it …" the clerk begins, then hesitates. "Actually, I'm not sure I should be telling you this, given you're not a party to the transaction."

"You got to be kidding!" Shane starts to rail, but he stops himself, realizing that a kneejerk angry reaction will torpedo the delicate situation. This is what has been explained to him in the past, that nothing good ever comes from succumbing to blind rage and abandoning control. He teeters on the tipping point, struggling to regain his balance and avoid calamity.

"Look, let me explain," he resumes, slowly and calmly, forcing his features to relax into a friendly cast. "You saw me come in here with Mrs. DeWitt, right? And I can tell you that Mr. Bronkovsky is my father. That money is meant for me. You see, I was robbed, and since I have no identification, my father wired me some money here, care of Mrs. DeWitt."

"Oh, sir, he could have wired you the money directly."

"How? I have no ID."

"There's a ten-digit PIN associated with each transaction. All you have to do is know that number. We actually deal with this problem a lot — people losing their wallets and such. In fact, even though I know her personally, and even with identification, Mrs. DeWitt would need that PIN in order to retrieve those funds."

"No kidding?"

"Not at all." Gassner pauses. "Under the circumstances, I suppose there's no harm in telling you this. The money transfer was, in fact, sent, but it went to Columbus, Ohio, not Columbus, New Mexico."

"Huh. How about that? So I guess the best thing would be to change it to my name instead, and for me to get the PIN."

"I'm afraid that's not possible. There's actual money in the system, now. What you're suggesting would require cancelling the original transaction, and our policy is to keep that money on hold before issuing a refund. So the sender would have to wait, or else issue a new transaction with new funds. The simplest thing would be for the sender to simply phone up, revise the transaction destination, and provide Mrs. DeWitt with the PIN."

Shane marvels at how helpful Gassner has been and cringes to think how close he came to berating the clerk. He actually likes the little old bald guy now.

"Do you have a phone I can use?" Shane asks.

Gassner gestures around the corner. "Yes, sir. There's a pay telephone next to the washroom."

Shane goes and picks up the handset. Connecting with the operator, he requests a collect call to his father. The phone at the other end buzzes distantly a dozen times without an answer. His father does not have an answering machine, which is probably a moot point, given that the operator likely wouldn't allow Shane to leave a message, anyway.

He hangs up the phone and goes into the bathroom, to kill time as much as anything else. When he looks in the mirror, he is shocked by the bedraggled stranger staring back at him. His hair is matted and greasy, his beard scraggly and untrimmed. The shiner he has been sporting under his left eye has progressed to the malignant yellowish stage. Although he knows he will regret it, he opens his mouth and flashes a smile. He has always been self-conscious of his missing teeth, has never even conducted a game interview in the past without wearing dentures, and the gaping black holes only make his appearance even more gruesome. He uses his good hand to splash some water on his face and try to smooth his hair somewhat. Deciding it is hopeless, he sighs and returns to the pay phone.

The rest of the afternoon is spent making dozens of unsuccessful attempts to reach his father. In between calls, he wanders outside to sit and watch the desert sun traverse Mexico en route to the Pacific.

Late in the afternoon, discouraged and hungry, he dozes, to be awoken by a figure eclipsing the sunshine. He opens his eyes and sees Mr. Gassner standing over him.

"Sorry, Mr. Bronkovsky, but we close at three o'clock," he says quietly. Shane opens his mouth to protest, but realizes there is nothing he can say.

"You eaten today?" Gassner asks. When Shane shakes his head, the clerk reaches into his pocket and forces something into Shane's hand. Shane opens his fist to see he's been handed a five-dollar bill, and he blinks, suddenly feeling disoriented, unsure of what the money means.

"You can pay me back when your transfer comes in," Gassner explains. "There's a cantina at the south end of town that's open until eight." He turns to go back inside. "They have a pay phone," he adds over his shoulder.

TEN

Shane finds the cantina and goes inside. After ordering a cup of coffee and a muffin, which is all Gassner's charity will buy, he occupies a seat near the phone and makes yet more unsuccessful attempts to reach his father. Eventually the cantina closes, too, so Shane pays his bill, taking his change in coins. To kill some time he takes a walk through the streets. It doesn't take him long to discover the defining moment in the history of Columbus, New Mexico. He comes across a state park at the edge of the town, commemorating a raid across the border by Pancho Villa a century ago.

Finding it odd that an American park would be named after a Mexican bandit, he wanders the grounds to learn more. He discovers that Villa, whose real first name was Francisco, was not, in fact, an outlaw, but a highly regarded revolutionary general. The incursion into New Mexico in March 1916, in which eighteen soldiers and civilians were killed and a portion of the town put to the torch, represents the only time since the War of 1812 that the U.S. was invaded. A retaliatory military expedition was launched into Mexico by the U.S. Army, led by legendary general "Black Jack" Pershing, involving ten thousand men and lasting almost a year. The park's museum houses examples of American military equipment of the era, including airplanes and trucks, that was used for the very first time by the U.S. Army in their campaign against Villa.

Shane's foray into the past manages to take up a couple of hours. When he locates a pay phone beside the park's campground and tries calling again, he is hopeful his father has returned. The operator is just advising him that there is no answer when a woman's voice comes on the line.

"Hello?" she answers, breathing heavily.

The operator asks if she'll accept Shane's collect call, and the woman assents with a bright, "You betcha."

"Uh, hello, who's this?" Shane asks.

"Hi, Shane. It's Oksana Kravchuk." It clicks that she is the caregiver his father mentioned, although the name tugs at his memory in some other way, as well.

"Hey, Oksana. Is my dad all right? I've been phoning for hours."

"Oh, he's fine. We've been out ... just pulled into the driveway this very minute. You're lucky I made it to the phone in time. Had to sprint." She laughs. "Whew. I'm out of shape." There is a pause, then she adds, "Your dad'll be a minute ... he's just getting to the door now. So, how you doing anyway, Shane?"

Her voice is warm and concerned. Shane feels a stab of self-pity and has to resist the urge to start crying over the phone. "Ask me no questions, I'll tell you no lies," he responds.

"That bad, eh? You hang in there, okay? Here's your dad now."

Shane hears Oksana identify the caller, and then Shane's father comes on the line, his breathing laboured. "Yeah?" he says grumpily.

"Dad. Where have you been?"

"What do you mean, where've I been? Out running a frig-ging marathon. What the hell's it to you?"

Shane is about to tell his father to fuck himself, but bites it back in time. He is starting to appreciate just how volatile his anger can be. "I … I was worried about you, Dad, that's all. I've been phoning all day, but there was no answer. I thought maybe something had happened."

"Oksana came by to take me to a doctor's appointment this morning, then we had to drive all the way to Dawson to get my prescription filled because the clinic in Peel's Crossing couldn't fill it. You're lucky she heard the phone ringing outside and got to it in time. Hey, come to think of it, what the hell you calling me collect for, with my money in your pocket?"

"That's just it, Dad, there was some kind of a mix-up. They sent the money to Columbus, Ohio, not Columbus, New Mexico."

There is a pause as the old man absorbs the information.

"Damn that Sally at the bank. If she could listen half as well as she can talk, she'd be a manager by now. I know I gave her the right address because I was reading it off the paper where I wrote it down, but she just kept going on and on about you … well, about the mess you're in, anyway. The whole town is talking about it. Hell, the whole damned country is talking about it. It's all I see on the news anymore."

"I was hoping it had blown over by now."

"A man's dead, son. That isn't going to blow over so quickly." For the first time since their conversation began, his father's bristle disappears, and he sounds sympathetic. It is so much bet-ter when he isn't angry, when he's normal, Shane tells himself … and then it hits him, like a sucker punch, that people must think the same thing about him.

"There's a lot of people on your side, Shane, I want you to know that. Not just here in town, either. Some guys sticking up for you on the TV, too. It's just that District Attorney in Chicago who's blustering about charges —"

His father trails off, as if he realizes he's not being helpful. "So what are we going to do ... about the money, I mean?" the old man asks.

"Dad, I need the PIN — the number they gave you."

"The what?"

"When you sent the money, they'd have given you this number. It's like a code we need at this end to unlock the transfer. Do you remember them giving you that number?"

"How the hell do I know? I recall them taking a hefty service charge, that's for sure —"

"I'm sorry, Dad. I'll pay you back, I swear."

"Oh, hell, son. I'm just bitching, that's all. It's not about you, it's about those bandits at the bank. Hang on, then, let me get the receipt they gave me. It must be on there someplace."

The receiver drops onto the tabletop, and Shane can hear his father grunting and the walker scraping on the floor as he shuffles around the room. There is murmuring in the background, and he hears Oksana laugh.

"Had to get my glasses, too," his father explains when he returns. "Now, lemme see here." There's more grunting and murmuring before his father exclaims, "Oh yeah, here it is. Transaction PIN. You got a pen handy?"

"Crap, no. I got nothing but the clothes on my back and some change in my pocket, and I'm at a pay phone in a parking lot."

"Then I guess you'll have to memorize it. It's like ..." He takes the time to count. "It's ten digits long."

"Oh, God. How am I going to remember that? I'm lousy with numbers."

"Bullshit. You got As in arithmetic when you were a boy. Of course, that was before hockey. There weren't nothing else you paid attention to after that. Anyway, ten digits isn't so bad, Shane. That's like a phone number with an area code, right? Come on, I'll read it to you a few times, then you recite it back to me."

They spend five minutes going back and forth until both are satisfied Shane has safely committed the PIN to memory.

"You best write it down as soon as you can, son. Keep saying it to yourself in your head until then."

"Thanks, Dad. I will."

There is a brief silence, as if his father is searching for the right words. "Where'd you sleep last night, son?"

"Don't worry. Tammy — that woman you were wiring the money to — she runs this ranch, and she's given me a place to sleep for the last couple of nights."

"You're lucky she's helping you."

"You got that right."

"So … you're okay?"

"Yeah. Sure. I will be, I guess … once I get that money. At least for now. Still have to figure out what to do about replacing my ID and stuff. And I don't even want to think about Kenny Linton and that business with the DA in Chicago."

"You can always come home to Peel Crossing, Shane. Might be just the thing for you."

"Maybe. Wouldn't even be able to get across the border now, though."

"You got a point there. Well, call me if you need me to vouch for you, or anything. Or just call." The old man chuckles. "Call collect, if you want. What's that PIN thingy again?" Shane recites the number. "That's right. Good boy. Okay, son. Bye for now."

"Goodbye, Dad."

Shane keeps repeating the numbers to himself as he contemplates his next move. Luckily, the phone booth has a telephone directory for the county, and while there is no entry for *Rancho Crótalo*, he does locate a number for DEWITT, R. Fishing change from his pocket to feed the pay slot, Shane dials the number, picturing the old rotary phone on the wall ringing.

It is little Gracie's voice that answers. "Hello?" she says.

"Hi, Gracie. It's Shane … you know, the man who's been staying at the ranch the last couple of nights."

"Uh-huh."

"Can I talk to your mom?"

"Mom's out in the stable."

"Could you get her for me?"

"It's that Shane fella," Gracie says to someone who is evidently standing nearby. "He wants to talk to Mama."

Abruptly a burst of Spanish cuss words erupts in Shane's ear.

"Yolanda! Wait! I sorted out the problem with the wire transfer and this time the money really is on its way."

There is a pause. He imagines her glaring at the phone. "You got the money for sure this time? You're not screwing with us?"

"I swear to God. There was a mix-up the first time — they sent it to Columbus, Ohio, by mistake, because that's where I used to live, but now it's fixed. Really."

"Okay. Gracie's gone to fetch Tammy. You just hang on. But if you're screwing with us —"

"You'll cut my balls off with a machete."

"More like a rusty butter knife, but, yeah, you get the idea."

Soon Tammy comes in, and Shane can hear Yolanda explaining things.

"Hello?"

"Hi, Tammy. Listen, I'm really sorry about the screw-up in town today."

"I figured for sure you were playing us for suckers."

"I'd never do something like that, especially, well ... to someone as nice as you."

There's a lull while she chews on that last statement. "Well, okay then, I'm glad we got it sorted out."

"Listen, can I spend another night at the ranch? I've no place to stay."

She sighs heavily. "No siree, I don't think that's such a good idea. I'm sorry for your troubles, but until I see that money, I ain't up to trusting you. I'm not a fool-me-twice kind of gal. I'll go so far as to come to town again tomorrow because we could really use that money you promised us. But that's about it."

"I'll pay you for another night."

He hears more air expel from her nostrils. "Sorry, Shane. You'll have to find some other Good Samaritan to carry the load for one night. I'll see you at the Western Union at nine o'clock in the a.m."

She hangs up, and Shane feels anger stir in the pit of his belly, like indigestion, but it is half-hearted. He can't really blame Tammy, especially after this morning's fiasco. He owes her and hasn't been able to repay the debt.

Shane leaves the park, planning to walk back into town, but the road leading in the opposite direction, toward Mexico, catches his attention instead. The sign says the border is only a mile and a half away, and this stirs Shane to try his luck in that direction instead. He occupies his mind by reciting the PIN over and over, adding some musical notes to turn the numbers into a jingle.

The road transforms into open highway again, surrounded on both sides by desert scrub brush, and Shane studies the landscape with a more discerning eye as he walks. Up ahead, something straight bisects the natural lines of the horizon, and only when he draws closer does he realize it is a fence that runs as far as the eye can see in either direction.

A phrase comes to mind, something he heard on a TV news broadcast in a hotel room during a road trip — the Great Wall of Mexico. President Trump made headlines during his campaign by proposing to build a wall between the two countries when, in fact, there has already been one for years, albeit not as grand as he proposed. Up closer, he sees that the existing wall is twelve feet high and rides the undulating wave of the terrain, running off into both horizons. It is overhung by a never-ending array of light poles spaced about fifty feet apart.

There is a gap in the fence where the two border checkpoints stand. On the American side of the wall there is also a staging area for cross-border shipments, with parked trailers and a couple of modest warehouses. Otherwise, the vicinity is chiefly desert. In contrast, when Shane looks over into Mexico, he sees an entire bustling town pushed up against the border, identified as *Puerto Palomas, Población 4,300*. Many of the buildings carry English signs advertising pharmacies and dental clinics, and Shane realizes that Americans must cross the border regularly to exploit these cut-rate services.

The sun is slinking below the horizon, and the airborne dust produces a spectacular blood-red sunset that soaks the entire sky. Shane pauses to watch the display, even though it spells the coming of darkness. As the light drops, the temperature does, too, and when the wind picks up, and the blowing grit with it, Shane realizes he will likely be spending this night outdoors. He turns to scout out the border's buildings for some nook or container to shelter him.

An unlit warehouse sits at the western edge of the parking area. It almost looks unused, and he wonders if it would be possible — or wise — to sneak inside. Circumnavigating the structure, he finds a small, high window, and with the use of his good right hand and a wooden pallet to stand on is able to pull himself up far enough to snatch a peek. An exit sign provides just enough illumination to see what's inside. The space has shelving along its walls, but is empty except for a large orange tarpaulin spread on the floor. The doors are all locked, however, and there is nothing else, not even a Dumpster, that can offer protection from the elements.

Shane feels bone-weary. He collapses on the ground and sits up against the side of the warehouse. He is half tempted to close his eyes and go to sleep on the spot, but the cold wind cuts right through him, and the blowing grit peppers his face. Reluctantly, he climbs to his feet and stumbles around the compound to continue his search. There are several other small buildings in the vicinity, plus a handful of storage containers and truck trailers, but every one proves to be securely locked. As much as he does not feel like walking back to the state park, he sees no viable options for overnighting here.

When he turns to plod toward the highway, a silhouette transverses a lighted window on the compound's periphery, compelling him to investigate. As he draws nearer, he recognizes Doc Sanchez's van and hears someone moving around inside. It dawns on him that he still owes Sanchez money and has already once been threatened at gunpoint by the man, but he thinks he can use the debt to his advantage. Besides, at this point he has nothing to lose. He knocks at the rear door.

Surprisingly, when the doctor sees who his visitor is, he breaks out into a big smile.

"*Buenas noches, amigo.* I was just thinking about you." Sanchez laughs.

"Look, Doc, I know I owe you money, and I swear —"

The doctor holds up his hand to cut Shane off. "No need. I was just speaking on the phone with the titillating Tammy, and she's explained the situation. I've arranged to meet her at the Western Union office tomorrow. I'll admit, though, I was curious where you'd be spending the night."

"I was planning to sleep in that Pancho Villa park tonight ... unless you have a better suggestion."

Sanchez breaks out into a giant, deep laugh. "Interesting choice. Come on inside, we'll talk about it."

Shane climbs into the van, relieved to escape the elements. It is as crowded as ever, but he notes that some of the medical equipment has been pushed out of the way, and a small table for two with accompanying bench seats has been unfolded from a niche in the wall. The doctor indicates one of these.

"Sit down. Relax. Are you hungry? Ha, ha, ha, of course you are. I'm afraid I don't have much to offer, but I'm sure I can scrounge something up." He opens a mini-refrigerator crammed with medical supplies and extracts a submarine sandwich wrapped in cellophane. Shane's stomach gurgles at the sight. There is a microwave oven amidst the clinical hardware, and the doctor places the sub inside to warm it up. Then he reaches into a beer cooler behind the driver's seat, extracts a bottle of Corona, and waves it at Shane.

"*Una cerveza, amigo?*"

"God, I'd love one."

Sanchez twists the cap off and places the beer in front of Shane. It is beautifully frosty, and although Shane is still shivering somewhat from the cold outside, he is dehydrated. He nearly drains the bottle in one big gulp.

Sanchez shakes his head with a chuckle and opens a second beer for Shane. "Go ahead, finish it off. Here's another to go with your food."

Shane eagerly complies, but before grabbing the fresh bottle, a thought occurs to him. "Um, how much you charging me?" he asks.

That earns the biggest laugh from Sanchez so far, causing his belly to bounce.

"*Touché.* No, sir, tonight you're my guest. *Mi casa es su casa.*"

"Thanks, I appreciate it. No offence, eh? But last time you did pull a gun on me."

"I'll admit I was a little rough on you when we met." The microwave beeps, and Sanchez goes to unwrap the sandwich and present it to Shane on a paper plate. He continues talking as Shane starts wolfing down his meal. "It was all a misunderstanding. I assumed you were with a motorcycle gang. Now, though, I know better."

Shane stops chewing. "Oh. So you know who I am?"

"Ho, ho, Shane 'Bronco' Bronkovsky. You're famous. Or should I say *infamous*? Anyway, *hombre*, you're all over the news. What I don't know is why you kept it a secret from me ... and also, I gather, from the ladies at the *rancho*."

"If you'd messed up the way I did, would you want people to know it?"

"Well, there's the difference between us. If I was royalty, I'd want *everyone* to know it."

"Royalty? Get real."

"Are you kidding? You're a professional athlete with eighteen seasons in the major leagues. Along with movie stars, that's about as close to royalty as we have in this country. You're at the top of the heap."

"Yeah, well, that was then, this is now. I'm washed up, broke, and now my dad tells me I could be in legal trouble."

"That Chicago DA does love the spotlight. With all the noise he's been making, he may have no choice but to bring charges now."

"Great."

"Relax, *amigo*. This isn't Chicago." Shane finishes the sandwich, and Sanchez opens a bag of potato chips and dumps them onto Shane's empty plate. Then the doctor holds up a bottle of amber-coloured fluid. "I was about to have a shot of mezcal. Care to join me?"

"Sure. Why not?" Glasses are produced, and two shots poured. "Don't I get some salt and a lemon wedge?" Shane asks.

For the first time since Shane's arrival, the smile leaves Sanchez's face. "If you weren't my guest tonight, I would shoot you for that comment." He manages to keep a serious look on his face for a few more seconds, then guffaws again. "Just try this first. But sip it, don't shoot it. I think you'll find it better than the piss they serve in most bars up north. *Salut!*"

They clink glasses and drink, and as Shane does so, his eyes light up. "Hey. That's good."

Sanchez beams knowingly and refills their glasses.

"So, Doc, is this where you normally hang out? No offence, but if I could park anywhere, this wouldn't be my first choice."

"The lot belongs to a friend of mine. He lets me park here whenever I want ... and tap into the electricity and water. The price is right, by which I mean it's free. I like it here. It's private and well policed by the border patrol. But what about you? You were planning to sleep in the park with the ghost of Generalissimo Villa — what brings you down to the border?"

"I don't know ... my feet just kind of took me here." Despite the doctor's admonition to savour it, Shane throws back the rest of the mezcal. "I'm glad they did," he adds. Sanchez chuckles and refills their glasses.

Shane rises. "Let me get by you, there, Doc. I gotta step outside for a piss."

"Why go outside into the cold and dust? I have a toilet in here. It's snug, but functional." He indicates a small doorway, which Shane assumed was some sort of storage closet.

When he is inside relieving himself, he sees that the compact, waterproofed chamber also doubles as a shower stall. "Hey, Doc," he calls out. "I haven't washed in, like, three days. Any chance I could grab a quick shower?"

"Be my guest. I was too polite to mention it, but you, *señor*, stink to high heaven. There should be plenty of hot water. I'll get you a towel and a plastic bag to protect your cast. I can even offer you a clean T-shirt and boxer shorts. A toothbrush and an electric razor, too, if you're interested."

"Oh, man, that would be awesome. You're a lifesaver, Doc."

"*Si*. That's what it says on my diploma."

✖ ✖ ✖ ✖ ✖

Shane emerges from the bathroom stall showered and clean-shaven. He feels and looks like a new man. Wearing nothing but a towel, he feels Doc Sanchez's eyes scrutinizing him and has a momentary suspicion there may be more to the doctor's generosity than simple hospitality.

"You're not, like, checking me out, are you, Doc?"

Sanchez guffaws. "You mean am I queer? Admittedly my life would be much simpler if I didn't relish women so much. No, it was purely occupational interest. I've worked with professional athletes before — boxers, in Las Vegas. You are in phenomenal shape, *amigo*."

"When you're low on talent and high on mileage, working out hard is pretty much the only way to stay in the game."

"Here, I promised you clean underwear." He tosses over the garments. Before Shane puts on the T-shirt, he studies the logo on the front that reads *Lobos de Chihuahua*. A stylized wolf crunches a hockey stick in its mouth.

"Hey, this some kind of a hockey team?"

Sanchez's stout figure inflates with visible pride. "That's *my* hockey team. It's owned by an old and dear friend of mine, Don Aléjandro Arguijo, but I'm the team physician, general manager, and chairman of the board."

"*Lobos de Chihuahua*, eh? I don't get it. I'm pretty sure *lobos* are wolves, but aren't Chihuahuas those yappy little hairless dogs that chicks like to carry around in their purses?"

Sanchez shakes his head with exaggerated sadness. "I expect that sort of ignorance from my fellow Americans, but I thought you Canadians were a little worldlier. No, Shane, Chihuahua is one of *Mexico*'s states." He points out the window toward the land beyond the illuminated Great Wall. "*That* is Chihuahua."

"No shit. And it has a hockey team?"

"Yes, we're an expansion team in the *Liga Mexicana Élite* — that's our national hockey league. In fact, we're just finishing building a new arena right next door in Puerto Palomas. You can see it right there, on the other side of the wall."

Shane has a look and then laughs out loud. "When I headed south on my motorcycle, I wanted to get as far away from hockey as I could. Now I find out that hockey is huge down here, right in the middle of the desert. Who knew?"

"They've been playing hockey down here in the Southwest for seventy-five years. Sure, the arenas are small, and it's not your calibre of play, but the fans are passionate. And now the sport's catching on in *Mexico*, too. I, for one, think it's a beautiful game. I was a big fan of the Albuquerque Six-Guns and the Houston Apollos as a boy." He holds up the mezcal bottle. "Another shot?"

"Sure."

"You should meet Don Aléjandro. He's a great man, and I know he'd love to talk to you, given your NHL experience. He and I go way back. We went through school together."

"You went to school in Mexico? I thought you said you were American."

"No, no, Don Aléjandro went to school *here*, in Columbus."

"Kids from Mexico go to school in the U.S.?"

"Why not? It's the closest school around. Those who can afford it pay for it. But a lot of mothers pay the tuition the hard way."

"What do you mean?"

"For decades, some Puerto Palomas women on the verge of giving birth, and I do mean on the verge — we're talking broken water, contractions, the baby practically crawling its way out — have been coming to the U.S. border checkpoint, where the guards feel they have no choice but to call an ambulance. The mother is taken to the hospital in Deming, the baby's born stateside, and presto, it's an American citizen, entitled to an American education."

Sanchez points outside at the shining wall again. "That border, *amigo*, is an illusion, although, as Einstein would say, it's a persistent one. We are all one people who were living here long before the bureaucrats decided where to place their fencelines. I have relatives north *and* south, and so does pretty much every other Chicano family hereabouts. Of course, once you leave this vicinity, your bloodline is unimportant. All the *gringos* see is your ethnicity, and as far as they're concerned, you're an illegal immigrant who just came scurrying over the border fence to steal their job or rape their daughter. Maybe that's why I came back here."

"Back from where?"

"I took pre-med in Tucson, then did med school and interned in Los Angeles, and finally, I tried private practice in Las Vegas. I'd had enough of dusty, rusty Columbus and was going to seek my fortune elsewhere. But the old WASP doctor who ran the clinic in Vegas was a great tutor in racial intolerance … among other things. He gave me every shit job he could find and insulted me constantly. In the three years I worked there he never called me anything other than 'Pancho Villa.' That was my own fault, I suppose, for trying to educate him about our little bit of local history, and the fact the *generalissimo* and I share the same first name — Francisco."

Sanchez stops talking and looks at Shane hesitatingly, like he's about to broach a matter of extreme delicacy. He leans forward and lowers his voice. "By any chance, would you care to smoke a joint?" he asks.

Shane's face becomes all grin and gratitude. "Hell, yeah! I'd love to. You know, I had some in that toiletry bag of mine that got stolen."

"No kidding."

"Yeah, but, frankly, I don't expect to ever see that again. Losing the cash and credit cards and ID is hassle enough, but it's losing my dental plate that really pisses me off."

"You lost some dentures, too? Hang on a minute."

The doctor gets up with a groan and goes to a small sink amid the medical equipment. He brings back a plastic cup with false teeth floating around inside.

"These yours by any chance?"

Shane recognizes them immediately. "Holy fuck, yeah! Where did *you* get them?"

"A patient of mine brought them to me. Said he found them on the side of the road. I've been cleaning and disinfecting them."

Shane fishes the dentures out and places them in his mouth. He chomps his teeth a couple of times and flashes a big smile. "How do I look?"

"Like a million bucks."

"Not anymore, Doc. Not anymore."

ELEVEN

Their two-man party goes on past midnight, and Shane wakes up in the passenger seat of the vehicle covered in a blanket, with the landscape rolling by his window.

"Good morning," the doctor's voice says beside him. Shane flops over and sees Sanchez at the wheel of the van, looking remarkably fresh. "I assumed we wouldn't want to miss our appointment with Tammy."

"Oh, crap. You're one of those early bird types, aren't you?" Shane moans. "All piss and vinegar in the morning. I've roomed with a few of your type over the years."

"Trust me, I'm hurting as bad as you are. But I'm used to getting my sleep interrupted at all hours — occupational hazard. Nobody wants to see their doctor dragging his ass, so I've just learned to disguise it. After a while, you almost believe it yourself." Sanchez suspends his right hand. "See that? Steady as a rock. Need your appendix taken out?"

"No, thanks. Say, have you seen my dentures?"

"They're in the bathroom. If you want to freshen up while you're in there, you've got ten minutes or so."

Shane splashes some water on his face, then brushes his teeth and combs his hair. Even though it's only been a few hours since he shaved, he decides to run the electric razor over his face again, too. They reach their destination, and Sanchez drops Shane off, promising to return after the doctor secures a cup of coffee.

When Tammy arrives, Shane comes around to open the door for her. She steps out, again wearing her town clothes, and her eyes take him in. "Wouldn't have recognized you except for the cast," she finally says. "My, my, you clean up real good."

"Why, thank you kindly, ma'am. And you're looking mighty purdy this morning, too, if you don't mind me saying," Shane replies, doing his best hokey cowboy impression.

That produces a smile, and Shane feels his heart beat faster.

"I was feeling guilty about leaving you out on your own last night," Tammy confesses. "But I see you managed to land on your feet all right. But where on earth did you find your chompers?"

"A patient of Doc Sanchez's found them on the road. The doc was kind enough to put me up last night, too. Otherwise I would have ended up sleeping outside in the park."

She touches his bare arm lightly, and the sensation goes right through him. "Okay, then, let's see if that money got here."

Today, there are no problems at the counter, and Tammy is issued a stack of fifties and twenties. She does not extract her share, instead handing the whole wad to Shane. It is almost as if she is testing to see whether he will grab the money and run off. Holding the cash in the fingers of his casted hand, he pulls out the agreed upon amount and passes it to her.

"I want to thank you again for all you did for me. I'll always think of you as my angel of mercy," he says.

To his surprise, Tammy blushes. She shoves the money into her pocket without counting it. There is something erotic in the way she sticks out her hip to push the bills into her jeans.

"I'll be honest, Shane, I figured I'd never see this money. I guess I misjudged you. And, well, it was handy having you help out, too. Good luck." She holds out her hand.

Shane shakes, but isn't ready to take his leave just yet.

"Say, I'm waiting around to pay off Doc Sanchez. But, after that, how about a cup of coffee? I mean, if you're not in a hurry."

Tammy tosses her hair and cocks her head sideways as she considers his proposition. "I got a couple of things I need to buy, but I ain't in no rush to get back to the ranch. Do you know where the Sierra Cantina is?" Shane nods. "Okay, then, meet me there in an hour."

Before driving off, she offers him an enticing smile that sets him tingling. He is standing there lost in thought, wondering what it is about that self-sufficient, unflashy woman he finds so attractive, when a horn jolts him back to attention.

"*Hola*, Shane," Doc Sanchez calls down from the driver's window of the van as it pulls up. "All good?"

"Awesome," Shane replies. He peels off more bills and passes them up to the doctor. Unlike Tammy, Sanchez does count the money, but his smile reveals all is in order. "*Gracias, amigo.* In future, I hope you'll think of Doctor Sanchez's Travelling Medicine Show for all your health needs in Luna County. Well, duty calls." He leans out to shake Shane's hand. "Say, what are your plans, anyway, now that you're flush again? Heading home?"

Shane looks down at the remaining money and does some mental calculations. "Actually, I could only hit my dad up for so much cash, and what I got left won't last long. No, I guess I'll hang around here for a while, maybe even see if I can get my bike back."

"And stay as far away from Chicago as you can?"

"There is that, but I was actually thinking of trying to talk Tammy into letting me stay at the ranch and help out for a while. I'm going to have coffee with her in a bit."

Sanchez erupts in a giant laugh. "If the rattlesnake don't bite you, something else does, eh? Well, if that doesn't work out, feel free to come knocking on my door. I'm generally parked in the same place. But, this time, *you* bring the mezcal. I prefer Del Maguey Minero. Don't forget." He waves a final farewell and puts the van into gear.

Shane finds a general store where he can buy some T-shirts, underwear, and toiletries before walking to the cantina. He orders a big breakfast and is working on his third cup of coffee when Tammy arrives. Shane rises and pulls her chair out for her, as much to sniff her scent as to make an impression. Tammy orders a cup of tea, and they make small talk about the weather and the town before the conversation drifts to Shane and his plans.

"You must be relieved to be back on your feet," Tammy says. "I expect you'll be heading back up north."

"Actually, I was planning on sticking around. It'll take a few days and a bunch of phone calls just to figure out my next steps, plus I'm still hoping the cops might find my motorcycle."

"There's a couple of motels in town. Nothing fancy, but they're clean."

"Well, actually, I was wondering what you'd think of me staying at the ranch for a while."

She opens her mouth to reply, but closes it again, and her lips contract. "I'm not sure that's such a good idea," she finally says.

"Why not? The stable is good enough for me, and I'd sooner the money go to you than some motel. Plus, I can do work … you said yourself it was a help having me around."

"Yolanda wouldn't like it."

"I get the feeling there's not much Yolanda does like. But is it really her decision?" Tammy sips her tea and says nothing, but Shane has a sense that she at least is thinking about it. "I'll pay you a thousand bucks," he adds.

"You ain't got a thousand bucks, remember?" she shoots back, but is smiling when she says it.

"Well, not in my pocket, but I'm going to arrange for more money. I need to pay my dad back, anyway."

"I don't know. I'm just not sure about a man staying with us, that's all."

"Haven't I proven that you can trust me?"

"You've kept your word so far, I'll give you that. But I barely know you."

"Well, if I ever lie to you, you can have Yolanda shoot me."

Tammy laughs and brushes her hair back with a hand. She drinks some more tea and scrutinizes Shane's face. He hopes that she is maybe contemplating other fringe benefits of having him around.

"Okay, how about this," he says. "I'll pay to rewire the stable, and do all the work. Now, how can you say no to that? Even with only one good hand, how often does someone offer to pay to work for you?"

"We sure could use the money," Tammy says, almost to herself, and Shane senses he has gained the advantage. He changes to a lighter approach.

"You know, you have to," he tells her with a grin.

"Oh? Do tell."

"Yup. You saved my life, so now you're responsible for me. I'm pretty sure it's some kind of cowboy code. You could have left me there on the side of the road to die, but you didn't, so the code says you're stuck with me. It's your own fault."

Tammy's laugh is soft but unrestrained, and Shane relishes the sound of it. "Well, okay then, I guess I just picked me up another stray." She spits on her palm and sticks her hand out across the table. Shane shakes it to seal the deal.

When he climbs back into the truck, he sees shopping bags and a box of groceries on the passenger seat, indicating that Tammy has made immediate use of the newfound cash. He moves the goods to the floor and sits sideways to face Tammy. As they drive back to the ranch, somehow they get on the subject of the legendary Billy the Kid. Shane was unaware that the outlaw's exploits took place largely in New Mexico and that he'd often hide out among the local Mexican Americans. As genuinely interested as Shane is in the story, he is more fascinated by Tammy's cheerful, animated face as she relates the details.

When they pull into the driveway to the ranch, Tammy grows quiet, a slight frown skewing her lips. No one greets them when they arrive, but when Shane carries the bags into the kitchen, Yolanda is sitting there shelling peas, and she explodes in anger.

"What's he doing here? Did this *bastardo* stiff us for the money again?"

"Would I have bought these groceries if he had?" Tammy replies. "Shane needed a place to bunk for a while longer, and I told him he could stay here."

Yolanda looks from Tammy to Shane and narrows her eyes before letting loose with a rapid-fire string of Spanish, all rolling R's and words spat out in staccato. Shane can't understand them, but he gets the gist.

"Listen here, Yolanda," Tammy says. "Just because you do it in Spanish don't mean you can cuss in this house. Now, he's gonna pay us room and board, he'll keep sleeping in the stable like before, and he's agreed to help out around the place, too. We could use the help, and you know darn sure we could use the money."

Neither one says anything else. They stand there glaring at one another, Yolanda with her legs planted, hands on her hips, Tammy with her arms folded and her head held high.

Maybelline comes hopping into the room. "*Shane, Shane, came back again,*" she sings when she sees him. Then she clues in to the tension between the other two women and her grin evaporates. "Oh, oh. No, no. Whoa, whoa," she burbles.

Shane has caused this situation and figures he needs to defuse it. Despite his reputation as a ruffian, he has always deplored locker room conflicts and has often played mediator, especially once he earned veteran status.

"Yolanda, I'm not trying to force myself on you here. And I'm not trying to take advantage of anyone's good nature. I figured this for a win-win situation, and I'm willing to pay my way and to work. But if you're not comfortable having me around, then I understand — I'll go, and no hard feelings."

Seconds pass, and Yolanda finally blinks. "How much did this one-armed bandit say he'd pay us?"

"A thousand for the next couple of weeks with two hundred up front."

"Actually, Yolanda, I also came back for your cooking. I was hoping for more of that rattlesnake chili."

Yolanda does not acknowledge the joke, but she sits down and resumes shelling the peas. "Well, at least the bum took a bath and shaved," she mutters, and with that, Shane has a place to stay.

He pulls out two hundred dollars and places it on the table where Yolanda can see. "There's the advance," he says. "Should I leave my balls, too?"

Yolanda's face still does not crack. "That's okay. I know where to find them."

Maybelline titters and pirouettes over to grab Shane by the chin. "Howdy do, look at you … you're all purrrrrrdy."

Shane catches a disapproving look from Tammy, and turns away from Maybelline's attention to address everyone. "Look, I know it's weird having me here. I just wanted to say, well, thanks a lot for everything, I mean it. I'll go and set up in the stable now. Then, if there's any chores I can help with, just say the word."

"Wash line's coming down," Maybelline says.

"Hinge is loose on the door of Vern's shack," says Tammy.

"You're going to need to dig yourself a shit hole, 'cause you ain't using the ladies' room," Yolanda says. This time she finally does smile.

✽ ✽ ✖ ✽ ✽

The snakes in their cages barely stir as Shane walks past them to the back of the stable, and he speculates that this is because they were recently fed. In the backroom, the mattress is still on the floor, although the bedding has been removed. He scrounges up some pieces of wood and constructs a crude platform to raise the mattress off the ground, then goes in search of the bedroll. He finds it airing out on the clothesline and sagging right down to the ground. One of the supporting posts has tilted inward, so he pushes it upright to restore tension to the clothesline, packs down the dirt again, and adds some bracing.

Next, he adjusts the door on the small outbuilding that Vern uses as his bedroom, relocating the wobbly hinge so its screws find fresh purchase, although this chore proves problematic what with the cast on his left hand. He concocts a workaround solution, wedging the door in position with his shoulder and using a wooden shim to lever the door off the ground.

When it comes to building himself an outhouse, he is able to do much of the crude carpentry once he locates a stack of second-hand lumber behind the stable, but digging a hole with just one hand is difficult. Only the softness of the soil allows any meaningful progress. He decides he will need to enlist the boy Vern for help with the excavation.

When Tammy walks out to the highway to meet the school bus, Shane tags along. Gracie seems shocked to see him waiting, and she skulks around to her mother's side. Vern, though, is visibly delighted by Shane's return.

"I thought you'd gone for good," he says.

"Oh, I came back to tackle that wiring job we started and help out around the place for a while until I get my shhh ... my stuff together."

Gracie is still looking at Shane uncertainly. He has a flash of inspiration. "Hey, I know it's not as good as a pony, but wanna ride on my shoulders?" he offers. The girl looks at her mother. Tammy just shrugs, so he squats down, and Gracie climbs aboard.

When he stands up, she squeals with joy. "Wow, I can see real far from up here." She grabs his hair and gives it a playful tug. "Giddy up, horsie." Shane gives a whinny, and imitating a horse's trot, canters homeward while the others follow, laughing at his antics.

✖ ✖ ✖ ✖ ✖

Shane does not wait to be evicted from the house after dinner. The previous night's carousing with Doc Sanchez and his bellyful of Yolanda's chicken enchiladas with beans and salad have him feeling drowsy, anyway. He thanks everyone for their hospitality, solicits chores for the next day, and bids them all pleasant dreams. He is a little surprised, but touched when Gracie comes over from the table to give him a good night hug. Outside, he and Vern linger for a bit discussing prospective work projects.

He occupies himself by tidying the workbench, staying up in the hopes Maybelline will come visit him again. Eventually, he undresses and turns down the lantern. That's when he hears the light crunch of her feet along the gravel aisle. She appears in the doorway waving the jar of moonshine, which only has a couple of fingers' worth of liquid left.

"Hey," she whispers. She kicks off her slippers and crawls right on top of his bed, even though he's clearly not dressed. "There ain't hardly but a little left, but I thought you might want a nightcap." She is wearing a flannel robe, and when she leans forward, it falls open, revealing a baby-blue nightgown beneath.

"Hang on," he says, and reaches for his pants, which are folded on the ground. "Here," he says, handing her a fifty-dollar bill.

Her playful expression dissolves. "What's this for?"

"I want to buy the next bottle. I've been drinking up all your booze."

"That's okay, you don't have to," she says, but slips the money into the pocket of her robe nonetheless.

Shane takes a swig and grimaces. "Maybe you can buy something that doesn't take the top of your head off."

She laughs and takes her own sip, wiping her mouth on her sleeve. "It ain't so bad once you get used to it. And you gotta admit, it's got a kick. The thing is, I can't buy no normal liquor. I mean, I got money, on account of Tammy pays us a share for working, but I don't never go into town without her driving me, and she watches me like a hawk. Thinks I'll get into trouble."

"Where do you get the hooch, then?"

"I buy it from a hand over at the Curly Q — that's the ranch next door. I go over there to buy eggs."

"Why don't you guys raise some chickens, too?" He points toward the adjoining stalls. "Instead of those."

She shrugs. "We've talked about it, but never seems to be enough extra money to get set up." She holds the jar up high and lets the last couple of drops of moonshine fall on her tongue, then seals up the jar. "We've talked about a lot of things." She's looking at Shane when she says this, but her gaze is faraway.

Then she catches herself being serious and jumps to her feet. "*Little ol' me has got to flee before Yolanda finds I'm free,*" Maybelline sings, bouncing up and down on the mattress as she does. She jumps off to step into her slippers, then pats him on the head, like he's a little child. "I'm glad I got my drinking buddy back. We *are* buddies, right?"

"You bet."

She puts her finger to her lips. "Shhh. Remember. Don't tell Tammy."

TWELVE

Late the next morning, after the kids are at school and the women are all working outside, Shane slips into the house to use the phone. With the operator's help he calls Morrie Getz, who, in addition to being Shane's agent, also serves as his informal financial manager. Or, more accurately, his financial conscience after bad decisions.

"Bronk! Thank God you called. Your ears must have been burning," Getz exclaims.

"How so? Am I on the Most Wanted List?"

"Not unless you're referring to being my most in-demand client."

"What are you talking about, Morrie? You said no club would touch me."

"Listen, Bronk, you know I always give it to you straight. I wouldn't count on lacing up your skates in the NHL anytime soon. But ... you're just about the most famous man in sports right now. We must have had a thousand requests for interviews."

"I don't want to talk to no reporters."

"Then don't ... not for free, anyway. But there's some seri-ous bidding going on for the rights to an exclusive interview."

"How serious?"

"I'm pretty sure it'll go to six figures."

Shane whistles. "What would I have to do?"

"Do? Nothing. Give them your side of the story. Answer their questions. Mind you, the big bidders want you on camera."

"I don't trust reporters."

Getz laughs. "Always said you were smarter than you let on. But look, Bronk, you should do this ... and not just because I get my cut. I know Brandi cleaned you out, so you need the dough."

"How do you know that?"

"She was bragging about it to one of the wives. You know, word gets around. Didn't I warn you about Brandi from the beginning? The girl might as well have been wearing a jersey with *Gold Digger* on the back. Oh well, that's water under the bridge now. Pick yourself up and get back in the game. Time to start thinking about a future outside of hockey and to grab all the dough you can. I know you're waiting for your playoff money, and eventually you'll get your league pension, but for now I've asked the club to hold off paying you."

"Hold off? What the fuck for? I'm broke."

"Calm down, Bronk. Everything's deposited directly into your joint account, remember? It'd be like handing that money straight to Brandi."

"Aw, shit, I didn't think of that."

"Yeah, well, I did. So, the first thing you do is open up a new bank account. Where are you, anyway? No, don't tell me, in case some cop shows up asking after you."

"Um, I can't open an account right now."

"Why not? Wait, you're not in jail already?"

"No, at least not yet. The thing is, Morrie, I got robbed. Lost my money, my cellphone, my passport, my ID — everything."

There is a pronounced sigh from the other end of the line. "Fuck, Shane. What did you do? Follow some hooker into a back alley? How many times have I told you —" Getz suddenly stops himself. "How broke *are* you, kiddo?"

"Well, my dad just wired some emergency cash to get me by … but that's going fast, and I really need some more. That's, er, kinda why I was calling."

"What kind of schmuck do you think I am? Don't you know an agent's supposed to suck money out of his clients, not vice versa?" Getz sighs again. "All right, all right. I'll save you from asking. I think I got two thousand in petty cash … will that tide you over? Just don't tell anyone, okay? You'll spoil my reputation as a shark. But, hell, Shane, all the more reason you should do an interview, don't you think? Strike while the iron is hot, and all that. Besides, who knows how long it'll be before you'll be able to sort the rest out. So? I got your permission to cut a deal?"

"All right, Morrie. But get some money up front when you do. I want to pay my dad back right away. And you can take that two K out of it."

"Oh, don't worry, Shane. I was going to. Listen, say hi to your dad next time you talk to him. It's only on account of him I'm so nice to you."

"My dad? I didn't think you even knew my dad."

Getz hesitates. "He never told you?"

"Told me what?"

"Why the hell do you think I've spent so much time on a hack like you all these years? It's on account of your dad. Just before you signed with me … what was that, like eighteen years ago? Anyway, he shows up in my office —"

"Your office? You mean in New York?"

"No, I mean Antarctica. Of course New York."

"Huh. I didn't know he'd ever been to New York."

"Oh, he has, because he came to my office without an appointment and wouldn't leave until he talked about you signing with me. I said you were legally old enough to do whatever you wanted, and he told me he knew that. Didn't want to see the representation contract, or talk about your draft prospects. He looks me in the eye, holds out his hand, and says, 'Just promise me you'll always take care of my boy.' There was just something about the way he said it. So, like the putz I am, I gave him my word. And here I am, stuck with you, and lending you money."

"I love you, too, Morrie." Shane says it laughingly, but inside he is choked up by what Getz has just revealed. Mostly he feels guilty about the years he's spent being angry at his father, thinking the old man resented Shane's success.

After arranging with Getz's assistant for a wire transfer in Shane's name, he hangs up and heads outside. It's a beautiful spring day, and the three women are all together, turning the soil in the vegetable garden behind the ranch house facing south. Although he has chores inside the stable, Shane would rather get some sun, so he goes over to offer his help.

Digging is impractical with the cast on his hand, so he contributes by hauling and dumping sixty-pound bags of fertilizer and black earth. Afterward he helps string the wire for a protective fence to keep animals out of the garden. Once the soil has been tilled and seeds pushed into the earth, he is assigned the task of carrying plastic pails of water from the kitchen pump. Shane is surprised to learn that an aquifer runs beneath this dusty desert land, albeit three hundred feet down. With this supply of water available, it seems to him that the ranch is not meeting its potential.

Everywhere Shane looks, he sees work that needs doing. On top of the obviously necessary repairs to structures and fences and machines, he envisions dozens of other improvements — a composting toilet, a windmill to pump the water, a solar-heated shower, sliding storage racks for the rattlesnake cages, even a small addition to the ranch house so Vern can have his own bedroom. Somehow, the place reminds him of his own hockey career, with grit, hard work, and determination compensating for a lack of natural gifts.

Shane realizes he has squandered a fortune, even as one of the lowest-paid players in the league. During the rambling mezcal-fuelled conversation in Doc Sanchez's trailer, the doctor related that Luna County is one of the poorest places in America in terms of household income. There are many stars in the NHL who earn more in a single period of a hockey game than men here earn in a year.

Shane has been called many things — a gladiator, a ruffian, even a clown. Most of Shane's fellow players are proud of what they do. They consider themselves the elite, the chosen few, performing at the highest level of human skill, bringing entertainment and a dash of passion to millions of ordinary lives. Because of his specialty, however, Shane has always felt like some sideshow freak of the sport, waiting in the wings to be unleashed. His job is to score punches instead of goals. Good players are respected by the fans of other teams, even where there are fierce rivalries. Shane, however, is vilified in most cities of the league.

The thing is, he loves the game, the sweet poetry of it — the speed, the finesse, the grace. He has always felt ten times better making a good play than landing a punishing hit or winning a fight. When he first started out in hockey, still a child, really, he was usually the best on the ice; he could skate through his opponents like they were standing still. He notched hat tricks and scoring titles. But as he progressed up the rungs of the sport and the competition tightened, it was his size and his bullish strength that caught the attention of the scouts. After that, he never stood a chance to become anything else.

And over the past few years, he has started to feel frequently depressed, worthless, and confused. For all his power, he is powerless. For all his strength, he is helpless. He is aware that bad things have happened to other hockey enforcers — several have died in recent memory. The coroner's reports may say drug overdose, or suicide, or death by misadventure, but Shane knows the truth. They simply lost their grip on the planet and fell off. Some blame the blows to the head they'd taken over the years, claiming they were punch drunk. Brain damaged. Shane doesn't know anything about that, and he'd like to think the Players' Association would do something about it if that was true, although he has also been in the game long enough to know that the lawyers wouldn't let the league admit liability.

And then — was it just a week or so ago? — then came the darkest moment of his soul, when the counterbalancing forces of his life — the camaraderie, the intoxicating rush of the game, the privilege and status offered him — were torn away and replaced by ignominy and persecution, and he found himself bilked and betrayed by the person closest to him. During the mad blur of his motorcycle ride south, he lamented more than once how he had left nothing to mark his passage through the world other than some undistinguished career statistics and a stack of newspaper headlines now dominated by one tragic incident. Only a desperate feeling that he still might accomplish something in life kept him from succumbing to the blackness suffocating his soul.

But now, during the few days he has spent at *Rancho Crótalo*, Shane has felt a strange new force, as if the impoverished soil itself is pulling at him. Here, your labour can produce a tangible result. Although you have to fight just to survive, the dirt under your fingernails, calluses on your palms, and sweat on your brow add up to something real. What does Shane have to show for his hockey years other than scar tissue, missing teeth, and ravaged tendons?

The people he has met here also have something to do with it. In many ways, they are as bruised and confused as he is. But he feels like he is on their team now, and as such, he will not let them down and will fight to protect them. It's what he does.

And then there is Tammy. He really does not know yet what to make of his feelings for her, and little voices in his head whisper warnings that he is desperate, on the rebound. Yet the very fact that she is not some primped and seductive cheerleader type smothered in beauty products, but plainer, and older, and worldlier than the sort of woman he's used to dating is what draws him to her. In the past he has been like a moth incinerated in the flames of disorienting beauty. Tammy's light is more like the soft, warming, life-giving glow of a wood stove in winter.

✳ ✳ ✖ ✳ ✳

Shane joins Tammy to meet the school bus. It may be his imagination, but he feels like she is starting to enjoy his company, too. They walk slowly and chat lightly about work the ranch requires.

Gracie leaps off the bus and sprints toward them. She greets her mother first, then gives Shane's thigh a hug, too. Then she stands, smiling up at him. He knows she is after a ride on his shoulders, but is too polite to demand it. First, though, he waits to greet Vern. The boy seems subdued, so Shane drapes his arm around Vern's shoulders and walks with him for a bit, telling him what progress has been made that day and giving the boy a

134

chance to talk about school, if he so chooses. Shane is emulating one of his first professional coaches, a tiny, sixtysomething leprechaun of a man with a reputation for being good with young talent. What that meant was treating the players with respect, keeping an even temper, and listening. Shane's been traded enough times since then to have endured virtually every coaching style there is, but the old coach's calm and caring approach has always stuck with him.

"Some of the other boys were hassling me today," Vern finally admits.

"You didn't get into another scrap, did you?" Tammy interjects.

"No, ma'am."

"Good," she answers, with no goodness in her voice.

"It's no fun when they pick on you, is it?" Shane says. "Bet it was over something really stupid."

"Yeah! Just because I dropped a fly ball playing baseball. I don't even like baseball. The teacher made us play."

Shane gives the boy's back a light pat. "They were just looking for an excuse. You're still the new kid — that's the only reason. It has nothing to do with who you really are. They'll accept you eventually. But stay out of fights, okay? They don't solve anything and only get you into trouble." The last statement is strictly for Tammy's benefit, and Vern does not look convinced. Shane decides that later, in private, he will also counsel the boy to stand up to bullies, perhaps teach him some fighting techniques. It's okay to be a pacifist, but not a patsy or a punching bag.

Shane gives Vern's arm a final reassuring squeeze, then he squats down to face the patient Gracie. "Want a quick horsie ride back home?" he asks. She gives a little squawk of delight and practically jumps onto his shoulders. "Hang on tight," he tells her, and takes off at as fast a gallop as his legs can manage.

135

✖ ✖ ✖ ✖ ✖

Later that evening, as the women of the house bustle around the kitchen preparing dinner, Shane sits beside Gracie at the table and watches her draw pictures. The little girl's doodles betray her obsession with horses, and obvious practice has resulted in renderings that are advanced for someone so young. When Shane catches her eyeing the blank canvas of his plaster cast, he offers to let her draw on it. Gracie selects coloured markers of permanent ink and sets to painstaking work. The finished piece is not bad, given her inexperience with drawing on rough, cylindrical surfaces. Shane includes Vern by having him draw some mountains and bushes as a background for the galloping mustang.

"It's cool," Shane decides. "Maybe when the cast comes off, I'll get a tattoo just like it. What's he called?" he asks.

"*She's* called Teotlalco."

"Wow, that's an unusual name."

"Unusual for you, maybe, *gringo*," Yolanda snipes.

"She was queen of the Aztecs," Gracie explains. "There's a city named after her in Mexico, too. I'm going to call her Teo for short, though."

Shane realizes this is the name she wants to give a real horse some day. "So, you want a girl horse?"

"It's called a mare, silly. I want to adopt a mare, and then I want to adopt a stallion, too. When I get one of each I'm going to raise a whole herd."

"Adopt?"

"Yup, from the BLM."

The acronym means nothing to Shane. He looks to Tammy for clarification. "The Bureau of Land Management," she explains. "They manage all the wild mustang herds on public land. Burros, too."

Shane returns his attention to Gracie. "And they'll let you adopt a horse?"

She nods. "It costs a hundred and twenty-five dollars."

"Is that all? Heck, I'll give you a hundred and twenty-five dollars."

Gracie's shriek of delight almost pierces Shane's eardrums. She throws herself at him and wraps him in an embrace. Her little arms enveloping him and the love that radiates through them create a tingling that flows through Shane like some amazing drug rush. He still feels it after she lets go.

"Did you hear that, Mommy? Shane's going to buy me a horse!"

"Oh yeah, honey, I heard it all right. It's getting late, sweetie. Go brush your teeth and get ready for bed. You git, too, Vern. Me and Shane are gonna have a little talk."

Gracie goes skipping out of the room, while Vern slinks outside to his shed. Through some unspoken communication, the other two women get up and depart as well. Once she and Shane are alone, Tammy reels like a striking snake. "Are you crazy? What the fuck's wrong with you, promising something like that?"

Shane doesn't know what's more shocking, that he's being dumped on for his generosity, or that Tammy is breaking her own house rule about swearing.

"It's only a hundred and twenty-five dollars."

"*It's only a hundred and twenty-five dollars,*" she mimics. "Well, Mister, it ain't that simple. First of all, we'd have to buy a horse trailer and drive up to the adoption centre in Oklahoma. Then we got to sign a contract saying we'll house and feed the critter. You got any idea what hay goes for? 'Cause we sure as hell ain't got no decent grazing. And, oh yeah, we'd have to renovate a couple of the stalls to meet their regulations. Then there's the vet bills ..."

"Sorry, I didn't know —"

"What you don't know about living here could fill a whole library."

"But I've got money coming. I'll pay whatever the costs are. Did you see how happy she was? We could make her dream come true."

"The sooner she learns that dreams are a lot of fairy-tale hogwash, and life ain't nothing but hard work and disappointment, the better off she'll be."

"That's not true."

"Oh yeah? Didn't you have dreams about having a loving wife and a happy family? How's that working out for you?"

"That's hitting below the belt."

"With a big galoot like you, that's where they tend to land." That last statement at least has a touch of humour in it. Tammy flops down onto the bench next to Shane, her anger waning. "Look, I love my little girl … love her more than anything in the goddarn world. I want to see her happy, I really do. But dreams are just silly notions when they ain't realistic. I had me some dreams, too, once upon a time. That's how I ended up here."

Despite the tension, Shane can't resist teasing. "You dreamt of being a rattlesnake rancher?"

"Very funny. No, I had me dreams of being a country singer once upon a time. I dunno, maybe it's because I was named after Tammy Wynette. Left my home in Throckmorton County, Texas, when I was barely seventeen and ran off to sing in honky-tonks and roadhouses. Wrote a fair bit of my own stuff, too. A lotta folks said I was pretty good … not just the young bucks trying to get under my skirt. The money was crap, and the living was rough, but I kept figuring someone would come along and whisk me off to Nashville, where I'd be a star. Then along comes Bobby DeWitt flashing a bankroll and a big smile and sweet-talking me about his big spread in New Mexico. Said he'd build me a recording studio and be my manager. Well, sir, all he managed was to get me knocked up. And see where I ended up?"

Shane places his hand on Tammy's and is relieved when she doesn't jerk it away. "But just because dreams usually don't pan out doesn't mean we shouldn't have them. Could you have lived with yourself if you hadn't given it a shot?"

Tammy shrugs. "I reckon not."

"For everyone that makes it, there's a hundred others just as talented who don't get the breaks. That's life. But this horse thing with Gracie isn't a pipe dream. It's just a matter of money, and I said I'd pay it."

"Shane, you do like to talk sweet, but it's not like you're here for the long haul, is it? Hell, we never even said you could stick around for more than a week or so, now, did we? No, sir, most promises ain't worth the spit that makes 'em."

"Hey, haven't I kept all my promises to you?"

She laughs and turns her own hand over so she can squeeze his fingers. "Well, I can't say I've ever caught you lying to me — yet. But it ain't like you've been an open book, neither. For instance, I don't even know where all this money you been promising is supposed to come from, when you've had to borrow from your own daddy just to get by."

It has bothered Shane that he hasn't been able to open up to Tammy, but he cannot bring himself to admit he recently killed a man and might be prosecuted for it. Still, he needs to open the blinds and let at least some of the truth shine through.

"I've got back pay coming from my old job," he tells her.

"And what old job is that?"

"I was a hockey player."

"You got paid for playing hockey?" He nods. "And how long did you do it?"

"Eighteen years … up until a couple of weeks ago."

"That's a long time. So, what ya fixin' to do now that it's all over?"

"Haven't decided yet."

"Well, from what I've heard, most of you fellas don't make more 'n' ten thou or so a year."

He realizes that she is assuming he was some bush-league semi-professional type. It troubles his conscience, but he doesn't correct her, preferring she not know how much money he's squandered, or the international scale of the scandal he's embroiled in.

"Seems to me you're gonna need that there money for yourself," Tammy continues. "The thing is, Gracie ain't eighteen, so she can't go signing adoption papers for no horse. It would be up to me, and I just can't see spending that kind of money."

"Even if I paid for everything?"

"There you go again. Next thing I know, you'll be promisin' to build Vern a hockey rink out back."

"Well, you sure got the space for it."

She smiles. "Have you told him yet?"

"Told him what?"

"That you were a professional hockey player."

"No. I mean, I could see how you wouldn't approve."

"It ain't that I don't approve, it's just … well, it's just not practical for us here, that's all. I mean, even if we could afford the equipment, the closest ice rinks are all up north, Albuquerque way." She sighs. "You must think me a real B-I-T-C-H."

"No, I get it. It's hard keeping all this together and being the one everyone leans on. I really admire you for it."

Her mouth opens, but she says nothing. Instead she stares into his eyes, as if trying to decide whether she likes what she sees there, until, from down the hallway, Gracie laughs, unhinging the moment.

"I'd best lock up now," she says.

"All right. Good night, Tammy," he replies and gets up to go. He pauses in the doorway. "At least think about it, will you? I mean about Gracie and the horse."

"Okay. I reckon I can do that much."

THIRTEEN

Maybelline evidently has not acquired a new supply of moonshine, for she does not appear in the stable that night. Shane therefore rises with the sun the next morning and with a clear head. After breakfast he volunteers to shepherd the kids out to wait for the school bus, and upon his return tracks Tammy down to beg a favour. She is alone in the kitchen sewing a patch onto a pair of jeans.

"Say, Tammy, I got more money arriving at the Western Union office, and I was wondering if I could get a lift into town. I wanna buy some stuff for the ranch, too, while I'm there."

"Keys are hanging on the wall. Help yourself," she answers. When Shane, surprised, does not move, she adds, "S'matter? Don't y'all know how to drive a stick?"

"Are you kidding? I'm a small-town boy. I was shifting gears before I was legal. I'm just surprised you're lending me the truck, that's all."

"You said I could trust you, didn't you? Well, there you go," she says matter-of-factly, returning to her sewing. "If you want to gas it up while you're there, I wouldn't complain. Just so you know, though, reverse can be a little tricky to find. First and second, too, for that matter."

"If you can't find it, grind it," he jokes.

"Not unless you're fixing to buy me a new transmission."

As he's starting up the truck, Maybelline materializes and sticks her head through the window. "Maybe you could pick us up some hooch while you're out," she whispers.

He smiles. "Already on my list. You like mezcal?"

"Love it. We'll have a party tonight."

Shane manages with some effort to get the truck into gear, but has to slam on the brakes when Yolanda walks directly in front of the vehicle. She remains planted there with her arms folded and a scowl on her face. He leans his head out the window to address her.

"Yolanda, Tammy said it was okay to borrow the truck."

"I know. And I know you wouldn't be so stupid as to steal our truck. Because if you do —"

"Yeah, yeah, I know. You'll hunt me down and feed me my own balls. Is that before or after you shove the scorpions down my pants?"

"After, of course." She walks over and hands him a piece of paper. "Groceries we need," she explains. "And you pay. *Está bien?*"

"*No problemo,*" he replies, taking the list.

✖ ✖ ✖ ✖ ✖

Shane returns from a prolific shopping spree that includes construction supplies for the ranch, work clothes, and several bottles of mezcal, and sees Doc Sanchez's mobile clinic parked out front.

The doctor is leaning casually on the side of his vehicle, grinning broadly as he talks to Yolanda, who is sour faced, as usual. The two are speaking in Spanish. Although Shane cannot understand the specifics of the conversation, judging by Sanchez's tone and the way he is holding his stetson over his heart, it appears that the doctor is attempting to sweet-talk the Chicana.

Something Sanchez says elicits a gush of words from Yolanda. Shane doesn't need a translator to know she is cursing the doctor. Instead of recoiling or showing any temper himself, Sanchez blows her a kiss.

"*Chinga su madre, pendejo!*" she spits at him and storms toward the house.

"Is everything all right?" Shane asks as he approaches Sanchez, who is fanning himself with his stetson.

"Terrific. I think I may be wearing her down."

"No, I mean, is everything okay in the house? Somebody sick or something?"

"Oh, no, I'm not here in a medical capacity. Actually, I came by to see you … and to ruffle Yolanda's feathers a little while I'm here. Someone needs to remind her that she's still a woman." He lets out a theatrical sigh. "And quite an attractive one at that."

"It didn't look like she was buying whatever you were selling."

He laughs. "Maybe. But, then, it wouldn't be any fun if she just threw up her skirts and said, 'Take me!' I'm a patient man … I think I can bring her around to my way of thinking."

"In this lifetime?"

"Ah, Shane, there's a lot you don't know about women. Don't let her display of temper fool you. The fact that she stayed and listened to me before blowing up was a good sign in itself. Actually, I think that last outburst may have been for your benefit."

"And you're not worried about what she might do to you if she ever got you naked? I mean, given her history and all."

The doctor delivers one of his patented belly laughs. "A naughty man like me needs incentive to keep from straying. And thanks to the way my sainted *madre* raised me, I'd never strike a woman. Actually, it's *you* being here that seems to have put a bee in Yolanda's bonnet. If I was you, I'd sleep with one eye open and my hands over my crotch."

"Gee, I thought she was starting to warm up to me."

"Ha! Then we're both optimists. But listen, like I said, I actually came here to talk with you. You remember me telling you about my friend Don Aléjandro Arguijo?"

"Yeah, sure, the school chum who owns your hockey team and the new arena across the border. The Lobos, wasn't it?"

"You remember. *Si, Los Lobos de Chihuahua.*" Shane finds it fascinating how the doctor's accent transforms seamlessly between the two languages. "Anyway, I mentioned you in passing to Don Aléjandro, and he's invited us to dine with him at his *rancho* tomorrow night. I'd really like you to meet him."

"Um, aren't you forgetting something, Doc? I've got no ID. How am I supposed to get to Mexico and back without a passport?"

"*Ah, Stupido!*" the doctor exclaims, slamming his palm into his forehead. "I'd almost forgotten. I've got great news for you. Wait a second." He climbs into his van and returns with something in his hands. Shane's eyes widen when he sees his stolen toiletry kit.

"Holy shit! It's my bag. Where the fuck did you find it?"

"Talk about luck. A colleague found it by the roadside." He watches Shane unzip the bag and start to examine the contents. "It's all there — your money, your credit cards, your driver's licence, your passport." Sanchez lowers his voice. "Even your, er, recreational stimulants."

"That's so weird ... I mean, that everything's still in here. Don't get me wrong, I'm not complaining, but I figured the kid would at least have stolen the cash."

"Must have been in a hurry to get rid of it. Perhaps he was being chased."

"Maybe. It's really whacked that the only thing he took out was my dental plate."

Sanchez shrugs. "Don't try to understand the criminal mind, and don't look a gift horse in the mouth. So, dinner tomorrow night, then? Or were you planning to take off, now that you have your stuff back?"

It has not occurred to Shane that his primary reason for staying around the ranch has just disappeared. He turns to stare at the ranch house.

"Actually, I just started some projects around here. Think I'll stick around for a while."

"Ha! I can just imagine what kind of projects you're talking about. Okay, *amigo*, I'll pick you up tomorrow about six o'clock."

Shane drops off the groceries and pays Tammy the next installment on his room and board, but he does not tell her that he has recovered his stolen money and papers. His conscience throbs because of it. Back in the stable he opens his reacquired toiletry bag and pulls out a plastic baggie of cocaine. Thanks to some binging during his ride south, there is not much of the drug left — barely a pinch. He pours it out onto the top of the workbench, uses a utility knife to form a straight thin line of powder, and snorts it down.

The familiar euphorigenic head rush and wash of energy comes over him. It seems more intense than usual due to his recent forced abstinence. Riding his hyperactive buzz, he collects some tools and starts out to tackle his first chore, feeling like a superman who can accomplish virtually anything.

It comes as a bit of a surprise to Shane at the end of the afternoon, after the high has worn off, that he has flitted from task to task like a manic moth, but hasn't actually accomplished anything. When he hears the voices of the children coming down the driveway, he realizes that he's lost track of time, and Tammy has gone out to meet the school bus without him.

He ducks into the stable, unsure whether to go out and greet the children now, or busy himself with some task and act like he was just preoccupied. He wonders why Tammy didn't fetch him and worries she somehow knows he has been snorting. He paces back and forth, causing the resident snakes to stir in their cages.

His current agitated state is totally at odds with the peace he has felt while staying at the ranch. It is like he found a sanctuary from the demons that have been plaguing him for the past few years and then invited them to walk right in. He realizes the cocaine is to blame, even as part of him aches for more of the drug. Feeling ashamed of himself, he retreats to the toolroom and flops onto his bed.

As he tosses on the mattress, feeling the darkness ooze out of the corners of his thoughts, there is a loud smack against the side of the stable, like some hard object has been flung against the boards. A few seconds later, the sound repeats then continues intermittently.

Feeling equal parts annoyance and interest, Shane goes outside to investigate. He finds Vern with a hockey stick and a puck, taking shots against the wall where a rectangle of the same dimensions as a hockey net is crudely painted. Shane has noted the shape a few times before, but never understood its significance.

"Hey," he calls over to Vern, just as the boy takes another shot against the simulated net. Vern drops the stick and backs away, as though he's in trouble.

"Whoa, relax," Shane says, coming closer. "That's a pretty good wrist shot you have there. Your bottom hand's too far down the stick, though. And try launching it from a little farther behind — you'll get more of a snap."

Vern still doesn't move, so Shane picks up the hockey stick and hands it over. "Go ahead. Try again," he urges. He holds up his casted hand. "I'd show you myself, but —"

Vern accepts the stick, and Shane helps him reposition his hands. The boy takes a few more shots using the suggested technique, and when he lets loose one especially hard shot, he breaks into a big smile of delight. "Cool!" he says, beaming.

"See?" Shane says. "But power isn't everything. A goalie will stop even the hardest shot if it's right in his pads. Accuracy's way more important. You need to learn to shoot for the corners." He points between Vern's legs. "And the good ol' five hole. How about tomorrow I paint some corner targets onto that net for you? But let me show you a drill they used to give us — I'll call out a spot, and you try to hit it."

"You played hockey?"

"Yeah, since I was five." He debates whether to confess to playing in the NHL, but doesn't want the information to get back to Tammy, who assumes Shane is some underpaid minor leaguer and doesn't know about the accident. "Keep it up, and who knows? Someday Vern ... er, what's your last name?"

"Draper."

"Well, keep it up and Vern Draper may become a household name someday."

"It's a stupid name. Who ever heard of a hockey player called Vern."

"Trust me, I've heard names a lot weirder, especially those Russian and Finnish ones. But, if you want, we'll give you a nickname."

"Did *you* have a nickname?"

"Well, it's kind of a no-brainer. My last name's Bronkovsky, so what do you suppose people called me?"

Vern thinks about it. "Bronco?"

"That's it. Pretty obvious, right? So, what should we call you?"

Vern shrugs. "I dunno," he says, although there is a hopeful tone in his voice.

Shane tries rhymes and alliteration, but *Vern* proves to be a thorny candidate. But then, as he thinks of the snakes on the other side of the wall, it comes to him.

"How about *Viper*?" he suggests. When the boy says nothing, Shane explains further. "You work with those rattlesnakes all the time, and you're not afraid of them … at least not compared to most kids. Think about it, a viper can strike as fast as lightning, and its bite is deadly. Plus, it begins with *V*, same as *Vern*. Well, what do you think?"

Vern shrugs. "I guess it's cool."

"Darn tootin' it is. Come on, Viper, we've got some time before supper. Let's practise some corner shots. And then I want to see your backhand."

✻ ✻ ✖ ✻ ✻

As Shane is being ushered out of the house at bedtime, he catches Maybelline's eye and gives her a significant look to indicate she should join him in the stable later. While he awaits her arrival, he cracks open a bottle of mezcal and takes some preliminary swigs.

When she finally dances into the stall, Maybelline sees the amount that he has consumed and chides him.

"Hey, Piggly Wiggly, you started without me."

"Well, go ahead and get caught up." She dives onto the bed and snuggles up right beside him. Shane finds himself unnerved by her closeness. He is concerned that she may try to initiate sex with him, and he has kept his clothes on for this reason. He is unsure how to handle it if she starts coming on to him. A few days ago, he imagined making a pass at her. Now, he is hoping their relationship stays platonic. It is his growing attraction to Tammy that spurs fidelity, although she has not yet displayed any reciprocal interest. Even the fact that he is drinking behind her back tweaks his conscience. This is becoming a persistent feeling.

As if reading his thoughts, Maybelline hands him the bottle, looks him in the eye, and says, "I ain't gonna fuck you, just so you know."

"That's cool. But we're still friends, right?"

"Of course we are, Silly Billy. Silly Shaney." She takes another sip. "This doesn't quite have the same kick as the moonshine, but it sure tastes better on the tongue, don't it?"

Shane grunts assent, just relieved to have avoided any sexual awkwardness with her — but he's not out of the woods yet.

Maybelline suddenly looks serious and sits upright. "You do *want* to fuck me, right?"

Shane chooses his words carefully. "Are you kidding me? What red-blooded man wouldn't want to make love to someone as beautiful as you, Maybelline? But your friendship means more to me, and I don't want to mess that up."

Seemingly satisfied with the answer, she collapses back against his body. She takes another sip of mezcal before elaborating. "Tammy told me she told you I used to turn tricks. I just didn't want you to think bad of me."

"Yeah, she told me, but it doesn't matter, May. What's past is past."

"The thing is, I never wanted to do it. I was all messed up. And my boyfriend, Jimmy ... he ... he made me do it." She starts to blubber and presses her face into his chest.

"That guy was an evil prick. If I ever came across someone doing that to a woman, I'd punch his face in."

"It's okay, he's dead. He ODed last year over in San Antonio. And I'm clean now." She takes another swig off the bottle when she says it and giggles. "Well, I still like to drink booze, but that doesn't count, does it?"

"Not in my books. But I guess Tammy would disagree."

She nods. "Yeah. Geez, that girl can be a tight ass sometimes. Don't get me wrong, I love her to death. She looks out for me like nobody ever did before. But sometimes I wish she'd just lighten up. She needs to get laid."

Maybelline's hand slides down and starts playing with Shane's zipper. "Hey, maybe you should screw her. I think she kinda fancies you."

"Why, did she say something about me?"

"Ha! I knew it. You like her, don't you?" Maybelline squeals with sophomoric delight. As she says it, she starts to rub Shane's crotch, and to his surprise, an erection starts to burgeon.

"Hey, I thought you said no sex," he protests.

"Well, I said I wasn't going to fuck you, but there's lots of other things we could do. And I said that before I got a nice mezcal buzz on and you started sweet-talking me about how beautiful I was 'n' all. Besides, you ain't a half-bad-looking guy, once you shave and get your teeth in. But I can stop if you want me to."

"Aw, fuck," Shane moans. It is not usual for him to achieve this state of sexual arousal. From a head that's always either throbbing or feeling like it belongs to someone else, to a gut that seems to be perpetually churning, problems above the beltline have monopolized his vitality. But despite this stimulation, his thoughts guiltily flow toward Tammy, and he is just about to tell Maybelline to stop when she ceases rubbing on her own and gets up from the bed wearing an elfish grin.

"Well, I'd best head back to the house before someone comes fussin' after me. I guess you'll just have to finish by yourself." She bends over and presses her lips to Shane's ear. "You can even think about me while you do it. I don't mind. It ain't really cheating if it's only in your imagination."

She waves at him from the doorway. "*Bye bye, Sugar Pie, I gotta fly.* Thanks, and save some drinks for me. But to answer your question, yeah, Tammy did say something about you."

She giggles, clearly not intending to elaborate, and skips out of the stable. The noise of her departure causes some of the rattlesnakes to stir, and Shane wonders if the serpents are waking from the torpor caused by their recent feeding. After that, he is too busy dealing with his own trouser snake.

FOURTEEN

Doctor Sanchez arrives punctually the next evening to take Shane to their dinner at Don Aléjandro's *rancho*. At the border crossing, Shane fumbles for his passport. Seeing his nervousness, Sanchez pats him on the shoulder. "Relax, I checked, and no warrants have been issued for you, yet. There won't be any problems." In fact, the guards seem altogether disinterested; they are waved through the border without scrutiny.

As they drive into Puerto Palomas, Sanchez points toward a large domed building to the west adjoining the border fence. "There ... that's our new arena. The ice-making equipment was just installed last month, and the players have already started skating. We're paying them to practise all summer so they'll be ready when the season opens."

"Why here?" Shane asks. "I mean, there must be bigger cities around with, like, a million people to support a franchise. Why put your team in a small town across the border from an even smaller village?"

"I told you. Don Aléjandro grew up in Palomas and went to school in Columbus, so this is his community. Besides, the arena isn't that large. It only holds thirty-five hundred fans. He'll easily fill that many seats. But, if not, Don Aléjandro's other business interests will offset any losses from the hockey team."

"So I take it the Don is loaded."

"Quite wealthy, yeah."

"Where does his money come from?"

Sanchez takes his time answering. "Import-export. But I wouldn't go probing into the man's business affairs at dinner if I was you. It would be considered indelicate. Just stick to hockey ... or whatever topic Don Aléjandro chooses to discuss."

"Don't worry, Doc, I'll be on my best behaviour. I know how to suck up to these robber barons. He's not the first rich guy to buy himself a hockey franchise as a hobby. Still, if they really care about the team, then the right owner can do a lot of good."

"Even though he's a self-made man who comes from humble roots, you'll find Don Aléjandro is a gentleman of the old school. And, yes, he's really passionate about hockey ... believes it's the sport of the future. You should have seen how excited he got when I told him we had a veteran NHL player staying right here. He's really looking forward to hearing your insights."

"I'll have to come up with some, then."

They leave the outskirts of the town and head out into the now familiar Chihuahuan Desert landscape. After about twenty minutes, they reach the ranch, which is surrounded by a high stone wall. The entrance onto the estate is blocked by massive spiked iron gates, which swing open automatically with a clank and a whir after Doc Sanchez announces their arrival into an intercom.

As they ride down the asphalt driveway, Shane can see that the place is *Rancho Crótalo*'s complete opposite. Lush and well tended, there are trees lining the road on both sides. The fences are all painted an immaculate white and form a line that ripples off into the distance with the terrain. Atop a faraway hill, Shane can see men on horseback ushering a small herd of cattle.

The two-storey ranch house itself is huge, certainly as big as any mansion Shane has ever been invited to in his time. It is done up in the traditional Mexican rural style, with a terracotta tile roof crowning white stucco walls and brightly coloured ceramic tile inlays throughout. Through an archway, Shane can see a massive inner courtyard surfaced in shiny old cobblestones, with a fountain bubbling away in the middle.

As soon as they clear their vehicle, the main door of the house opens, and out steps a middle-aged Hispanic man casually attired in blue jeans and a cowboy shirt, his arms spread wide in welcome. He sports the obligatory big moustache, but his greying hair is neatly coiffed and greased back. Although the man appears to be of the same vintage as Sanchez, he is trim and solid looking in comparison to the doctor.

"Francisco! *Cómo estás?*" the man says, and the two wrap each other in a big hug.

"*Muy bien, gracias*, Don Aléjandro. And may I introduce Mr. Shane Bronkovsky of the Columbus Blue Jackets."

"Welcome to my home, Mr. Bronkovsky," the Don says in flawless English, flashing a bright, toothy smile. "You honour me with your presence." When he shakes hands with Shane, there is iron in his grip. "Please, come inside."

It is only then that Shane notices the two moustached men who have followed Don Aléjandro out the door. They have the same sombre and dangerous look as the men who stole his Ducati. It is clear they are not run-of-the-mill domestics, but provide some kind of security. Both are wearing loose-fitting denim jackets which no doubt conceal firearms.

Don Aléjandro doesn't seem to even notice the men. He guides Shane into the house, jabbering away about his first boyhood job selling refreshments at a hockey game. He proves to be a very charming and hospitable man, and Shane soon forgets about the bodyguards. Although Doc Sanchez and his longtime friend are obviously on intimate terms, Shane notices that the doctor never drops the respectful honorific *don* before his host's name, and thus Shane adopts the same formality.

During a tour of the mansion, Shane is shown a massive dining hall containing a table that can seat twenty, but their dinner tonight is served on a patio, with the three of them sitting around a small table. The five-course meal is delicious. The quality and presentation of the dishes and matching wines remind Shane of the upscale restaurants Brandi insisted on frequenting. The impression is complete when a chef in white uniform and hat emerges during dessert to chat briefly with Don Aléjandro and receive their compliments.

Brandy, liqueur, and cigars are proffered, and the men push back their chairs to sip from their glasses and blow smoke up at the star-laden sky. During the meal, Don Aléjandro seemed more interested in recounting escapades from his and Sanchez's naughty schoolboy past and discussing prospective match-ups for the next round of the NHL playoffs than picking Shane's brain. Now he refills Shane's glass and fixes him with a probing look.

"So, Shane, what are your plans for the future?"

"Assuming you manage to stay out of jail, that is," Sanchez quips.

"Please, Francisco, that's not fair. We both agree that Shane here is innocent of any wrongdoing and is being treated unfairly. God protect us from ambitious prosecutors."

"Thanks, Don Aléjandro, but the doc's got a point. It's pretty hard to make plans when you've got something like that hanging over your head. But, honestly, I haven't really given the future serious thought. I've been way too busy just trying to deal with stuff as it happens ... which is pretty fast and furious, lately."

"Do you think you might stay in hockey? In some other capacity, I mean."

Shane shrugs. "Hockey's all I know. Right now I'm a leper, and no one in the game will touch me, but I have thought before that I'd like to try my hand at coaching. Not in the bigs, mind you — that's way too cutthroat for me. But maybe in the minor leagues." He gives a self-effacing grin. "I've never told anyone that before. A lot of guys would probably say I don't have the smarts to be a coach."

"Never let others set limits for you. Look at me. I was just an impoverished boy from the poorest *barrio* in Puerto Palomas, but I made my fortune. Or take Francisco here, once a lazy trouble-maker expelled several times, but now an esteemed physician."

Sanchez laughs. "True, I managed to make it through med school. But esteemed? You exaggerate. Still, thank you for the compliment, Don Aléjandro."

"My point, Francisco, is that our teachers had us both pegged for either jail or the poorhouse. But we showed them, didn't we, *compadre*?"

"Yes, we did," the doctor replies, and the two men clink their glasses.

Don Aléjandro leans toward Shane. "I was wondering, Shane, if perhaps you'd be interested in helping with our hockey team?"

"You mean, play for you?"

"Oh, no, as much as I would welcome your talents, *La Liga* wouldn't allow it, at least not without you getting Mexican citizenship, which would take some time. But I could use someone with your experience and knowledge of the game as a special consultant."

"Consultant?" The word does not fit into Shane's conception of the hockey universe.

"A paid consultant, of course. Someone to advise the coach of game strategies, suggest practice drills, and perhaps evaluate the players."

"You mean like an assistant coach, or something?"

Don Aléjandro waves his cigar in a small impatient circle. "The title isn't important. The coach ... well, let's just say he's an obligation of sorts, and a figurehead. You wouldn't have to treat him as your superior. You would answer to me and Francisco."

Shane blows out a ring of smoke from his own cigar. The idea has definite appeal, not the least of which being that the job would keep him close to Tammy and the ranch. Plus, what with the legal storm brewing in the north, Mexico seems like a great place to hide. The only thing keeping him from sticking out a hand to shake on the deal is a voice in his head reminding him that no contract should be undertaken without first talking to Morrie Getz.

"I'd love to work with you. A lot of guys I've played with were kind of cocky. They'd do what the coaches told them to because they'd be benched otherwise. But I don't think they ever really listened. Me? I always figured I needed all the help I could get, so I paid attention." He taps the side of his skull. "I've got all that information stored right here. Just let me run it past my agent, though."

Don Aléjandro is grinning until Shane mentions his agent. A scowl cuts across the older man's face, but stays there only a few seconds. The smile that returns seems a little slyer.

"I understand, but I wasn't necessarily thinking of something so formal. You could come and watch my team a few times, tell me what you think, give me a few suggestions, and I'd pay you under the water. No, wait, that's not right." He turns to Sanchez. "*Cómo se dice 'bajo el agua'?*"

"Under the table," the doctor replies.

"Yes, yes. That's it. I would pay you under the table. I'm a simple man with an aversion to paperwork. I'm used to doing business with just a handshake."

"Well, I can't see anything wrong with that —" Shane starts to say, but is interrupted by raucous voices from inside the house.

"Ah, my son, Enrique, has returned," Don Aléjandro explains, rising from the table. "I'm sure he would enjoy meeting you." He calls out into the next room. "*Enrique, salga aquí en la terraza!*"

The young man who walks out onto the patio is the very one who pulled a gun on Shane and stole his motorcycle on the highway. He is flanked by the two older men who rode in the back of the pickup that day — carbon copies of Don Aléjandro's own tough-looking bodyguards, right down to the thick moustaches crowning their scowling lips.

Enrique doesn't recognize Shane at first, but when his eyes take in the cast on the arm, something evidently clicks, judging from the sneer that appears on his face.

"That's the son of a bitch that stole my motorcycle!" Shane yells, jumping to his feet and pointing. As he takes a step forward, guns suddenly appear in the hands of Enrique's companions and point straight at Shane. They are nasty-looking automatic machine pistols, compact but clearly meant for serious firepower. When the companions pull back the bolts of their firearms, the sound causes Don Aléjandro's bodyguards to come running onto the terrace, guns raised, although they appear unsure as to where to point their own weapons. Shane freezes, realizing the moment is perilously tense. Out of the corner of his eye, he sees Doc Sanchez slide beneath the table, like a snake slipping under a rock.

"*Alto!*" Don Aléjandro suddenly barks. "*Dejen sus pistolas ahora!*" The raised voice is at odds with the soft-spoken, affable man Shane has seen so far. It has the confident tone of someone used to commanding men, with an underlying note of menace. The Don's gunmen instantly obey, but Enrique's bodyguards hesitate and look to their young boss for guidance. Enrique gives a tiny, barely perceptible nod — only then are the weapons put away.

"What's all this about, Shane?" Don Aléjandro demands.

"Your son and those goons of his, they stole my motorcycle after I crashed. When I tried to stop them, they pulled a gun on me."

"Yes, Francisco has mentioned that you were robbed, but you're positive these are the men?"

"Damned sure. I recognized the bastards the second I saw them. They stuck my Ducati in the back of a tricked-out black pickup truck and just took off with it."

Don Aléjandro turns and addresses his son in Spanish. Shane has no clue what they're saying, but carefully observes the body language of the two men. The Don is initially patient, like he is addressing a child, but when Enrique replies, there is nothing defensive or repentant in his tone. If anything, his whole demeanour oozes arrogance. At one point he actually spits in Shane's direction.

Don Aléjandro does not appear to like what he is hearing from his son. The patient fatherly patter is replaced by a rapid-fire series of staccato words. Shane manages to parse *stupido* and *idiota* and so deduces that Enrique is being chastised. This is confirmed when the son's face turns red with rage and he starts screaming at his father. Droplets of spittle fly into the Don's face, but he says nothing, until finally some line is evidently crossed, and he delivers a hard slap across Enrique's face.

For a second Shane is convinced the son will attack the father. Despite the age difference, he thinks the old man would be able to hold his own in an all-out brawl. But Enrique is clearly trying to get a hold of himself; his jaw is clenched tight, and his whole body is visibly trembling. The palpable tension unnerves the various bodyguards as well; both Enrique's protectors and the Don's slide their hands inside their jackets and shift uneasily from leg to leg, their eyes darting from man to man all the while.

When Enrique does finally move, it is not toward Don Aléjandro. He turns to Shane, and his lips pull back into a snarl. "I should have put a bullet through your brain when I had the chance," he hisses, then turns on his heels and storms out of the room, his bodyguards hastening to follow him.

After all the shouting and tension, the room lapses into silence, except for the sound of the nocturnal animals calling outside. Don Aléjandro stands with his back to his guests. Shane can see from the slump in his shoulders that the man's anger has been replaced with a great sorrow.

Doc Sanchez evidently picks up on it, too. Having emerged from under the table, he indicates to Shane with a jerk of the head that they should leave.

"It is getting late, Don Aléjandro," Sanchez says, his voice full of sympathy, "and we have a long drive back. Thank you, as always, for your splendid hospitality."

"Yeah, I had a great time, and the food was delicious. It was really nice meeting you," Shane echoes.

The Don's back straightens, and when he turns around, he wears a forced smile. "It was a great pleasure meeting you, too, Shane. I hope you will seriously consider my offer."

"Um, yeah. I'll do that." What Shane really wants to talk about is his stolen motorcycle, but he senses it is not wise to force the issue, under the circumstances. When they shake hands, the firmness is gone from the older man's grip. The Don and the doctor embrace and exchange some soft, private words, then one of the bodyguards leads Sanchez and Shane back though the house and outside to their vehicle.

Sanchez is uncharacteristically quiet as they start their drive back, so Shane kickstarts the conversation.

"That was a bit of excitement, eh? For a second, I thought World War Three was going to break out."

"Don Aléjandro would never allow it, especially under his own roof."

"Yeah, well, it looked to me like Enrique might have had ideas of his own. Is it just me, or is that kid a psycho?"

"He's always been a difficult child. Now that he's grown up and his father's brought him into the business, they don't see eye to eye on how to do things. His father is a gentleman and a diplomat, who plans things to the last detail. Enrique is … let's just say he can be pigheaded and impetuous."

"You mean like when he stuck a gun in my face and stole my Ducati?"

"That was stupid of him. Don Aléjandro was very angry. Enrique knows better than to make trouble on the American side."

"Oh, so it would have been okay for him to do that to me in Mexico?"

Sanchez laughs. "Oh, *amigo,* in *Mexico,* the cartels do what they please."

It takes a few seconds for the information to sink in. "You're saying those guys are mobsters?"

"Don Aléjandro is a businessman. Most of his enterprises are totally legitimate, but okay, some of his longstanding import-export operations aren't exactly legal, though they are quite lucrative."

"Holy shit! You took me to dinner with a drug lord?"

"Don't be so fucking naive. You smoke and snort the stuff, don't you? It's got to come from someplace. You create the demand and then you condemn the guys who fill it? You're like one of those people who love eating meat, but try to ignore that animals are killed and butchered in the process. Besides, the hockey team is totally above board, or I wouldn't be associated with it. And the offer he's making you is a generous one. Given your situation, Shane, you should jump on it."

"I'm not going to go work for a drug lord! Don't they, like, murder people left, right, and centre down here? Holy shit, some of the stuff I've heard on the news —"

Sanchez slams on the brakes, bringing the vehicle to a screeching halt in the middle of the road.

"Don Aléjandro isn't like that! He hates violence. His territory goes back over thirty years to when the Godfather of all *Mexico*, Félix Gallardo, originally carved up the country's drug trade into smaller *plazas*. Don Aléjandro has managed to prosper without excessive bloodshed. What's happening in the country now is madness. Fifty thousand killed in five years, a lot of them innocents! It's like the gates of hell have opened up. No one hates the violence more than Don Aléjandro. He's told me as much. He has two of the most violent cartels to either side of him, and he's placated them by staying neutral. He's relinquished control rather than fight with them and stoop to their level of evil. I'm proud to call him my friend."

Behind them, a car lays on its horn before pulling around their stopped vehicle and accelerating past them. Doc Sanchez presses down on the gas pedal, and they resume driving.

"Shit, and you call *me* naive?" Shane finally responds.

"I don't involve myself in the illegal side of his affairs, even more so now that Enrique has taken charge. I'm afraid the son is not as benign or wise as his father, and certainly he is far greedier.

He not only endorses the tactics used by the other cartels, I think he relishes them."

Shane has been searching his memory for any news items he has absorbed from hotel television sets about the Mexican drug war.

"I seem to recall hearing about mass graves full of corpses with body parts cut off. That's pretty nasty shit."

Sanchez clucks his tongue. "It just gets worse and worse. All the big cartels have got armed squads of enforcers now, and they're totally ruthless. Down south, for example, they have *Los Zetas*, all former commandos or members of the elite Special Forces who deserted and worked for hire as a private army, then went into business for themselves as their own cartel. They've upped the ante for violence, so now other gangs are bringing in ex-military from Central America. They're all monsters with no conscience. Cutting off the heads and hands, that's to make identification harder, and to intimidate the hell out of the public.

"It's bad enough when they're killing one another, but a lot of innocent people suffer in the process, too. Next door, in Juárez, for instance, is *La Línea* — most of them are ex-cops. One day a bunch of them show up at a birthday party full of teenagers and shoot it up with AK-47s. Sixteen kids killed, another dozen injured, all because they thought one of the kids had squealed on them to the cops. They're devils."

He turns to look at Shane. "You heard what happened to the cops in Columbus, right?"

Shane shakes his head.

"The FBI came in and busted the mayor, the city manager, the chief of police, and most of his men. Got them for running guns to *Mexico*. The whole Columbus police department's been disbanded."

"And you're still saying Don Aléjandro isn't getting his hands dirty?"

"That wasn't his doing, and he chose not to interfere. Enrique disagreed — wanted to grab the guns for himself, or at least charge a tax — but he was overruled. I shudder to think what would happen if Don Aléjandro were no longer here to keep a tight rein on things."

They drive in silence for a while, each man wrapped in his own thoughts. Then Sanchez speaks again. "I have a confession to make, Shane."

"What's that?"

"Your stolen bag ... it wasn't really found by a patient of mine. When you described the motorcycle that Mormon kid was driving, I knew right away it was Enrique's. I saw it parked at the arena, and I went and peeked in the sidecar ... first I saw your dental plate lying there, then later I found your bag down on the floor."

"And you didn't figure that it was Enrique and his men who stole my Ducati? What the fuck, Doc?"

"I ... I didn't want to get involved. It was on the American side. Don Aléjandro has ordered Enrique not to cross the border, where he can't guarantee protection from the authorities the way he can in *Mexico*."

"And Enrique went anyway, didn't he?"

"Yes. Yes, he did."

Shane turns to stare out his window into the darkness. "I wonder what happened to the poor Mormon kid," he asks the night.

FIFTEEN

Shane awakens to the sound of animated voices outside. Curiosity and the need to urinate override the desire to cover his head with a pillow and cling to sleep. Shane staggers to his feet, dresses, and stumbles outside for a pee, muttering curses at the serpents as he passes. Rounding the side of the stable, he is surprised to see the entire household assembled in the driveway and heads over to find out what has them so energized.

His stolen Ducati stands in their midst as they speculate about its presence. Vern is sitting sidesaddle on the leather seat, but he slides off when Shane approaches. Yolanda, however, continues to squeeze and manipulate the controls on the handlebars. Shane wonders if she really is that interested in how the machine operates or is only trying to annoy him.

Tammy looks up at him. "This here the bike they stole from you?"

Shane nods. He doesn't see the value in disclosing his newfound revelations about the identity of the thieves.

"Coulda sworn I heard you drive in with Doc Sanchez around eleven," Tammy continues.

"I did," Shane replies. He gestures at the Ducati. "This wasn't my doing."

"Then how do you reckon it got here?"

"I guess the thieves had a change of heart."

Tammy snorts. "Ain't like any thief I ever heard of."

Shane shrugs. "Maybe they were feeling too much heat from the law to hang on to it."

"Then they would have just dumped it somewhere. Seems like they took an awful chance bringing it here … and pushing it all the way up to the house. I sure didn't hear no engine, and I'm a pretty light sleeper. And, come to think of it, how did they know exactly where to bring it? Don't like the thought of a bunch of criminals prowling around my property."

Shane gives her a big smile, which has the desired effect, now that he is wearing his dentures again. "I'm sure Yolanda would have blasted anyone who tried to get into the house. Those guys obviously snuck over here to do right instead of wrong, so I say, let's not look a gift horse in the mouth."

He climbs aboard the Ducati and looks it over. Everything is clean and polished — even the scratches from his crash have been retouched. The key is in the ignition, and he starts the motorcycle up, listening with satisfaction to its healthy roar. He revs the throttle a couple of times, mostly to determine whether he can still operate the vehicle with one hand in a cast. He decides it would be technically possible to drive it, though tricky, but shuts the machine down.

"Not sure I can ride it yet with this busted arm," he announces, studying Tammy for a reaction.

"So, you still figuring on staying some?" she answers.

"If you'll have me."

"Well, just as long as you pay your room and board like you promised and keep helping with the chores, I won't kick you out just yet." Tammy takes one last wary look at the Ducati and retreats to the ranch house.

✖ ✖ ✖ ✖ ✖

Although rewiring the lights in the stable is the biggest job on his list, Shane wants to save that project to do alongside Vern. Instead, he opts to fulfill his promise to add corner targets and a low centre bull's eye to the painted hockey net on the side of the stable. When he finds Vern's hockey stick and puck stored against the wall, Shane attempts to take a couple of practice shots, but cannot properly grip the shaft of the stick with his casted left hand. He gives up on the exercise, but turns to see that Yolanda has snuck up and been watching the entire time.

"Typical man ... work to be done, and he'd rather play games," she comments.

"It's for Vern," he explains.

"Yeah, well, that little *baboso* needs to spend less time thinking about hockey and more time helping out around here."

"From what I can see, the kid more than holds up his end, but you gals still ride him pretty hard."

"He's got hockey on the brain, that's all. It's a waste of time, but he don't got no sense about it."

"Like Gracie and her horses?"

"That's different."

"Why, because she's a girl? Seems to me, Yolanda, that you pick on Vern just because he's a guy. For that matter, you haven't given me much of a chance, either. Aren't I paying my way? Haven't I been helping out around here?"

Yolanda gestures at the painting on the wall. "*Si*, some help."

"Well, is there something specific you want me to do for you? Just say the word."

Yolanda snorts and grabs her crotch. "Is this what you had in mind? Just try it!"

Shane lets out a belly laugh, and is amused to see a veil of confusion come over Yolanda's face. "Don't get me wrong, Yolanda, you're an attractive woman, but between your knife and Doc Sanchez's gun, there's no way I'm going there."

"Sanchez? What's he got to do with anything?"

"Can't you tell? He's carrying a torch for you."

Her mouth opens and closes a couple of times, but nothing comes out. Finally she spits on the ground and walks away. But then she stops in her tracks and turns to face him again. "There's kindling needs cutting, if you think you can manage with one hand," she tells him. There's a twinkle in her eye — or maybe it's just a trick of the sunlight.

Shane goes around the back of the house and finds Tammy swinging an axe at some thick chunks of firewood. Although her energy and enthusiasm are obvious, her technique is poor. Rather than aiming at the outer quadrants, where it's easier to pare off a length, she is striking the logs in the middle, getting the axe lodged in the process, and having to use her foot to lever the head back out.

"Need some help?" Shane asks.

"I can manage," Tammy replies, just as she gets the axe stuck again.

Shane walks over so he can face her. "Aw, c'mon. I grew up feeding a wood stove. Let me give you a hand."

Tammy pulls the axe out, then wipes her brow. "A hand is pretty much all you got, ain't it," she retorts.

"Bet I can do better with one hand than you're doing with two. It's not how hard you hit it, but where. Let me show you."

Tammy relents, so Shane repositions the piece of wood on the chopping stump. He arcs the axe high above his head with his good hand, and lets the tool's weight propel it downward, closer to the outer edge. A piece the width of a milk carton gets neatly lopped off, although the remaining section of log topples over in the process. He puts down the axe to prop up the fallen log again.

"Here — you chop, I'll stand 'em up," Tammy says. Shane realizes this is her way of admitting he was right. He likes the fact that she is flexible enough to concede a point. Together they tackle the stack of wood, then further reduce some of the lengths into smaller sticks of kindling.

Once they finish the chore, Tammy fetches some lemonade. As they sit side by side on the stump, admiring their handiwork, Shane again broaches the subject of getting a horse for Gracie.

"I told you I'd think about it!" she snaps back. "I don't get why you're so doggone hell-bent on tossing your money away on a kid that's not even yours."

"Excuse me for caring. I'm just trying to be nice to the poor kid."

"Poor kid? We're poor, all right, but that don't mean my little girl don't get everything she really needs. And that sure as hell don't mean you can come waltzing in here flashing money around and tell me how to raise my own flesh and blood."

"Aw, for fuck's sake, that's not what I meant. I'm just trying to be nice."

"What you're being is a real a-hole," Tammy says, stabbing Shane hard in the sternum with her forefinger. "If I want anything from you, I'll be sure to let you know. And if you're offering to buy that horse because you think it's going to make me all weak-kneed for you, forget about it — I ain't easy like that one inside you got the hots for."

From the direction of the house comes a whimper like that of a dog whose tail has just been stepped on. Shane turns to see that Maybelline has been standing on the porch listening to the entire exchange, unbeknownst to them. She turns and runs back into the house, slamming the screen door behind her.

"Aw, shit, now see what you've done," Tammy sighs. It's unclear whether she's chiding Shane or herself. She collects the empty lemonade glasses and hurries into the house. Shane vacillates about following to help soothe Maybelline's ruffled feathers, but decides to stay outside and stack firewood.

Eventually he ventures inside, carrying an armload of kindling as an excuse for his presence. There is no sign of Tammy, but Maybelline is sitting at the table, peeling potatoes and whistling merrily.

"You okay?" Shane inquires.

Maybelline smiles up at him. "Of course I am, silly. Why wouldn't I be?"

"Well, because of what Tammy said out there."

She laughs. "That didn't bother me."

"You seemed pretty upset."

"Naw, I know she didn't really mean it. I just like screwing with her head from time to time, that's all. I mean, don't get me wrong, I love Tammy, she's great. But sometimes she can be a little bossy. So I keep her on her toes. Besides, she was starting to get pretty pissed with you … figured I'd better get her mind on something else before she smacked you across the side of the head with a chunk of firewood and sent you packing. Then we'd *never* get you two together."

"I doubt that's going to happen. I don't think she likes me."

"Oh, she likes you, even if she's afraid to admit it to herself. We just need to give her a little more time, and she'll come around. Meanwhile, though, you gotta stop acting like such a doofus. Be nice to her. Stop trying to tell her what to do. She don't like that. Wouldn't harm none to take your shirt off from time to time, neither."

Shane finds himself blushing. "She thinks something's going on between us."

"Well, she ain't wrong, now, is she?" Maybelline answers with a wink. "She just don't know exactly what."

"Maybe you should stop, you know, sneaking in at night and drinking behind her back."

Maybelline's pale face darkens. "Is that what you want?"

"No, no, I really enjoy partying with you. It's just, Tammy —"

"Never mind Tammy. I saw you first, and I figure I coulda had you anytime I wanted. Just because I'm going to let Tammy have you don't mean I'm gonna give you up altogether."

Shane has encountered this kind of talk from women before, and it has always irked him to be treated as if he has no will of his own in these matters.

"Just like I'm some kind of dog you lead around by the leash?"

She laughs. "Oh, Shane, you men are *all* dogs. And it ain't a leash we lead you by. But don't go frettin', now. We ain't gonna go breakin' Tammy's heart, but that don't mean we can't have some fun. I'll see you tonight. Now, *howdy doody, do yer duty*. Go show Tammy what a big, handy he-man you are."

Shane exhales irritably, but can't think of a retort, so he leaves to tackle some more outdoor chores. He even goes so far as to take Maybelline's advice and work shirtless in the hopes that Tammy will catch a glimpse.

When it's time to meet the school bus, Tammy comes out back and invites Shane to join her, stealing glimpses of his musculature with little coyness. After Shane dresses, they head down to the road. He tries to initiate small talk as they walk, carefully avoiding the subject of horses. Tammy, however, adds little to the conversation. When prompted, she answers questions about the kids' grades, the garden's prospects, and the minutiae of rattlesnake ranching, but she seems otherwise withdrawn. If she is crushing on him in any way, she is doing a top-notch job of hiding it. Shane is disheartened by the time they reach the highway.

Gracie explodes from the school bus with a laugh of delight, offering Shane some solace in the fact that her happiness does not only stem from seeing her mother. In fact, the hug she gives Tammy seems short and perfunctory compared to the intense wraparound affair she bestows on Shane. When the hug goes into overtime, Shane looks up at Tammy to see if she resents her daughter's overt affection, but Tammy's look is cryptic.

After Gracie lets go, Shane makes a point of approaching Vern.

"Hey," he greets the boy.

"Hey."

"How was school?" Vern shrugs. "Play any sports today?" Shane persists.

"Baseball again, during gym class."

"How'd that go?"

"I don't care about baseball. It's not my game."

"You should care. It's great practice. A lot of college hockey players play baseball in the off-season."

Vern perks up. "They do?"

"Sure. Reacting to a baseball is a lot like reacting to a puck. And hitting a ball is all about timing ... just like one-timing a shot. You've seen guys bat a puck out of mid-air, haven't you?"

Vern nods. "Uh-huh. I've done that, too."

"Well, there you go. Timing and reflexes. If you can hit a puck, you can hit a baseball. You just have to give it a chance."

"I never thought of it that way."

"Oh yeah, there's lots of stuff you can do to improve your game off the ice ... and your conditioning, too."

Gracie has been walking alongside Shane. She has one hand in her mother's and the other in Shane's, but her gaze is directed squarely at him. Knowing what she wants, he stops and squats down to her eye level.

"You want a ride, don't you?"

"Yes, please."

"You know, riding me is like riding Opie, that big ol' work-horse I told you about. Wouldn't you rather ride a mustang?"

Gracie looks confused, and Tammy shoots him a dirty look. He gives Tammy a wink to calm any concerns.

"How about Vern gives you a ride? He's more your size."

No one seems enthused by the suggestion.

"It'll be great for building up the legs ... and it'll help your cardio, too," he tells Vern.

"Well, okay," the boy assents, and he squats down to be mounted.

"Give him a try. It'll be like a riding a pony," Shane urges Gracie. She climbs aboard with Shane's help, and Vern takes off in a sprint, showing excellent speed. Judging from Gracie's shrieks of delight in the distance, her new mount is proving an adequate replacement. Vern has his head down and is working hard, having evidently taken Shane's coaching to heart.

"It's a pity you never had kids of your own," Tammy comments. "You got a way with them." Shane meets her gaze. The earlier hostility seems to have dissipated.

"Yeah. You're lucky," he answers.

"It's never too late for a feller. Hell, some of them old coots at Holy Waters are still fathering kids into their sixties."

"Fathering's the easy part. Kids need a mother, too. How about you, Tammy ... ever consider having more children?"

She shrugs. "Kind of got my hands full as it is." She gestures across the landscape. "Guys ain't exactly lining up for a piece of this life, neither."

"I find that hard to believe. A beautiful woman like you has a lot to offer."

A blush paints Tammy's cheeks. "Oh, there's no shortage of guys looking to get under my skirt, if that's what you mean. But finding a man with a heart as well as a hard-on who'll stick around and treat you right, well, that's something altogether different. So no thanks. The dogs that come sniffing around I send a-packin'."

"Don't you ever get lonely?"

"Mister, the loneliest I ever been was when I was married."

Up ahead, Vern, zigzagging, loses his footing and goes tumbling to the ground. Tammy gasps, and she and Shane sprint over. It is clear, at least to Shane, that no damage has been done. Both kids are lying there laughing, Gracie bouncing up and down on top of her cousin. Tammy, nonetheless, immediately tears into her nephew.

"You stupid idiot, Vern, why don't you watch what you're doing!"

"Sorry, Aunt Tammy. I got tangled up."

"Sorry don't cut it, boy. You mighta hurt Gracie."

"No, I was careful, I made sure she landed on top of me."

"You was lucky, that's all. Clumsy galoot. I got a mind to take my belt to you."

"I said I was sorry."

Gracie tries to intervene. "I'm okay, Mama. Vern made sure I didn't get hurt."

"What are you talking about, child? It's Vern that done sent you tumbling."

As Shane helps the children up, he sees a chance to play peacemaker. "Nobody's hurt, and that's the important thing, right, kids?" They both nod. He wraps an arm around Vern's shoulders. "Hey, you looked good out there, bud. You're pretty darned fast. Felt that in your legs, though, didn't you?"

"Sure did."

"Well, keep it up and you'll build up the ol' quads and glutes in no time." He sees Tammy about to say something and hastens to intercept. "But you heard your aunt — you have to be extra careful whenever you're carrying Gracie. She's precious cargo."

"I wouldn't let anything happen to her, really I wouldn't."

He squats down to meet Gracie eye to eye. "That was fun, huh?"

"Uh-huh. He was fast, almost like a real pony."

"See, what did I tell you? Well, maybe you can do it again ... but only if your mom doesn't object."

All eyes are on Tammy. She knows when she's outgunned. "Oh, heck, I guess it weren't no big thing, but for land's sake, children, be careful."

Gracie remounts, and Vern gallops off again, albeit more slowly. The adults resume their stroll, but their words have dried up, and they walk the rest of the way in silence.

× × ✖ × ×

In the handful of hours before supper, Shane and Vern make excellent progress on the electrical upgrade of the stable. The exposed posts and beams of the building make stringing new wires easy, and the duo manage to get new fluorescent lights hung overhead and connected to a regulation replacement light switch. Shane watches with amusement and a little pride himself as Vern repeatedly flips the light switch on and off, a self-satisfied grin on his face.

After dinner, Shane coaxes the women out to the stable for the big reveal. He gives Vern the honour of switching on the lights, adding a "Ta-dah!" for emphasis. When Shane turns to read the reaction on Tammy's face, he is disappointed by the lack of enthusiasm.

"Isn't it great?" he asks. "Nice and bright. Vern did practically all the work himself."

"Aw, heck, that ain't true," the boy demurs, but his grin runs ear to ear.

"I dunno. It's awful bright," Tammy answers. Shane actually sees Vern's shoulders slump.

"That's the idea," Shane replies.

"Might disturb the critters."

"They don't seem any more riled up than normal to me." He turns to Yolanda. "What do you think?"

The Chicana shrugs, which at least is not a condemnation of the idea.

"Don't know what was wrong with the old ones," Tammy persists. "They worked just fine. Don't mean to sound ungrateful, but I'm the one's gonna have to pay the extra electricity costs."

"No, no, these new fluorescents are way more efficient. They'll actually cut down on your lighting bills. Besides, that old wiring was a fire just waiting to happen. If a building inspector ever saw it, he would have shut you down for sure."

"Well, I just *love* them," Maybelline chirps. She raises her arms up toward the ceiling as if basking in sunlight. "*Hark, hark, say goodbye to the dingy dark,*" she sings.

"I guess now I won't have to worry about slicing off one of my fingers when we're filleting," Yolanda adds, having formed an opinion after all.

The hard set of Tammy's mouth shows she has nothing more to say. She turns and leaves the stable. Shane senses Vern's disappointment and rushes to fill the void. "Way to go, buddy.

High-five," he says, offering up his palm for slapping. The boy has to jump to reach it.

Maybelline waltzes over and presses her lips to Vern's cheek. "Good job, Vern." Judging from the resulting blush on the boy's cheek, the kiss has more than a casual impact. Maybelline reads this and giggles. She catches Shane's eye and winks. "See you later," she mouths silently.

Shane turns to see Yolanda studying them. At first he worries that she spotted his secret exchange with Maybelline, but Yolanda's look actually seems benign.

"Don't expect a kiss from me," she tells Vern, "but better an electrician than a hockey player. *Bueno.*" Vern's face breaks into a gigantic goofy grin.

Gracie has been watching the scene sullenly, seemingly unsure what to make of Vern's ascension into the limelight.

"I could teach you some things about being an electrician, too, Gracie ... if you want," Shane tells her.

"Girls aren't 'lectricians," she counters.

"That's not true. Girls can be whatever they want to be. Isn't that right, Yolanda?"

She smiles, amused not by the question but by its source. "*Si, chiquita.* Don't let any man tell you different."

Gracie has little time to ponder the revelation, as her mother's voice echoes into the stable.

"Gracie! Come on, child. It's time for bed."

The little girl reacts immediately, but stops in her tracks to go over to her cousin. "Good job, Vern," she says and offers up her palm to be slapped.

SIXTEEN

Maybelline sneaks into the stable shortly before midnight, giggles preceding her entrance. Shane is lying on the mattress fully clothed, already two swigs of mezcal ahead of her. Instead of walking around the bed, Maybelline climbs over top of Shane, her breasts pressing against him, lengths of her legs liberally exposed. Shane eases away from her once she has settled into place.

As she reaches for the bottle, Maybelline rubs her other hand across his abdomen, then slides her fingers down inside his beltline. Shane is irritated by her continued, deliberate teasing, but he does not want her to feel rebuffed, so he takes the wandering hand in his and makes a show of examining her palm.

"Wish I could tell your fortune," he says.

"Yolanda can. She already read my palm." Maybelline hands over the bottle and uses her free hand to trace the lifeline. "See this break here ... that's from when I was all fucked up 'n' stuff. But from here on it's clear sailing. Yolanda says I'm going to end up having a long and contented life." She turns over Shane's hand, and a puzzled look clouds her face. "Wow, you're really messed up," she comments. Shane's palm has a large, ugly scar, the result of getting badly sliced by a skate blade early in his professional career.

"Here, try this one," he suggests.

"Actually, I don't really know nothing 'bout it … reading palms, I mean. Except one hand's supposed to be your potential, and the other shows what's already gone on in your life, but I forget which is which for a guy." She drops his unblemished hand and reacquires the scarred one. "Hell, if this ain't the one that shows the life you've lived, then it should be," she chuckles.

"Not my whole life … just one bad season," Shane replies. He takes another swig of mezcal.

Reflected on the surface of the liquor bottle, he catches sight of a standing figure and suddenly feels the booze backslide up his throat. Tammy is in the doorway, silently observing them. He has no idea how she managed to enter the stable and traverse the gravel path to sneak up on them without making any sound, but it's clear she is upset by what she is seeing. Her fists are clenched, and even in the dim lantern light, the trembling of her frame is clearly visible.

"Aw, shit," Maybelline mutters when she follows Shane's gaze to Tammy. The redhead jumps to her feet, but wavers when she realizes she cannot escape with Tammy blocking the exit. She looks down at the floor like some sorry little girl.

The mezcal bottle in Shane's hand feels like it's burning him, but there's no point in trying to hide it now. He recorks the bottle and places it down on the ground, then searches for something reassuring to say. Tammy's continued silence is unnerving.

"We were just having a friendly drink," he finally offers.

"Yeah, I can see that. Real friendly," Tammy retorts. She walks over and nudges the bottle with the toe of her boot. "She chargin' you for her company, or is this one a freebie?" Shane recognizes a verbal snare when he hears one, and stays mum.

Although Maybelline's path out the door is now clear, she does not make her escape. Neither does she affect crocodile tears. To Shane's surprise, her face colours to match her hair.

"Up yours, Tammy! I'll always be grateful for what you done for me, but I don't have to take that kind of crap from you. 'Tweren't *nothin'* going on between us, and that's a fact. Yeah, I snuck out here to have a few drinks behind your back 'cause I know you don't like it, but that's all, so spare me your Miss-High-And-Mighty disapproving attitude." It feels surreal to Shane, observing someone else succumbing to anger.

"And that's another thing, come to think of it," Maybelline surges on. "What the hell gives you the right to tell me what I can and can't do? Yeah, this is your place, but you know darn well I pull my own weight and keep to your rules the rest of the time. I don't need you to remind me how messed up I once was. I remember clear enough. But screw you if I can't have a few drinks at the end of the day, like I'm gonna end up back on the streets or something if I do. I love you to death, Tammy DeWitt, but you're a real tight ass, y'know. Maybe you should have a couple of drinks yourself and loosen up for a change. Wouldn't do you any harm to get laid, either." She jabs a finger in Shane's direction. "That one there'll help you out in a heartbeat. He's crazy for ya."

Finally Maybelline heads out the door, but Tammy doesn't let her off scot-free. "Yeah, get out of here, you loco bitch! Go back to the gutter where I found ya."

Now Tammy turns on Shane. "Shoulda known you was no good when I picked your sorry ass up off the side of the highway. All that sweet talk don't amount to nothing when push comes to shove. So, you like to party with drunks, do you?"

She reaches down and plucks the mezcal bottle off the ground. Pulling the cork out with her teeth, she spits it at Shane. "All right, then. Let's have a party, you 'n' me. That crazy bitch thinks I'm a tight ass. Well, I've done my share of honky-tonking … all those years I was singing in joints even she'd be too scared to step into." She throws back her head and gulps down a good quarter of the bottle, then wipes her mouth with the back of her hand.

"Mezcal, eh? Good shit, too. Well, you got money in your pocket now, don't you? Yessiree, I've been down the bottom of a bottle more than once. That's how I ended up with Gracie. She's a bottle baby, on account of I was too drunk to make sure Bobby was wearing a rubber." She takes another swig and breaks out into laughter. "Bottle baby … ha, that's a good one. If I was still writing songs, that'd be a natural."

"Tammy, don't —" Shane pleads.

"S'matter? I thought this was a party," Tammy answers and takes another swig.

"Stop it, you'll make yourself sick."

"You weren't complaining when it was Maybelline doing the drinking. Oh, but of course, she flashes a lot more skin, don't she? Here, let me help you out." Tammy unbuttons her shirt, but has trouble pulling the right sleeve off over the bottle in her hand. She giggles, drains the bottle, and tosses it onto the mattress so she can remove her shirt. Finally, she stands there in a sleeveless men's undershirt. Shane cannot help but admire the defined musculature of her arms. She is not wearing a bra, and her nipples are pushing at the fabric. She catches Shane ogling her breasts and laughs.

"Whaddya think?" she asks, pulling back her shoulder blades. "Not as perky as they once was, but not bad for a gal coming onto middle age." She swirls her hips in an exotic dance, and at the same time cups her breasts and flaunts them the way Shane has seen strippers do.

"Here, let me give you a real show." Tammy begins removing her jeans, but once they're down around her calves, she teeters, loses her balance, and falls directly on top of Shane.

"So much for foreplay," Tammy laughs. "All right, then, let's get straight to the screwing." Ramming her lips onto his, she forces her tongue into his mouth, where it squirms like an agitated serpent. Meanwhile her hand gropes around Shane's crotch in search of an erection.

"C'mon, Big Hoss, let's see what ya got," she urges. Her speech is beginning to slur.

Shane pushes her off and stands up. "Stop it!" He's concerned by her behaviour, but also he is embarrassed by his lack of arousal. This has become a chronic problem in recent years. Aside from his basic humiliation over his impotence, he doesn't want Tammy to think that he doesn't find her attractive.

Tammy starts to clamber to her feet, but now the alcohol is clearly showing its impact. She sways like an aspen in the wind, and when she steps toward Shane, she tumbles to the mattress. Squirming onto her back, she stretches her arms out toward him.

"Shane! Shane! Come back and fuck me, Shane!" she laughs.

"Not when you're like this."

"I thought you liked drunks."

"I told you, there's nothing going on with me and Maybelline other than sharing a few drinks. I really like you, Tammy — a lot — but you're hammered."

"I think you're right. The room's spinning." She rolls onto her side and squeezes her body into a ball. "Oh, shit. I don't feel so good."

Shane figures she is going to throw up, and although it's likely the best thing for her at the moment, he doesn't want vomit all over his bed.

"C'mon, Tammy. Let's get you outside, then we'll put you to bed." Despite some awkwardness due to his cast, he manages to pick her up. She hangs limply in his arms, pressing her face into his chest.

"Thash wha' I've bin tryin' to tell ya, ya big galoot," she slurs, barely coherent. "Take me t' bed. I wanna make shweet love to you."

"I'm taking you to bed, but just so you can sleep it off."

"Nooo!" she shrieks, astonishingly loudly given her inebriated state. Seconds later, the door of the ranch house slams, and the other two women come running out. Yolanda is carrying her shotgun, and she points it toward Shane when she sees Tammy hanging in his arms, half naked.

"What are you doing to her, *puerco*? I'm going to blow your balls off," she growls.

Tammy raises her head. "That's right, Yolanda. Shoot him. I begged him to fuck me and he won't do it, the queer cocksucker." A noticeable spasm shakes her body. She adds a feeble "Oh, shit," before unleashing a gush of vomit.

Having anticipated this, Shane puts her down and keeps her head forward so that the spew arches away from her, landing harmlessly in the dirt. The other two women cringe in disgust, although there is amusement written there, as well.

"She's drunk," Shane explains.

"You think?" Yolanda retorts. She and Maybelline share a snicker.

"Here, the two of us can carry her," Maybelline offers.

"That's okay. I already got her. Just show me where to put her. But we should try getting some water down her before she passes out."

Maybelline pirouettes and flits like a shadow into the house. Yolanda is still eyeing Shane and has yet to lower the shotgun. Finally she breaks open the weapon, shakes the shells into her hand, snaps the barrels shut, and gestures toward the house.

"Bring her."

"Hang on a sec. Let's make sure Tammy's unloaded, too." Shane lowers his head to where Tammy's is hanging down. "How you doing, sweetie? Anything more needing to come out?"

At first the only answer is a groan, then an animal sound issues from deep within her and she upchucks again. Finally, she is only dry heaving, aftershocks rocking her body.

"All right, I think she's done," Shane says. He picks her up again and kicks dirt over the puddle of vomit. "Let's get her some water and put her to bed."

Maybelline meets them at the door with a pitcher and a glass, and Shane deposits Tammy on the stoop so they can force her to drink two glasses of water. At the suggestion of a third, she shakes her head petulantly, lets out a little burp, and passes out. When Shane goes to pick Tammy up again, Yolanda pushes him away.

"We can take it from here, *hombre*."

"You sure? I don't mind carrying her."

"Just because she was acting all hot and horny for you don't mean I'm letting you into the house. Back to the stable, now. *Vamos.*" The Chicana turns to Maybelline and scowls at her. "And don't you go sneaking out there, either. You've caused enough trouble for one night. Come on, *loca*, give me a hand."

Together they grab Tammy's arms and legs, hoist her off the ground, and start lugging her into the house. Shane heads back to the stable. He hears Maybelline call out, "Good night." To his surprise, Yolanda's voice follows. "*Buenas noches*, Shane. *Gracias.*"

SEVENTEEN

Shane spends another uneasy night haunted by troubling dreams. He wakes up with the sun and a pounding headache, feeling like he's fighting his way through a fog. He blames the booze, although in reality, last night was a temperate one, by his standards. Still, he prefers not to delve into other possible causes of his pain and haziness at the moment and closes the case by self-prescribing two Percocets.

There is nothing in the stable to wash down the pills with, so Shane heads to the ranch house in search of water. Tammy, rock-solid team player that she is, is up and active in the kitchen. Even though they are alone, his greeting and subsequent attempts at conversation are met with stony silence.

"Do you want to talk about what happened last night?" Shane suggests. Once upon a time, the need to discuss another person's feelings was as foreign to Shane as this desert terrain is now, but thanks to persistent coaching from his ex-wife, he added a new dimension to his interpersonal game.

Tammy reels back and fixes him with dark-rimmed, blood-shot eyes.

"Nothing happened last night, okay? So there sure as spit ain't nothing for us to talk about."

Shane stands paralyzed, his anger rising. He resents her rebuffing him when he was only trying to be supportive and communicative.

"Screw this," he rumbles, turning to leave before he can damage anything. The old floorboards of the kitchen vibrate beneath him as he stomps toward the door. But somewhere between the third and fourth step, a feeling of déjà vu washes over him. *You're always running into someone or running away from everyone. Get a grip, Shane! Go back and talk to the girl.* It occurs to him, too, that Tammy's rough words might have been her gruff attempt to initiate the discussion.

He turns back and hovers, searching for words that will not ignite the volatile situation. He realizes that he should simply confess his fear of not being able to perform sexually. Perhaps if he offers this innermost secret to her like some precious gift, she will understand how much she has come to mean to him. And, yet, despite his impulse for intimacy, the prospect of revealing his impotency to her is still too humiliating, striking at the very core of his manhood.

Tammy, too, looks like she wants to speak, but cannot form the right words. She stands there limply, scouring the same frying pan over and over. Shane is not sure, as he's standing behind her, but he thinks she might be crying. This only adds to his indecisiveness. Women's tears have always been an enigma to him. On various occasions in the past he has misinterpreted them, been manipulated by them, or been chided for trying to stop their free flow.

"I'm … sorry," he offers, but Tammy whirls around like she's been slapped.

"Sorry! Sorry for what, exactly? For drinking behind my back when you know I don't allow it? For sneaking around with Maybelline and making me think she's back to her old ways?" The anger collapses, and her voice breaks. "Or … or … for making me care when I know I'm just going to get my heart broke again? Damn you!"

Shane is spared from having to answer, as Gracie walks into the kitchen then. "What's wrong, Mama?" she asks, absorbing the tension. Her gaze bounces between the two adults in search of an explanation.

"Nothing's wrong, sweetie," Tammy replies, turning back to the sink and wiping her eyes with the back of her hand. "Y'all ready for school? Bus'll be here in a minute."

"Yes, ma'am," Gracie replies, unconvinced.

"Come on, let's go get Vern, and I'll walk you out to the road," Shane offers.

Gracie wavers. "What about you, Mama?"

Tammy doesn't turn, but her steadier voice indicates she has recovered somewhat, or at least put on a brave front. "You run along with Shane now, Sunshine. Mama's got things to finish up. Love ya."

"Love you, too, Mama."

✖ ✖ ✖ ✖ ✖

Long after the school bus rumbles away in a shroud of dust and exhaust fumes, Shane hesitates by the side of the road, reluctant to return to the ranch house, where Tammy's anger lingers like radioactive fallout. Eventually he takes a roundabout route back onto the property, meandering through the scrub brush. He pictures himself settling here and imagines how, with time and money, he might help the ranch thrive.

Wandering in from the back of the property, he stumbles across Yolanda sitting astride his parked Ducati. She is clearly pretending that she is racing it down some imaginary highway, complete with accompanying sound effects coming from deep in her larynx.

"You're revving it too high, Yolanda ... shift, shift!" Shane calls out as a joke.

Yolanda turns, shocked to be caught play-acting like a child. She dismounts, but is too proud to slink away. Instead she stands there, hands on her hips, as if daring Shane to make a snarky comment.

But Shane, who knows a thing or two about confrontation, avoids eye contact and walks up to run his hand along the motorcycle's windshield.

"The seat height's actually pretty good for someone who's shorter," he comments. "Personally, I feel pretty crunched up on her, especially doing longer runs cross-country." He finally ventures a glance into Yolanda's face. She actually looks more surprised than hostile. "You ride?" he asks her.

Yolanda hesitates, but her expression softens. "My brother had a couple of motorcycles. I'd ride his dirt bike, but sometimes he'd let me take out his Five Hundred ... mostly to keep me quiet when he'd done something he didn't want my *padre* to find out about." She reaches out and gives the handlebar a twist.

"You want to take her for a little spin?" Shane offers on impulse. He has never let anyone else ride his motorcycle, but senses an opportunity to make peace with Yolanda.

"No shit?" she asks, her dark eyes hovering between delight and suspicion.

"Sure, what the hell." He extracts the key from his pocket and fires up the machine. It emits a deep roar from the exhaust system that makes Yolanda smile. "You like that, eh? The sales-man called it desmodromic ... comes from the L-twin cylinders. Go on, hop aboard."

Yolanda mounts, and Shane helps her push the motorcy-cle off the kickstand. "She's a lot of machine, so be careful. You probably won't have to take her past second." He is relieved when, instead of gunning it for power, Yolanda slips the cycle into gear and gingerly applies the throttle. At first it appears she is having a little trouble keeping her balance, and Shane ques-tions his decision to let her ride, but with additional speed the motorcycle straightens out, and Yolanda rolls down the driveway. He watches her turn around at the ranch's entrance, and on the return leg it is evident she has quickly gained some confidence in handling the Ducati. She pulls up, waves off Shane's assistance, and labours to put the motorbike up on its kickstand by herself.

She turns the engine off, and looks up at him, a wide smile on her face that makes her seem years younger.

"*Madre de Dio!* That's some bike," she exclaims. "I never even got it out of first. How fast can it go?"

"I've had it up to one eighty, but they say it'll do two hun-dred. Zero to sixty in, like, three seconds." Shane flashes his cast. "Of course, it's the coming back down to zero you have to watch out for."

"What's something like that go for?"

"A lot ... too much, I guess, but I could afford it at the time. Let's just say that it costs a hell of a lot more than most cars do."

"*Ie, Chingao!* Boys and their toys," she comments. She swings her leg over and swivels sideways on the seat so she can face Shane. "Tammy's real riled up at you, in case you're too thick to notice."

"Gee thanks, but I kinda figured that out already. It's why I'm out here instead of in there."

"Can't make you out. Not many guys would have done what you did last night."

"I didn't do nothing."

"That's my point. All the *hombres* I know pour liquor down a woman's throat just to try to get her in the state Tammy was last night."

"Sounds like you've been hanging around the wrong kind of men."

She laughs. "Do tell. But there ain't many of the right kind around here ... or anywhere else, for that matter. You must be some freak that blew in with the wind. Hey, you're not queer, are you? That would explain why you're driving this fancy over-priced Wop-cycle instead of a homegrown chopper."

For a moment, anger stirs inside Shane, but he realizes Yolanda's insults are made in benign jest. He cracks a smile and strains to think of a retort. Shane's job required him to learn how to take jabs — physical ones on the ice, as well as verbal ones in the locker room — but his hair-trigger temper often set his education back.

"You got me pegged. How else could I withstand your sexy Latina charms? Maybe I should just give the Ducati to you, man up, and buy a Harley instead, huh?"

"*Órale!*" she laughs. "Now you're talking. Who needs a man with that hunk of machine purring between your legs?"

"I dunno. A bike won't cuddle you afterward or take care of you when you're sick."

"Ha! Like a man would, either." She spits in the dirt to emphasize her point. "You know what they say. Men are like horoscopes. They always tell you what to do and they're almost always wrong."

"Hey, I'll admit there are a lot of assholes out there, but that doesn't mean you just give up, does it? I mean, the right man could be just around the corner."

"Sure, sure, I've heard it all before. There's someone for everyone. Trust in true love. You have to kiss a lot of frogs before you meet Prince Charming. *Ay caramba*, you *are* queer. You sound like some teenage girl who's been reading romance novels. That is, until the men come sniffing around, and she finds out they expect her to spend the rest of her life on her knees, either scrubbing or sucking."

"I get it, Yolanda. You hooked up with the wrong man and got a raw deal. Think I can't sympathize? Let me tell you, I've just been played for a sucker and cleaned out but good by a gold-digging bitch ... does that mean I should figure every single woman is an evil witch? You tell me, aren't there any good women out there?"

Yolanda pounds herself hard on the chest. "I'm a good one." She flicks a thumb toward the ranch house. "And there's good ones in there, too ... even that *loca puta*."

"That's just my point. I'm telling you there are plenty of good men out there, too."

She laughs. "Sure, if you say so. But, believe me, the second they hear *my* story, they're gonna go running for the hills."

"What about Doc Sanchez?"

"*No manches!* That pig? He's always hitting on every skirt for a hundred miles around — *and* on both sides of the border." She spits again, but then looks up at Shane, a peculiar shine in her eye, like a crescent moon reflected on the surface of a dark lake. "Why ... did he say he was interested?"

Yolanda suddenly looks like a lovestruck schoolgirl and Shane has to fight not to laugh. "He said he needed a woman like you to keep him in line." She snorts, and Shane senses she's disappointed by the answer. "I think all that flirting and stuff with women is just, you know, some kind of macho act," he offers. "I got the distinct impression he's seriously sweet on you."

"Ha! For what? For me to go live in his truck?"

"Well, I guess that depends on what you're looking for, don't it? Maybe you'd be happy to stay right here on Tammy's ranch forever. If not, maybe the doc is the sort of man that needs a woman lighting a fire under him. I'll be honest, first time I met the guy I wasn't too keen on him, either. Hell, he stuck a gun in my crotch. But I truly think that behind that big hat and big moustache —"

"And big belly."

They both laugh at that.

"Yeah, and behind that big belly, too, there's what you say you're looking for — a decent man. My game sheet may not be so hot when it comes to women, but as far as men go, I'm a pretty good judge of character."

She makes a sour face, but it looks to Shane like she's processing what he's said. "What you gonna do about Tammy?" she asks, changing the subject.

"I don't know. Keep my distance for a while, I guess. I tried apologizing, but she only got madder. Anyway, I got things to try to figure out."

"You planning on staying a while, or what?"

"I dunno. Yeah. Maybe."

"'Cause, I'm telling you right now, if you're fixing to take off soon, then don't go messing with my girl."

"I thought you didn't want me here."

Yolanda shrugs. "What do I know? Sounds like my track record with the opposite sex ain't no better than yours. But let me give you one piece of advice, *hombre*. If you're serious about Tammy and plan on hanging around, then don't go giving her no space, figuring she'll come running to you. A gal likes to be wooed, you know. Oh, sure, she may take a strip off you, but, *órale*, you look like you've been in a scrap or two in your time. I'm sure you can take it."

As she has been talking, Yolanda has unconsciously taken the Grim Reaper necklace out from under her blouse and started rubbing it, evidently out of habit. Shane nods at the piece of jewellery. "That's a weird-looking piece of bling, Yolanda. I've been meaning to ask you about it."

She frowns. "You don't know? This is the Skinny Lady, *Santa Muerte* … Sacred Death. I worship her, and she keeps me safe."

"No offence, but from what I've heard about your past, I don't think she's doing such a great job."

"Oh, no, I turned to her after, when I was in prison. A lot of the Latina women there believe in her. Tammy don't approve, but she lets me be. The Catholic priests preach against her, too, but I think they're scared how popular she's become down South. Millions worship her now. Trust me, Shane, *Santa Muerte* can work miracles. Her magic is very old and very powerful."

✘ ✘ ✖ ✘ ✘

Shane spends the afternoon working on the ranch's outdoor hand pump, which evidently seized up some time ago. Despite his manual handicap, he manages to take apart the pump's housing and lubricate the individual interior pieces with grease. He then reassembles the mechanism. Grunting like an old boar, he labours at the handle, and just as he is about to give up, is rewarded by a trickle of rusty liquid dribbling from the spout. Another minute of pumping delivers a steady gush of cold, fresh water with each downstroke.

He grins and, stripping naked to the waist, begins washing off some of the perspiration coating him, finally sticking his head directly under the flow of water. As he does so, his eye catches the flutter of curtains in the kitchen, and he makes out a silhouette standing at the window. He realizes that he is hoping it's Tammy watching him — not so she can admire his physique, but so she can see what he has accomplished and how much of a help he is to her and the ranch. At that moment, the depth of Shane's feelings for Tammy becomes undeniable.

He hikes into the sun-soaked desert to dry off, and while he's at it, to try to crystallize the fuzzy thoughts in his head. Standing in appreciation of the arcane beauty around him, he notices splashes of colour among the scrub brush's plants. Upon closer scrutiny, he finds a variety of small blossoms that have popped up with the coming of spring.

Given that he has no plan of his own, Shane decides to take Yolanda's advice, and he begins gathering flowers to bring to Tammy. Despite encountering prickles and spines, he cuts a few paddles of the yellow and pink blossoms from prickly pear cacti and stalks of the red flowers of ocotillo plants.

Once he has assembled an improvised bouquet, Shane goes looking for Tammy. He finds her in the stable, cleaning out snake cages, and with an audience of vipers, he presents her with the flowers.

Her eyebrows arch in surprise, but she accepts the gift and stands mutely sniffing the blossoms. Her expression is indecipherable.

"Look, Tammy, I'm so, so sorry for what I did," Shane blurts out. "Drinking behind your back was wrong. It was lying to you, and I never want to keep anything from you again. But I swear, nothing went on between me and Maybelline, and that's the truth. We had a few drinks and chatted ... mostly about how great you are, although I didn't need her to tell me that."

Tammy continues sniffing the flowers, but she is at least looking up at him now. Shane can see both sides of her life written in her face — hardship etched in lines around her eyes, vitality sparkling in her grey irises.

He pauses briefly, hoping she will join in the conversation and save him from having to forage for words to express feelings he barely understands himself. But still, she says nothing, so he plunges forward. "But, damn it, I'm not sorry for what I did last night, or, rather, didn't do ... not jumping your bones when you were all over me. I mean, you were really pissed off and piss drunk, and it just didn't feel right, Tammy. It's not what I want with you."

"What *do* you want?" she asks, finally breaking her silence.

"I ... I wish I could give you an easy answer. I mean, we just met, and we're not kids, and as for me, well ..." He wants to tell her about his fear of not being able to please her in bed and the legal problems dogging him. He told her he didn't want to keep things from her and meant it, yet he still cannot utter the words that will humiliate him and possibly obliterate his chance with her. "I just want you to know me, the real me. God, I wish you could be inside my head right now, Tammy, and feel what I'm feeling. I really want to be with you. You're different than all the other women I've known, especially since the divorce. They've all been these really beautiful women —"

"And I'm not?"

"No, no, I mean, yes, you're beautiful. But in a different way, a real way. From the inside, not just the outside. Those other women, once you took away their clothes and makeup, there was nothing to them. Like some of those nancy-boy hockey players from Europe. All fancy skating and showing off, but afraid to take a hit or go into the corner after the puck. Funny, all my life I've been hearing how true beauty comes from within, but I never knew what they meant until I met you."

He is pleased with that last statement, at having verbalized his feelings almost poetically — at least by his standards. There is a peculiar look on Tammy's face, and for a second he is hopeful that she is about to kiss him. Instead, however, she shoves the flowers into his chest.

"Sweet talk, that's all it is. Bobby was real good at that, too. That man could talk his way out of the doghouse or into my bed real easy. Well, just look where it got me. When push comes to shove, I ain't met a feller yet who knows how to put his money where his mouth is." She turns her back on Shane and goes back to the cages.

Shane stands frozen, confused as to what she does or doesn't want from him.

"I meant what I said, Tammy. It's not just words. What do you want me to do? How can I prove it to you?"

She sighs and shakes her head. "Look, I ain't havin' a good day, okay? Why don't you just give it a rest." A wry smile squirms onto her face. "Unless you want to help me clean these cages."

"Clean? Sure, I can do that."

"Of course, you gotta git the snake out first."

Shane feels a shudder crawl up his spine and onto the back of his neck, knowing he is trapped by his own words. "Show me what to do," he says, his mouth suddenly dry.

Tammy demonstrates the technique: she opens the cage and uses her metal wrangling rod to pin the rattler to the floor. Then, as Shane witnessed on milking day, she grabs the serpent behind its triangular head and tosses it unceremoniously into a new cage. After that, she removes the mat from the bottom of the used pen, shakes it off, and rinses it clean.

"All yours," she says, her tone mocking, "assuming you're man enough."

Shane hands back the blossoms, takes the wrangling rod from her, and approaches the next cage in line. When he unhooks the door, the rattlesnake opens its mouth and hisses at him, offering an excellent view of its nasty-looking curved fangs. Shane wavers, but after catching Tammy's look of doubt, he opens the door a crack. The snake initially undulates backward, but then, like a bolt of lightning, it lunges toward him. Even though the wire of the cage protects him, Shane cringes and jerks his hand away.

"Ha! Macho man. Even Gracie did better than that first time out," Tammy laughs.

Shane feels anger rise up and spill over his face. He turns to spew heated words at Tammy — his mouth even opens to deliver the first phoneme — but when he sees her amused smile and shining eyes full of humour but devoid of malice, he realizes that he's actually mad at himself for having flinched. Using his anger to motivate himself, Shane flings the door open and pins down the serpent in one quick motion. He changes hands so the left one with the cast wields the metal rod, then reaches in with his good hand and seizes the rattler behind its head. Before he can fully contemplate what he is doing, he pulls the snake out and tosses it into a clean cage.

His hand is shaking as he withdraws it and quickly closes the door. In fact, his whole body is awash with adrenalin and residual anger. He takes a look at Tammy and sees that she is now standing with her mouth open.

"Well, I'll be darned," she says softly, as if to herself. Then she seems to collect herself, and her face sets again. "See, what did I tell you? Nothin' to it. And don't go patting yourself on the back quite yet. There's another couple of dozen cages to go, yet." But then she touches him on the arm, and her tone softens. "Sorry, I forgot about your broken hand. How's about we do 'em together? It'll go faster that way. I'll wrangle and you clean. I mean, if it's okay by you."

EIGHTEEN

D inner that night is the most convivial one Shane has yet had at the ranch. The atmosphere is downright festive. Thanks to his contribution to the house larder, they enjoy a hardy meal of chicken-fried steak, spinach, and candied yams, with an abundance of extra helpings, plus cherry pie for dessert. There is plenty of joking and unabashed laughter, led by Maybelline, who has clearly patched up her differences with Tammy. Even Vern has abandoned his usual hangdog look and is grinning between forkfuls.

For the first time since he hopped across their threshold, Shane doesn't feel that anyone at the kitchen table resents his presence. Yolanda still sends periodic barbs his way, but they are accompanied by smiles and lack malevolence, as well as being directed more at his gender than at him personally. Shane suspects Yolanda knows no other way of dealing with the opposite sex. Or perhaps she is merely pandering to her audience; any man-bashing joke generates instant horse laughs from the other two women. So Shane chuckles along and contributes some stories of particularly gross or ignorant teammates he has known.

Perhaps the greatest contributor to Shane's upbeat mood sits in a vase in the middle of the table. Tammy has relented and taken Shane's offering of wildflowers after all. On several occasions during the meal, she has looked at the makeshift bouquet and then back to him, and their eyes have met and lingered. She has even taken to smiling at him, although in all honesty, Shane still has no clue what she is thinking or what his next move should be.

After the house is locked for the night, he takes a stroll around the property. His head is buzzing a little tonight, and he tries deep, restorative breaths of cold desert air. A set of head-lights bounces up the driveway, and Shane is pleased to see they belong to Doc Sanchez's van.

"What's up, Doc?" he greets Sanchez as he climbs out of the cab.

"*Buenas noches, mi amigo.* Glad to find you here still. I take it you've found reason to stay for a while?"

Shane shrugs. "It's as good a place as any right now."

Sanchez laughs. "You bet. Outlaws have hidden out in New Mexico for centuries."

Shane blanches. "Are you saying they've charged me?"

"No, no, at least not yet. I was just making a joke. You're not officially a wanted man —" Sanchez gestures toward the ranch house. "Although presumably you aspire to being one there, am I right?"

Shane shakes his head. "I have no freaking idea. Yolanda seems to think I have a chance, though. She says I need to be nicer to Tammy. You know, woo her and stuff. She says that's what women want."

Sanchez's ears perk up. "Yolanda said that? Hmm. Interesting. Who would have pegged her for a romantic at heart?"

"As a matter of fact, I put in a good word for you today."

The doctor cocks an eyebrow. "Really? How so?"

"Well, she was going on about how there are no good men around, and I told her I think you're a good guy. Oh yeah, and that you're sweet on her. Shit, I hope that's okay." Shane looks at the six-gun hanging from Sanchez's hip. "Please don't shoot me for meddling."

"That would be a quick way to drum up some business. Of course, it all depends on how Yolanda took it."

"Hard to say. I mean, she called you a bunch of names, but that doesn't necessarily mean anything with her. Oh, I don't know, Doc. You're talking to the wrong guy. When it comes to women, I'm clueless."

"We all are, *amigo*. But as a physician I can tell you that women are a condition to be taken seriously. You don't just take two aspirin and call them in the morning. They require around-the-clock intensive care. Ha! Now who sounds like a romantic? My business here is with you, but perhaps I'll stick around."

"Business? What kind of business?"

"Don Aléjandro and I were wondering if you've considered his offer."

"Seriously? After what happened the other night? You expect me to go work for some shady drug lord?"

"Careful what you say, Shane, or I *will* pull my gun. Remember, Don Aléjandro is a close friend, and in all other respects he is a perfect gentleman. I told you, he's giving up the drug business and the hockey team is a hundred percent legitimate." He pounds himself on the chest. "Remember that *I'm* in charge. We're both making you this offer."

Shane realizes he's on the verge of offending Sanchez. "Sorry, Doc. I guess I'm still rattled by that gong show with his whacko kid. You gotta admit that was pretty hairy." He places his arm around the doctor's shoulders. "It's not like I got a lot of job prospects right now, is it? Still, I'd like to stick around the ranch for a bit. You understand, right? There's no hurry, is there? I mean, it's the off-season, right? It'll keep for a week or so, won't it?"

"I suppose, although there's no off-season for management, as you'll find out. We've already started recruiting for next fall, and there are players to be evaluated. Still, I do personally understand the allure of *Rancho Crótalo*. I'll tell Don Aléjandro you're leaning toward taking our offer. Meanwhile, I have a thought. Are you any kind of a crooner, Shane?"

"Say what?"

"I mean, how's your singing voice?"

"I dunno. Average, I guess. Why do you ask?"

"Well, I say we take Yolanda's advice and go serenade the *señoras* beneath their window. It is a time-honoured Mexicali tradition. I have a guitar in my van. Had I not been a physician, perhaps in another life I would have been a *yolandachi*. Come on, let's pour our hearts out to the ladies, tell them how we feel."

"Won't we look kind of stupid?"

"I assure you, that's half the point. Women want us to make fools of ourselves over them."

"I don't know if I should even bother. It's kind of embarrassing, but ... hell, I guess technically you're my doctor now. The thing is, even if Tammy gets in the mood, I'm not sure I can deliver the goods, if you know what I mean."

"Ah," the doctor says with a nod and a sympathetic smile. "Believe me, I understand. It's not that common yet for a man in his thirties, but not unheard of, especially given your profession."

"What do you mean? What's hockey got to do with it?"

"Not the hockey, per se. More like your specialty within the game. When I worked in Las Vegas, I moonlighted as a ringside doctor at boxing matches. I've seen this before. The human brain wasn't meant to take the repeated shocks those pitiable fighters sometimes suffered — mostly poor Latino and black kids hoping to make it to the big time while the fat cats just sat back and raked in the dough. And I've been reading up on the subject in my new capacity as team physician for *Los Lobos* ... although I hope my advice will be more preventative by counselling the players to less violence."

"Fighting's part of the game ... always has been," Shane rejoins.

"And the Romans used to send gladiators out to die for the amusement of the crowd. That doesn't make it civilized. Tell me, how many concussions have you suffered in your career, Shane? Don't answer. You probably don't know yourself, especially since the word *concussion* has become a touchy one in professional sports and the leagues are trying hard to conceal the extent of it. Tell me this, then. Do you suffer from any of the following?" Sanchez holds up his hand and starts ticking items off on his fingers. "Sensitivity to light and sound? Short-term memory loss? Loss of appetite? Do you feel the need to sleep long and late? And, to the immediate point, loss of sex drive is one of the common symptoms, as well."

Shane's brow sags as he processes this. The doctor pats him reassuringly on the arm. "It's nothing to be ashamed of. Now that you're retired, hopefully you'll recover, although the long-term data on the subject is still sketchy. But, as your doctor, I advise you not to go crashing your motorcycle again, and to avoid any other traumatic blows to the head."

Sanchez reaches into his pocket and produces a foil packet containing four blue pills. "Meanwhile, we live in an age of miracles. Here. Fortunately I never travel without these."

"What's this? Viagra?"

"*Si*. One of my more popular items. And since we are being candid, even I find need of a boost in the pants these days. They'll take care of your short-term problems, although I should warn you, they're not cheap. Damn those thieving drug companies. But you need to know that there are other, more serious symptoms that come of repeated head trauma. Maybe you're already familiar with some of them."

"Like what?"

"Ever found yourself on the brink of tears for no apparent reason? Have you ever suffered from depression, *amigo*? Maybe contemplated suicide?"

"If I've been blue lately, I've had plenty of reasons to be."

"Before your recent misfortunes, I mean. Look, you don't have to answer me now. I just want you to know that there's a medical reason for the things you've been feeling. Start there. Maybe that will help you through the bad moments. But if you do want to talk about it, well, I'm around."

Shane flips the foil packet in his fingers a few times. "Thanks, Doc. What do I owe you for the boner pills?"

"Tonight the going rate is one song. I was serious. Let me fetch *mi guitaro*, and we'll show those women that there's a soft, romantic side to *machismo*."

Sanchez practically runs into his van and emerges with an ornately inlaid acoustic guitar. He tunes it, then turns to Shane. "Know any good ballads?"

"Not really. I'm more of a rock 'n' roll kind of guy, although I don't know the lyrics to many songs."

"Hmm. How about Elvis Presley? Everyone loves the King, right?"

"Sure."

"Okay, let's try 'Can't Help Falling in Love.' Know that one?" The doctor sings a few bars.

"'Heartbreak Hotel' would be more up my alley, but, sure, I know it. Don't really remember all the words, though."

With Sanchez coaching him through the lyrics, they rehearse the song. Shane soon gets the hang of it, gaining confidence and volume with each run-through. Suddenly a window opens at the side of the ranch house, and Tammy's voice shouts out, "What in tarnation is going on out there?"

"Quick," Sanchez whispers. "Now's our chance."

The duo hurry around the building. The lights are on and the ranch's women are each hanging out of a window.

The men nod at each other and launch into their perform-ance. The doctor strolls as he plays and sings, sidling up to Yolanda's window. Shane takes his cue and approaches Tammy, putting all the feeling he can muster into his performance. Tammy's hair is down, and she is wearing a simple nightgown, which, backlit by the bedroom light, shows the silhouetted shape of her naked body beneath.

She looks so alluring that it stirs something in Shane's chest, groin, and stomach simultaneously. He feels intoxicated. He strains to sing in tune and to add vibrato, wanting his song to be as poignant and soulful as the feelings exploding inside him. The look on Tammy starts somewhere between irritation and suspicion, but as the performance progresses, a smile takes over.

As the song finishes, Doc Sanchez stretches out the last note, strumming his guitar so furiously it seems the strings might break. Then he removes his giant stetson, leans closer to Yolanda, and earnestly whispers something that sounds like Spanish poetry. Shane has no poems of any language in his repertoire, but he steps forward so his face is only inches from Tammy's.

"Aw, Tammy, I'm sorry for every stupid thing I've done. If there's anything I can do to make it up to you, just say the word.

All I want is a chance to show you how much I really care about you … and how special I think you are. God, you look amazing tonight. I wish I was in there with you."

To his chagrin, Tammy turns to watch Sanchez and Yolanda. She seems more interested in spying on them than in Shane. "Lord have mercy," she whispers, "is she actually giving that no-good skirt-chaser the time of day?"

"He's not as bad as he makes himself out to be. It's all an act, really. I think deep down he's a lonely guy who knows a great thing when he sees one. Maybe Yolanda sees the good in him."

Evidently this is not the case, for eventually Yolanda unleashes a torrent of words in rapid-fire Spanish that is decidedly not poetic and then slams the window shut. Sanchez laughs and blows her a kiss through the glass.

"Good riddance," Tammy murmurs. She turns back to Shane. "You say you want to do something for me? Go to bed, right now." And with that, she, too, closes her window, leaving Shane standing there deflated.

He turns to Sanchez. "I figured it wouldn't work, but I guess it was worth a shot."

"Surely you didn't expect her to drag you through the window and start humping you on the spot? I actually think that went well."

"Oh yeah? Didn't sound like it to me. What was Yolanda going on about, if you don't mind me asking?"

"She said it would take more than sweet songs and flowery words to win her over. She said I was fat and crude and should be embarrassed to be living in a van. She told me that a doctor should be honourable, a leader in his community to be looked up to, and that that's the greatest compliment he can give to his woman."

"Phew! And yet you think it went well?"

"Of course. I can read between the lines. And what I see is a road map to Yolanda's affections." He pats his stomach. "She's right, of course. I've allowed myself to get soft and lazy. I should certainly lose a few pounds, I know it. Maybe I'll take up skating with *Los Lobos* at our new arena." He looks at Shane. "How about you? Any luck with Tammy Girl?"

"Naw. She was too busy gawking at you two."

"Well, I still think we made a favourable impression. It's like they say in hockey — 'keep putting the puck on the net, and good things are bound to happen.'"

"Sure, provided you're not up against a hot goalie. Or a cold woman."

"Ha! Good one. Well, I'll leave you to your bed. Tomorrow's another day. *Buenas noches*, Shane." He walks off humming a tune and softly strumming his guitar.

Shane turns for one last look at Tammy's bedroom window — just in time to see her light go out. He sighs, but decides she is right. Getting a good night's sleep is probably the best thing to do. The fresh air and the crooning seem to have cleared most of the buzzing in his head and dulled any desire to get high. Or maybe it is the doctor's knowledge of Shane's ailments and the revelation that they are the side effects of years of concussions.

Shane always prided himself on his endurance. He never missed a game if he could help it, even lying to the team doctor about his symptoms sometimes to make sure he got to dress for the next match. His ex-wife, Veronica, often joked about his thick Ukrainian skull. Maybe it wasn't thick enough.

Shane strips off all his clothes and crawls into bed. To ease his frustration and to try to induce drowsiness, he tries masturbating, but finds he has trouble staying erect. That's when he remembers that Doc Sanchez has supplied him with a remedy for the problem. It occurs to him that he should be saving the pills for sex with Tammy, then he chortles at the improbable thought.

I don't think me and Tammy are going to be bumping uglies anytime soon, he tells himself. *Besides, sounds like there's plenty more pills where these came from.* He retrieves the foil packet from his pants pocket, swallows a pill, and then lies back to wait for the drug to take effect.

To get in the mood, Shane conjures up the recent memory of Tammy hanging out the window in her nightgown. He still can't put his finger on precisely what it is about her that attracts him so. In the past, he has dated models, dancers, and other women whose entire stock in trade was their physique and their looks. But over time, Shane began to feel they all came out of the same mould, like a series of interchangeable plastic dolls. Even the treacherous Brandi, despite distinguishing herself by her extraordinary greed and duplicity, is practically a clone of her predecessors. The compulsion to chase and bed these women was as much about bragging rights as about sex, let alone companionship. Compared to Tammy, the others all seem artificial — and he's not referring to the breast implants and other cosmetic surgeries that many of them routinely underwent. Tammy is, well, *solid,* like the living ideal of real womanhood, not some shallow caricature afraid to gain weight or break a nail.

Shane hears the stable door creak open and footsteps come down the gravel path toward the toolroom. He assumes it is Maybelline wanting another drinking party, and the idea that she is brazen enough to visit Shane again after the previous night's ruckus irritates him. Plus, not having anticipated her appearance, he is naked beneath the sheets. There is no time to scramble out of bed to get clothes on, so he feigns sleep.

The footsteps enter the room and stop. There is a pause before the visitor speaks.

"If you're really sleeping, I'll scream." The voice is Tammy's.

Shane opens his eyes and sits up. "I was just faking it," he tells her.

"Oh, that's just what a gal likes to hear."

"I mean, I was afraid maybe Maybelline snuck out again."

"Maybelline's in the sack and she's gonna stay there." Tammy is wearing a worn old housecoat that hangs down to her calves and has cowboy boots on her feet.

She wavers, as if unsure of her next move. "Well, I ain't drunk tonight, but I don't go nowhere I'm not wanted. If you don't want me here, just say so."

"I want you more than anything in the world," Shane replies. It is clearly the right answer, for Tammy smiles dreamily, unties her robe, and steps out of it. She is not wearing the same utilitarian nightie she had on earlier, but is now attired in a sheer, low-cut black-lace negligée. The cowboy boots make the sight even more arousing.

"Wow!" is all Shane can say.

She giggles like a schoolgirl. "Like it? Wore it once for my honeymoon and ain't had it on since." She walks over, lowers herself onto the mattress to lie beside Shane, and gives him a long, lingering kiss. "Of course, I don't plan to have it on for long."

Tammy pulls down the sheet so she can study Shane's body. "Saints almighty, I ain't never seen a feller built like you outside of the movies." She begins kissing the middle of his chest before sliding sideways to suck on a nipple.

Any concern of Shane's that the Viagra hasn't had enough time to work evaporates as his penis leaps to attention, feeling like a rocket ready to launch into outer space.

Suddenly, Tammy stops and fixes him with a serious look. "Look, I gotta make one thing clear. I don't normally do this.

Hell, I don't *ever* do this. It's been a really, really long time since I been with anyone, but that ain't the reason I'm here. And it ain't just because you're built like a brick shithouse. It's 'cause of what you're doing with the ranch, and with the kids, and, well, I'm sick and tired of not trusting any man and hating the whole damn lot of you. But if you ever lift a finger to hurt me or my gals, or ever lie to me I'll … I'll —"

Shane interrupts her with a long, deep kiss. "You can trust me, I promise. I'll never hurt you."

"Well, maybe you can hurt me in a good way." She laughs, reaching beneath the sheet. "Get your guns up, Big Hoss, you got me wetter than a gully washer."

NINETEEN

Shortly before the sun comes up, Tammy jolts awake in Shane's arms.

"Damn. I hadn't figured on staying this long. It's near light. I hope Gracie ain't woken up yet. She sometimes likes to come snuggle with me." She pulls on her robe and stomps into her cowboy boots. The entire time, she has not cast a glance in Shane's direction, let alone looked him in the eye. He starts to wonder whether she regrets last night. The thought that she may be ashamed of spending the night with him or that he may have again misread the depth of a woman's feelings for him causes anger to rise inside Shane. He immediately makes an effort to smother it.

As if she has read his thoughts, Tammy comes over, kneels beside the mattress, and gives Shane a kiss. "Look, honey, we need to talk about things ... or maybe not. Maybe we just oughta let it be what it is. My hubby did use to say I liked to talk things to death, but then again he was a fella liked to let his fists do the conversing a lot of the time. Just so you know, last night was special for me … and not just the screwing part. But I hope you don't mind if we keep it our little secret for now, especially from Gracie, until we can get a sense of what exactly's happening between us and all. Is that okay with you, Big Hoss?"

Shane nods. The smile he gets in return transforms Tammy's face into a younger, carefree version that looks so much like Gracie, it's as if the universe has condensed, and nothing separates the mother's past from the daughter's future.

"See ya at breakfast, then," she says, and delivers a farewell peck.

✳ ✳ ✖ ✳ ✳

It is obvious from the knowing smiles that Yolanda and Maybelline exchange over breakfast that they sense — or perhaps scent — the lovers' union that has taken place, but they do not pass comment. Tammy tries unsuccessfully to avoid their eyes, but after seeing that there is no disapproval there, she allows a half grin of contentment to remain on her face.

When Shane escorts the children out to the school bus, he feels that a seismic shift has occurred in his feelings toward them: they are now charges in need of his protection and nurturing. The sensation is satisfying, as if a part of him previously missing has now clicked into place.

He listens to Gracie's free-flowing little-girl babble, dipping in and out of her words occasionally to pass comment or offer encouragement. She again raises the subject of adopting a wild horse, and despite Tammy's previous admonishment for raising false hope, he feels confident enough to make a tentative promise — though not confident enough to make the offer without requiring Tammy's approval first.

With Vern, fewer words are necessary; the boy seems content just to be in Shane's presence and accepted on equal footing. Perhaps it is only Shane's imagination, but lately Vern seems to be standing straighter and laughing more. Shane briefs him on the day's renovation plans, soliciting feedback on a few design issues and negotiating the boy's after-school involvement in the work.

Shane is almost sad to see the bus arrive. Gracie gives him a big hug around the neck, and warmth spreads throughout his insides like melting toffee. He and Vern shake hands formally, in the manner of adults, but they are both grinning in appreciation of the half joke as they do it, and Shane cannot resist tousling the boy's hair after. He watches the children depart, then strides back to the ranch, whistling a happy tune and imagining what the landscape around him will look like after a few years of applied improvements.

�֗ ✗ ✖ ✗ ✗

Shane is outside banging down loose pieces of the stable's barn board when Maybelline comes fluttering out of the ranch house to tell him he's got a phone call.

It is Morrie Getz on the line. The agent is audibly excited. "Bronk, you're gonna want to kiss me when you hear the deal I cut for you! Two hundred and twenty K for a half-hour interview, just so long as we keep it an exclusive. Am I the best, or what?"

"Sweet! Who's it with?"

"*CelebTV.*"

"*CelebTV*? I thought they only did movie stars and musicians and whatnot."

"Are you kidding? Right now you're a gazillion times bigger than any of them. Only thing is, it's got to be on camera."

"You mean, like, live?"

"No, no ... but they're a TV show, right? They want video they can air."

Shane suddenly pictures a camera crew invading the ranch and grilling him in front of the others.

"I dunno, Morrie. Isn't there anyone else? I mean, I'm not sure I want to be on TV."

"Sure, there's plenty of others, but these guys are offering the most by a long shot. And *all* the top bidders are TV shows. Look, right now the media is making you out to be Public Enemy Number One. Not the hockey press, necessarily, but the mainstream guys are on a feeding frenzy. You've got to try to tell your side of the story, so why not make some nice coin doing it? I'll level with you, Bronk, you may need to hire a good lawyer if that DA in Chicago goes ahead with charges."

"Shit, Morrie. You know I always come across looking like a doofus in interviews."

"Frankly, kiddo, at the moment it would be pretty hard to look any worse than you already do. Might as well get paid for it."

Shane sighs. "You're right, Morrie. I can't keep hiding from this, and it's a damned good payday. So, how's it going to work, the taping? I don't want them coming here where I'm staying."

"Shit, Bronk, I don't even know where 'here' is ... no, that's a lie. I can tell from the area code you're somewhere in New Fucking Mexico, of all places. Look, we can do the interview wherever you want, but I'd suggest someplace quiet, someplace neutral. Maybe a hotel suite. I know a couple of nice joints in Albuquerque. That work for you?"

"I think it's about a four-hour drive."

"Okay, then. And I'll book you a suite so you can freshen up beforehand and look presentable for the interview. So, do I give them the thumbs-up?"

"Yeah, sure. I guess."

"Great. I'll get back to you. They're chomping at the bit, so I figure it'll happen in the next day or so. Still got to nail down the contract and arrange for a big chunk up front. And we have to figure out what we're doing about a new bank account for you."

"No problem there. I got all my ID back. Everything that was stolen, as a matter of fact."

"No kidding! That's great, Bronk. But what about a home address?"

"Home? What the fuck's that, Morrie? I don't have a home anymore. I've lived in nine different cities over the past eighteen years and I don't have a damn thing to show for it."

"Well, you're going to need one for the bank. They're going to want to see ID or something official with your home address on it." There's a pause, and when Morrie speaks again, his voice has softened. "You know, I could swing it for you to use my home address. Hell, kiddo, if you need a place to live for a while, you can come and bunk with Gertie and me. Stay for as long as you need to."

Shane is annoyed to feel his eyes misting up. He blinks away the tears before they can fully form. "Thanks, Morrie. That means a lot to me. Really, though, for now I'm okay where I'm staying." He wonders if sometime in the future he'll be calling *Rancho Crótalo* his official home. Then he realizes his green card will soon be revoked, now that his pro-hockey days are over. He has plied his trade in the States for eighteen years now, but in the end, Shane is still a foreigner.

"Hey, you just gave me an idea. When I first broke into the league, I bought ninety acres outside my hometown in the Yukon. Pretty much the only thing Veronica didn't get in the divorce. Never got around to building anything, but there's a trailer home parked there I've been paying taxes on. And I've got a post office box in town where they send the bill. My dad's got the key and collects all the mail. So I guess technically I do have a home after all."

"Well, there you go. You'll need to get your dad to send you a copy of the tax notice, but that and your passport should be enough to get a bank account set up. Once you do, let me know where to send your dough, and I'll call back to tell you when and where to meet *CelebTV*. Look, Bronk, it was an accident. We both know that. This is your chance to try to get the rest of the folks believing it, too. Okay, kiddo?"

"Sure." He pauses, fumbling for the right words. "Hey, Morrie. You, know, um … you're a good friend. Thanks for everything."

"Someone's got to look out for you, you big schmuck. Take care of yourself, and I'll be in touch soon."

There is a Yellow Pages on the floor below the wall phone. Looking under *Banks*, Shane chooses one in Deming, then phones to get their fax number, plus instructions for setting up a new account. Afterward, he calls his father's house. The caregiver, Oksana, answers, explaining that his dad is preoccupied in the bathroom. Shane tells her what he's after.

"Sure, Shane. Your dad may be a while, but I know where he files your papers. He keeps all your stuff in the shrine."

"The what?"

She laughs. "Sorry. That's what I call it. He's filled your old room with pictures and posters and memorabilia, along with albums upon albums of clippings."

"What clippings?"

"Didn't you know? Your dad has probably got a copy of every article ever written about you anywhere. Even bought himself a PC and learned how to use it, just so he could print off all the online stuff, too."

"You're kidding. I thought he'd disowned me. All he ever seemed to do was chew me out for my mistakes and tell me to try harder."

"Oh, you know your dad, Shane. Has to show the world how tough he is by barking at it, but deep down he's got a caring heart. At least I've come to think so, since coming to work with him. He really loves you — don't believe otherwise." Her voice softens. "Your dad and I have spent so such time going through those scrapbooks together, I feel like I know you intimately. Well, not *intimately* like, you know ... oh, darn, if you could see me blushing right now. Twenty-five years later and I still feel like a gawky, stupid girl when I talk to you. Not that you would have noticed, but I had a big crush on you back then. Of course, every girl did. But you were only interested in Helen Dubrovich. My, she did fill out a sweater. Mind you, these days she fills out just about everything else, too. Ooh, that's catty, forget I said that. She still lives here, you know. Brags about how hot and heavy you two were, even when her husband's right there. Cripes, listen to me prattle."

"I remember," says Shane.

"Helen? I should hope so. You guys went out for, what, two years?"

"No, I remember you, Oksana. You used to come out and play shinny with us. Skinny little thing with pink laces on your Tacks, but a damned good skater with a wicked shot, and you weren't afraid to go into the corners."

"Yeah, that was me. I'd get myself beat up if it meant you might talk to me. Improved my game, though. Good enough to get a hockey scholarship to Michigan. Paid for my nursing degree."

"And you came back to Peel Crossing? Why?"

"Why not? Oh, I worked in Vancouver for a while, but I didn't like it. I missed the Yukon. More room to breathe, and a better place to raise kids."

"Oh, you got kids?"

There's an awkward silence. Even over the phone he senses she's flustered. "No … well, not yet. Hopefully still time. Listen, I've jawed long enough. Where do you want me to send the tax papers?"

Shane relays the bank's fax number and tells her what to write on the cover sheet.

"No problem," she tells him. "Your dad has a scanner on his PC … and a fax app. I can do all that right from here. It was really nice talking to you, Shane. I hope this trouble blows over. For what it's worth, I watched that hit — the whole play, not just the couple of seconds they keep showing over and over — and it was a hard body check, but it was clean. Looks to me like you caught Linton off balance with his head down, that's all. It was an accident. I mean, don't get me wrong, it's a tragedy he's dead, but it's a damned crime what the media's doing to you. I hope it all works out for you, Shane. Come say hi when you're up this way next. You know, you really should come visit your dad. He's not getting any younger."

TWENTY

Two days later Getz phones back with final arrangements for Shane's interview in Albuquerque with *CelebTV*, along with confirmation that an advance of fifty thousand dollars, less what Morrie is owed, has been deposited into Shane's new bank. Shane ponders how, at one time, the amount of money in question would barely have registered in the shadow of his NHL earnings. True, Shane's pay was closer to the league minimum than to the multimillions commanded by the superstars, but it was still enough to make him once brag to his father (somewhat maliciously, he now recalls) that he earned more in a single eight-month season than the old man had in a lifetime.

But now this money shimmers wildly in Shane's imagination. A larger payment will follow the interview, but he has the power to put some plans into action right now.

First, however, he must get to Albuquerque for the interview. The cast on his hand makes him hesitant to try driving there on his motorcycle, so he sets out to borrow the ranch's pickup, which he has been using regularly, anyway. But Shane seeks not only Tammy's permission, but also her company. He envisions a little honeymoon-like excursion to the city, with a couple of carefree nights spent in a luxury hotel. He especially wants to wake up with Tammy in his arms, and not have her slinking off before the sun comes up, as she has every night since their first together. The tricky part will be getting away to do the actual interview … unless he finally comes clean about his predicament. He resolves to do so soon so he can stop hiding things from Tammy, and goes looking to tell her about the trip.

She is in the kitchen hemming a skirt. Coming up behind her, Shane slips his hand under her shirt and begins kissing her neck.

"Stop that!" she snaps, jerking away from him. She seems genuinely angry.

"No one's looking. The kids are outside," Shane says, hurt by the rebuke.

"That ain't the point. If you expect me to drop my drawers and do you right here on the floor in the middle of the afternoon, just 'cause you're feeling randy, you got another think coming."

"Take it easy, sweetie. I was just saying hi."

"You're the one that needs to take it easy. I ain't no floozy you can just come in and start pawing whenever you feel like it."

"I'm sorry, okay? I didn't mean any disrespect by it. I guess I got a little carried away when I came in to give you the good news."

"And what good news would that be?"

"Well, I landed an all-expenses-paid trip to Albuquerque for the weekend, and I thought you could come along and spend a couple of romantic nights with me in a posh hotel."

"Did you, now? You figured I'd up and go gallivanting with you, just like that? What about Gracie? Not to mention that thick-skulled nephew of mine. And who's going to run things here while I'm gone?"

Tammy's reaction confuses Shane. "Don't be like that, sweetie," he protests. "I just thought we deserved a little holiday together. Surely Yolanda and Maybelline can take care of the kids, and the ranch can survive for a couple of days without us. Don't you want to be alone with me?"

She stands up and tosses her sewing onto the floor. "What I *want* is a man who'll buck up and carry his share of the weight," she shouts. "I want someone who won't go running off the first chance he gets."

Shane cannot comprehend Tammy's anger and feels his own stirring. "It's not like that, damn it. This is work."

"You saying going away with me would be work? Like I'm some kinda hard-luck case needs tending to? You're one to talk."

He has stepped into the sort of verbal snare that the women he's with always seem to have a knack for laying, and he resents it. But even though his pulse is elevated and his face flushes with heat, for once his ire does not spill out into loud words or violence the way it has so many times in the past. Outside the game, he has never attacked anyone, and certainly he's never struck a woman, not even in his worst fits of rage. He did, however, habitually punch walls or smash furniture in furious accompaniment to heated words. Now, however, he is separated from his anger. While it is still there, burning like a red-hot coal, it feels contained — caged — as if it's not really his own, and he's watching from the outside.

"No, that's not what I meant. I have to go to Albuquerque for work, so I thought it would be great if you came along."

"Work? What kind of work? You fixing to leave the ranch?"

"No, honey, I'm still staying … if you'll let me. But I have to do an interview — for television — and they're paying me, and springing for the hotel room, too."

"Why the heck would anyone put you on the television?"

This is Shane's golden opportunity to confess everything, but Tammy's acerbic mood stops him. He is afraid an unbridgeable gulf could open between them. Accident or not, he has killed a man.

He shrugs nonchalantly. "It's about my hockey career."

"I thought you were done with hockey."

"I am, but it looks like hockey's not done with me. So, how about it? You interested?"

He moves in to try for a hug, but Tammy pushes him away. "Goddarn it, I said leave me alone. Look, if you gotta go, then go, but I ain't feeling up to it right now. If you must know, I'm fixing to fall off the roof."

"The roof? What are you talking about?"

"You know. Aunt Flo is coming to visit."

"Oh. You never mentioned that. Is she coming, like, tomorrow? We'd be back in a couple of days."

"Geez, Louise, you can be thick sometimes. What I'm trying to tell you is there's gonna be a crime scene in my pants and I'm doing the time right now."

Now Shane is totally confused, and his face shows it. Tammy rolls her eyes.

"You know … the red badge of courage … riding the crimson tide. Oh for Chrissake, Big Hoss, I'm trying to tell you, that time of the month is comin' and I ain't feeling none too good, okay?"

"Oh, geez, I get you. Sweetie, that doesn't have to stop you."

"Well, you ain't the one that has to deal with it, are you? I said I'm not up to it, and that's that. Now leave me be."

Shane opens his mouth to ask about borrowing the pickup truck, but thinks better of it.

"Whatever you want," he acquiesces and leaves.

On his way out he almost falls over Maybelline, who is sitting on the back stoop, munching through a large bag of potato chips.

"Watch where you're going, dickwad," she says, not looking up from her snacking.

"Sorry, May. Didn't see you. What're you doing sitting there, anyway?"

She glares up at Shane. "I'll darn well sit wherever I please. What's it to you, Mr. Motorcycle Man ... Mr. Fix It Even If It Ain't Broke ... Mr. Won't Drink With Li'l Ol' Maybelline No More Now That He's Bopping Tammy?" She finishes by flinging a potato chip at him.

"What's the matter with you?"

"I'm getting ready to punctuate. Go away and leave me be."

This time Shane is a little faster to clue in.

"Punctuate, as in ..."

"A period with an exclamation mark. That's right. So just go away and leave me alone to die in peace, Mr. Broken Teeth, Broken Arm, Broken Promises."

"Maybelline, I'm sorry we don't party together anymore, but, you know ... Tammy and all."

"Oh, I know, so go blow, Joe."

"Don't worry, I'm going, all right. Going to Albuquerque for the weekend, as a matter of fact. Better Albuquerque than here, with two women PMSing at the same time."

"Ha! You don't know the half of it, or two-thirds ... whatever! Just take my advice: stay away from Yolanda. That *chica* gets really nasty this time of the month."

Shane walks off shaking his head, still trying to fathom the situation as he rounds the corner of the ranch house. Vern is lurking there, and he practically jumps on top of Shane.

"Did I hear you saying you're going to Albuquerque? Take me with you, Shane! Please, you gotta let me come along. I can't take it again. Last time they practically tore me apart."

"Let me get this straight. This has happened before? All three of them got their period at the same time?"

"It happened once before, about a year-or-so back. They all turned into monsters. No word of a lie. It was horrible. I don't think I'd live through it a second time. Please, *please*, take me with you!"

Shane has an idea. "All right, but only if you can wrangle us using the truck. I mean, they're not going to need it here, are they?"

Vern brightens. "No, they never go anywhere on the weekends, especially when they're crabbin' like that." His face gets serious again as he contemplates the enormity of the challenge. "Aw, man, I ain't sure I want to go in there an' ask Aunt Tammy for the truck, though. She's already mean enough to me when she ain't playin' for the Red Wings."

"Ha! Playing for the Red Wings — good one. I almost played for them once —" He stops when he sees Vern's confused look. "Never mind, long story. But we're going to need that truck, Viper. No way I can ride my motorcycle all the way to Albuquerque and back with a broken hand."

Vern sighs heavily and hangs his head. "Shoot," he mutters, kicking the dirt. Suddenly his face pops back up with a giant grin pasted on it.

"Beñat!" he exclaims.

Shane cocks an eyebrow. "What are you talking about?"

"Beñat. He's this old feller up in the hills … we bring him supplies, and in exchange he stocks us up with snakes and mice.

They've been trading with him for years, and we're overdue for another visit. Aunt Tammy hates making the drive up there ... she'll lend us the truck for that, for sure."

✗ ✗ ✗ ✗ ✗

Shane wrestles the pickup into gear, and as it grumbles down the driveway, a crate of groceries in back, he and Vern exchange a look of relief. They soon reach the interstate and turn north toward Albuquerque.

The remains of derelict roadside businesses and abandoned homesteads give way to true countryside. The truck has no radio, so Shane attempts some small talk, but Vern seems disinterested. He sits erect in his seat and stares out the window, scanning the landscape intently.

"Horses!" he suddenly shouts as they near a field where two sad-looking roans lean over the fence, looking laconically out over the highway. "Two for me."

Shane is unsure what exactly the boy means, so he gives a neutral, affirming grunt. A few minutes later, however, Vern again hollers loudly. "Horses! Oh, boy, a whole bunch of them ... four, no, five! Ha! I'm winning seven to nothin'."

"Winning? What is this, some kind of horse-counting contest?"

"Ain't ya never played Bury Your Horses? Gracie and me and Aunt Tammy always play it when we're travelling."

"Sorry, never heard of it. Mind you, you've got an advantage when it comes to looking around. I have to keep my eye on the road."

"Yeah, but you're way taller ... you can see farther."

Shane chuckles. "Okay, you're on."

The two of them prove fiercely competitive in their horse-spotting game. Shane closes the gap in the score with a string of single-horse sightings, but Vern has a knack for finding small herds, and he surges to a comfortable lead again as the scenery wavers between brown, stunted scrub brush as sparse and dry as *Rancho Crótalo* and lush, tree-filled terrain testifying to the life-giving presence of water. Then they round a curve, and there, grazing on a hillside, is a riot of horse flesh — palominos, Appaloosas, creams, greys, and several with pure black coats. The herd is so large it's hard to count them all.

Vern's eyes widen, but although his mouth pops open, he is mute in his amazement. It is Shane who first calls out, "Horses!"

"Shoot! I saw them, too," the boy gripes.

"Maybe, but I called it first," Shane says and hastens to tally up the horses before they're out of sight. "Wow, there must be fifty of them, easy. It'll be tough to catch me now."

"I don't want to play no more," Vern whines and slumps down in his seat.

"Come on now, Viper," Shane urges, "for all you know there might be a herd even bigger than that one up ahead somewhere. Never give up — that's the secret to life. Always keep trying your best. But you can't win them all, so it's important to learn how to take your losses in stride. Don't you want to be a good loser?"

"I'd rather win," Vern says.

"Everybody wants to win, buddy, but not everybody can. The important thing is to try your hardest and have fun. I knew guys who went their whole pro careers and never even made the playoffs, let alone won the Cup. Heck, take that rabbit we saw." Shane is referring to earlier in the drive, when a jackrabbit dashed across the highway in front of them, narrowly avoiding their vehicle and giving them both a scare. "For that rabbit, winning is finding enough to eat and not getting eaten by some coyote."

"And not getting squished by a car," Vern adds.

"See, kid, you've got it," Shane replies, and they both laugh. There is a warmth spreading inside him. Shane has spent much of his adult life being looked down upon as a brute good only for his bulk and his fists; he almost started to believe it himself. It is a revelation to realize that he has enough wisdom, much of it hard won, to offer guidance to the young.

As they approach Albuquerque, the roadside becomes progressively more industrialized, and opportunities for spotting horses all but disappear. Shane consults a map and chooses an alternate two-lane highway that loops through more countryside before feeding into the city. But although they encounter suburban estates and golf courses, no ranches or farm fields appear.

Suddenly, however, Vern springs upright in his seat, spins around to look behind him, and shouts, "Bury your horses! Bury your horses!"

"What the heck are you talking about?" Shane asks. "I didn't see any horses."

Vern gives him a look of disbelief. "We're playing Bury Your Horses, remember?"

"You get a point for every horse you call out first, you said."

"Yeah, but you *lose* all your points if someone sees a cemetery and calls it first. And I saw one back there."

Shane considers the situation for a few seconds, then pulls over onto the shoulder. "I didn't see any cemetery," he says.

"I swear, I'm not lying. I saw it. Back there. It was really little, but it was a cemetery, all right." The boy looks like he's about to cry, and his manner is so earnest Shane cannot bring himself to dismiss the claim. He puts the truck into reverse and slowly backs along the shoulder.

"There it is," Vern calls out.

In front of a large field sits an anomalous parcel of land, barely the size of a tennis court, surrounded by a stone wall. In front of it the highway's shoulder widens into a parking area, which Shane steers into. A stone obelisk about five feet high stands in the middle of the plot.

"Looks more like a monument to me," Shane comments, but seeing the sincerity in Vern's face, he suggests they get out for a closer look.

Sure enough, there are also headstones, most lying horizontal, practically buried in the grass, but also a handful of polished marble grave markers standing upright at the back, eclipsed by the obelisk.

"Well, it's the smallest one I've ever seen, but I'd have to say this officially qualifies as a cemetery," Shane announces.

"I win! I win! Ha, ha, I beat you!"

Vern's taunting irritates Shane, but he has decades of experience losing. Moreover, he has just admonished the boy to be a good loser. He smiles and pats Vern on the shoulder. "Nice play. Way to beat the clock and pull out a come-from-behind win. But, um, remember what I said about being a good loser? It's even more important to learn how to be a good winner."

Vern blanches. "Holy cow. You're right … I hated it when other teams rubbed it in after they beat us." He straightens up and offers Shane his hand. "Good game, Shane. I thought you had me … I was lucky to win."

"That's better," Shane tells him. "Hey, we're both winners in my book, so when we get to Albuquerque, I'm going to buy us some ice cream." He turns back toward the stone monument. "That's one flashy chunk of marble. Must belong to some rich guy." He bends over to read the inscription. "Didn't die too long ago, either. Oh well, even with a private plot and big-ass gravestone, rich is just as dead as poor."

They climb back into the truck and finish the drive into the city. Shane's interview is still several hours away, and he wants to buy some conservative attire for his interview, so he finds a shopping mall where he and Vern can use the bathroom and grab some lunch, and he can fulfill his promise of ice cream.

They check in at the hotel, where Morrie Getz has booked them a modest-sized suite. There are two king-sized beds, and they each choose one and spread out over the mattress, relishing the indulgence after the spartan sleeping arrangements of the ranch.

There is a message asking Shane to touch base with the *CelebTV* crew upon arrival. Once he has confirmed the time and location of his interview that evening, he takes the opportunity to use the bathroom. After luxuriating in a hot shower, he shaves, taking great care not to nick himself.

When he comes out, Vern is channel surfing on the TV, mesmerized by the cavalcade of images on the screen. Suddenly apprehensive the boy might stumble across coverage of Ken Linton's death, Shane helps him locate a kid-friendly movie to watch.

Between worrying about his interview and concerns that Vern might see Shane being vilified by the media, Shane's mood blackens. When he's ready to leave for his session, he turns to Vern. "I'll be back in an hour. I don't want you watching any adult stuff, got it?"

Something about Shane's intense manner clearly disturbs the boy. He instantly slumps and refuses to make eye contact. "Yessir," he mumbles.

This has a sobering effect on Shane's mood. He realizes that Vern, so lively and happy during the trip, now feels picked on again and is folding back into his usual unhappy state. Suddenly, Shane's petulance seems self-indulgent, petty, and hurtful.

"Hey, sorry, Viper. I'm not mad at you, all right? I'm just a little worried about leaving you by yourself. I'm responsible for you, and I don't want anything to happen, or I would never forgive myself. But it's okay, because I know I can trust you."

Vern brightens. "You bet you can. Don't worry about a thing."

Shane smiles and gives the boy's shoulder a squeeze. "Atta boy. I knew I could count on you. If the movie finishes before I get back, you can watch cartoons or something like Nickelodeon, but it's got to be kid stuff. Promise?"

"Okay, Shane. I promise."

"All right, then. I won't be long."

Shane realizes that, sooner or later, everyone's going to find out what he is hiding. *But maybe if I give a good interview and tell my side of the story, it'll help smooth things over*, he thinks.

He checks the time and hurries out.

TWENTY-ONE

The hospitality suite where Shane is being interviewed is on a lower floor. During the elevator ride down, he tries to clear his head and concentrate on what he's going to say. As before an important game, he feels the stirrings of anxiety in his abdomen. His earlier mall meal is all but McHappy as it roils in his stomach.

Thanks to the bouncer-like attendant standing outside, the suite is easy to find. Shane enters to find a dozen people waiting for him. It's a larger crew than he anticipated, which unnerves him, but there's no turning back now. Heads turn in unison as he enters, but the range of their expressions is less uniform. Some look curious, some excited, some outright hostile — or so it seems to him. A beautiful woman in a pink silk blouse and a form-hugging skirt breaks through the milling bodies and extends a hand. Her smile is friendly, almost seductive, showing bright white teeth. She looks vaguely familiar. Shane realizes she is the host of the *CelebTV* interview segment.

"Hi, Shane. I'm Julia Jansen. I'll be interviewing you. I'm thrilled that you've agreed to talk with us." She introduces him to various members of the crew, but all the names and titles wash over his head.

"Okay, then," she says when the preliminaries are dispensed with. "Just sit down here and we'll get you miked up."

He takes the indicated seat in the glare of portable lights while a ponytailed sound technician steps in and starts snaking a cable down the inside of his shirt. Once the techie has clamped the lapel microphone to Shane's shirt front and retreated back behind the wall of lights, Julia looks at her subject appraisingly. "You don't mind if we dab a little makeup on you, do you?"

Shane has done many in-studio interviews during his career, and he knows the drill. They often apply powder to take away the shine and sometimes blush to add colour to the cheeks. The makeup artist introduces himself as Fabian and, after Julia whispers some instructions into his ear, goes to work. Fabian seems to take a lot of time, but Shane is relieved when he feels makeup being applied to his recent wounds. From past interviews, he appreciates how much of an impression stitches and abrasions leave and is grateful *CelebTV* wants him to look normal.

"All right, then," Julia says, smiling radiantly as she takes a seat in front of him. "I know you've probably done this a gazillion times before, but just speak naturally. We're not live, so if you flub something, don't sweat it ... we can fix it in the edit. Always look at me, not the lens. The main camera is right behind me, but we'll be taking some fill-in shots with a handheld." She gestures off to the side, and Shane notices, for the first time, a woman holding a formidable-looking portable video camera.

"Okay, then," Julia continues. "Let's get a sound check. Say something."

"Um. Hi, everyone, my name's Shane Bronkovsky. And this is my interview. How's that?"

Julia receives a thumbs-up from the sound guy. "Fabulous. Let's get started, then." Abruptly, her smile disappears and her eyes narrow.

"Shane Bronkovsky, thank you for agreeing to talk with us exclusively here on *CelebTV*. I guess my first question is … how *are* you?" She says it like they're on intimate terms and she really cares about his welfare.

"I'm doing okay, Julia, you know, all things considered. I mean, I've been through a lot."

"So, where have you been the last couple of weeks?"

"Well, my team's done, and I always take some time off at the end of a season. I've been doing some travelling on my motorcycle."

"So … you just killed a man and you go sightseeing?"

Shane feels a rush of adrenalin. *Look out, Bronk*, he thinks, *she's coming after you*. He struggles not to let the emotion reach his face. "I feel bad about what happened, Julia. It was a horrible accident, but there's nothing I can do about it now except learn to live with it."

"You claim it was an accident. What do you have to say to the people who believe you deliberately set out to hurt Ken Linton?"

"That's ridiculous! It was a clean shot. He had his head down, that's all."

"That's *all*? The man is dead. Do you deny you had a heated verbal exchange with Ken Linton earlier in the game?"

"Yeah, there was some trash talking. Linton is … was … a chirpy little, um … player."

"So he got under your skin, and you decided to get even with him, is that right?"

"No, that's not right. Please don't put words in my mouth."

"We're trying to get to the bottom of a great tragedy, that's all. We're asking the things that all of America wants to know."

She pauses and glances down at her clipboard before resuming. "So, are you saying you had no intention of making contact with Ken Linton — that you ran into him by accident?"

"Well, no, obviously I meant to hit him, but it was a clean check. I mean, it's a contact sport. What I did was part of the game."

"Really? Killing people is part of the game? Come now, Shane. Didn't the referees feel differently? Didn't they try to remove you from the game? And didn't you fight them, too?"

"No, they didn't. The crowd was going crazy, so they said they were doing it for my protection. And I didn't fight them. We all got tripped up and fell down. It was an accident."

"I see, you all tripped. Another accident."

Shane can feel sweat forming on his forehead as the lights radiate heat, and the portable camera moves in for a close-up as if they've been waiting for it to happen. He finds himself wondering if walking out of the interview now would invalidate his fee.

"Let's talk a little about you, Shane," Julia resumes. "You're paid to fight, correct?"

This question he can field easily. He's been asked it countless times before. "Well, no, Julia. I'm paid to play hockey."

"Yes, I'm sure you'd prefer to think that. But you are expected to fight, correct?"

"Fighting is part of hockey. A lot of players get into fights. It happens."

"Yes, but in your case it happens all the time." She looks at her clipboard. "Would it surprise you to know that you've been in over two hundred fights since joining the NHL? That's more than a professional boxer."

"A boxer doesn't play eighty games a season."

"What about those wounds you're sporting right now? Did you get them in a recent fight?" The portable camera swoops in even closer until it is right in his face. Across the room, a video monitor catches his eye, and suddenly he realizes that the makeup artist did not, in fact, cover his stitches and cuts, but enhanced them so they look raw and recent.

"You bastards set me up!" he shouts.

"Please, Shane, control yourself. In fact, let's talk about that famous temper of yours. Isn't it true that while playing in Los Angeles, you were enrolled in anger management therapy as part of a plea bargain following an altercation at a night club?"

"Yes, it's true, as you obviously already know. But did you know that the judge who sent me there used to send half the people that went through her court to anger management? It was a dozen night classes at the local community college, a big waste of time."

"So, you're saying the class did nothing for you?"

"Look, lady, over the years I've been enrolled in classes on confidence building, assertiveness training, self-esteem, effective communication, lateral thinking, leadership, yoga, figure skating, crystal therapy, and even past-life regression. This sport is big business, and as soon as some yahoo in the front office realizes that the game isn't really played on the ice, but played between the ears, there's nothing they won't do to mess with the players' heads, especially if you're on a losing skid."

"It sounds like you're carrying a lot of resentment."

"Oh, so now you're a shrink, too? I suppose this is where you'll cut away to game footage of me breaking a stick over the edge of the bench, or that time in Philly I went after the fan in the stands." Out of the corner of his eye he sees two producer-types exchange a look before one of them writes something down on a clipboard. *Shit*, he thinks, *I handed that one right to them.*

He plunges onward. "The thing is, every one of those times, I was provoked. I'm not some simmering volcano about to explode. But when push comes to shove, I fight back."

"And did Ken Linton provoke you?"

"No. I mean, yeah, he pissed me off, but I didn't go after him, if that's what you're implying. I mean, they've got their tough guy, too, you know?"

"What guy?"

"Their enforcer, Toby McNeil. If I go after Linton, then I've got to answer to McNeil. Same as if someone tries to go after one of my guys — they have to answer to me. That's what I am, you see. A protector ... a guardian."

"You were afraid of Toby McNeil, so when you saw a chance to vent your anger on Ken Linton, you took it."

"Of course not! I've fought McNeil lots of times. I mean, he's no pushover, but I'm not afraid of him."

"So you say, but isn't Toby McNeil the one who gave you those stitches in a game just two days before you killed Ken Linton?"

Again the secondary camera swoops in for a tight shot. This time she gets in so close he could lick the lens. "Get that thing out of my face," he growls. The videographer scampers back into the wings.

He turns back to Julia. "Yeah, McNeil gave me these stitches." He holds up his right fist. "He also gave me these bruised knuckles, 'cause he wouldn't take off his headgear. Me, I fight fair. As soon as I know we're gonna go, I drop my gloves and flip my helmet off. So yeah, he got some good shots in. But I bloodied him up, too. Like I said, it's all part of the game. I'm just giving the fans their money's worth."

The fans! he thinks. *That's it. Screw her, I've got to get through to the fans.* He turns and looks directly at the camera, ignoring a flurry of hand signals from the crew telling him to look at Julia.

"The reason I agreed to come on and do this interview is because I want the fans to know that I never intended to hurt

Kenny Linton. What I did was legal — a clean hit. He had just dished off the puck, and the rules say he's fair game. Honestly, I expected him to dance out of the way, he's a great skater. The rest of it — the helmet coming off, him hitting his head on the ice — that was a million-to-one chance. I can't begin to tell you how bad I feel about it. I'll have to live with it for the rest of my life."

"At least you *have* the rest of your life, unlike Ken Linton. You say it's all part of the game. Are you aware the Chicago District Attorney is considering bringing homicide charges against you? Or have you been too busy sightseeing?"

If her intention is to distract Shane from the camera, she succeeds. He glares at her. "If it happens, I'll welcome my day in court."

"Perhaps we can give the courts something else to consider. What I want to talk about now, Shane, is your history of violence against women."

"My *what*?"

"I'm referring to an incident last July when your fiancée, Brandi Simpson, called the police to your penthouse apartment —"

"Okay, first of all, she was never my fiancée. Second, she only called the cops to get even with me because I threw her dog out the window —"

"You threw her dog out the window?"

"It wasn't a *real* dog. It was a stuffed toy. She has, like, a hundred of them. And *she* started it … she threw my Cream LP out the window first."

"But you don't deny that you were living with Ms. Simpson at the time and that the police were called to your home to investigate a case of domestic violence."

"Sure, we were shacked up, but I'm telling you, the whole thing was bogus. There were no charges. The cops came, they asked a bunch of questions, they had a look around, and they left. I mean, they were just doing their job, and you could tell they pretty much knew she was making the whole thing up just because she was pissed at me."

"That's not what Ms. Simpson has to say. She told *CelebTV* in an exclusive interview that she called the police after you assaulted her, and that she only withdrew her complaint for fear of her life."

"Fear of her life? That's bullshit. Look, I grabbed another of my albums out of her hand before she could throw it out the window, too — that's all. I mean, they're vintage vinyl. The cops asked her if she felt threatened and wanted to go with them to a women's shelter, and she said no. I figure she realized her little stunt had gone too far. If she had any problem with me she could have left anytime. Like you said, this was last July. We were together almost a year after that."

"But victims of domestic abuse often stay in the abusive situation due to fear, a misguided sense of loyalty, or financial hardship. Ms. Simpson says that only after the public outcry over the death of Ken Linton and the rise of the #MeToo movement did she find the courage to come forward and tell her story. Would you like to see what she had to say? We can play it for you."

Oddly, Shane's surging anger suddenly dissipates, like the heat of a red-hot iron doused in water. He was so very close to calling Brandi a lying bitch on camera and shouting that she is using them the same way she used him … but what Julia has just said about domestic abuse victims hits home. Brandi's lies are an insult to real victims of domestic abuse. Women like Tammy, Yolanda, and Maybelline have been mistreated, battered, and hurt so badly that their emotional wounds may never heal. They deserve better than to have their suffering exploited by the likes of *CelebTV* and Brandi, who's not even in the same league as them in terms of courage and strength. *And you know what, Shane?* his suddenly wiser inner voice tells him. *You deserve better than to let these media vultures exploit you and try provoking you into a temper tantrum on camera.*

When he resumes talking, he is so calm that he almost feels disembodied, like he's watching himself from the other side of the lens. "Julia, for the record, I never hurt Brandi Simpson in any way, nor have I laid a hand on *any* woman in my entire life. Also for the record, yes, I've had some off-ice incidents and have lost my temper on occasion, but I am not a violent man. I never tried to hurt Kenny Linton. I'm sick about what happened, but it was a terrible accident. I didn't do anything wrong."

He stops. "What time is it?" he asks.

Julia glances at her watch. "Six thirty-two," she says. "But we'll stay all night if you want to talk some more. You owe the world the truth."

"Seems to me the truth is the last thing the world's going to find here." With that, he removes his microphone and gets up to leave.

Behind him he hears Julia firing more questions in rapid succession, like a tabloid journalist's version of shooting drill. "Shane, don't you have any remorse? What do you have to say to Ken Linton's family? What do you think will happen to you if you have to go to prison? How did you get that cast on your arm, Shane? Were you in another brawl? Is it true that substance abuse was the reason for your divorce?" He pulls the door shut behind him, careful not to slam it, and goes out into the serene silence of the hallway.

TWENTY-TWO

"**T**his is the place. Turn here," Vern exclaims. Following a crack-of-dawn breakfast at the hotel, they have been driving for two hours. For the past five minutes, Vern, in addition to asking for regular odometer readings, has been scouring the roadside for the turnoff into the mountains. Shane is still a little vague about the nature of their errand, besides dropping off a crate and making a pickup in exchange. Seeing as this side trip was the key to Tammy granting permission for the journey, he assumes it is important. Still, there is something oddly furtive about the entire mission.

"You sure this is it?" he asks Vern. All he can see is a vague tract heading off into the wilderness.

"Uh-huh. See, there's the marker." He indicates a small pyramid of stacked stones practically overgrown by brush.

"All right, if you say so. Looks like a pretty rough road. Let's hope this old truck can take it."

They drive for another forty-five minutes, and as the dirt road grows steeper, changing into a series of switchbacks, Shane has to turn on the four-wheel drive. The pickup rattles and groans, but doesn't fail them. The trail dead-ends at a small clearing in front of a sheer face of rock. Shane was expecting to see a building of some sort, but there is only wilderness all around. The cliff in front of them rises at least ten storeys into the air. Although majestic, like something out of one of Shane's Westerns, it is not promising as an end destination.

"We're here," Vern declares, flinging open the door.

"Where? There's nothing. The road stops."

"We go over there," Vern says, pointing at the rock face. Shane follows his finger, but sees only a sheer wall of stone.

"You're kidding. How are we supposed to haul that huge honking box up *there*?"

"Don't fret none. Beñat'll help us. There he is now."

Turning around, Shane now sees a narrow footpath emerging from a crack in the cliff, which he hadn't spotted before. A laden burro is being led along it by a small, ancient-looking man who appears to have stepped out of centuries past. He wears a white tunic and trousers woven from coarse cloth, and his footwear consists of homemade, ankle-high rawhide moccasins with ornate beading around the top. The one incongruity in his pre-Columbian attire is a giant black beret, several times larger than the common variety, sitting atop his head.

The man has a peculiar gait, like he is gliding over the ground rather than walking upon it. He comes up to Vern and kisses both cheeks, much to the boy's embarrassment, then places his palm on top of the youngster's head.

"*Bienvenido, chico. Eres más alto.*"

"*Buenos dias, Señor Beñat.* Yeah, I reckon I've grown maybe two inches since I seen ya last."

"And I have probably shrunk as much," the old man replies in heavily accented English. When Beñat turns his attention to Shane, a look of astonishment lights up the old man's face.

"*Mon dieu!* It's you! So, so, so ... here you are at last. *Bonjour, mon ami. Bienvenue!*"

Shane shakes the man's hand and is surprised by its iron-like grip. This moment of welcoming has a dreamlike déjà vu quality. Shane wonders how the man happened to arrive on the scene just as the pickup pulled up. The impression he'd gotten was that their visit to Beñat was spontaneous, so he would not know they were coming. Unless the old man was perched up high in the rocks, watching, how did he know they had arrived? Why did he greet Vern in Spanish but Shane in French? And what did he mean by *here you are at last*? Most likely he was referring to their delivery errand, but the way he looked at Shane — or almost *into* him — made it seem like Beñat meant he was waiting for Shane personally.

Shane opens his mouth to get some of these questions resolved, but Beñat has already started the exchange of cargos. When Shane steps over to help, Beñat shoos him away and starts placing boxes into the bed of the pickup in a precise manner. The containers have holes drilled in their sides, and Shane realizes they contain living creatures. As he leans in for a closer look Beñat catches his interest and gestures to where the boxes now sit in two neatly arranged rows.

"Death row," he says, then grins impishly as he indicates the other line of boxes. "And row of death."

Shane peeps through the holes and gets the joke. The first row of boxes contain a half-dozen different kinds of wild rodents, while the second row houses a collection of rattlesnakes, their natural predators.

"Well, I guess we'll get going," Shane says, anxious to return to *Rancho Crótalo* and Tammy, but Beñat, Vern, and the burro are moving down the path that plunges into the tower of rock.

Shane follows, fighting claustrophobia as the cliffs squeeze in on them. Only a tiny swatch of sky is visible overhead. The trail looks to be a combination of natural fissure and manmade pathway through the rock. The amount of labour necessary to have hewn the rock and made the trail passable seems monumental.

The zigzagging nature of the route makes it hard to estimate distance, and time itself seems to dim in the shadow of the rock. When they again emerge into the open, the sunlight is blinding. Even after spots stop dancing in front of his eyes, Shane has difficulty processing the scene before him. They are in a small, lush ravine that runs, like the green slash of some titanic painter's brush, up into the hills. In the near distance, hundreds of sheep are grazing, their occasional bleats echoing off the canyon walls. Presided over by a hyperactive black-and-white dog, they add a surreal soundtrack to the scene. Vern immediately runs over to pet and play with the dog, who responds with barks and spins.

What commands Shane's attention, however, is a collection of square-shaped dwellings high up in the cliffs on the far side of the valley, nestled beneath a gigantic natural dome in the canyon wall. The view is impressive on a scale that defies his perception. Some parts of the abodes have been hewn out of the rock, and the rest of the construction has been done using red-coloured brick. Wooden poles project from the rooflines of the buildings like tines of forks. A path winds halfway up the cliff, and a series of ladders provide the final access. The houses are clearly ancient, yet they appear to be perfectly preserved.

"Oh, hey, I read about these places back in school. This is, like, one of those pueblos, right?"

Beñat nods. "*Oui, c'est ça.*"

"Wow ... and you live here?"

"I am a shepherd, so mostly I make my home wherever the sheep graze. But, yes, I sleep here whenever I can ... the animals are especially fond of the grazing in this part of the valley, and it is always nice to have a roof over your head."

"So, are you Indian … oh, shit, sorry, that's not politically correct. What is it I'm supposed to say — First Nations?"

Beñat laughs. "No, this is my second nation … although it has been my home longer than my first. No, not Indian. *Je suis Basque.*"

"Basque? That's, like, in Spain or something, isn't it?"

"Or something. And you are a Canadian, no?"

"Yeah. How did you know?"

"The sheep told me you would be from the far north, at the end of the earth."

"Not quite, but close. The sheep told you I was coming, eh? Pretty smart sheep."

"*Dios!* These sheep? *Non, monsieur.* Truly they are among God's most stupid animals, but they sometimes talk to their cousins — the wild sheep in the mountains."

"I see. And *those* sheep are smart?"

"Oh, no. They are stupid, too, although definitely not as stupid as these. But the mountain sheep talk to the raven. Now, the raven — ah, she is very wise."

"So, the raven knew I was coming."

"No. Lusio, he says you will come. He and the raven, they are good friends." There is a twinkle in Beñat's eye, and Shane can't figure out whether this is some obscure foreign humour or if the old man actually expects Shane to believe the nonsense about talking animals. The thought that Beñat might be playing him for a fool irritates Shane, and he feels the first flushes of anger stroke his cheeks.

"So what's this Lusio … a coyote or something?"

"Ha! The coyote, he is also very smart, but a liar … you cannot believe a word he says. No, Lusio is a man. A very great man."

"Do tell. How did this Lusio guy know I was coming?"

"Ah. That is a very long story ... one we save for later." Beñat stretches his hand toward Shane. Out of reflex, Shane pushes it aside. Beñat clucks his tongue.

"Please, permit me." He reaches out again, slowly, and places his palm against Shane's chest. After a few seconds he nods his head. "Yes, Lusio said you carry much inside of you. Tell me, why are you so mad?"

"You were just starting to piss me off with this sheep and raven stuff. It's no biggie. We're cool."

"No, no, I am talking about your great anger. I say the word *mad* because in English, you use the same word for 'angry' or 'insane,' no? Think about this, *mon ami*. It is not some accident of the language." Beñat taps Shane's chest. "You carry it here. You try to lock it up, but sometimes the beast escapes, no? Other times it scratches you from the inside and ... I forget the English word ... what a dog does with its bone —"

"Gnaws?"

"*Si. Oui.* Gnaws at you. I know, because I was once exactly like you."

"Exactly like me, eh? No shit. And did you play in the NHL, too?"

Shane would not have thought it possible, but the grin on Beñat's face spreads even wider. He seizes Shane's hand and pumps it wildly. "NHL! *Mon dieu!* This the sheep did not tell me. But that is wonderful. *Incroyable!* Not me, *mon ami*. I was not, I think, good enough, although I did not have a chance to find out. In my time only some Swedes, and then, later, a few Russians were able to come from Europe to play in America. I hoped only to play for *Txuri Urdin*, my local club, but fortune was not so kind. But, ah, the NHL ... yes, what player does not dream of it?"

Dan Dowhal

Beñat twirls his shepherd's crook around and holds it like a hockey stick. He takes aim at a rock on the ground and smacks it down the valley in a good imitation of a slap shot. "Rocket Richard. Gordie Howe. Bobby Hull. Bobby Orr," he chants like some sort of mantra. "Of course, I dreamed of playing for a Basque team in the Olympics, and there it was necessary to admire the Soviets. Bobrov, Firsov, Kharlamov, Mikhailov, Yakushev."

"You're kidding. You played hockey?"

"*Bien sûr.* Back home in San Sebastián." He laughs and taps Shane lightly on the shins with his staff. "Maybe I see now why Lusio sent you to me. Come, I will make us some tea and tell you my story." He gestures up the cliff toward the stone dwellings.

"Hold on, I can't just leave the kid."

"Do not worry, *mon ami.* He will be okay. Children need to play, not listen to grown men making serious talk. Napoléon will watch over him." He whistles, and the sheepdog that has been gambolling with Vern comes sprinting over. Beñat says something to the canine that Shane cannot understand. Then Napoléon goes racing back to the boy at full tilt.

"Was that Basque?" Shane asks.

"Yes, my native tongue. It is the language the dog prefers, although his first language was Spanish."

Shane no longer finds Beñat's impish tone irritating. He suspects the old man is one of those persistent jokesters who perceive a punchline in every heartbeat.

"Never heard it before. Strange language ... no offence."

"No, no. It is true. It is unique, for sure. The academics cannot find a root linking it to any other language on earth. Some say it is the tongue of ancient Atlantis. But, like many of my countrymen, I also speak the languages of the nations that still hold us in their grasp — France and Spain. And I have been in

246

America for more than forty years now, so I have tried to learn its language as well. But this is not so easy when you are talking only with sheep."

They reach the cliffs, and Beñat indicates the series of ladders that rise in stages up the rock face. "We go up there."

Shane casts a last look at Vern. The boy's laughter indicates that he's enjoying himself, so Shane follows the old shepherd skyward.

TWENTY-THREE

Beñat leads Shane up to the rooftop terrace of the largest adobe-brick building. From there, an entrance that is half doorway, half window leads to an inner chamber carved out of the rock. The room is small and sparsely furnished. Along one wall is a low sleeping platform covered in blankets. A simple plank table with two chairs dominates the middle of the space. Nooks carved into the sandstone hold candles and some pottery. A small two-burner propane stove sits on the floor, surrounded by a meagre assortment of well-used pots and pans. It is here that Beñat turns his attention, firing up the stove and putting on a dented, fire-blackened kettle.

Shane ponders his own recently lost home in the sky — the spacious condo where he lived with Brandi, which had closets bigger than this entire room.

"You live simply," he comments to the shepherd.

"I simply live," the shepherd replies with a hearty laugh. "See, my English is not so bad. I can make jokes."

"Good one," Shane replies. He surveys the surrounding houses. "Must have been hundreds of people living here once, eh?"

"Yes. But even then this was a holy, sheltered place."

"I'm surprised the government lets you stay here. Aren't these all, like, protected historical sites? State parks and whatnot?"

"The government does not know about this place. It hides from the world."

"Really? After centuries, nobody's stumbled across it? I find that hard to believe. I mean, this area isn't *that* remote. Hell, you found it, didn't you?"

"I did not find it. I grazed my sheep in these hills for many years and never knew it existed."

"What do you mean you never found it? You're here, aren't you?"

"Lusio showed me. He took me here."

"Oh yeah, right. Lusio. The guy who told the raven who told the mountain sheep who told your sheep who told you I was coming. So who is this Lusio, anyway?"

"Wait, my friend. First we drink tea and I tell you my story, and then we will talk about Lusio." Right on cue, the kettle starts to whistle, and Beñat busies himself preparing their refreshment. He brings the teapot and a pair of mugs to the table and bids Shane sit down. Suddenly the shepherd bangs his forehead. "*Coño!* Forgive my rudeness. I have lived alone for too long. I have been talking and talking and we have not shared names."

"The sheep didn't tell you that?"

Beñat guffaws. "Ha! The sheep think everyone is called *Baaa*! Allow me to begin." He removes his oversized beret and gives a deep bow. "My name is Beñat Koldobika Goikoetxea. I was born near the village of Auzoberri, in Euskal Herria — what is called Basque Country. I am happy to be making your acquaintance." He offers his hand formally.

"My name is Shane Alexander Bronkovsky. I was born in the town of Peel Crossing in the Yukon Territory, Canada." They shake hands, and again Shane is impressed by the strength of the old man's grip, although now he senses the rugged life behind it. He is reminded of the old trappers and prospectors he knew in his youth — cantankerous, unkempt, stubborn men who were all sinew, gristle, and gumption.

"As you can see, I am a shepherd. My father and his brothers and their father and their grandfather were all shepherds. But that is not to say I have always been one. No, *mon ami*, and this is why I share my story with you. When I was a boy I became angry, *mad*, that I was expected to spend my life tending sheep. I shouted and cursed and kicked and threw stones at the sheep. My mother cried and pleaded with me. The priest threatened me with hell. My father beat me without mercy. But all that only made me more angry."

"But you see, we're not the same. I had it good as a kid. I mean, my mom died when I was twelve, and sure, that sucked, but I always had my hockey. Things were cool, you know?"

Beñat tolerates the interruption with a smile, then proceeds as if Shane has not spoken.

"I fought my parents with so much fury they sent me away. I went to live in the city, in San Sebastián, with my mother's brother. Now, you may perhaps think that when a young man obtains that which he has fought for since he was a little boy, he will stop his anger, but that was not how it went with me. The anger — it remained, like some wild animal that has climbed inside to make a nest. Soon I found other people to feed to the animal within. At school, I fought every boy in my class. Not just with my fists, although that I did every day. No, I also fought with this." Beñat taps his temple with his forefinger.

"What, you mean, like, head games?" Shane asks, drawn into the tale despite knowing that its moral will ultimately be directed at him.

"No, no, I mean that I fought even harder in the classroom to be the best student, the one who knows the most and gets the most distinctions for his examinations. I beat the other students and overcame the laziness of the teachers, and this earned me a scholarship for the *universidad*. You may perhaps think that when a young man beats all others around him, and he rises to the top and has the chance to be the most educated and successful man his family has ever seen, in all its generations, that man should stop being angry, no?"

"Let me guess. You were still pissed, right?"

"Pissed? This expression I do not know. Is this what you do when you have knocked someone you are fighting down to the ground? Do you then stand and urinate on them?"

"God, no. It's just a figure of speech. It means being angry."

"I told you my English needs work. Yes, I was still *pissed*." He grins with childlike enthusiasm, delighted to use his newly acquired slang. "I was pissed at the girls, who I felt did not offer the worship and feminine rewards I had earned. I was pissed at my uncle, who did not appreciate my genius and complained about having me under his roof even though I was willing to pay for it. At the *universidad*, where I studied languages and politics, I discovered socialism, and soon I was pissed at the capitalists who controlled the means of production and exploited the proletariat. I was also pissed at the students who now performed better than me in that bigger arena. Anger alone could no longer lift me to the highest distinction in my *programmes*. But my constant burning, now famous anger drew the attention of some other students and professors. They came and seduced me to their political cause, convincing me to turn my anger into a weapon against the Spanish government in the fight for the independence of the Basque people. I joined the separatist rebels, *Euskadi Ta Askatasuna* — the ETA. You have heard of them?"

"Didn't they used to blow shit up and stuff?"

Beñat throws back his head and unleashes a colossal laugh. "*Piss, shit.* Pardon me, but your English language likes to run to the bathroom. Although I should not be so cruel — she is not alone in this regard. Yes, *mon ami*, there were some in our organization who felt the need for violence, but despite my angry nature, I did not seek blood. I only attacked the government with my words. However, in the end this did not matter."

Suddenly, Beñat jumps to his feet and rubs his hands together. "But, wait. I did not tell you about my hockey! One of the men in my group, when he discovered that in the mountains we skated on the ice all winter, he took me to join in the hockey. I liked it immediately, perhaps because it was different. I felt that the football — what they call soccer here in America — that is played by all the young men, I felt this was the sport of the oppressing Spaniards."

"I thought you Basque guys were into *jai alai*."

"True, we have many sports of our own, including *cesta punta* — what you call *jai alai* — but they are played *mano a mano*. No, hockey appealed to my angry nature. The more angry I was, the more superior my play."

Beñat puffs out his chest with evident pride. "I became one of the best players, scoring many goals. True, we had not many teams in my city to compete with, but sometimes we did play exhibitions against other cities, and I saw that I truly had skill. Alas, I was made to leave for America the year before Spain's national hockey league, *La Liga Nacional de Hockey sobre Hielo*, was born and San Sebastián formed a team, *Club Hockey Hielo*

Txuri Urdin. If I had stayed, I am confident I could have played there. Several of my hockey comrades did so."

"Why'd you have to leave?"

"Ah, yes. To return to my story of stupid anger. As I said, although I shot only words at the enemy, I did so openly, in public, and soon became well known to Franco's secret police. When other members of my ETA cell exploded a bomb — one meant only to destroy a building, but it killed two people — my name was attached to the arrest warrant, and soon I was hunted for murder. So, I was taken onto a fishing boat and fled to America. The only work I was wanted for here was shepherding. *Ironique*, no? I, who fought so hard to escape my destiny as a shepherd, was saved from imprisonment and torture and death by becoming one." Beñat flips his thumb toward the window, where the sheep can be seen down below, grazing. "And so I remain one now, over forty years later."

"I didn't realize they brought shepherds all the way from Europe."

"Oh, yes, my friend. It is a hard, lonely life that pays *shit*. Americans do not want to do it. For almost a century there was a diaspora of Basques who emigrated here to mind herds of sheep, although I was one of the last. Finally, Basque men grew tired of working like slaves, so America now obtains its shepherds from even poorer places ... El Salvador or Nicaragua."

"So you learned your lesson, is that it? You stopped being angry?"

"Oh, no, *mon ami!*" Beñat laughs. "I was more angry than ever." He starts counting on his fingers. "I was angry the authorities falsely hunted me for a murder I did not do. I was angry to be pulled away from my studies, my politics, my hockey, my people — my *life*. I was angry to leave the green hills and beautiful shores of my homeland to end up here in a dry, strange land where everything, animal and vegetable, tries to stick something sharp into you. I was angry about the pay and the hours forced upon me by the rich capitalist pig who employed me. Most of all, I think, I was angry to end up as a shepherd like my father after all. I said it was ironic, but that is not to say I enjoyed being carried on the shoulders of *ironía* like some helpless little lamb.

"I hated my new life. Whenever my bosses allowed me to come down from the hills for a few days, I would take all my pay and spend it on alcohol. I would become as drunk as my little money would allow, but before I reached the oblivion that swims in the bottom of the glass, I would fight — anyone, and for any reason." Beñat leans closer and points out an assortment of scars concealed among the wrinkles of his face. "The fights left their marks, but I did not care. Until one day I badly hurt a man, some stupid cowboy, and I was arrested. Now, I thought, they will find out about me and send me back to Spain, and even though Franco is dead and we have a new king, the ETA are still called terrorists. I will be executed. For, you see, in that very year, 1978, five comrades were sent to the wall and shot by the government."

"Obviously they didn't send you back, though."

"No. This rancher, a big shot whose father had just died and who now owned many, many sheep — I think he was also related by marriage to the sheriff — this fat *porc* came to me in jail, and he said, 'We know who you are. If you want to stay here, I can obtain your release, but you work for me now.' So, I thought, what choice do I have? I went to work for him, but now I was even more angry, for I no longer received any money, and never got to come down from the hills. The rancher, he trusted no one else with our secret. He said he protected me, but I think he was afraid to lose his slave. He himself drove the truck once a month to bring me water and propane and cheap food in bags and cans, and once a year I sheared the sheep and he took away the wool. And all the time I was angry, so angry. Even in my sleep, my dreams were filled with big oceans of hate and fury that banged against my brain like giant waves crashing in a storm."

"Wait. Are you telling me you've been stuck up here working for free for, like, forty years? Holy cow, no wonder you're angry!"

"I am not angry, my friend. That is the point of what I am telling you. And that is where Lusio enters the story."

"Finally. This is the guy who told the raven who told the mountain sheep —"

"Who told my sheep who told me you were coming. *Si.* That Lusio."

Beñat rises to refresh Shane's tea and to look out the window at Vern playing below. Evidently satisfied, he returns to his seat and resumes his story.

"I reached a point of great despair. Perhaps another man would think about taking his own life, but I was much too angry inside for that. I attacked the world around me instead. I tore up bushes and smashed the cactus and pounded rocks against rocks. One day I caught a coyote trying to steal one of my sheep, and I beat it to death with my *cayado* — my shepherd's stick — and kept beating it long after the life had left the body. Then I heard someone laugh. I looked up, and was surprised to see an old man sitting on a boulder watching me. I saw from his face, his complexion, and his clothes that he was a Native ... one who clearly still followed the traditional ways."

"And that was Lusio?"

"Yes, Lusio ... although I did not yet know his name. When he spoke, it was in Spanish. 'You cannot kill a coyote twice,' he said to me. I replied, 'I am a shepherd. I am only doing my job.'

'He is a coyote. He is only doing his,' Lusio replied. I cursed him and told him to go away before I took my *cayado* to him, too. He just shrugged, said I was the one he had been looking for, and then asked me why I was so angry."

Shane realizes that Beñat asked him the very same question. *Mind you,* he tells himself, *I wasn't beating the crap out of a dead coyote at the time.*

"I was surprised," Beñat continues, "and perhaps because he surprised me so, or because I was ashamed by what he saw me doing to the poor coyote, or because I had spoken to no one for a long, long time, I let him approach, and I listened to what he said. He was from the Zuni people and was what we would call a shaman or medicine man. Some might also call him a sorcerer, although he did not use any of these words himself. He told me there was no good word outside his own language for what he was. We spent many days and nights together. Lusio led me on a dream quest to the hidden world that was all around me, and he taught me how to untie myself from my anger."

Beñat pauses and stares into his mug for a few seconds, as if something is revealing itself there. Finally he lifts his head and grins. "I will not bother you with all the little details of my long journey to becoming enlightened, but I can tell you that Lusio taught me to laugh at the world, and to be at peace. So, the day before the rancher who made me his slave was to arrive for his monthly delivery, I counted out a number of sheep that I felt was a fair payment to me for my years of slavery, and for the remaining sheep I built a pen where I left them safely for their new shepherd. Then Lusio brought me and my new flock here, to live in freedom and without fear."

"Without fear? Dude! What do you suppose that rancher will do if he finds you? At best, he'll send you back to live out your days in a Spanish prison. But he sounds like a mean son of a bitch who might do worse, like hurt, or even kill you, and who the hell would even know?"

"That was twenty years ago, Shane, and as you can see, this rancher, Señor Mack Black, has not located me, and he will not. I explained to you before, this canyon and its pueblo are protected ... by magic."

"Magic? You really expect me to believe that?"

"I simply tell you what is true. If you do not believe, that is your concern. Over four hundred years ago, the Spanish came through this region, forcing their will and their religion upon the people. Have you heard of the *conquistador* Oñate — or, in full, Don Juan de Oñate y Salazar? He was a very, very cruel man. One time, when the local natives revolted, he ordered the right foot to be cut off from dozens of prisoners as punishment for this resistance. Many pueblos were destroyed by the soldiers of Oñate, but this — this was a sacred place, so the holy men made a great magic to protect it. It can never be found, except by those who are admitted by a guardian."

"It doesn't look that special. When was the last time anyone even lived here? I mean, before you," Shane says, feeling the need to push back against all the nonsensical talk of magic.

"Spirits live here, Shane. And now it is my home, as well. I am very happy here — finally at peace. But Lusio has explained that I am like water in a stream that flows onward, and he has given me a mission to complete. And you are the key to that."

"Look. Let me talk to this Lusio guy. I think there's been some kind of mistake. I'm not the guy you're looking for. I mean, it's a million-to-one shot I'm even here, you know? I don't believe in destiny and all that crap. It's just plain dumb luck."

Another hoot of merriment erupts from Beñat. Shane has to admit that if nothing else, the little old shepherd certainly seems to be sitting with his bum firmly planted on the bright side of life. Of course, maybe the loneliness has simply driven him around the bend.

"Talking to him will be difficult," Beñat chortles. "Lusio's ashes were scattered to the winds two winters ago. He walks in another world now. That is why he now only speaks to me through the animals … or sometimes in my dreams. But you will understand much more when you take your own dream quest. We have some hours before the sun sets and the boy goes to sleep. Then we can begin."

"Begin what?"

"The ceremony. Like the one Lusio did for me. It is a sacred tradition, older than these walls. A journey of the inside mind … of the spirit. You are lost. You must find yourself."

"Yeah, right. Look, Beñat, I like you and all, so please don't take this the wrong way, but I'm really not into all that weird-ass spiritual stuff."

"The choice is yours. Stay for supper and think about it. I will go and prepare the peyote anyway."

"Peyote! Well hell, Old Timer, why didn't you just say so? Sure. Why the hell not? Let's go tripping."

TWENTY-FOUR

Darkness washes across the valley, and eventually an over-sized moon slides over to hang in the slash of sky visible from the canyon. Beñat and Shane sit cross-legged in front of a large firepit on the terrace outside the shepherd's abode, chatting lightly about past hockey exploits as they watch the flames licking and squirming before them, teased by a lazy evening breeze. Vern is sound asleep in one of the nearby adobe buildings, perhaps dreaming of hockey exploits of his own.

"It is time," Beñat finally announces and stands up. "We begin the ceremony by honouring the earth, the sky, and the four directions of the wind." Shane smirks — it is the sort of new-age neo-paganism he has been anticipating — but he rises and plays along. Still, although he is only humouring the old shepherd, when they turn toward the north, which is where the breeze is coming from tonight, Shane actually feels the wind's presence, going so far as to whisper, "Well, hello, old buddy." During his early boyhood it was the north wind he watched for in the fall, since it brought down the Arctic cold that spawned the ice for hockey. That was when he still played on the back-yard rink that his dad painstakingly flooded for him, long before the journey to progressively larger arenas with artificial ice and hockey all summer long.

Beñat pushes a handful of some brown herbal substance into Shane's hand, puzzling him. He knows it is not the peyote — he watched that being prepared earlier that afternoon, marvelling at how much work was involved. He had assumed you simply ate the peyote buttons as they were, and was amazed by Beñat's elaborate process of cutting, mashing, pulping, and cooking the cactus into a soup.

"Tobacco," Beñat explains, reading Shane's confusion at the stuff in his hand.

"Uh, thanks, but I don't smoke."

"Not for you … for the spirits. An offering," the shepherd replies, indicating the tobacco should be thrown into the fire. Shane complies — the tobacco generates a whoosh of excited flame — and is instructed to sit down again. Now Beñat passes over one of the small clay bowls containing the peyote, keeping the other for himself. "Drink this — all of it — and wait for the other world to reveal itself to you. Open your heart and call for your spirit guide to come and show you the path."

Shane puts the bowl to his lips and drinks. His first reaction upon tasting the peyote is that he wants to spit it out. He can't recall ever tasting anything quite so awful, even with all the honey he saw added to it, but Beñat smiles and gently urges him to persevere. Shane chokes down the rest of the repulsive con-coction, screwing up his face in disgust as he sets down the bowl.

"Yuck! That's horrible!" he complains, but Beñat does not appear to be listening. Having consumed the contents of his own bowl, the Basque has closed his eyes. He begins a guttural chant from deep in his throat. Shane turns to stare into the frenetic flames, waiting for the drug to kick in. All of a sudden a violent spasm shakes his stomach, and he pitches forward to vomit into the firepit.

"Good, good," Beñat says. "That is you releasing all the bad things from your past." He smiles and resumes his singing. Shane rolls over onto his side and curls into a ball until the queasiness goes away. A couple more paroxysms rock his system, but these quickly pass, and soon he finds the nausea being replaced by a tingling euphoria.

He opens his eyes. The fire appears to have grown higher and more animated, with hues more vibrant than any he has seen before. The flames begin dancing in tune to Beñat's chanting. Shane sits up and sways in union with the sight and sound. He feels warm and safe, as though the huge rock dome overhanging the pueblo village is shielding him from all the ills of the universe. The shadows cast onto the dome by the rooftop fire resemble dancers, as if hidden inhabitants of the abandoned houses have come out to join the celebration. He feels wonderful — lighter, younger, freer — like he has slipped out of his broken and battle-ravaged body and become a creature of pure spirit. "Okay, spirit guide," he whispers. "Come and get me."

His friend the north wind stirs perceptibly, bringing with it scents from across the canyon. Their richness washes over Shane like a breaking wave, and amid the delightful deluge, he imagines he can pick out the individual smells of the canyon's animals, plants, soil, and rocks. It seems to be coming to him not so much through his nose, but via his mouth — he opens his lips and flicks his tongue into the night air, tasting it.

Above him, the moon is pulsating with luminosity and tossing off spiralling satellites of electric colour that pinwheel through the sky in a cosmic fireworks display. Some of the lights detach themselves from the heavens and come fluttering down to flit around Shane. It all reminds him of the laser light shows projected onto the ice at big league hockey games.

"Ladies and gentlemen, tonight's first star ... *la première étoile* ... number thirteen, Shane 'Bronco' Bronkovsky," he calls out in his best over-the-top arena announcer's voice. In his head comes a roar of approval from the unseen spirits of the canyon.

"Way to go, Bronk!" a voice calls out, and then a figure forms in the flames and towers above him. It is a giant bear, pure white, standing upright on its hind legs. Shane assumes this is some sort of drug-spawned hallucination, although, like the moment itself, the vision seems intensely real.

"Wow. Who are you?" he asks the apparition.

"A friend," the spirit bear replies.

"And what's your name, friend?"

The bear shakes its head. "I have a lot of names, but you wouldn't be able to pronounce most of them. Wait, I know one that's perfect for you. Call me Puck. I've been called that in the past."

"Are you a polar bear, Puck? If so, you're a long way from home."

"That depends on what dimension you're in, but then again, look who's talking."

"You got me there. Mind you, I don't even know where home is anymore."

"Yeah, you've managed to get yourself pretty lost."

"Can you help me? I mean, aren't you supposed to be my guide or something?"

"I can coach you, Bronk, but I can't play for you. Only you can do that. Only you can play the game. You're behind, but you can still win."

"Gee, thanks for the pep talk, Coach. I'm surprised you didn't tell me to keep my stick on the ice and my head up."

Puck laughs, revealing formidable-looking fangs that are several inches in length. "Actually, Bronk, up ahead you're going to want to keep your head down and hold your stick up high."

"I have no idea what you're talking about."

"I know. That's okay, it's not your fault. You're tied to the human world. You don't see things the way I do."

"So, what are you saying ... you can see my future?"

"I see ... *possibilities*. What I can tell you is that your yellow road first runs red, then black. But no matter where you go, Bronk, you can't run away from yourself. Let go of the anger and hurt and confusion and despair inside of you, or they will destroy you, my child. There's courage and love and strength and wisdom inside you, too. Let that guide you now. Be the wise man, not the dunce. Be content, not sad. Seek love, not hate. Be merry, not angry. Be free, not a prisoner."

In Shane's head, the dull background buzzing he has lived with for years abruptly starts to quicken in tempo and fury — it feels like his skull is about to be blown apart. He opens his mouth to scream, but instead of sound, out comes a swarm of tiny bees into the night air. As the last one tumbles out, a beautiful, quiet calm is all that's left inside, more peaceful than anything he has felt since he was a boy. The bees swirl playfully around Shane, then they join into a column that spirals up into the sky, heading directly toward a cluster of stars. He follows the swarm until it disappears from sight, and only then does he realize he is staring at the Big Dipper peeking over the canyon rim. He uses that to locate Ursa Major, one of the only constellations he still remembers from childhood sky-watching with his dad.

"Great Bear," he whispers to himself and smiles. He realizes he has not properly thanked his guide, but when he turns, Puck has returned to the flames.

x x X x x

Time has lost all its authority, and Shane has no idea how long he has been in his trance. Beñat is in exactly the same spot, and his chanting has ceased. The fire, too, is diminished. Shane, now finding the desert night chilly, adds wood to the coals and wraps himself in a blanket.

He no longer feels the peyote's psychoactive effects, but the serenity that flooded into him earlier still lingers, and his head remains clear and free of discomfort. He sits contentedly watching the flames — it's a subdued, ordinary fire, he notes, without any supernatural dimensions — and ponders what has just transpired.

Beñat stirs, and Shane looks over to see the shepherd watching him.

"You have returned," is all the old man says. He stands, grunting softly as he stretches his back and legs. "*Mon dieu.* I miss the days when it felt like there was nothing my body could not do," Beñat comments. He smiles at Shane and winks. "What a pity I had no head to go with my body then, eh, *mon ami?*"

"That was quite an experience," Shane finally comments. "Thank you. I can't explain it, but I feel like … I dunno, like I've let go of all this bad stuff inside me." He taps his casted hand softly against the side of his head. "I've had this wonky feeling in my head for years, and now it's gone, just like that."

"It was the spirits, *mon ami.* I am happy that they blessed you. Did any talk with you?"

"You're not going to believe this … then again, you probably will, but, yeah, this big-ass bear paid me a visit, and we chatted." Shane proceeds to relate his encounter with Puck. "I know it was all in my head, but, man, it sure felt real," he concludes.

Beñat smiles. "Some say *that* world is real and this one is not, for it is from the spirit world that ours was born. But, my friend, you say this bear was large and all white?"

"Yup. Like a polar bear."

"The Great White Bear is a very powerful spirit. You are fortunate to be blessed with such a guide."

"Well, no offence, but I don't feel very blessed. My crappy life is still the gift that keeps on giving. If I wasn't just tripping, and if it really was a spirit, would it have killed him to speak plainly, not in crazy, colour-coded riddles? I could use some direction right about now."

"Ah, my friend, but he did give you direction. The colours he spoke are the answer. It is part of the ancient wisdom of this place."

"How so?"

"Yellow — it means north. Red is south. It means you will go home to the north, where you came from. But first you must go south."

"Really? What about the black?"

Beñat frowns. "That only time will tell. Black means down — underground. It can also mean the place of the dead."

"You mean like a graveyard?"

Beñat shrugs. "Who is to say? With the spirits, much of their meaning is hidden."

"Great. But the bear did say that first I should go south — that seemed pretty clear. I just wish I knew how far south." Shane stares into the fire and weighs the job offer in Mexico to help coach *Los Lobos de Chihuahua* against the prospect of a life at *Rancho Crótalo*. "Did you get a message from the spirits, too, Beñat?" he asks after a while.

"With me it is not so clear. I know my place is here in these hills … even if prison was not waiting outside."

"Oh, right. The trouble back in Spain and the blackmailer you're hiding from. What was his name again?"

"Mack Black, like his father and grandfather, an easy name to remember. But he is not what concerns me."

"No? Then what?"

"I am growing old. Someone must become the next guardian of this sacred place. My heart tells me the spirits will find an answer, but still, I worry." He smiles at Shane. "At first I thought perhaps you were to be the next keeper of the canyon. Now I know it is not so, but still, I do not fully understand why you were sent here. There must be a reason. I suppose I must wait and see. But you will go south. Even to *Mexico*, perhaps?"

Shane nods. "Maybe. Hockey's all I know, and I'm a journeyman, after all. Besides, I'm too beautiful for jail."

"Be careful, my friend. We have a saying in my country. *Arrotz-herri, otso-herri.* It means, 'A foreign land is a land of wolves.'"

"Thanks for the advice. It would be okay, though. If I went to Mexico, I mean. I'd be one of them — a wolf. The team is *Lobos de Chihuahua* — the Chihuahua Wolves."

TWENTY-FIVE

S hane and Vern rise with the sun and bid Beñat and the hidden canyon goodbye. Driving home, they play another closely fought game of Bury Your Horses, but as they enter Luna County, enthusiasm for the contest seems to wane as man and boy alike becomes tangled in his thoughts. Shane sees Vern slump and fidget as they approach *Rancho Crótalo*, and given the premenstrual moodiness they left behind, Shane can empathize.

Upon their arrival, Tammy comes out to inventory and help offload the animals procured from Beñat. Although Shane knows better than to expect any public gesture of affection, he hopes for some indication that his lover missed him. But Tammy does not oblige, hardly making eye contact the entire time. When she's done, she gives Shane an enigmatic glance before turning toward the ranch house. "Thought you mighta been back yesterday," she comments over her shoulder.

That night's dinner is a sombre affair despite the ample meal of pork chops, mashed potatoes, and greens. The women of the ranch all seem withdrawn, eating with their heads down. Taking their cue from the morose adults, the kids chew back their words along with the food. Shane feels like the nexus of the uncertain mood, as if somehow the acceptance and trust he previously gained has diminished during his absence.

"How did you happen to meet that Beñat fellow?" he asks in an attempt to spark conversation. "Seems like a real hermit type, and he lives way off the beaten path, to put it mildly."

"Some Injun feller took Bobby … my husband … up there for the first time when word got around he was fixin' to start raising rattlesnakes. Me and the young 'uns been making the trip regular since Bobby passed. No way we'd be able to make a go of it without the snakes and critters he rounds up for us. All he asks in return is a box of vittles and some camp supplies. Works out pretty good for us."

"Bit of a weirdo, don't you think?"

"Weirdo? Do tell. Compared to what? A man with a wife and baby who decides he wants to wrangle rattlers and gives away his cattle? Maybe he needs to get drunk and smack a woman around some … that's certainly not considered weird around these parts."

"I like him," Gracie says, her face looking serious and grown up, like a magistrate passing judgment. "He's always laughing. And he lets me ride his burro." She turns to her mother. "Mama, if we can't have a horse, can we at least have a burro?"

Shane opens his mouth to reiterate that he is willing to cover all the expenses of a horse for Gracie, but a pre-emptive don't-you-dare look from Tammy cuts him off.

"We'll talk about it some other time, Gracie," she tells her daughter kindly but firmly. "School tomorrow. If you're done eating, then you're excused. Go fetch your homework books and we'll have a look at what needs doing."

That signals the dissolution of the dinner gathering, and Shane takes on clean-up duties in the hopes of getting a chance to talk to Tammy alone, but the opportunity never manifests itself. At the end of the evening, as he and Vern are being ushered out of the ranch house, he waits until the boy has ambled out of earshot before asking Tammy softly, "Will I see you tonight?"

There is, at least, a moment of vacillation before she shakes her head. "It's that time of the month, remember?"

"I don't care. I mean, I'm happy just to hold you. I've missed you."

"Maybe tomorrow," she murmurs in response and closes the door. Shane stands looking into the kitchen window until the interior light goes out, then he finally turns and heads to the stable.

The rattlesnakes in their cages herald his arrival with scrapes and hisses. "Fuck this," he tells them, "I'm going to get drunk." After all, first as the paramour to a teetotaler, and then as the conscientious shepherd of Vern, he has gone several days without even a beer, peyote trip notwithstanding. But when he gets back to the toolroom he discovers his bottle of liquor is empty. At first he supposes Maybelline snuck in during his absence, but then he remembers Tammy's drunken episode involving the consumption — and subsequent expulsion — of the remainder of the bottle.

Shane does, however, still have a bottle of premium mezcal gift-wrapped for Doc Sanchez. He could just drink it, given the doctor doesn't even know of its existence, but feeling the need for some sympathetic company, Shane decides to deliver the gift — and then suggest that they drink it together. When Shane starts the truck, not caring that he hasn't asked permission to borrow it, he sees a shape silhouetted at Tammy's bedroom window as he drives off.

Doc Sanchez seems genuinely delighted to see Shane, even before the mezcal is produced. The doctor rips the wrapping paper from the bottle and exclaims with delight when he sees the label. "Del Maguey Minero! You remembered."

"I've been meaning to drop it off for a while now. Sorry, I've been a little preoccupied."

"Yes, yes. The yummy Yolanda told me you'd gone to Albuquerque." Doc Sanchez winks at Shane and nudges him with his elbow. "She also said you've been doing the nasty with Tammy. Congratulations! At one time I figured that fortress was impenetrable. I assume the little blue pills have worked their magic."

"What the fuck? That's supposed to be a secret. Tammy and me, I mean."

"Ha! You think there's such a thing as a secret between three women sharing a small house? Don't worry, *amigo*. Yolanda says the children are still in the dark."

Sanchez produces two glasses and pours a hefty shot into each. "To you and Tammy," he toasts. "I have to be frank, though. I hope you're not resting on your laurels. Yolanda is skeptical your hookup will last ... no offence intended."

"So, you and Yolanda are bosom buddies now?"

"No, but I sure would love to buddy up with those bosoms." He laughs heartily at his own joke. "Actually, I have made some progress on that front. Today, we just talk. Tomorrow?" He pats his tummy and laughs again. "What woman can resist such a hunk of *machismo* for long?"

"Yeah, well, you might want to get your hunk of *machismo* to a gym, Doc ... no offence intended. Why does Yolanda think Tammy and I are iffy? Has Tammy said something?"

Sanchez frowns. "Let's just say the woman has trust issues ... and who can blame her? I saw first-hand the abuse she suffered from her husband. Many a night I got called to the ranch to treat her, and I was expected to believe she was the world's clumsiest woman, allegedly always tripping on stairs or bumping into doors."

"And you never reported it — the physical abuse?"

"I had suspicions, but that's all they were without corroboration. Tammy would never admit what really happened, at least not until after her husband got himself blown up in Iraq. But, as far as *you* and Tammy go, the gist of it is that Tammy feels you're hiding something from her ... which we both know is true. Never underestimate women's intuition."

"Yeah, I feel bad about that. I've wanted to tell her the truth, but it just never seems like the right moment. I mean, it's not exactly a great opener, is it? 'Hi, I'm one of the most hated guys in North America right now, and by the way, some yahoo DA in Chicago may charge me for murder. Want to hook up?'"

Sanchez chuckles. "Nonetheless, I would advise you to take care of that before tomorrow evening. When the shit hits the fan, it's always messy."

"What's happening tomorrow?"

"*CelebTV*, of course."

"You know about that?"

Doc Sanchez jerks his thumb toward the flatscreen television mounted to the wall above them. "Hell, yeah. They've been promoting the crap out of it all weekend. 'No-holds-barred interview with disgraced hockey goon Shane Bronkovsky. Monday night, exclusively on *CelebTV*.' Frankly, I'm surprised you'd take that chance. They're shamelessly sycophantic panderers most of the time, unless they go after someone for ratings ... then their jaundiced journalism is like doing surgery with a screwdriver. The patient always dies a gruesome death."

Shane shrugs. "They're paying really, really well, and I need the money. Besides, I got a chance to tell my side of the story. How bad can it be?"

Doc Sanchez's derisive laugh gives the answer. "This is *CelebTV* we're talking about. Trust me, there'll be no 'my side of the story' by the time they get through with you."

"Who cares what people think? Half of them are already after my head anyway," Shane says, and shoots back the rest of his mezcal. He is not as blasé as he is trying to sound, however, as he recalls the way he was verbally ambushed in the studio.

Sanchez refills Shane's glass. "And what about Tammy?" he asks. "Do you care what she thinks?"

"She won't see it, though, will she? I mean, there's no TV or internet at the ranch."

Doc Sanchez shakes his head sadly. "Shane, Shane, Shane. For someone who's performed in the media spotlight, you're pretty naive when it comes to appreciating the intensity of that spotlight's glare. We're not talking about a Northern sports story anymore. No, sir, *CelebTV* has tens of millions of viewers. Sooner or later, Tammy *will* find out, if only through the grapevine. I think it should be sooner, and it should come from you."

Shane swirls the mezcal in his glass, studying the liquor's eddies as if a solution to his dilemma might be hiding there. "You're right, Doc. Tomorrow, when the kids are at school, I'll tell her everything. Like I said, I've been meaning to do it for a while now."

"*Buena fortuna, amigo.* I'll be rooting for you. I hope it works out, I really do. But — and sorry if I sound like the voice of gloom and doom here — what are you going to do if it all goes south?"

"You mean if Tammy gives me the boot?"

"Well, there's that, but I was thinking more along the lines of what'll you do if they charge you with Linton's death? Will you go back to stand trial?"

"Don't see that I'll have a choice."

"Of course you'll have a choice. When things go south you can always go south."

"You mean Mexico?"

"Exactly. Don Aléjandro is hoping there are no hard feelings, now that you've got your motorcycle back, and that you'll help coach *Los Lobos*. You did promise us an answer soon."

"I guess it would beat hiding out in the mountains for the rest of my life."

"It would be perfect for you, Shane. At least come and check out the new arena. Technically, it's the off-season for *La Liga*, but we're paying our new recruits to practise all summer ... get a leg up on next year. That's how serious we are about building a top-notch team. You could meet the guys, watch them skate ... you know, get a feel for things. What do you say?"

"That psycho Enrique isn't involved with the team in any way, is he, Doc?"

"He's too busy with other business to concern himself with *Los Lobos*. Look, I'm his godfather. I've known him since he was a little crybaby filling his diapers. Trust me. I know how to handle him."

Shane recalls the crazed look on Enrique's face as he put a gun to Shane's head out on the highway. "Somehow I doubt it, Doc."

"Don Aléjandro considers the matter between you and his son closed. You're under his protection now. In this precarious world, Shane, there are worse places to be, believe me."

Shane's face must betray his skepticism, because the doctor tops up their glasses and tactfully changes subjects. "Will you be watching your big *CelebTV* broadcast tomorrow night? You're welcome to catch it here."

"Thanks, but no thanks. I never watch my own interviews. I hate the way I look on camera, even when they're *not* doing a hatchet job on me. No, hopefully I'll be having dinner as usual at the ranch."

"Rattlesnake fillet?" the doctor asks, a grin cleaving his face. He holds up his glass. "I don't know how you can handle it without a stiff drink."

"Actually, now that I'm springing for the groceries, the menu has improved a helluva lot. Next I'm thinking of buying one of those big-ass stainless-steel grills. Then I'll be grilling big thick steaks every night."

"Careful, *amigo*. As your doctor, I must advise you that too much red meat is bad for you. Say what you will about rattle-snake, it's lean and low in cholesterol."

TWENTY-SIX

I t is afternoon by the time Shane gets a chance to approach Tammy alone out in the stable. This is just as well, given he is nursing a Category 3 hangover and is having trouble working up the courage to confess his troubles to her.

"You were out late last night," she says before he has a chance to compose his opening remarks. Her back is turned to him as she repairs the latch on one of the snake cages.

"Doctor's appointment," he answers. It is meant to be light-hearted, but comes across as evasive.

"Do tell. I guess that liquor I'm smelling on you was taken for medicinal purposes, huh?"

"Doc Sanchez and I had a few drinks, sure. As a matter of fact, he offered me a job."

"He gonna dress you up in a short skirt with white stockings and make you his nurse?"

"Very funny. Actually, he offered me an assistant coaching job with his Mexican League hockey team."

"The *Lobos*? Shane, do you know who owns that team?"

He shrugs. "If I'd worried about the moral character of all my team owners, my hockey career would have been a short one. But, speaking of my career, I need to tell you something —"

"The man's a *narco*. Do you have any idea what that means?"

"I'm not stupid, Tammy. Of course I know what that means."

"No, I don't think you do. This was a quiet, law-abiding town until their drug money snuck across the border, and our mayor, police chief, and city manager done got caught up in it. I thank the Lord Almighty we have the wall to help keep that filth and their violence and drugs out of the U.S. of A."

"The drugs are coming across anyway, despite the wall, and you know why? Because the U.S. *wants* them, that's why. We create the demand. They just fill it."

"Who cares about a bunch of heroin junkies? We should round 'em all up and ship *them* behind the wall ... it would serve 'em right."

"Heroin? That's only a tiny part of it. There's coke, and pot, and ecstasy — all the party drugs. The kids, their parents, their teachers, businessmen, cops, senators ... hell, everybody does it, Tammy."

"Well, *I* don't do drugs, and I won't tolerate anyone who does." Her eyes, to this point narrowed in determination, suddenly open wide. "Great balls of fire! You ain't just drinking ... you're doing drugs, too, ain't ya?"

"Of course not." It is technically true. Shane long ago exhausted what little cocaine and marijuana were left in his bag. Still, his conscience starts to pulse. It occurs to him that for something that started out as an attempt to come clean with Tammy, the conversation has stumbled off the path and gotten lost in the underbrush.

Tammy has not said another word, and Shane can feel the searchlight of her scrutiny looking for telltale signs of treachery. He decides to wait for a more suitable moment to confess his predicament. He is confident that he has time. She has not seen any of the previous media sensationalism surrounding Shane and is equally unlikely to know about the *CelebTV* interview yet.

"Look, babe, the only job I really want is being your man and helping out around here. You know you can trust me, don't you?"

Tammy bites her lower lip. "I don't know what I know anymore. I hate myself for trusting you and I hate myself for not trusting you, all at the same time."

She steps closer and pounds her fists on his pectoral muscles softly, almost tenderly. Suddenly, like a fountain gushing forth, she starts bawling and presses her face into his chest, wetting the front of his T-shirt with her tears. Shane just stands there, no suitable words finding their way to his tongue. Women and their tears have always been a deep mystery, seemingly straightforward on the surface, but concealing a multidimensional maelstrom of meaning.

When several seconds go by and she is still sobbing, he begins stroking her hair gently. He is not completely sure, but it sounds like the crying ebbs somewhat, so he rubs her back. He is fairly certain the massaging is having a soothing effect, so he follows the next logical progression in his mind, sliding his hand down to caress Tammy's buttocks.

She jerks back like she's been jolted with a thousand-volt cattle prod and punches his chest again, this time with unambiguous rancour. "What the heck d'ya think you're doin'?"

"I was just trying to, you know, comfort you. Get you to stop crying. See? It worked … you're not crying now."

"You big galoot, you was trying to feel me up. I'm bawlin' my eyes out and all you can think of is to try to get it on with me?" She suddenly sends her fist flying at him — not some feeble, half-hearted swing, but an all-out attempt to injure directed at the vicinity of his head. Out of well-honed reflex Shane blocks the blow. Unfortunately, it is his injured hand that he uses to parry the punch, creating consequences for them both when Tammy's swing thuds into the plaster cast.

"Ow!" she yelps, bending over in anguish.

"Aw, fuck!" Shane grimaces as his broken arm pulses with pain.

They both stand there, groaning. When the initial rush of agony subsides to a tolerable aching throb, Shane opens his eyes. Tammy is flexing and relaxing her fist.

"You hurt me," she says with an accusatory tone.

"Girl, you hurt yourself. I was just protecting myself."

"I think it's busted," she says. "Shoot! That's all I need."

"Here, let me see." When she looks skeptical, he adds, "Trust me. I've thwacked my knuckles on more helmets than I can count."

She allows him to examine her injury. He squeezes the fingers to see if there's any lateral pain, but she doesn't express any. Before releasing her hand, he kisses her fingers. "Looks like a bruised knuckle. Put some ice on it for the next couple of days and it should be fine. If it's still giving you trouble after that, you can go have it X-rayed."

She sits staring at her hand, as though it is somebody else's. "I guess I lost my temper," she finally says, looking up at him. "But you sure ticked me off something fierce when you started pawing me like that in the middle of a good cry."

Several retorts spring to mind, but Shane wisely dekes around them, settling on what he has been taught is the only appropriate response a male can utter following an argument. "I'm sorry."

"The kids'll be getting home from school soon. D'ya mind goin' to fetch 'em? I'm gonna ice this down."

"What are you going to tell them ... about the hand, I mean?"

"I dunno, maybe I'll tell them the truth: I hurt it walloping a big doofus."

✗ ✗ ✗ ✗ ✗

Shane offers to help the injured Tammy out by cooking dinner, but Yolanda steps in to take charge instead, resulting in a low-key meal of tortillas, beans, and rice. Although the children are told Tammy's injury is due to some vague misfortune with the washing machine, Shane is certain, based on the way Yolanda is looking at him, that Tammy has told her the truth. It is not that Yolanda regards him with outright hostility, but more like she is hedging her bets, afraid her fledgling trust in him might have been a mistake.

The children, sensing the shadow over the meal, seem more interested in engaging with each other than with the adults. Watching them, Shane is convinced that a new friendship has blossomed between the pair since his arrival.

After helping to wash up, Shane leaves the uncommunicative kitchen clique to their moods and goes outside for some fresh air. It is a clear, warm night, and an almost-full moon lights the horizon, a half veil of thin clouds diffusing its light. He walks over to his Ducati and sits down on its seat to stare up into the sky, trying to find a point of balance for his teetering emotions. Behind them comes the squeak of the screen door followed by a slam as someone exits the ranch house.

He turns to see Yolanda walking toward him. She comes over and starts squeezing the controls of the motorcycle, making neither eye contact nor conversation.

Shane breaks the silence. "How's Tammy's hand?" he asks.

Yolanda shrugs. "She says it hurts. Worried she might have broken something."

Shane knocks on the plaster of his cast. "This is hard, but not *that* hard. Her punch kind of glanced off. It's not totally impossible that she has a hairline fracture of the proximal phalange or metacarpus, but I think it's just a subperiosteal hematoma — a bone bruise."

Yolanda clucks her tongue. "Does Sanchez know you're invading his turf?"

Shane smiles and shows her the discoloured, oversized index knuckles on his right hand. "Tools of the trade."

The sight seems to unsettle Yolanda, and she steps back from him. "Didn't she tell you what happened?" Shane asks. "She started it."

"And you just finished it, is that it?"

"It wasn't like that. She was punching at me and hit the cast. What are you saying, if a man hits a woman he's a monster, but if a woman comes after a guy he's just supposed to take it?"

She shrugs. "Maybe … if the guy's as big as you. What were you two fighting about, anyway?"

"It started with her being pissed about me going out for a few drinks last night. I honestly don't know how it went off the tracks after that. Maybe she's PMSing."

"Careful, *hombre*, we get to use that as an excuse — you don't. Anyway, she doesn't seem to be holding a grudge, so I guess I won't, either. It's just, we've been through a lot, the three of us. I hope we haven't made a mistake, you know, letting you into our lives. We'll see … until today, I didn't think so."

There's another slam, and Maybelline comes dancing out to join them.

"*Shame, shame. Blame Shane for the pain,*" she sings. "*He's afraid of a punching bag, just because she's on the rag. Tick-tock, the see-through Doc. X marks the ray, today, today, today.*"

Shane glances at Yolanda. "Lord help me," he says, "I think I'm learning to speak Maybelline." He turns back to the redhead. "Tammy wants her hand X-rayed pronto?"

Maybelline's answer is an exaggerated bow at the waist and an Elvis impersonation. "Thank you, uh, thank you very much."

Shane goes inside to check on the patient. While he remains convinced the injury is not serious, he doesn't begrudge Tammy her desire for medical attention. She is sitting at the kitchen table with an ice pack on her hand watching Vern, who is helping Gracie with her arithmetic homework.

"Really hurts, huh?" Shane asks sympathetically. She nods, not looking up. He tries to examine her hand but she shakes her head, keeping it under the ice pack.

"Okay. Should we call the doc?"

"He don't usually come out at night, less'n it's life or death. I figured since you're such a buddy of his now, you could drive me out to see him. It'll beat going all the way to Deming and sitting around in the emerg."

"Sure. What about the kids?"

"It's Gracie's bedtime, anyway," she says — as much an announcement as a reply. "I'll tuck her in and meet ya outside. Figured you could drive. I ain't up to it."

Outside, Yolanda announces she will accompany them. Shane wonders whether the Chicana is now reluctant to leave him alone with Tammy, or is seizing the opportunity to visit Doc Sanchez. The threesome pile into the truck and drive down to the border.

As they pull up, interior lights and the flickering of a TV screen indicate the doctor is at home. Shane has a brief moment of panic that his *CelebTV* interview might be on, then figures that since the show broadcasts from the Eastern Time Zone, it must be long over.

They approach the van, and Shane knocks on the door. Doc Sanchez throws open the door and bellows in greeting. "Shane! Speak of the devil. Bad news, *amigo*, you're all over the news. It's official, you've been charged with manslaughter." Then he sees that Shane is not alone. "Oh. *Buenas noches, señoras.*"

"What's he talking about, Shane?" Tammy asks. It's clear from her tone that whatever isthmus of goodwill the couple has been tiptoeing across has been abruptly swept away.

"You didn't tell her?" Sanchez asks. He smiles at Yolanda. "I told him to tell her, really I did. I'm all about honesty in a relationship."

"Tell me what?" Tammy demands.

"I was involved in an accident in a hockey game in Chicago, and now the District Attorney is charging me. I'll explain everything later. Let's get you taken care of first." He urges her inside. "Tammy's hurt her hand, Doc. We were hoping you could do an X-ray. I'll cover the expenses."

"I don't need your money," Tammy spits out. "Besides, sounds like you're going to need all your dough for a lawyer."

An all-news network is playing, and the doctor goes to turn the TV off. "Leave it," Tammy insists. "Might be something interesting on." Her words drip with sarcasm. The doctor flashes Shane an apologetic look and goes about his examination.

Four people make for a tight fit in the mobile clinic, so Shane goes to sit in the passenger seat while Yolanda squeezes onto a stool offered by the doctor. The news channel has moved on to international coverage, but Shane knows from experience that they will soon come back around to any juicy story.

"How did it happen?" Sanchez asks as he studies Tammy's hand.

"I was trying to punch this one here in the head and he blocked me with his cast." The doctor cocks an eyebrow but stays silent. "Didn't know plaster could be so goddanged hard," she adds. "Hurts like heck."

"My special mixture," Sanchez comments with pride. "Let's see if I'll have to mix up another batch for you."

As the doctor moves the X-ray machine into position, Tammy turns to look at Shane. "So? Do you want to explain what's goin' on?"

"Here? Now? In front of the others?"

"*He* already seems to know all about it, and *she* sure as Moses should."

"Look, it's just like I told you. It happened during a hockey game a few weeks ago. Me and another player collided. The guy fell and smacked his head on the ice. He died, but I swear to God, Tammy, it was a freak accident."

"Then how come they're charging you?"

"The guy that died was a big star, and now some DA is looking to capitalize on that and make a name for himself ... at least that's how it seems to me."

"How come you didn't tell me?"

"I was trying to put it all behind me, all right? My team ... the league ... they pretty much threw me out with the garbage. That's how I ended up down here in the first place. Then when I first met you, well, it's not exactly the first thing that comes out of your mouth under the circumstances, is it?"

"But you still kept it from me after we ... you know."

"I wanted to tell you, Tammy, I really did. I was trying to tell you earlier today when you ... um ... when we had our little spiff."

"I told him he should tell you," Doc Sanchez interjects.

"You're not helping, Doc," Shane hisses. Anger is stirring, and he needs to take it out on someone.

"Tryin' ain't doin', Mister," Tammy fires back. She is clearly wrestling with the reins of her own wrath. "Don't you think I deserved to know what kind of man was sleeping under my roof?"

"The same man I was ten minutes ago … but I'm not exactly sleeping under your roof, am I? You kick me and Vern out every night and lock the door, like you're putting the dogs out."

"Don't get sassy with me, Mister. You know what I mean." Now she turns on Doc Sanchez, who has been sitting back, watching the exchange. "Well, what in tarnation am I paying you for? Is it busted or ain't it?" The doctor frowns and turns to consult a computer monitor nestled in the middle of his medical gear. He works the mouse and leans closer until his nose is practically touching the screen.

"There's no sign of any fracture," he proclaims after several seconds of intense scrutiny. "The knuckle bone's badly bruised. Just keep icing it, and take some extra-strength Tylenol for the pain. Or I can write you a prescription, if you want something a little stronger."

"I don't need no pills makin' me stupid, thanks just the same, Doc. I'm a woman — I reckon I was born to hurt." Yolanda snickers at that one.

"Have it your way," the doctor replies. "I'll submit the paperwork. You're not, in fact, paying me, though. Bobby's GI insurance will cover it. You can go now, if you want. We're done."

Tammy shoots him a look but says nothing. She rises to her feet and turns to face Shane. "I want to believe you, Big Hoss, I want to trust you." She lets the words hang.

"Then do. Trust your —"

"Don't say it. Don't say *heart*. Right now my heart feels like it's been stomped by a Brahma bull, and my head's spinning like that bull just took it for a ride at the rodeo. If my hand wasn't so sore I swear I'd punch you in the nose."

"I have some Percocet that will take care of that pain in no time," Doc Sanchez interjects.

"You're not helping, Doc," Shane growls again.

"Oh, take a Valium. I can write a prescription for that, too. I'm just trying to lighten things up. This is too painful to watch. Look, both of you, I'm not saying this isn't a serious situation. Shane, what with everything Tammy's been through, you can't expect her to just shrug this off. Trust is easily broken and more easily bruised. But, Tammy ... I realize I've only known Shane a short while, but despite what you might think of me, I'm a good judge of character. I can tell you this man is just an oversized pussycat. More importantly, he deeply, genuinely cares about you ... all of you. As for the incident, I've watched the footage several times, and it's pretty obvious to me that it was an accident. I'm ninety percent certain Shane will never get convicted ... even if he is, I'm equally certain he won't go to prison."

Shane feels the floor lurch beneath him, as if the van is suddenly moving. Until this moment, he hasn't seriously entertained the possibility that he might go to prison.

"You don't really think I'll actually do any time, do you?" he asks weakly.

"No ... as long as you don't get a jury of Blackhawks fans. But what do I know? I'm a doctor, not a lawyer."

Yolanda has not said a word since entering the mobile clinic. Now she reaches into her blouse and pulls out her *Santa Muerte* necklace. She kisses the grinning skull on its mouth, then hangs the medallion around Shane's neck. "Here. I think you may need this more than I do."

At that moment, the grinding wheel of television journalism comes full circle. "And now, our top story," the anchorwoman announces from the screen above them. A highly unflattering photo of Shane appears on screen, complete with black eye and missing teeth. "Former Columbus Blue Jackets player Shane Bronkovsky has been charged with manslaughter in the death of Chicago Blackhawks star Kenny Linton during a hockey game at United Center earlier this month. We warn viewers that they may find some of the footage they are about to see disturbing. We go now to our crime specialist, Bill Maloney, reporting live from Chicago."

Shane is almost relieved that Tammy will see the incident first-hand and be able to judge for herself. The fatal accident is shown from multiple camera angles, then the report cuts to the press conference held less than an hour earlier where the charges were formally announced.

A reporter asks from off camera whether the charges were sparked by the episode of *CelebTV* that aired earlier this evening, and the DA looks displeased. "Absolutely not," he asserts, then hastily leaves the podium.

Despite the prosecutor's assertion, the news report nonetheless cites the *CelebTV* episode as if it was the groundbreaking piece of investigative journalism that cracked the case, even rebroadcasting some of the more salacious footage as if it was fact. Shane's feelings quickly disintegrate into horror that Tammy is seeing it all. The reporter paints Shane as a known substance abuser and violent brawler, though he is experienced enough to tack the work *alleged* onto every accusation.

The coup de grace is the sound bite from Brandi, Shane's ex-girlfriend, accusing him of abuse. Not a single word of Shane's side of the story appears. The report concludes by saying that police in Columbus, Ohio, are investigating whether additional charges of domestic assault should be filed.

If Shane didn't know the truth, he would figure himself for a monster after that heavy-handed coverage.

Tammy, having no such inner knowledge, has clearly bought into the TV version. "I trusted you!" she exclaims.

"Tammy, I swear I'm not who they're making me out to be."

"And what about your wife? Is she lying, too?"

"That wasn't my wife, that's the woman I was sharing a condo with in Columbus. And, yeah, as a matter of fact, she's lying through her teeth and probably getting paid to do it. I swear to God, Tammy, I never laid a hand on her … at least not like that."

"What's that supposed to mean?"

"It's just, you know, she liked it rough … during sex, I mean."

"'She was asking for it.' 'She liked it rough.' That's what men always say. It's never their fault. No, sir, I can't believe you." She points at the screen, which has mercifully gone on to cover the latest legislative dysfunction in Washington. "It was on the news!"

"Just because it's on TV doesn't make it true."

"Well, just because you say it, that sure as shootin' don't make it true." She lowers her voice, and a ridge of tension runs along her jaw. "If I can trouble you for the keys, Yolanda and I are going home now."

"Tammy, please … I love you." Shane's words are desperate. He doesn't even know if they're true.

"No, don't you dare! Don't start with 'I love you' or 'I swear I'll change.' I've heard it all before and it don't cut custard with me. Now, are you gonna give me the keys or ain't ya?"

Shane fishes through his pocket for the keys and hands them over. Tammy makes no move to take them, as if she is reluctant to even come close to Shane. It is Yolanda who leans over to take them from Shane's hand. There is no anger in her brown eyes, just a vague sort of world-weary sadness.

"How do you expect me to get home?" Shane asks.

"I don't care. But even if you crawl, get one thing straight: it ain't your home and never will be. I expect you to clear out tomorrow."

Tammy exits, and Yolanda climbs off the stool to go with her. At the door, the Chicana turns and opens her mouth to say something to Shane, but ultimately just sighs and shakes her head. "*Buenas noches*, Frank," she says to Doc Sanchez instead.

"*Hasta pronto*, Yolanda."

For a few minutes, neither man says anything. Shane fights back tears. Doc Sanchez eventually gets up to turn off the television, then he starts rummaging through a cupboard. He emerges with a half-full bottle of tequila, which he hands to Shane.

"As your doctor, I should warn you that alcohol is a depressant. As your friend, I advise you to take a few big slugs of this, and go ahead and cry."

TWENTY-SEVEN

Doc Sanchez offers to drive him to the ranch the next morning, but Shane chooses to walk instead. It is blossoming into a beautiful spring day, and he has a hornet's nest of buzzing thoughts to sort through.

The two men stand outside the mobile clinic, heads down, each awkwardly searching for words. Finally, Shane looks up and says quietly, "Look, Doc, do you mind if I keep my options open on that coaching job for a couple more days? I'm, you know ... still figuring stuff out."

Sanchez shrugs. "What's a few more days? But a word of advice, *amigo*, whatever you decide, take control of your life. Don't let other people shape your destiny."

"Thanks, Doc ... for everything." Sanchez looks at the hand being offered and wraps Shane in a hug instead. After a while, Shane reluctantly unwraps himself from the comforting contact. "*Hasta luego*, Doc," he says and turns toward the highway.

"Hang tough, Shane," the doctor calls after him.

× × ✖ × ×

When Shane turns off the main highway onto the county road that leads to the ranch, his thoughts and resolve are no closer to crystallizing. The sun gains some altitude, and with it the day heats up. He is reminded of his first day here, just after he crashed his Ducati. For some reason, he thinks of the gangly, oddly attired teenager who robbed him not far from where Shane is walking at the moment.

Once he got his stuff back, Shane put the incident out of his mind. For the first time — perhaps due to a newly acquired empathy for fugitives — Shane gives the boy's fate some deeper thought. He remembers the deputy's belief that the youngster had been run off by the polygamous elders of the renegade Mormon congregation, Holy Waters, who didn't want competition for the young girls. Shane recollects how he screamed in rage after the boy robbed him, and the threats of bodily harm he yelled at the fleeing youth. Now he feels profoundly sorry for the teenager. "Poor little fish out of Waters," he comments aloud, shaking his head sadly. If Enrique, that twisted son of Don Aléjandro's, had caught up with the fugitive, homelessness and dispossession would have been the least of the boy's problems.

Shane reaches the ranch glazed with perspiration. Not wanting to face Tammy a sweaty mess, he goes behind the stable to pump some water for washing up. As he stands to let the sun and air dry him, he thinks of all the projects and improvements around the ranch he still was planning to undertake. It seems so unfair — not just to him, but also to the ranch — to be denied the chance to complete the work. It is like being sent to the dressing room while a game is still in progress.

When Shane comes back around the stable, Yolanda and Maybelline are standing there waiting for him, but Tammy is nowhere in sight.

"At least you're not toting your shotgun," he jokes to Yolanda as he approaches them. "Even so, I guess there's no chance she's changed her mind and I can stay?"

The Chicana shakes her head. "Not a snowball's chance in hell. She's acting all tough, but she don't fool us … you really done a number on her." Shane opens his mouth to protest, but Yolanda raises her hand to silence him. "I know you didn't mean to, that's the only reason you and me are still talking, but you hurt her real bad, and that's a fact."

Maybelline steps up to him and stretches onto her tiptoes to kiss him gently on the cheek. "Goodbye, Shane. Nice knowin' ya." The fact that she makes her farewell without spins or pirouettes or little snatches of silly verse makes the moment feel as sombre as a funeral.

"Where is she? I have to talk to her."

"It's no use," Yolanda insists, but he's already gone to find Tammy. The front door is locked, and when he goes around back to the kitchen, that entrance is shut as well.

He taps on the window and calls out, "Tammy! Open up, let's talk about this." When there is no answer, he starts rapping sharply on the glass with the back of his plaster cast. A shape becomes visible inside — Tammy approaches the door, but doesn't unlock it.

"Go away. Take your stuff out of the stable and leave, or so help me, I'll call the sheriff." She turns her back on him and disappears again.

He gives up, but now anger has taken hold. As he heads to the stable, he hoofs the dirt, upturns a wheelbarrow, knocks over a rake, and tosses a bucket across the compound. Entering the stable, he gives the old wooden door a few kicks for good measure, and on his way to the toolroom to gather his possessions, he thumps every post he passes, agitating the rattlesnakes in their wire cages.

"Aw, shut the fuck up!" he tells the rows of snake eyes watching him. "I'm not afraid of you fucking snakes!" He steps forward and starts shaking the stacked up pens. Suddenly he imagines hearing a voice, Puck's voice, counselling him not to be angry, not to vent his frustration on the blameless serpents. When he stops, it is like a fever breaking, but it is too late.

The end cage tumbles off the wobbling stack onto the ground. Its door springs open, and a large rattlesnake starts to slither out. In a panic, Shane reaches for the cage door, hoping to prevent it from escaping, but as he does so, the viper lunges toward his hand. So fast does the rattler move that Shane feels the bite before his vision registers it. The snake recoils after striking, and Shane has the presence of mind to slam the cage door shut before letting out a wail and rushing out of the stable.

"Help! Somebody help me!" he screams. "A snake bit me!"

Yolanda and Maybelline are digging in the garden. They exchange a look, but don't even put down their tools.

"Tammy!" Maybelline calls toward the house.

"Yeah, yeah, I heard," a voice shouts back. "Land's sake, how could I *not* hear?"

The realization soaks in that the women mean to let him die, and the idea has a surprisingly calming effect. He wonders if it will be painful. He sinks to his knees and closes his eyes. His thoughts flutter to the other tough guys he's battled on the ice over the years. A number of those fellow enforcers are now dead, including three who took their own lives. The hockey world has closed ranks and denied the deaths are related, but his beat-up brain knows better. Hasn't he himself contemplated suicide, after all? *Perhaps this is for the best*, he thinks. *My life's basically over, anyway.*

But, no, the truth is Shane wants to live. Even though his past has caught up with him and destroyed his fantasy of a life on the ranch with Tammy and the kids, he has experienced something profound over the last few weeks. It is as if he was lost in the woods and spotted a path to salvation.

"Please, I don't want to die," he sniffles.

"Oh stop it, ya big baby, no one's gonna die," Tammy's voice says, and he looks up to see her staring down at him impassively. "Yolanda, go git the snakebite kit, will ya?" she calls out and bends down to inspect the wound. "Which one got ya?" she asks Shane.

"The really big one on top ... in the end cage."

"Good," she replies.

"Can't say I blame you for wanting to see me hurt."

"No, stupid, good 'cause that's a fully growed Diamondback. The old ones store up more venom but don't tend to waste it less'n they got to. It's the young 'uns you gotta look out for ... ain't learned to control themselves yet. Good thing it wasn't one of the littler species, like those tiger rattlers Beñat caught. They'll pump some nasty juice in ya." She drops his hand. "Looks like a dry bite ... no venom. Just trying to warn you off, I reckon. Besides, we milked 'em not long ago."

Shane looks down at the bite, which is turning purple around the puncture marks. He doesn't understand how Tammy can be so dismissive. "That's it? What if you're wrong? What if it did squirt some poison in me? How long before I die? Shouldn't I get a shot of antivenom just to be safe?"

She shakes her head. "Big Hoss, you got it wrong. I ain't sayin' a rattler can't kill you, but it ain't likely. More people in these parts die from bee stings than snakebite."

Yolanda shows up with a small case that she hands to Tammy, who hesitates before opening it. "All right, I'll give you a shot. I was just trying to save some cash. This stuff ain't cheap, but I reckon you've been generous enough with your money ... if not the truth." She extracts a syringe from the kit and administers the injection — more roughly than necessary, in Shane's estimation.

"How the heck did you get bit, anyway?" she asked.

"Knocked the cage over and the snake tried to get out. It was an accident."

"An accident, you say. I heard you yelling and cursing in there, Big Hoss. I've been on the receiving end of those kinds of 'accidents' too many times."

"Tammy, I'm sorry, about everything. Mostly I'm sorry I didn't tell you everything up front about my … you know, my situation. But you have to believe me, I'm not a criminal, and I never hit my girlfriend, I swear."

"Doesn't matter. Maybe you're telling the truth, maybe you ain't. I can't take that chance. Got my girls to think of." She rises and is about to turn away, but instead hikes up her skirt above the knee and tilts her leg slightly sideways. Shane makes out the faded white dual scars of a puncture wound. "Bit once, twice shy," she whispers.

✖ ✖ ✖ ✖ ✖

It takes Shane barely two minutes to pack. He carries his meagre possessions outside to stuff in the saddlebags of the Ducati and in his backpack. His connection to the ranch has become so intense and profound that it feels surreal to sever it so easily.

He starts the motorcycle's engine, dons his helmet, and climbs aboard. Fortunately the throttle and one of the brakes are on the right grip; otherwise he'd have no chance of piloting the bike with a broken hand. As long as he goes slow and avoids any sudden movements, he should be okay. Taking one last woeful look around the crooked structures and the mesquite-filled landscape, Shane leaves *Rancho Crótalo*.

As he exits onto the county road, he catches a flash of motion and hears his name being yelled. A figure comes scrambling out from behind some bushes and begins chasing the Ducati. Shane brakes and turns to see Vern running after him.

"Shane! Shane! Wait up!" the youngster is shouting.

Shane dismounts and walks back to the boy. "Vern, what are you doing here? You're supposed to be in school."

The boy wraps Shane in a desperate hug. "Don't go, Shane. Please don't go." Tears are welling up in Vern's eyes. "Maybe Gracie and me can talk to Aunt Tammy and get her to let you stay. Please, Shane, I don't want you to leave. I ... I don't want to be alone there again."

Shane tilts the boy's head back and looks him in the eye. "Hey, buddy. You're not alone ... they're your family. They love you."

"They hate me. They're always picking on me ... at least they did until you came along. That's why you need to stay."

Shane has to fight back the tears that are starting to mist his own eyes. "I can't stay, Vern. I was really only passing through. I have to go back to my own life."

"Then take me with you. You said I was a good helper ... I could do that. I could help you."

"Aw, Vern. I'd love to. You *are* a great helper ... and a great kid. That's why you have to stay here. They need you. You have to finish those projects we started, but more importantly, you got to take care of them, especially Gracie. You have to protect them."

"Protect them?"

"That's right. That's what I do ... what I did. Protected my teammates. It's a tough job, really tough. Nobody'll thank you, people will call you names, and they'll go out of their way to pick on you. Not everybody can do it. But you can, Viper. I know you can. I've seen it. You're tough. And it'll get easier as you get older."

"No, I don't think I can do it."

Shane has heard countless inspirational quotes from all the coaches and managers he has served over the decades, but the words that come to mind now are those of his very first coach — his dad. "'Easy makes you lazy, son. Hard makes you strong.'" He bends down to look Vern directly in the eye. "They really need your protection, Viper, even your Aunt Tammy. Maybe her most of all."

"Yeah, but who's going to protect me from *her*?" The self-pity is gone from the boy's voice, and there's a note of humour in this last statement. It tells Shane that Vern is going to be okay. He offers his hand to the boy.

"Sir, it's been an honour and a privilege working with you."

The line is borrowed from numerous movies, but that doesn't diminish his sincerity. Vern shakes the proffered hand, his shoulders squared back, looking two inches taller.

"Likewise."

"Need a lift back to school?"

"Nah, that's okay. I'll walk. No point strolling into class half-way through and drawing attention to myself. I'll just show up after lunch, and no one'll even notice." He fixes Shane with a very adult look. "Besides, I figure I got lots to think about."

"You and me both, Viper. You and me both."

Shane gets back on the motorcycle and drives away without looking back. When he reaches the intersection with the main highway, he stops and presses his forehead down on the handlebar. Whatever resolve he has been clinging to is dissolving. Familiar dark thoughts emerge from the shadows the way dusk floods back following the all-too-brief afternoon of a Yukon winter. Feeling the beasts of despair begin their gnawing, Shane starts to cry. He can't do this. He can't go on. It's hopeless. But then he remembers Doc Sanchez explaining how Shane's depression is a result of the blows he's taken to his head during his hockey career. *Don't let it win*, he tells himself. *You're a fighter, after all.*

Shane looks to the right, to the north, and pictures the long drive back to Chicago, where a criminal trial and possible imprisonment await him. Turning himself in would be the smart play, he supposes, but he cannot shake the conviction that he is being unjustly persecuted. He realizes his drive would take him past the valley where Beñat, himself a fugitive, has hidden happily for decades. This conjures up recollections of the peyote trip and the guidance given by his spirit guide or hallucination, Puck. After a few seconds, Shane tightens his jaw in determination and turns south.

TWENTY-EIGHT

Stepping inside the *Pista de Hielo de Puerto Palomas*, Shane is transported back to his past, to the time of two-thousand-seat arenas with spartan cinder-block dressing rooms. Although it is brand new and workers are still applying finishing touches, the building already has the almost-seedy feeling endemic to small hockey arenas with all the ambiance of a subterranean bunker. By his late teens Shane was already playing to sizeable crowds in small cities, but this place has the feel of his formative years.

First and foremost, Shane wants to get the feel of the rink itself. He finds the way down to the ice surface and discovers a half-dozen young Hispanic men scrimmaging. Shane stays in the shadows and sizes the athletes up. They are better players than he imagined, albeit with much room for improvement. Still, if this is the calibre of some of the players Shane will be working with, he might just enjoy the job after all.

"Why am I not surprised to find you here, *amigo?*" Doc Sanchez laughs from behind him. Shane turns to receive a giant bear hug from the doctor. "I'm really happy you accepted our offer, Shane. I know our young players can learn a lot from you. And hopefully the arrangement will benefit you, too ... I mean, beyond offering refuge from your legal troubles."

"I was worried they might stop me at the border, especially riding in on my motorcycle, but the guards just waved me through ... didn't even look at my papers."

Sanchez snickers. "It's not coming into *Mexico* you have to worry about. It may be trickier getting back into the States."

Shane shrugs. "Nothing there for me now."

"Well, there's plenty for you here. I see you're already check-ing out some of our talent. Come on, I'll introduce you."

They walk down to the players' bench, and Doc Sanchez calls the skaters over. The introduction is in Spanish, but Shane nevertheless gleans the big buildup he is getting. The players step forward to shake Shane's hand, and a chorus of enthusiastic but unintelligible greetings spills out. Shane looks helplessly to Sanchez.

"For some reason I thought they'd all be like you and Don Aléjandro ... you know, bilingual and all."

"I'm afraid not. We're border babies, after all. Oh, the odd guy will speak a little English, but most won't. Not to worry ... we'll fix you up with an assistant who can be your translator."

"Well, tell the guys I'm really pumped to be working with them. Say I'll be stressing the fundamentals — skating and stick-handling and conditioning — and I expect hard work, but it will pay off in the end as they hone their skills."

Doc Sanchez translates. As he speaks, a derisive laugh echoes down from the stands. They glance up and see Enrique stand-ing there with his two henchmen. He walks down to join the gathering, and Shane swears he can feel the temperature drop ten degrees just from the sheer menace the young *narco* exudes.

"Come off it, *gringo*. Skills? Fundamentals? Not exactly what you're known for, is it, tough guy?" derides Enrique. "No, you should teach these players how to hit hard and play dirty ... how to fight." He slams his fist into his hand. "Turn them into the meanest, toughest team in *La Liga* — the team everyone's afraid of. Then we're guaranteed to win."

Shane glares at the young drug lord, but is unnerved by the chilling sadism he finds there. Even Tammy's rattlesnakes have more humanity in their eyes than Enrique does. The tension between them arcs, ionizing the moment.

Doc Sanchez breaks the silence. "I must remind you, Enrique, that while your father put you in charge of the building, you have no say in running the team itself. That's the agreement. If you have a problem with how we are doing things, I suggest you take it up with Don Aléjandro." The doctor speaks in English. At first Shane thinks this is for his benefit, but then he notices the hockey players watching the exchange with rapt attention and realizes Doc Sanchez does not want them privy to the argument. Shane turns and waves them back to their scrimmage.

"My father will not live forever, *porco*," Enrique hisses, turning to leave. "Soon I'll deal with you ... and this brain-dead goon, too. Go on, play your children's game. I have men's work to do." He climbs up to rejoin his minions, saying something to them that elicits loud laughter as they exit.

"Ignore him, Shane," says Sanchez. "He's all smoke and no fire." The doctor is trying to act nonchalant, but his face is pale, and perspiration beads on his forehead despite the coolness of the arena.

"Gunsmoke, maybe. That kid is bad news."

"He won't dare disobey his father. If you see him around the building, just avoid him. You answer strictly to me and Don Aléjandro, and we're giving you a free hand with the players."

"Trust me, Doc. I'll make a point of staying out of that little psycho's way. What's he doing around the hockey arena, anyway? I thought he was in the, um ... the family import-export business."

"I told you, Don Aléjandro's interests are mainly legitimate. He put Enrique in charge of this building's construction and managing its operation afterward. I think he's hoping to spare his son from the sins of the father, especially now that the drug business has degenerated into such a mad and deplorably violent affair. I told you, he wants no part of that. Get to know him ... you'll find Don Aléjandro's an honourable man." Doc Sanchez grins and reaches into the inside pocket of his jacket. "And a generous one. Here ... your first payment." He offers up a small stack of brightly coloured Mexican currency.

"Wow, that's a lot of zeroes," Shane comments, examining the denominations.

Sanchez guffaws. "Welcome to *Mexíco*, *amigo*. We're not *that* generous. You'll have to learn to do the exchange rate in your head. Now that you've seen where you're going to work, let me show you where you can bunk — at least for now."

Shane's accommodations turn out to be a trainer's room in the arena's basement. Doc Sanchez apologizes for the small windowless space, but Shane proclaims that the snug apartment is to his liking, especially compared to the toolroom of *Rancho Crótalo*. It has the accoutrements of business — a desk, a blackboard, filing and equipment cabinets — but there is also a sitting area, a bed, and an ensuite bathroom that includes a shower stall.

"Settle in. Next week we'll find you a *casa* to rent. You'll soon find that your money goes a lot further here in Palomas."

"No hurry. Somehow, being in an arena feels like home. But what about you, Doc? How come you haven't bought yourself a nice crib here in town, instead of living in a converted van?"

"I'm not licensed to practise medicine on this side of the border. I'm American, remember?"

"I keep forgetting that. Sorry, no offence, I kind of think of you as Mexican."

"I'm only offended that you think I'd be offended. My family has lived in New Mexico for almost three hundred years. It's only been part of the United States for one hundred and fifty of those years. But, as a matter of fact, I have been considering buying myself a spread on the other side of the Great Wall. In my youth I liked to think of myself as footloose and unfettered. Now the idea of putting down roots has its appeal, especially if I have someone to share my life with."

"You mean Yolanda?"

Doc Sanchez's shrug is non-committal, but the sheepish smile on his face betrays the truth.

"So things are going okay with you two."

"Yes, in fact, we have our first official date tonight. Mind you, we have to meet in town, thanks to you. I'm *persona non grata* at the ranch now."

"Sorry, Doc. But why? You didn't do anything. I was the one who messed things up."

"Guilt by association — and my gender. Apparently Tammy's circled the wagons and returned to her old man-hating ways. From what I'm told, I'll only be allowed on the ranch in case of extreme medical emergency."

"It's Vern I worry about most, Doc. Poor kid will likely get picked on again, just 'cause he's a guy. Well, I worry about Gracie, too. I know her mother loves her, but that's one little girl who's likely to grow up with big problems if she inherits her mom's baggage. Maybe if I could have gotten her that horse she wanted —"

"You can choose your friends, but you can't choose your relatives, Shane. Besides, who's to say Gracie might not be better off treating all men with suspicion? Around here, the girls end up knocked up and dirt poor all too easily. We have a saying: *cada cual hace con su vida un papalote y lo echa a volar*. 'We each make a kite of life and fly it, as well.' It means that in the end, we control our own destiny. Tell me, did *you* do everything your father wanted you to?"

"Sure ... until I was twelve years old. Then all I did was fight with him about everything. For a while I even thought I hated him. I feel pretty bad about that now. The thing is, I wouldn't have become a pro-hockey player without him."

Sanchez slaps Shane on the back. "This is way too philosophical a discussion to have without a bottle of mezcal. I expect you to stock up the liquor cabinet, seeing as I'm paying you so handsomely, and next time I'll tell you about *my* dear ol' dad. Get settled in, and tomorrow you can start working with the players. I'll find you a translator in the meantime. Now, I'm off. Got to go get some signatures from Don Aléjandro."

"Say, Doc, is there somewhere safe I can park my bike overnight? I don't like leaving it out in the parking lot."

"No local criminal would be stupid enough to steal from a property owned by Don Aléjandro, but if it makes you feel better, park it in the equipment garage. I'll give you the access code for the automatic door."

After the doctor has excused himself, Shane strips and hops into the shower. As he is towelling off afterward, he hears a distant sound like someone shouting. It almost seems to be coming from within the walls themselves. He presses his ear up against the concrete and briefly hears the noise again, louder but still indistinct. Then the shouting ceases abruptly. A few minutes later it is replaced by distant scraping and a faint sporadic pounding.

Dismissing the sounds as leftover construction work, Shane dresses and thinks about the rest of the day ahead of him. The emptiness of his new life in exile suddenly unfolds before him. He misses the calming domesticity and sense of purpose he found — and lost — at the ranch. For the first time in days, Shane's head begins to throb. An all-too-familiar cloudiness shrouds his mind, and he feels the weight of his unhappiness pulling him downward. Tears well up, and he collapses onto the bed, burying his face in the pillow as he strives to fight off the bleakness suffocating him, but the pain seems more than he can endure. He looks up at the ceiling and, taking into account his height and some allowance for the length of a rope, he wonders whether the sprinkler head is high enough off the ground and whether it would support his weight.

"No!" someone shouts, and Shane looks around, puzzled, finally realizing it was his own voice. "No," he repeats at normal volume, but with no less conviction. He knows that he does not really want to die. He has faith in a better future ahead. It is a small faith — a journeyman's faith, a fourth-liner's faith — but he can feel its crystalline promise, provided he can gain control of it.

Shane gets up and splashes water on his face. An inner compulsion urges him to counter the depression by getting high. There must be a place in a town where he can find something to get him stoned. Or he could just go out and get stinking drunk.

He shakes off the impulse, realizing it would solve nothing and potentially send him onto a downward spiral again. Instead, he fishes out his cellphone and dials his father's number. As the line rings, he takes some slow, deep breaths.

Shane realizes he's half hoping Oksana will answer. It is supremely comforting, nonetheless, to hear his father's voice.

"Hey, there, old man," he says.

"Everything okay, son? Have they arrested you?"

"Nah, I'm good. Just phoned to hear your voice and see how you're doing."

"Ha! I'm crippled, half blind, and my medicine cabinet's got more pills in it than a pharmacy, but I'd have to say I'm doing a damned sight better than *you*."

Shane laughs. "You got me there, Dad. You got me there."

TWENTY-NINE

Despite Doc Sanchez's contention that Shane's Ducati will be safe on the arena grounds, Shane opts to park his motorcycle inside before the sun goes down. The underground maintenance compound is surprisingly crowded. In addition to a small flatbed truck, a panel van, and a team bus sporting the *Lobos* logo on its side, there is rolling boom lift and even a trio of golf carts, presumably for scooting around the arena corridors.

At the far end, near a gate that leads to the ice rink, sits a Zamboni. Despite the thousands of times Shane has seen similar ice-cleaning machines in action, he cannot resist inspecting one up close. He walks around the vehicle, then climbs up into the driver's seat. As he is studying the controls, there is a loud clank from the far end of the chamber, where gigantic fans provide ventilation for the icemaking plant next door. Two are whirring away, doing their job, but a third fan is motionless. To Shane's astonishment, the entire fan housing swings open, like a giant door, and one of Enrique's henchmen comes through the portal wheeling a crate on a dolly. Shane slips down from the Zamboni and slides out of sight.

The *narco* loads his cargo in the rear of the parked van before opening the garage door and driving off. Through the entrance-way, which has been left open, Shane can clearly make out two voices, one low and guttural, cursing angrily in rapid-fire Spanish, while the other, younger and in English, is pleading to be left alone and released from something. Then there is an audible smack, a shout of pain, and both voices fall silent.

Puzzled, Shane goes to the opening to investigate. He sees that the fan's entire housing swings on mammoth hinges, designed for easy egress. Through the portal he can make out a tunnel that runs for a considerable distance. It is wide enough to easily accommodate small vehicles; not only is another golf cart parked there, but also, clearly visible even in the dim lighting, is what appears to be the same Indian motorcycle with sidecar that the youth who robbed Shane on the highway was driving. Beyond that are two shadowy figures, one sitting on the ground, bent over in apparent pain, and one standing over him in a threatening posture.

Whatever is going on, Shane decides it is none of his business. He hastily exits the maintenance compound. In the corridor outside his new quarters, his cellphone rings. The call display indicates it is Doc Sanchez.

"Shane, Shane, get the hell out of there!" the doctor shouts over the phone, without salutation or preamble. "Run, *amigo*, run! It's a fucking catastrophe."

"What are you talking about, Doc? What's going on?"

"Don Aléjandro, he's dead ... murdered," Sanchez blurts out. The anguish in his voice is evident. "Enrique claims it was a rival cartel, but I know it was him, the little monster ... he resented his father for abandoning the drug business and now he's taking over."

"Holy shit," is all Shane can utter in response.

"It's over!" the doctor wails. "I'm on my way back to Columbus, and you should get out of there, too." Then there is a loud crashing noise over the line followed by something uttered in Spanish before the call abruptly ends.

Shane stands there stunned, knowing he has his own skin to consider now. He is all too cognizant of the death threats Enrique has voiced on multiple occasions, and without Don Aléjandro's protection, there is no reason to believe his twisted son won't follow through on them.

A metallic clack echoes from behind Shane — the unmistakeable sound of a round being racked into a handgun's chamber. His mouth goes dry and his knees begin to buckle. "Don't shoot," he yelps and raises his hands in the air. Turning slowly, he sees the henchman he spied in the tunnel earlier. The unfeeling eyes and menacing smile on the thug's moustachioed face are as frightening as the gun in his hand. He says something Shane does not understand and waves the gun's muzzle in the direction of the maintenance area. The meaning of the gesture is obvious enough. The *narco* comes around behind Shane and prods him forward with spine-rattling jabs of the pistol.

They pass through the fan opening and down the tunnel, squeezing past the golf cart and the parked motorcycle and coming to a stop in front of the huddled figure Shane observed earlier. It takes him a moment to realize he has seen the odd clothes before, although they are now much worse for wear. And, indeed, when the face meekly lifts to see what fresh torture is coming, Shane recognizes the Indian-riding youth who robbed him seemingly an eternity ago. However, dark circles are etched under the teen's eyes, his face is blemished with dirt, and there is a scraggly growth of blond beard. The old-fashioned clothes are now torn and stained with perspiration and, in several spots, blood. A rank odour, like a hockey bag that hasn't been washed all season, wafts from him, hanging in the air like a cloud of spring blackflies. Shane realizes the kid has been kept prisoner here, evidently wearing the same clothes for weeks.

The teen's enslavement is confirmed when he stirs, causing chains to rattle. Shane cannot believe what he is seeing. There is a line of ankle shackles and chains — enough for another half-dozen prisoners, it seems — cemented into the wall of the tunnel. It is like something out of a Hollywood dungeon.

A blow across the back of the head knocks Shane to his knees. A sharp pain shoots across the circumference of his skull, and stars swirl before his eyes. The henchman barks more unintelligible Spanish, and Shane gleans from mimed motions that he is expected to shackle himself. He gauges his chances at tackling the *narco* and wrestling the gun from his hand, but he is feeling dizzy and having difficulty focusing, so he sits and does as instructed.

The shackles close with a snap, and Shane tries to concentrate on their locking mechanism, wondering whether they might be picked, and if so, what tool he might procure to do so. The attempt to focus through his mental haze causes a sudden sweep of nausea, and he throws up.

Some of the vomit lands on one of the henchman's shiny cowboy boots, and the man curses and jumps backward. Examining the splatter, he steps forward and wipes the boot on the captive teenager's pants. Shane promptly pukes again, this time spewing on the *narco's* pant leg, as well.

The thug erupts in anger, cursing wildly, and begins to kick at Shane, who curls up into a ball and tries to protect his head and ribs.

"*Para, pendejo!*" Enrique's voice screams down the tunnel. The kicking ceases, and Shane opens one eye to see the young drug lord shambling toward them. A green canvas bag is slung over his shoulder, and he is brandishing a military-style assault rifle with not one, but two large drum cartridges which suggest its sole purpose is firepower. Then Shane sees that Enrique is tugging two men behind him: Doc Sanchez and one of Don Aléjandro's bodyguards. Both men have their hands tied behind their backs, and a rope secured around their necks.

Enrique tugs his two prisoners forward and forcefully yanks them down to the ground. He orders his henchman to shackle Doc Sanchez's ankles, leaving the doctor's hands tied, while the other prisoner is left bound and kneeling on the floor. Enrique begins to berate his henchman, emphasizing his points with occasional slaps to the head, then he abruptly swings his rifle down and to the side and pulls the trigger. A hail of bullets all but obliterates the head of the captive bodyguard, splattering blood and brain matter everywhere. Enrique keeps pumping bullets into the lifeless body until his rifle is empty.

Shane's stomach heaves again, but there is nothing left to bring up. The youth chained next to him rolls his eyes heavenward until the pupils disappear, and he passes out, slumping against Shane. Doc Sanchez is evidently made of sterner stuff. He wipes his face as best as he can on his own shoulder and glares at Enrique.

Having made his point, the drug lord retrieves fresh drum cartridges from his shoulder bag and slams them onto the rifle. He then uses the weapon to prod his henchman back down the tunnel and out the fan housing, haranguing him the entire way.

"Shane, thank God you're okay," Doc Sanchez whispers once they are alone.

"Ditto, Doc, but who knows for how much longer. We're royally screwed, if you ask me."

"Who's your boyfriend?" the doctor asks, gesturing at the teen slumped against Shane. It is gratifying to see that Sanchez has retained his sense of humour.

"Believe it or not, it's the kid who robbed me out on the highway. I think they've been keeping him here as some kind of slave labour. Might be what they have in mind for us."

Sanchez jerks his head in the direction of the mutilated corpse. "Or else that. Who knew Enrique was this ambitious ... a tunnel, slave workers. I had no idea, and I doubt his poor father did, either. *Dios bendiga su alma.*"

"C'mon ... you don't think the Don was in on it? He was a smuggler his whole life, and he built an arena smack dab on the border. It would have taken some serious cash to dig a tunnel this size. He had to know about it."

"Absolutely not. Clearly Enrique diverted men and machines from the arena's construction and hid the costs." Sanchez pauses as something else comes to mind. "*Madre mía*," he murmurs. "Those poor men."

"What are you talking about?"

"There was a bizarre construction accident. Three workers died. One of them operated the drilling machine we used for the service tunnels. Afterward, we paid a huge bribe so the officials would whitewash the inquiry. Now I suspect Enrique must have had those men killed to keep this a secret, like some deranged Egyptian pharaoh."

"Well, you can see why he'd want to keep it on the down low. This isn't a tunnel — it's a gold mine. You could drive a small truck through here. Imagine the drugs you could move."

"Not just drugs ... people, too. Enrique wanted to get into human trafficking, but his father refused to exploit the poor and desperate. Plus there's a tidy sum to be made the other way, bringing guns back into *Mexico* ... although I suspect he wants those for himself, judging by the hardware he was sporting. I think that lunatic actually plans to compete against the other cartels." He shakes his head. "We should have suspected something when Enrique was so quick to accept the job of building the arena right after he'd argued for so long with Don Aléjandro about giving up the narcotics business."

The unconscious youth beside them groans. His eyes open, then dart around the tunnel as he assesses the situation. When he sees the defaced corpse on the ground, he whimpers.

"Hello again," Shane opens the conversation.

The youth glances sideways. "I don't know you, Mister."

"Sure you do, you little bugger. The injured guy out on the highway who you robbed and left to rot a few weeks back. Remember?"

The teen looks Shane over. "You look different ... you got teeth 'n' stuff now."

"Is that all you have to say for yourself?"

"Look, Mister, I'm sorry, okay?"

"Shane. My name's Shane. This here's Doc Sanchez."

"And for what it's worth, I'm Abraham. But what I did to you out there ... I was runnin' for my life. You've seen these devils. They've had me prisoner here for weeks. I done got out of my chains and stole that there motor-sickle and tried to get away. That's when I ran into you out on the highway. I ... I didn't want to do it ... I done known it was a sin ... but when you showed me the money, I saw it was my only chance. I mean, you was all busted up. You couldn't help me, and if I stayed to help you, they was gonna catch me." He starts to cry. "They got me anyway," he blubbers. "Whupped me somethin' fierce."

"Geez. All right, kid, all right. It's okay," Shane consoles the sobbing youth.

Sanchez clears his throat. "Sorry to interrupt this touching reunion, but did you say that you got out of your chains? Seems to me that's useful information, given the current situation."

Abraham shakes his head. "'T'ain't no good. They took away the key. Used to keep it hangin' on the wall for when someone would release us to work every day. Now they each have a copy they keep on 'em. Won't leave the key in the motor-sickle no more, neither."

"Us? There are others?" Sanchez inquires.

"There was a couple of other fellers when they first brought me here, though they was in mighty bad shape. Both dead now." He starts crying again. "I don't want to die!" he moans. "Ain't I been punished enough for stealin' one li'l bag of food?"

"What food? You took money and, um ... other stuff from me," Shane interjects.

"Not from you. From them. That's how I ended up here in ... in hell. Funny, 'cause I was born and grew up on a spread up north called Holy Waters, and I was told that was as close to heaven as we could get, here on Earth. Then, outta the blue a coupla months ago, I got shunned by everybody — even my folks — and they done run me off the land. All on account of me 'n' my gal Zaylie was in love, but one of the elders, Jebediah, wanted her for his bride. I drifted around some, and eventually I ended up down here, at the border, where I couldn't go no farther. I tried to snatch a lunch from some guys I done seen in a warehouse. Next thing you know, they catch me, stick a gun in my face, and drag me down here. I figure they're gonna shoot me, but when the boss man hears I'm all alone and nobody knows where I am, they look at each other and laugh and knock me around and chain me up and ... well, you know the rest."

"But if the tunnel already goes on through to the other side, what are they still working on?" Shane asks aloud.

"Never no end to the work. The ground's pretty soft, so we're always shoring things up," Abraham explains. "Then there's these extra caves they're carving out, like they're expecting to hole up a bunch of people down here or somethin'."

"Well, whatever they have in store for us, we're about to find out the hard way," Doc Sanchez says grimly. They follow his eyes and see Enrique walking back down the tunnel, alone, the assault rifle resting casually on his shoulder.

THIRTY

A t Enrique's approach, Abraham gives a soft cry and tightens up into a ball, his head between his knees. The drug lord laughs and taps the teenager on the shoulder with the barrel of his gun. "That's right, you should be afraid."

"Oh, God," Abraham whimpers and begins to tremble.

Enrique grabs the youth's hair and pulls his head up to glare into his prisoner's face. "I've told you before. I'm the only God down here." He yanks Abraham forward violently. "Get on your knees and pray to me. I'm your God of Abraham."

"Leave him alone, you puny little piece of shit!" Shane shouts, surprising himself. Seconds ago he was cowering, hoping not to call attention to himself, trying to clear the cobwebs in his head. But he can't stand this any longer. He is angry, but not with his usual mindless animal rage. No, this is a new anger, a righteousness anger.

Enrique recoils as if bitten. He releases Abraham and steps forward to slam the butt of the rifle into Shane, who manages to twist his body just enough to take the brunt of the blow on his shoulder.

"What's that you say, tough guy? You think you can stand up to *me*? You think this is some hockey game with its play fighting? This is my world. I own you."

"Oh yeah, you're a big man with a gun in your hand beating up on helpless kids. Why not unchain me, and we'll see how tough you really are. You know, *mano a mano*."

Enrique actually laughs at that one. "You've been watching too many movies, *gringo*. Do you really expect me to put down my gun and fight some big stupid goon just because you've insulted my *machismo*? You're a bigger moron than I thought. No, I'm the brains who commands the stupid, disposable beasts. I have the balls my weakling father never had! I called our hockey team *Los Lobos* because that's what we're meant to be, wolves who feed on the sheep, on the weak."

"Your father was twice the man you'll ever be," Doc Sanchez interjects. "The only weakness he ever had was you. He spoiled you. You're a disgrace."

"Shut up, Francisco," Enrique snarls. He slings his assault rifle over his shoulder, and from his pocket he pulls out a pearl-handled switchblade, flicking it open melodramatically in front of the doctor's face. "I'll deal with you in a minute. You could be useful to me, but if you'd rather be stubborn, I'll carve you up like the fat pig you are."

The drug lord turns and points the knife at Shane. "First I'm going to take care of you. I was going to let you live and work you like the dumb ox you are. I figured that even with that broken arm, you'd give me twice the work as this scrawny runt. Now I've changed my mind. I said before that I should have killed you out on the highway. Well, now I'm going to fix my mistake. But first, I'm going to make you scream ... starting by cutting out your eyeballs."

As Enrique slowly brings the tip of the blade up toward Shane's eye, Shane throws his head backward, causing the Grim Reaper necklace Yolanda gave him to jump into view. Enrique stiffens before switching the knife to his left hand in order to make the sign of the cross with his right. "*Santa Muerte*," he murmurs.

Seizing the opportunity, Shane swings his broken arm, using the plaster cast like a club. Enrique stabs at him, but gets the tip of his blade embedded in the cast's plaster. Then Shane sweeps with his shackles, and as Enrique's feet get tangled up in the chains, he collapses sideways. The *narco* scrambles to sit up, bringing his rifle to bear.

He does not get the chance to pull the trigger. Another set of chains, these belonging to Abraham, appear from behind. He drops them down over Enrique's head and yanks violently backward against the windpipe. As the steel necklace tightens, the *narco* gasps, groans, and gurgles, his face turning red. In desperation, he tries to point the rifle behind him, but Shane rolls over on his side to generate some extra torque, tugging at the chains with every ounce of his strength. There is a crunching sound, and Enrique goes limp, his neck broken. A wet stain appears and blossoms across the front of the dead man's slacks.

There is a long silence, except for the sound of heavy breathing. "Hmm. That's too bad," Doc Sanchez finally observes.

"Screw that! The guy was trying to kill me. I'm glad he's dead," Shane retorts.

"No, not that. Good riddance, and I hope the little shit rots in hell." Sanchez spits on Enrique's corpse. "But, as it happens, his bladder expelled upon death, and now someone has to fish through those piss-soaked pockets to look for the key."

"You do it, kid," Shane tells Abraham. "You killed him."

"I didn't kill him. You did when you yanked his legs."

"Oh, whatever. Let's just say it was a team effort." He offers his palm. "High-five!"

Abraham stares blankly at Shane. "Um, Holy Trinity?" he replies uncertainly.

Shane sighs. "Never mind. Help push him a little closer, kid, I'll do it."

They find a ring with several keys, and Abraham points out the one that opens all the shackles. Shane then uses the switchblade lodged in his cast to cut through the ropes binding Doc Sanchez's hands. The first thing the doctor does is pat the cast. "Another reason I prefer plaster of Paris," he chuckles.

Abraham leaps to his feet. "C'mon, let's mosey. America's that way," he says and starts walking. No one follows. "Whatcha doin'? Come on before one of the others shows up," the youth pleads.

Meanwhile, Doc Sanchez has picked up the assault rifle. He turns to face south.

"You're going back?" Shane asks. "What about Enrique's men?"

Sanchez flourishes the weapon. "You know what the *narcos* call this puppy, Shane? *Huevos de Toro.* The Bull's Balls, on account of the double drums. A hundred rounds in each. The way I see it, that's two hundred opportunities to drum some sense into whatever parts of the snake's body are still thrashing around now that the head's been cut off. I'm still general manager and chairman of the board of *Los Lobos de Chihuahua*. No, I've worked too hard for what's back there. I'm not giving it up."

"Look, don't hate me, Doc, but I'm not going with you. That cocksucker deserved to die" — he points to Enrique's corpse — "and I'm not sorry one bit. Shit, I don't even know whether technically it happened in Mexico or the States, or whether they'd give me a medal or a lethal injection for it. Either way, I'd rather not have to answer for it." He indicates the northern end of the tunnel. "I'm going that way."

"I figured as much, and it's okay with me. I accept your resignation as coach without prejudice."

"Fuck!" Shane curses suddenly. "I've got my wallet on me, but my passport and my Ducati are back there."

"*De nada.* Drop me a line to let me know where you land. I'll send you your passport. And I'll take care of your bike for you."

"Fuck it, Doc. Sell the Ducati. The fucking thing has been nothing but bad luck. You know what? Start a youth hockey program with the money. Buy Vern some equipment. Hell, get Gracie a horse."

"I'll do that, *amigo.*"

They embrace. "*Vaya con dios,* Doc."

"Good luck, Shane." The doctor takes the rifle in both hands and hefts it. "Pancho Villa rides again," he chortles and marches back toward the arena.

Shane hastens after Abraham. "Wait. Let's take the Indian," he suggests, and jogs back to find the key on Enrique's corpse. When he finds it and returns to the motorcycle, Abraham is sitting in the driver's seat. Shane shakes his head. "No way, kid. I've seen you drive. Broken hand or not, I'm the pilot. You ride in the sidecar."

✕ ✕ ✖ ✕ ✕

The tunnel exit is hidden in the same stateside warehouse Shane visited earlier. No guards are on duty, nor do any pursuers materialize, but still Shane wants to put as much distance as possible between them and the border, so they ride non-stop for almost two hours — up through Columbus and Deming out of Luna

County toward Albuquerque. Eventually, Shane's broken arm starts to ache, and since the sun is going down, he decides to find them some food and a place for the night. They locate a truck-stop motel and go inside the restaurant. Heads turn as they choose a booth. At first Shane attributes the rubbernecking to Abraham's strange attire, but when Shane excuses himself to go to the washroom, he sees himself in the mirror and understands. His face is sprayed with the blood of the man Enrique executed back in the tunnel. His T-shirt and jeans are also spattered, but here Shane's predilection for black has paid off, as the stains are less noticeable. He cleans himself as best as he can and returns to the diner.

A worn-out waitress with box-red hair comes to take their order. Shane finds he has to teach Abraham the basic principles of eating in restaurants, as if he were a child. Once assured that Shane will be covering the tab, Abraham ends up ordering enough food for three people, while Shane, his head still pounding and his stomach in knots, settles for the only salad on the menu, which is otherwise a grease-filled carnivore's delight.

Although he is thinking ahead to his own legal predicament, he is wondering what to do about Abraham. He is grateful to the youth, knowing that in all likelihood, he owes Abraham his life. Still, Shane has problems all his own and does not want to be saddled with the teen. And, yet, it would be cruel to simply abandon him.

Shane sighs. "What the hell are we going to do with you, Abe? You have any relatives you can go live with?"

The teenager shakes his head, dislodging bits of food from his mouth. "Nope, all my kin are at Holy Waters, and they done shunned me." The remembrance moves the youth to begin weeping openly.

Shane grimaces and offers Abraham an extra napkin. "Look, I can give you a few bucks to get you started, but you're going to have to figure out what to do with your life. Find a job, maybe learn a trade. What schooling do you have?"

"Well, sir, I got my ABCs and can do my sums, but I wasn't fixin' to be no preacher. Them's the ones got the extra book learnin'."

"Computer skills?"

"What's a computer?"

"Fuck. Okay, how about carpentry? When I played for Philly I used to see some great Shaker furniture in the stores. You handy with a hammer and saw?"

"Well, sir, there's a few families who are mighty good at buildin' ... make all our furniture and barns and whatnot. Not mine, though."

Shane shakes his head. Abraham will have to find menial physical labour somewhere, but in this part of the country, the odds are he will be competing with illegal immigrants who have slipped across the border. If he is lucky enough to find employment, he will likely be paid a pittance and risk being exploited by his employers.

Abraham can read Shane's face well enough. "I'm in trouble, ain't I, Shane? Oh, don't I know it. I been wanderin' around for a couple of months now, and I feel like Adam, cast out of Eden and landing smack dab in the middle of Babylon. I know I'm not right for this world. Even before those bad men grabbed me, everywhere I went people were lookin' down at me, and callin' me names, and runnin' me off. I felt like I was sinkin' lower and lower every day. How am I supposed to live in this world run by machines and business 'n' such. It's all movin' so darn fast I don't even know what's goin' on half the time. No, sir, it just ain't fair for a poor fella who don't know nothin' but how to be a shepherd."

Shane freezes mid-bite, a piece of lettuce dangling from his fork. "A what?"

"A shepherd. You know, I tend sheep."

Shane starts to laugh. Abraham shifts in his seat, and his face reddens. "What's so darn funny? Ain't nothin' wrong with being a shepherd. I don't mind saying I liked it, and I was good at it, too."

"It's all right, Abe, I'm not laughing at you. I just got the punchline of a joke. A cosmic joke. Trust me, kid. I'm the one that's feeling small right now." He leans closer. "I know this is going to sound crazy, but I actually think we were meant to meet, like it was preordained. You know what I'm talking about?"

Abraham frowns. "I used to be devout, but I don't believe anymore, not since they cast me out just so some elder could take my Zaylie for his sixth wife and say it's all God's will. No, sir. Was it preordained that I should end up stealin'? And ... and kill a man?"

"You didn't kill him, Abe. I did."

"It was a team effort." Abraham holds up his palm. "Holy Trinity."

Shane can't help but smile. "No, kid. It's 'high-five' and what you do is ... oh, never mind. You won't need it where you're going."

"What do you mean? Where am I going?"

"I have a job for you. As a matter of fact, I have a whole new life for you. It's perfect. It's better than perfect — it'll be your own private Eden."

"An Eden without Eve," Abraham whimpers.

"Well, technically, you wouldn't be Adam ... but I get your point." Shane shakes his head and rolls his eyes at the ceiling. "I should have known it wouldn't be quite so easy. Life always seems to want to buck Bronco." He aims his fork at the youth. "Okay, Abe. If I take you back to Holy Waters, do you think you can sneak in and get your Zaylie to run off with you?"

"But I told you, she's married now."

"Seriously? With everything you've just seen and done, *that's* where you're going to draw the line? Okay, then, let me help you out. I don't know what they taught you growing up, but here in America polygamy is actually against the law. So technically, the marriage isn't valid. Get it? That means she's *not* really married. Eat up, then let's go get your gal."

THIRTY-ONE

After hearing about how the inhabitants of Holy Waters live and work, Shane realizes it is best to wait until daytime to rescue Zaylie. As much as operating under cover of darkness initially seemed like a good idea, he learns that the girl will now be sleeping inside the elder's home with his other five wives, and although the door to the house will not be locked, the chances of slipping in, finding her bedroom, and getting her out — all undetected — are slim. (Also, the newest bride will likely be in her husband's bed, Shane surmises, but he keeps this theory to himself.) Abraham suggests that they approach Zaylie in the daytime, while she works at her job tending the communal vegetable gardens, since the women work separately from the men.

They take a room at the motel, which Shane pays for in cash, and spend a sleepless night. Abraham tosses and turns, no doubt thinking of the mission ahead, and possibly filled with longing for his sweetheart and uncertainty over whether she will actually run away with him. Shane's insomnia stems from a different source. He is still traumatized by his bloody near-death ordeal in the tunnel, as well as concerned about Doc Sanchez's fate. But mostly he is agonizing over whether to turn himself in and face justice. His indecision is coloured by visions of being publicly vilified, then sent to prison. Part of him wonders whether it isn't wiser to go home to Canada and fight extradition.

He thinks about the prestige and income he commanded as a professional athlete, all now lost. But what did he ever do with all the privilege and opportunity he had, except squander it in selfish hedonism? And his vocation has certainly taken a toll exacted in pain and trauma; his brain is as battered and scarred as his face.

And yet, Shane still loves hockey and feels blessed to have had the career he did. Even if he was only a fourth-line enforcer and never hoisted the Stanley Cup, he wouldn't change a thing if he had it all to do over again — at least, none of the things he did on the ice. And in that moment, he knows what he has to do. It will be a struggle to take his jumbled thoughts and turn them into convincing words, but he must return to Chicago to defend himself and proudly tell the world what he stands for.

This resolve calms the anxieties that have been jostling through his thoughts like ravens flocking at a garbage dump and allows him to snatch some sleep. When he awakens, dawn is declaring itself through the dirty curtains of the motel room window. On the next bed, Abraham snores lightly. Evidently he, too, finally succumbed to sleep in the dregs of the night.

Shane rouses the teenager, strong-arming him into the shower to wash off months' worth of grime and perspiration. He tells Abraham this is so he'll look his best when meeting his sweetheart, Zaylie, but it is just as true that Shane can't bear to smell his companion's body odour anymore. Afterward, they both study the fledgling beard that has grown on Abraham's cheek. Even after prolonged growth, the whiskers are sparse and downy. However, by mutual consent, they are spared execution.

"Ready or not, you're an adult now, Abe," Shane comments. "Might as well start looking the part."

The youth's clothes, however, present a problem. Shane is all for throwing the badly soiled, foul-smelling garments away, until it occurs to him Abraham will need to be as inconspicuous as possible when sneaking into Holy Waters. They compromise by buying a change of clothes at a roadside mall, then running Abraham's shirt and pants through the wash at a local laundromat.

They plan their rescue mission for early afternoon, after the women return to the fields from their midday meal. Plumbing Abraham's memory, they locate Holy Waters on a road map and set out on the Indian with a roar.

As they turn off the main highway and head toward their destination, the countryside starts to look familiar, and Shane realizes this is the detour he and Vern took during their recent road trip to Albuquerque. Sure enough, as they pass the tiny cemetery that was a point of contention during their travelling game, Shane finds himself murmuring, "Bury your horses!"

They reach Holy Waters, and Abraham guides them around the property's split-rail fence to a spot on the road offering an elevated view of the garden plots where Zaylie toils. The location is several hundred yards away, but the women are clearly distinguishable amidst the rows of plants. Even in the warm spring weather they are all wearing bonnets and long-sleeved dresses that reach to the ground.

"I see her!" Abraham exclaims, squeezing Shane's arm in his excitement. He tries to point Zaylie out, but to Shane the tiny, amply-dressed figures all look alike.

"All right, Abe. This is it. You're going in alone, and I'll be waiting here with the engine running. You won't likely have a lot of time before the men are onto you, so don't waste it giving her your life story, okay? Do what it takes to convince her to come with you, then get the heck out. You guys can work out any fine details later, when you're by yourselves."

"What if ... what if she won't come with me?"

"Yeah, Abe, I didn't want to be the one to bring that up. There's no guarantee that she will want to leave, so you'd better be prepared to come hightailing back here alone ... well, except for the bunch of angry men who'll likely be on your heels." He reads Abraham's uncertainty and places a reassuring hand on the youth's shoulder. "Look, buddy, if you meant as much to her as you say you did, you've got a good shot. But it'll be a shock for her to see you, and you'll be asking her to decide her whole future on the spot ... to leave behind the only home she's ever known."

Shane recollects the many times he's been called into a manager's office to be told he's been traded. "Just tell her you know it's a shock, but she's getting a once-in-a-lifetime opportunity to be with a man that really wants her, and to have better prospects for the long term. Oh, hell, Abe, just tell her you love her and she's all you've been thinking about."

Abraham nods and slips through the fence as Shane anxiously watches his progress. Initially Abraham stays hidden, slipping behind trees and hillocks, but eventually he needs to cross a large, open field. He pauses behind a tree, and for a moment Shane thinks Abraham has lost his nerve, but then he picks up a fallen log, slings it over his shoulder, and strolls nonchalantly over toward the women.

"Nice touch," Shane chuckles, although he feels his pulse quicken with suspense. Witnessing the drama unfold from a distance is like watching a scene in a silent movie. Abraham enters the garden area, and the first two women he passes take no notice. A third woman, more stout than the others, is on her knees weeding. She raises her head as the youth goes past, and even from a quarter mile away, Shane can see her shock of recognition. The woman gets up and runs to one of her fellows, gesticulating excitedly. They confer briefly, then the second woman leaves as quickly as her long skirts will allow.

"Here we go," Shane says to himself. "C'mon, Abe, clock's running."

Abraham reaches a girl hoeing amidst the plants, and the two young people stand there looking at one another. Then, in a promising development, log and hoe are tossed aside, and the couple embrace. However, after Abraham's overture, it is evident Zaylie has things to say about the proposal, as her hands start to wave wildly in the air. The boy reaches for the girl's arm, but the girl shakes him off. The debate continues.

The stout woman who first recognized Abraham approaches and begins to berate him. Zaylie, however, turns and argues with the woman, seemingly telling her to mind her own business. Shane wonders if the stout woman isn't perhaps one of the other wives with whom Zaylie now lives, and if so, whether there is bad blood between them.

Meanwhile, the woman dispatched for help reaches a large outbuilding. Soon, six men come spilling out, heading in the direction of Abraham. To complete the movie-cliché scene, some are carrying pitchforks and long-handled shovels. Fortunately, the bearded man in the lead appears to be elderly and is not making fast progress. Apparently, protocol prevents the younger men from passing him and hastening ahead.

"It's now or never, Abe," Shane whispers. This is as nerve-wracking as watching the opposing team on a power play during overtime in the playoffs.

Abraham has resumed pleading with Zaylie, despite the stout woman's interference, but now he spots the arriving rein-forcements. Finally, with less than fifty yards remaining between himself and the posse, who are now shouting and waving their makeshift weapons, he steps forward and flings Zaylie over his shoulder. The stout woman tries to intervene, but Abraham pushes her away, causing her to stumble backward and sit down hard on the ground. Abraham turns and runs back toward Shane, as Zaylie shouts and pounds on his back.

"Oh, way to go, kid," Shane sighs, going over to fire up the motorcycle. "You've already got petty larceny, grand theft auto, and homicide on your resumé — why not add kidnapping?" With his load, Abraham moves slower than the posse, who are closing ground. As Abraham reaches the final slope leading up to the road, two of the younger men abandon protocol to dash past the elder in an attempt to catch the abductor. Capitalizing on the high ground, Abraham reels around, using Zaylie's torso to knock down one pursuer, then he kicks the other downhill.

"Here, catch!" a red-faced Abraham pants, flinging his pay-load over the fence to Shane before clambering through the rails himself.

Holding Zaylie in his arms, Shane gets his first close look at the object of affection. Her bonnet has flown off during the flight, and she is bareheaded. Her strawberry-blond hair is rolled back in a bun, and she has a pretty, tapered, freckled face and large, intelligent blue eyes, which at the moment pierce Shane with a look of indignation. Despite her young age and diminu-tive size, her shape is decidedly womanly, and Shane can see why a dirty old man would covet her.

There is no time for introductions or pleasantries. Shane dumps Zaylie into the sidecar and leaps into the driver's seat. He begins pulling forward as Abraham closes the last few feet.

As soon as the teen dives in on top of the girl, Shane cranks the Indian's throttle. They take off with the prerequisite cloud of dust just as the pursuers come through the fence. One angrily tosses a shovel after them, but it thuds harmlessly in their wake.

Shane and Abraham's immediate troubles are not over, however. Squeezed into the bottom of the sidecar, Zaylie squirms and thrashes about violently. Her curses are loud enough to be heard even over the engine's roar and the rushing wind, leading Shane to wonder how a girl who has supposedly led a sheltered life has managed to accumulate such a rich portfolio of profanities. Poor Abraham looks like he's riding a bucking bronco as he is bounced and jerked about forcefully. Eventually Zaylie works a leg free and starts kicking at Shane, causing the Indian to swerve across the road.

Fearing for everybody's safety, Shane looks for a place to pull over. Up ahead, he spots the now familiar little private cemetery. "Bury your horses," he mutters and turns into its driveway. As soon as the motorcycle comes to a stop, Zaylie sends Abraham tumbling onto the gravel. The young woman climbs out and looms over him, shaking her fist.

"How dare you, Abraham Johnson? I ain't some sack of taters to be picked up and carried over your shoulder!"

Abraham gets to his feet and approaches his sweetheart, though he wisely keeps some separation between them. "Zaylie, darlin', please. I didn't have time to argue with you. The menfolk were comin' and you know darn well what they woulda done to me."

"That still don't give you the right to do what you done!"

Shane speaks up. "You're right, Zaylie. He shouldn't have forced you. If you insist on going back, we'll turn around right now and drop you off."

Both boy and girl shoot him dirty looks. "And who, sir, are you?" Zaylie demands.

"My name's Shane. Nice to meet you. I'm just a buddy of Abe's. I'm going to take him to meet another friend of mine … and set him up in a new job as a shepherd."

Zaylie turns back to Abraham. "That's the shepherding you was tellin' me about, I reckon, but you was mighty short on details."

"That's 'cause I ain't got no details yet."

"And you're just gonna follow this fella on blind faith, and 'spect me to come along, too?"

Abraham's face tightens. "If you knew what I've been through … well, you'd know blind faith is just about all I got goin' for me."

"Well, it ain't been no picnic for me, neither, Abraham Johnson. You think I wanted to marry Jebediah Carson? You think I wanted him to take me to his bed?" She starts to weep. "The older wives, they came and held me down just so he could have his way with me."

Abraham stands with his arms dangling at his sides, paralyzed by Zaylie's tears and the image of her rape. Shane surreptitiously signals to the youth that he should comfort her. Abraham nods, then steps in to take his sweetheart in his arms.

"Why didn't ya come back for me sooner?" she sobs.

"I tried. I snuck back a buncha times, but I guess they figured I would, 'cause a bunch of 'em was always waitin'. They'd whup me, but I kept comin' back. I was cold and starvin', but I didn't care. You was all I could think about. Then they tol' me it was too late, that you'd done gone and married Jebediah and it weren't no use … that you said to tell me you was a married woman now and didn't want me no more. I didn't believe them, Zaylie, but then they gave me this." He reaches into his pocket and pulls out a plain-looking brass ring. "Nobody else knew I'd gave you a pledging ring. We agreed we weren't gonna declare till you was eighteen, so we wouldn't need your folks' okay."

She takes the ring from him and rotates it slowly between her fingers. "They done stole that from me. The first coupla weeks I kept a travellin' bag hidden under my bed, hopin' you would come back for me. I invented every excuse I could think of to put off the weddin'. Then my pa found the bag and beat the livin' tar out of me. I kept the ring in that little heart-shaped box you carved for me ... the one with both our initials, remember?" Abraham nods with a sad smile. "I guess they figured out easy nuff who it was from."

"You can wear it now, though. Put it on, Zaylie."

"Abraham Johnson! What kind of a girl do you take me for? For better or worse — and believe you me, it's been nothin' but the worse — I'm a married woman now. I ain't gonna go a-sinnin' ... no matter how much I hate my husband."

"But that's what I was trying to tell you. You *ain't* married. It ain't legal."

"I know I was shy of my eighteenth birthday when we tied the knot, but my folks gave Jebediah their say-so, so I only had to be sixteen. You very well know our ways, Abraham."

"Yeah, I know our ways and have the bruises to prove it. Seems to me, Zaylie, the bride should have to give her say-so, too. But that's not the point. Jebediah can't marry you, not legal like, on account of polly ... polly ... aw, heck, you explain it to her, Shane."

"Polygamy. Having more than one wife. It's against the law in the good ol' U.S. of A. Most countries, actually."

"But it's sanctioned in the Book of Mormon."

"Yeah, well, the Bible also says we should put witches to death, but the government doesn't look too kindly on that, either. Plain and simple, Zaylie, not only is your marriage invalid, but I'm guessing you could get randy old Jebediah in some serious hot water if you took it to the authorities. Maybe even send him to prison."

"I ain't married?"

"That's what I'm trying to say!" Abraham cries. "Now will you put on the ring?"

"Just hold on a minute, Abraham. Assumin' this fella here ain't makin' the whole thing up, it's still not that cut and dried."

"What do you mean?"

"I've just spent the last coupla months being treated like some man's slave. I prayed every night for deliverance and maybe … maybe the good Lord listened to me. But from now on, I ain't gonna be no man's chattel, and that's that. Ain't no feller's ever going to tell me what to do or raise his hand against me, d'ya hear?"

"If things don't work out, I know a rattlesnake ranch that would love to have you," Shane jokes.

Zaylie spins to face him. "Look, Mister Shane, it may very well turn out that I owe you some thanks, and, if that's so, then I'll say I'm sorry in advance. But right now, if it ain't too much trouble, I wonder if you could give me and Abraham a little privacy. We still got some things we have to figure out."

Shane raises his hands in mock surrender. "Hey, no problem. I'll just be over here hobnobbing with the dead people." He looks from the gangly, uncertain boy to the plucky little firebrand of a girl and smiles. Assuming they can reconcile, he's pretty sure he knows which one is going to be the sheep and which the shepherd.

Wandering among the small cluster of headstones, it doesn't take long for Shane to glean the story of the people buried there. As he surmised on the first visit with Vern, it is a family plot going back several generations. He reads the inscriptions and dates and follows the thread to the most ostentatious and most recent of the monuments, the one that originally caught Vern's attention when they drove by. Shane goes to check it out, vaguely remembering that the owner's passing had been recent. The inscription confirms that the death date was just four years ago, at the less-than-ripe age of forty-three.

As he reads the name, Mackenna Black III, something clicks in Shane's memory. If this was one of his beloved movies, the Basque shepherd Beñat's voice would now be echoing in voice-over: "Mack Black, like his father and grandfather, an easy name to remember."

"Holy shit!" Shane shouts, garnering a dirty look from Zaylie, who is still laying down the law for Abraham in the parking area. Shane takes the hint, and the rush of thoughts continues inside his head. *This is the bastard blackmailing Beñat. If he's dead, that means the little sheep-dipper is in the clear. Hell, if there's someone else to watch the herd, he doesn't even have to stay in the valley anymore.* And then Shane's knees weaken, and he is forced to sit down hard on the stone dais. He is overcome with a dizzying sense of déjà vu, as if powerful and unfathomable cosmic forces have been channelled through him — like the dancing electrical arcs of some Hollywood Tesla machine — to manipulate causality in the physical universe. When his thoughts rebalance, he feels strangely at peace.

Abraham is waving him over now. Shane joins the couple, curious to know what they have decided. Zaylie, unsurprisingly, is full of questions.

"This valley, does it got water?"

Shane nods. "There's a well, and a stream, too ... it's pretty lush."

"So you reckon Abraham and I could grow our own vegetables?"

"You bet."

"And we're gonna have a stake in the flock? Our very own sheep?"

"That's my understanding. You can ask Beñat about numbers."

"You can count on that. Okay, now let's talk 'bout living arrangements. Assumin' this polygamy thing checks out, until Abraham and I are married, I'm gonna need my own room."

Shane laughs, remembering his astonishment upon seeing the abandoned pueblo village. "It's a bit of a fixer-upper, but you can have your own town, if that's what you want."

THIRTY-TWO

Before heading to Beñat's valley, the threesome detours to Albuquerque to supply proof to Zaylie that her polygamous marriage to Jebediah Carson is illegitimate. Because of his own status, Shane is reluctant to visit the police, and is relieved that the girl is willing to accept the authority of the public library once Shane explains the institution's purpose. The female librarian who politely answers their legal query studies Zaylie's clothes and puts two and two together. Zaylie is taken aside for a conference, and while the two whisper earnestly, as much as he would love to see the Holy Waters elder get some worldly retribution, Shane worries the police may get involved after all.

Therefore, he is relieved when Zaylie rejoins them and suggests they leave. "That library gal tol' me the same thing you did," she informs them as they exit onto the street. "What Jebediah done is wrong, and he could go to jail for it … maybe. It would depend on how all the lawyerin' works out. She also said I could think about it if'n I didn't want to go to the police right away … said somethin' about some statue that don't have no limitations for a buncha years, but I didn't quite make no sense of it. Anyway, I'm thinkin' I'll just let it sit for a spell and get on with my life."

She looks up at Shane. "I reckon it's about time I said thank you for everythin' yer doin' for us. From what Abraham tells me, you've been a real friend in need." She surprises him by getting up on her tiptoes and delivering a chaste little hug. Then she turns to Abraham and proffers her hand. "Now, Abraham Johnson, if you please, I'd like to be wearin' my ring."

The day is waning, and Shane is anxious to get to the hidden valley before sunset. Given that it is her first time in the city, he is concerned that Zaylie's curiosity and excitement will slow them down, but it is soon obvious that she is overwhelmed by the urban environment. As they head back to where the Indian is parked, she clings to the arms of her male escorts like she's afraid the crowds will carry her off.

✳ ✳ ✖ ✳ ✳

They reach Beñat's valley just as the sun is starting to flirt with the horizon. Shane is somehow not surprised that the Basque is waiting for them when they pull up.

"Let me guess, the sheep told you we were coming," Shane jokes as he embraces the old shepherd.

"It was not necessary for anyone to tell me, *mon ami* … I can hear the sound of that engine miles away. You have traded vehicles, I see."

"It's a long story."

Beñat laughs, and Shane realizes how much he has missed the little fellow's indefatigable good humour. "You have only been gone two days. How long can it be?"

"You'd be surprised. Two days? You sure? Feels a lot longer." But Beñat is no longer paying attention to Shane. He has moved forward to stare incredulously at Zaylie and Abraham, who stand there meekly, arm in arm.

"*Dios!* Can it be? He found you!" Beñat emits a giant laugh that echoes through the hills, then does a little dance. He hastens back, hugs Shane, slaps him hard on the back, then returns to face the young couple. Removing his giant beret, he flourishes it in front of him and bows formally.

"Beñat Koldobika Goikoetxea, at your service. You are most welcome."

"Howdy, I'm Abraham Johnson, and this here's Zaylie Hutchinson. Shane there was saying —" But he does not get a chance to finish. Beñat laughs again, then hurries away, beckoning for them to follow.

"Come, come, come," he exclaims with unbridled glee. "You will want to see the valley and the sheep before it grows dark." He turns to Zaylie. "And you, my lovely child, will want to see your living quarters and the garden, of course."

The Basque continues talking away as he leads them into the entrance crevice and along the claustrophobic path into the canyon. "I have only a little garden right now, but the soil there is good, and we can make it bigger very easily. The stream runs for almost all the year, but we can bring water from the well if the rains are inconstant. The sheep still have their coats from the winter, so we must plan the spring shearing soon. The Zuni elders say they can use all our wool and offer a good price this year for our share."

Bringing up the rear as they move through the tight passageway, Shane can only imagine the expressions on the young couple's faces. When they emerge into the lush valley with its grazing herd of sheep, he is gratified to see them exchange a pleased look as their fingers intertwine.

Napoléon, the little sheepdog, comes running over and barks excitedly at Abraham. The youth bends over and pats the dog's head. "Well, hello there, little feller."

"Napoléon says welcome, and he is anxious for you to meet the sheep. He apologizes for his bad English and promises we will all work on it together. Go, go with him while you still have the light. Shane and I will show Zaylie the houses and the garden, assuming *mademoiselle* is comfortable to be left in our care."

Zaylie nods. "Don't be long," she calls after Abraham. "We still got a heapa chores before bedtime."

The youth and the dog walk toward the hillside, with the latter running circles around his new colleague in excitement. Zaylie, meanwhile, is eyeing the pueblo houses and the ladders leading up to them.

"Nobody said we was gonna be livin' in caves ... and there sure are a heap of ladders to climb," she grouses as they begin the trek upward. When they reach the rooftop terrace, she stops to take in the view and wave at Abraham in the distance before nosing around in the dwellings.

Shane wants to get Beñat alone, in order to tell him about Mack Black's gravesite, but the little Basque is far too eager to play tour guide to Zaylie. He greets every one of her concerns with good humour and a ready remedy, and soon the young woman is clearly being won over. The coup de grâce is a large storeroom Beñat leads her to, urging her to take whatever she and Abraham may need, now and in the future. Hewn deep into the stone hillside, the storage area looks like a small general store. Not only are there sundries, canned goods, and preserves, but also camp supplies, carved wooden furnishings, bedding, even an assortment of clothing.

"The Zuni shamans send gifts all the time, but my needs are small," Beñat explains. "I think perhaps some of these gifts were meant for you," he says, his eyes twinkling. He indicates a rack of skirts and women's blouses. Zaylie immediately goes over and starts examining the garments. Meanwhile Beñat flits to a shelf and fishes around for a minute, muttering something softly to himself in Basque, before exclaiming, "Aha! There it is." He hands Zaylie a small wooden box. Shane cranes his neck to have a look as she opens it. Inside are two silver rings, one smaller than the other, ornately worked with an intricate geometric pattern. "A welcome gift for you two," Beñat says, handing her the box. "*Ongi etorri!* Welcome to this valley."

The delight shines on Zaylie's face as she accepts the jewellery. Her freckles shimmer upward, and Shane realizes it is the first time he has seen her smile. The change is profound, the way the sun emerging from clouds can transform an entire landscape. Poor Abraham must have been powerless the first time she unleashed the power of that smile on him.

"Them houses are a darn sight bigger than they look from the outside," Zaylie comments, as they re-emerge onto the terrace. "Land's sake, a couple hundred folks could live here."

"Close to a thousand in the old days, I believe," Beñat says, igniting a fire in the stone hearth and fussing over his teakettle.

"And you been livin' here all by yourself? Don't it get lonely?"

Beñat gives his trademark shrug. "A man can be in the city with a million people around him and still be lonely. I, on the other hand, have been content. When I first came here, I needed refuge and time for contemplation, and this valley gave me both. The shamans visit and hold their ceremonies — in fact, they come for their spring blessing tomorrow. And I have made a few friends who come to call. I am happy." He laughs. "And now I have you. You will stay?"

Zaylie nods. "I reckon so. It's queer … I can't rightly put it in words, but this place sits right with me, especially now that

I've been here a spell. I only ever called one place home before, but for the last coupla months it ain't felt like that at all. I felt trapped and set to, like I been tossed to the dogs."

She looks at Shane. "I know I only spent a coupla hours in that city you took us to today, but that were plenty for me. All them folks livin' on top of one another and rushin' round like starving rats loose in a granary … and the air itself stinkin' of all them machines. And from what little I know of Abraham's ordeal, there's a heapa wicked folks out there, too. He says he's flat out stopped believin' in God. I won't go that far, but I sure been reconsiderin' some of what them elders preached to us … a lot of it beat into us with a switch." She looks over to where the waning sunset has tinted the tops of the canyon's far walls. "But I gotta say, this place feels like a godsend in every sense of the word."

Abraham climbs up to the terrace and joins them around the fire, cuddling up to Zaylie. "That's a mighty fine herd of sheep you got there, Beñat," he reports. "Nice and fat and healthy. And that little dog of yours, if he don't beat all, the way he keeps them critters gathered all up. I swear there ain't much for me to do when he's around."

"Don't you worry your head about that, Abraham Johnson," Zaylie says, patting his arm. "I can find you plenty to do. Startin' with right now. I done picked out a fine house for us to live in, and Beñat has been kind enough to stake us to everything we need. I'd like to get our bed set up before it gets pitch black."

"Our bed? But you said —"

"I don't need some fool boy to tell me what I said." She frowns and studies him for a minute, then rises to her feet. "Listen to what I'm sayin' now. Abraham Johnson, I'm gonna ask you a question, and you give me yer honest answer. Do you love me, and do you promise you ain't gonna have any other gal but me, and you're gonna take care of me and stick with me, no matter what happens, and spend the rest of your life makin' sure I'm happy and taken care of?"

"You know I do."

"Say it. Say you vow it, with the Almighty and these here men as witnesses."

"I vow it, Zaylie Hutchinson, I vow it with all my heart and soul."

"Well, Abraham Johnson. I'm givin' you my solemn vow that you're the only man for me, and you always will be, and I'm gonna love you, and I'll never stop lovin' you 'til the day I die … and then some. And I'm gonna be at your side through thick and thin, come hell or high water, and no woman could ever be a better wife to you than what I'm gonna be."

She produces the rings Beñat gave her earlier. "Here, put yours on and put this one on me," she says, handing over the rings and offering her finger for the second time that day. Abraham obeys, and when the act is complete, she leans forward for a kiss. Abraham doesn't respond immediately, still somewhat confused, with his mouth agape. "Abraham Johnson, ain't you gonna kiss your wife?"

"My what?"

"Well, you can sure as shiz believe we ain't part of no Holy Waters Temple no more, and good riddance to them, I say. So I reckon we's our own temple now, so *we* get to say what's right and wrong. Now, seeing as both of us have reached our eighteenth birthday, we can speak for ourselves, and we just gave our solemn vows in front of God and these witnesses and had our very own sealing ceremony, and that's good enough for me. As far as I'm concerned, this is a celestial marriage, and you 'n' me are gonna be bound together for all eternity. And seein' as we're now man and wife, startin' tonight we'll be sleeping in the same bed. Anyhow, them's my thoughts on the subject. But I ain't gonna do your thinkin' for you, Abraham. Do you agree with me or not?"

"Oh, yes, Zaylie!" Abraham cries and plants a big kiss on his bride's lips.

"A wedding! A wedding! We must celebrate!" Beñat shouts and leaps to his feet. He goes running first to the storeroom, then into his house, emerging with two bottles and four brass chalices.

Overrun with excitement, the little shepherd hands Zaylie and Abraham each a chalice. "Am I correct that you will not drink alcohol?"

"No, sir," Zaylie shoots back. "I still believe in Joseph Smith and his Word of Wisdom, the law of health the good Lord gave him in 1833. Now, my good husband here has seen a little more of the world than I have, so I'll let him make up his own mind if he wants to go messin' with intoxicating spirits on his wedding night."

Abraham casts a glance at his wife. "No liquor for me, neither. Our bodies and our minds are precious gifts from God, so we gotta keep 'em healthy and strong," he replies, clearly reciting from memory.

"That is what I thought, so this is some sparkling grape juice — exquisite, but without alcohol. Here, Shane, *aide-moi.*" He passes the things in his hands to Shane, and then begins working on the top of what resembles, in all other respects, a bottle of champagne. The cork pops and goes flying off into the dusk to cheers from the assembly, and Beñat fills up the young couple's cups. He then retrieves the remaining bottle from Shane. "You have not taken up abstinence during your recent adventures, have you, *mon ami?*" the little Basque asks.

"If I had, I'd give it up for a special occasion like this," Shane replies, holding out his chalice.

"Excellent! Because this is a bottle of very rare cognac I have saved for such a moment."

When the cups have all been filled, Beñat offers the first toast. "*Osasuna!* To your health. May your hearts always be filled with love and your house filled with the laughter of children."

"To the bride and groom!" Shane shouts, and after the chalices clank in a communal toast, he takes a sip of the cognac. It is smooth and easy on the tongue, with a hint of fruit and spices. He wonders if it might be the best he's ever tasted, given that most of his experiences with cognac — coming at the end of meals that typically involved gallons of beer, cocktails, and wine — are somewhat of a blur. In his previous life, a world of testosterone-filled, nouveau-riche, twentysomething millionaires, even the most outrageously expensive spirits were consumed in large volumes during hedonistic riots of excess. He and his teammates, filled with a sense of entitlement and urged on by the sycophantic encouragement of hangers-on, acted as though they were rapacious demigods, and the universe itself was meant to be devoured. He takes another small, appreciative sip of the cognac and experiences a pang of regret at the waste and folly of his youth.

"Music, we must have music!" Beñat now shouts. Again, he dashes off into his room. He surprises Shane by reappearing with an MP3 player and battery-powered speakers. Reading Shane's expression, Beñat laughs as he plugs in the cables. "What, you expected pan pipes or a lute? Not all technology is foreign to this valley, *mon ami.* I can assure you, this little music box is like a gift from the gods to a shepherd." He scrolls through the device's contents. It is clear when he finds what he's looking for by the impish delight plastered over his face. A lively bluegrass tune starts to play, and Shane suddenly feels his foot start to tap, as if it has a mind of its own.

"First the bride and groom must dance, and then it will be my turn," Beñat calls out. Abraham and Zaylie look at each other, unsure what to do. "What, do you people not dance at weddings?" the Basque demands.

"I've heard tell other temples allow it, but we never did at Holy Waters," Abraham says. Zaylie nods agreement.

Beñat frowns, the stern expression looking alien on his nearly always happy face. "This is not right! Everywhere around the world, north and south, east and west, they follow this tradition. Come, come! Celebrate! Take each other and dance!"

The young couple glance at each other questioningly for mutual consent before obeying, and although their style is initially stiff and uncertain, soon their knees rise with each step and they are stomping around to the infectious music as Shane slaps his thigh in time. Beñat, prancing like a show horse, comes over to replenish Shane's chalice.

More foot-stomping fiddle tunes ensue from the playlist, and next Beñat, then Shane dances with the bride. Zaylie is radiant, the effort of dancing adding to the glow of her flagrant joy. Beñat, the self-appointed host of this celebration, now conjures up a large plate of cheese, sausages, flatbreads, olives, and pickled delicacies, which he places on a low table in front of the firepit for the revellers to consume at their leisure. When Zaylie takes time out for a rest, the menfolk keep the party alive by dancing with each other. Although Shane drinks more cognac, he finds he is not getting drunk, and he is happy to derive his intoxication from this magical moment, which he has helped birth. He watches the sparks from the flame dance skyward, though not in time to the music the way they seemed to during his psychedelic experience. There, too, the urges have passed, as he has no compulsion to elevate his mood with some hallucinogen, nor, for that matter, with cannabis, cocaine, or codeine.

Yet, as much as he feels deeply satisfied, he knows it will soon be time to move on. He is also content in that knowledge.

He remembers his spirit guide's prediction that his road home would first run red and black. That has come true in more ways than one. But he was also counselled that, in the end, the future consists of possibilities, and that he, Shane "Bronco" Bronkovsky, not some preordained fate or magical force, ultimately holds the reins of his own destiny. He smiles at the knowledge, and as he does so, he seems to see the shape of a bear amidst the flames, dancing briefly on its hind legs before disappearing heavenward.

His meditative moment is interrupted by the bride and groom announcing that they are going to call it a night.

"Luddy Mussy! Who ever would have thought when I woke up this morning that my day was going to end up like this?" Zaylie chuckles as she takes her husband's arm. As a final gesture of goodwill, Shane and Beñat help Abraham carry a frame, headboard, and mattress from the storeroom and wrestle them through the narrow doorway to set up a bed in the house that the young couple will inhabit, while Zaylie follows with the bedding she has selected. There is much laughing and backslapping and hugging and congratulating as Shane and Beñat take their leave.

They return to the firepit for a nightcap, and Shane finally has the opportunity to tell Beñat about the death of his nemesis, Mack Black.

"It's true, Beñat, he's dead. I've seen his grave myself." He is about to add that it was by sheer fluke that he stumbled across it, but given everything that's happened, he questions how random the event really was.

Beñat, meanwhile, sits mutely, staring into the flames. The smile is gone again. "This, the spirits did not tell me," he says softly.

"Well, now *I'm* telling you. Isn't that great news? For starters, it means you can get the hell out of this valley ... especially now that you've got those two lovebirds to watch the sheep."

"*Mais, mon ami*, why would I want to leave this valley? This is my home now ... my refuge."

"But that's just it. You don't need a refuge anymore, now that there's no more Mack Blackmail."

Beñat laughs. "Mack Black drove me here, but he did not keep me here. I stayed because I found inner peace and *l'illumination*. I looked for this my whole life. No, when I say it is a refuge, I mean it is a refuge from the madness of the outside world, from the anger and greed and selfishness, from the evil that people do to each other every day."

"But don't you want to travel, to see more of the world?"

"Oh, my good fellow. In this little place I have travelled farther than I ever imagined I could ... to worlds you cannot comprehend." He glances at Shane. "Or perhaps you can comprehend a little ... now."

Shane contemplates the fire. "I thought you would be happy."

"But, Shane, I am very happy. Just not for the reason you think. I stopped fearing Mack Black many years ago. But his ... his badness, it was always there in my mind. It was like smoke, hiding the sun, making it difficult to breathe. Now I can feel peace, knowing his veil has lifted, and the sun is shining again. For this, I thank you."

Shane nods and finishes his cognac. "Well, I figure I'll turn in, too. Like the lady said, it's been a long, crazy day. Tomorrow ... well, I start the next leg of my journey."

"I will make up a room for you to sleep in tonight," Beñat tells him.

Shane smiles and pulls his blanket tighter. "Thanks, buddy, but no thanks. I don't know exactly when I'll see the sky and stars again after tomorrow. So, if it's no trouble, I think I'd like to sleep outside tonight."

"As you like, *mon ami*. If you wake up, throw some more wood on the fire. It will keep you warm." He rises to go.

"Hey, Beñat?"

"*Oui*, Shane?"

"Those shaman guys coming tomorrow, how are they getting here? Are they, like, riding wild horses, or do they just materialize out of thin air?"

"You joke. No, they have their own air-conditioned autobus. Why do you ask?"

"I was thinking maybe they could drop me off at an airport, and I'd fly to Chicago instead. Do you figure they'd be willing to do that?"

"I am sure they would be honoured. But what of your motorcycle?"

"Doesn't belong to me, and I'm not a big fan of sidecars or vintage bikes, anyway. I was thinking of leaving it behind for Abraham. Call it a wedding present. The kids might want to get out from time to time. Once Abraham has a few more driving lessons, that is. Say, to visit Albuquerque ... or, as Zaylie called it, Babylon. Unless leaving the valley is, like, against the rules, now that they're here."

Beñat sends another monstrous guffaw flying out into the night. "Rules? This is not a hockey game, Shane. Everyone makes their own rules. Hmm. Perhaps *I* will drive the motorcycle sometimes, too. I formerly had one, a 400cc BMW, while a student in San Sebastián. We shall see. We shall see. I told you that I do not feel a compulsion to leave the valley. But that is not to say it is not possible. Now, I will say *gabon* ... good night."

"Hey, Beñat, guess what?"

"What?"

"Las Vegas has an NHL team now. Phoenix has had one for ages."

"*Mon dieu!* The universe is full of miracles!"

✖ ✖ ✖ ✖ ✖

Waiting at the Albuquerque airport for his flight to Chicago, Shane phones his father.

"Dad, I'm going to turn myself in," he tells the old man. "I'm through with running."

"That's good, son. You're innocent, and we'll fight this. Mr. Getz says the Players' Association is with you, too. In fact, they're going to pay for your lawyer. There's a lot of people on your side, Shane."

"Dad, listen, I want to tell you something. You, and all the help you gave me growing up, well, that means so much to me. I'd be nothing without you. I'm sorry I never said thank you often enough. I'm … I'm sorry for everything. I just want you to know I love you."

The statement is met with silence. It is Oksana's voice he hears next.

"Oh, hi, Shane. Your dad's going to need a minute. He's having a good cry and doesn't want you to know it. That's a man for you." In the background Shane hears his father curse Oksana for her honesty.

"It's going to take a couple of days for the two of us to get there, Shane, but he wants to be by your side."

"The two of you?"

"Yeah, I promised the doctor I'd come along and take care of your dad. Oh, hang on." There is an exchange of voices, and his father comes back on the line.

"Damn that woman. So, okay, I was crying. Who cares? I love you, too, son."

EPILOGUE

Ten Years Later

On the way to pick up his daughter, Shane stops by the post office to gather the family mail. Among the usual bills and flyers is an envelope postmarked Boise, Idaho, and addressed by hand. Shane studies the letter, his interest piqued, but he does not want to be late picking up little Desirée, especially not on hockey game day. He tucks the envelope into the inside pocket of his parka and returns to where his vehicle is idling, its exhaust wafting ghostlike shapes into the twilight of the frigid January afternoon.

Later, sitting in the stands at the town arena, as his daughter's team warms up under the watchful eye of their coach, Oksana — also Desirée's mother and Shane's wife — Shane, having no interest in the gossip of the other parent spectators, opens the letter. Even after so many years, he still receives occasional mail from supporters and disparagers alike rehashing the accident of a decade ago and the trial thereafter. This letter, however, brings the past flooding back in an altogether different way.

Dear Mr. Bronkovsky:
I hope you remember me. You stayed briefly
with us at our ranch in New Mexico ten years
ago. If you don't remember me, maybe you
remember the rattlesnakes? I recently came
across one of those "Where Are They Now?"
articles in *Hockey World* magazine, and it was a
real surprise and delight to read the interview
they had with you.

Shane's brow knits as he remembers the article in question.
He had tried to avoid the interview, but the journalist came
uninvited all the way to Peel Crossing and pestered half of the
town until Shane finally relented. Oksana thought the resulting
story was a balanced piece that portrayed Shane in a favourable
light. Shane has to concede that at least it wasn't a hatchet job.
He returns his attention to the letter.

I know I was only a boy at the time, but after
you left the ranch I was shocked to discover
how totally clueless I had been about who you
were and the trouble you were involved in at
the time. What I remember most about you was
that you were a real friend to me. You helped
me with my wrist shot and taught me electrical
wiring. You'll be pleased to know both of those
skills have been useful in my life.

But it wasn't just that article that made
me want to write to you. A couple of days
later, while I was driving home for Christmas,
a motorcycle pulled up just outside of
Albuquerque, and the driver waved for me to

pull over. It was a cool old Indian model with a sidecar, and wasn't I surprised to discover it was Beñat, that shepherd fellow we used to visit up in the hills to trade for snakes and rats, riding it. After the two of us said hello and such, he said to make sure I sent you his regards when I wrote you. He said to tell you the valley had been blessed with a whole bunch of new sheep and two babies. That sure threw me for a loop, because I was just beginning to think I might write you.

The kicker was when I mentioned you to Doc Sanchez while visiting on Boxing Day, and he let me in on the secret. He told me it was you who came up with the idea for the youth programs they offer at the Palomas arena, and that you paid for my cousin Grace and me. That's when I knew I had to write to say thank you, and to tell you how you changed our lives.

You see, Shane, I am a college senior now, attending Boise State University on a hockey scholarship. I'm an average player at this level — I know there's no chance of cracking the professional ranks, and that's okay. The scholarship paid for my education in electrical engineering, and I have a good future ahead of me. I plan to return home to New Mexico and set up a business providing low-cost solar energy for the folks there. I'm hoping my hockey career isn't over, though. I'm engaged to a really nice gal from Puerto Palomas, and after we're married I plan to get dual Mexican-American citizenship — I hope to eventually play for *Los Lobos de Chihuahua*. That's assuming I can make the team. They've got a pretty good bunch of players.

Let me tell you about Grace. You may remember how crazy she was about horses. When Aléjandro Arguijo and his son were murdered by the Juárez cartel, Dr. Sanchez became owner of the hockey club. He also arranged to buy some of Señor Arguijo's horses and incorporate them into a *Los Lobos* youth athletics program. Well, Grace took to riding like a duck to water, and guess what? Now she's one of the youngest professional rodeo riders in America. Her specialty is barrel racing, but she's pretty good at roping, too. She's not earning much money yet, but she really loves it, and her career's just getting started. At first Aunt Tammy was dead set against her girl going off rodeoing and being away from home so much, but Grace has a way of getting what she wants. Now Aunt Tammy's proud as punch, and there's pictures of Grace in action hung up all over the sitting room.

Shane looks down at the ice where his own little girl is going through the pregame drills. He imagines her ten years in the future and wonders whether she will achieve her oft-stated goal of playing women's hockey professionally. He has neither fuelled nor discouraged Desirée's dream, believing that it is up to her to find her own path, but it's not surprising that hockey is in her DNA. As if she senses him watching her, Desirée looks up and gives him a little wave. From the bench, Oksana tracks the gesture and turns to blow Shane a kiss before returning her attention to her charges.

Shane resumes reading.

> Speaking of Aunt Tammy, you wouldn't believe what she's done with the ranch. The rattle-snakes are long gone, and now the place is a state-funded shelter for abused women. She fought long and hard to make that happen and has pretty much made it her whole life. There's a new irrigation system, and the stable's been expanded and turned into a two-storey bunkhouse. The gals all work together growing avocadoes and tomatoes for market. There's chickens and a few steers, too, but mostly — as Aunt Tammy is fond of saying — they raise hope and self-esteem.

> To boot, Aunt Tammy is a country singer now, too! She and Maybelline (you remember her from the ranch) have an act together and sometimes play around Southern New Mexico. Aunt Tammy writes all their music and plays guitar, while Maybelline writes the words and sings. They've even put out their own CD, with all the money going to the shelter.

> And as for Yolanda, well, she's Mrs. Sanchez now. She and the doc courted for a couple of years and then got hitched and bought a spread just outside of Columbus. These days she's real busy on both sides of the border, not to mention being mama of twin baby girls. She and

Aunt Tammy are still tight. Yolanda comes by regularly to help out with the shelter's paperwork and whatnot. She was the one that used to drive me and Grace across the border to use the arena and the riding stable a few times a week, until I was old enough to get my licence. Otherwise, I don't think Aunt Tammy would have let us go, even though it was all paid for.

Anyway, I guess I'll wrap up now. Like I said, I mainly just wanted to say thank you and let you know that you made a difference in my life. You were only at the ranch for a bit, but I'll never forget you and the things you taught me, or how well you treated me when I was going through some rough times.

Both Yolanda and Doc Sanchez say hi, and so does Grace. The magazine article says you went home to Canada after the charges against you in Chicago were dismissed, and that you found peace and a sense of purpose coaching kids. I'm really happy for you. But if you're ever in this neck of the woods again, be sure to look us up.

Yours truly,
Vernon "Viper" Draper

Buried recollections of Shane's time in New Mexico come gushing out. It is like a flash flood in a canyon, a relentless torrent in which pieces of memory and regret bob to the surface and spin like flotsam caught in the supercharged current. Should he feel guilty for having forgotten these people so thoroughly, for having been so oblivious to their triumphs and tragedies?

No, he finally tells himself. It's not that he suppressed the past …
but the future took hold of him with an unyielding grasp, and in
the process hypnotized him with its gleaming promise.

By the time Shane left Chicago, he was already in love with
Oksana, although his father's failing health was the reason he
cited for returning home to the Yukon. Reconciling with his
father and helping to care for him during his last days, dealing
with the legal and emotional aftermath of his death, convincing Oksana to marry him, the birth of their child, the building
of their new home — each of these things has been an all-
consuming chapter in the story of the past decade. In many ways
Shane feels like his life only truly became his own after he was
finished with pro hockey. The time spent in New Mexico was
like a punctuation mark separating the two segments of his story.

The arena buzzer sounds to signal the start of the game, and
Shane refolds the letter and tucks it away. For the next hour he
devotes his attention to cheering his daughter on, although he is
equally vocal in support of every girl down on the ice. Oksana,
too, plays cheerleader, taking care not to show favouritism or
obsess about winning. It is one of the many ways she and Shane
have proven to be well matched.

By the time the game finishes at five o'clock, it is pitch black
outside. Peel Crossing is in the midst of a prolonged cold snap,
with temperatures hovering near minus forty, so even though
the walk to where their truck idles in the arena parking lot is
short, Shane makes sure Desirée is properly bundled up, despite
her protests.

To compensate for her displeasure, he hoists her onto his
shoulders and lets her pretend she is riding a horse. This little
game, a treat for the child, he now remembers originated with
little Gracie back at *Rancho Crótalo*. They reach the truck, and
the family piles in, purring at the warmth and coziness of the

cab. Oksana takes the driver's seat, an unspoken concession to Shane's history of concussions. Although the doctors have pronounced him fit to drive — and, out of necessity, considering the hectic family schedule, he does so regularly — both parents prefer Oksana to take the wheel whenever possible.

Desirée bubbles merrily about the fun she had at hockey and about her budding friendships with new teammates as they head for the outskirts of town and the road that will take them up the side of the mountain to the log house Shane and Oksana built with their own hands. Shane stares contentedly out the window, conjuring phantoms from the darkness outside. While the letter from Vern has stirred memories and thoughts of alternate possibilities, it has not disturbed the inner peace that characterizes his life here in Peel Crossing. In the old moments of despair and confusion that once haunted his life, Shane would never have dared ascribe such a joyous outcome to his own life.

The road takes them past the pioneer cemetery, where only old-timers — those who have spent the better part of their lives in the Yukon — are allowed to be buried. His father is there now. If the priests are to be believed, he, too, is at rest. Out of reflex, upon spotting the headstones, Shane murmurs aloud, "Bury your horses," realizing that this habit, too, was born during his odyssey down south.

"What's that you said, Papa?" Desirée asks, interrupting her monologue.

Shane smiles and wraps his daughter in a hug. "Nothing, baby. It's just a game Daddy once played."

ACKNOWLEDGEMENTS

My sincerest thanks to the Canada Council for the Arts and the Writers' Trust of Canada, who provided financial support for the writing of this book. My profoundest gratitude to Patrick Boyer, for championing it, and to Elsa Franklin, who started everything. Also, a tip of the hat to the hardworking editorial team at Dundurn Press, especially freelancer Catharine Chen for her editing. Thank you to my first readers, Gabriela Sgaga, Laura DiCesare, Peter Jagla, Jim Miller, and Brian Bell. A special thank you to Santiana Guiresse for helping me with my Basque words and facts. Thanks also to the Columbus Train Depot Museum, Columbus Village Library, and Pancho Villa State Park for supplying local knowledge, past and present, and to the Chiricahua Desert Museum in Rodeo, New Mexico, for their rattlesnake tutelage. And, finally, a bow to the members of the Dawson City Writers' Circle and the Imperial Literary Society for their feedback and camaraderie while this book was writ.